THE NEMESIS LIST

R. J. FRITH

TOR

First published 2010 by Tor

This paperback edition published 2011 by Tor
an imprint of Pan Macmillan, a division of Macmillan Publishers Limited
Pan Macmillan, 20 New Wharf Road, London N1 9RR
Basingstoke and Oxford
Associated companies throughout the world
www.panmacmillan.com

ISBN 978-0-330-51997-7

1 3 5 7 9 8 6 4 2

A CIP catalogue record for this book is available from
the British Library.

Typeset by CPI Typesetting
Printed and bound by CPI Group (UK) Ltd, Croydon CR0 4YY

R. J. Frith is the winner of Tor UK War of the Words competition which was run in conjunction with Sci Now magazine in 2009 to find a new publishing talent.

R. J. is a prolific writer of ~~~~~~~~~~~~~~~~~~~~~~~~~~~~ d has be~~~~~~~~~~~~~~~~~~~~~~~~~~~~~~~~~~~~~ ~~~ is R. J. Frith's first novel.

R. J. Frith lives in the East Midlands.

Praise for *The Nemesis List*

'Jeven in particular is a very interesting creation, part science experiment gone wrong, part cocky, murderous con man. His illnesses and drug dependences make him unpredictable and at points quite terrifying, and as a reader it is a treat not to know what a character is going to do next'
Fantasy Book Review

'At last, a sci-fi book that doesn't bombard you with techspeak from page one. Story and character are at the fore here . . . I bet you a fiver this author goes far'
Scott Pack, Me and My Big Mouth

'R. J. Frith has a light style that quietly sketches in his characters, as well as a knack for blindsiding you just when you think you know where a plotline is heading. A surprisingly intimate and personal book that sets up the major conflict still to come'
Total Scifi Online

'There's plenty of intrigue and complexity to keep even the most paranoid conspiracy theorist guessing'
SFCrowsnest

As colonists, you have elected your Colony directors, your station masters and your heads of law enforcement. You thought these people were in charge of your lives. Untrue: only the Planetary Heads of State have ever been in charge of your lives. You thought you voted for them in fair and just elections, but, I can reveal to you now, these men and women are bred, trained and taught the art of leadership. You didn't vote a single one of them into office. Since the last wars blighted Earth's past hundreds of years ago the Planetary Heads have abandoned democracy, the same way they have now decided to abandon our futures.

Why upset humanity's equilibrium with endless upgrades? Why confess to unimplemented advancements? Why not simply explain how dangerous innovation is? How much it might hurt us. Do any of us remember the days when scientists weren't herded together like prisoners in Government enclaves? Does the Government consider us foolish enough not to understand that these people are now working not to advance the human race but to stifle it?

Our bloody past has taught this Government to treat us like

perpetual children never to be let loose with anything that might harm us. Never to give us a free choice in our own lives.

Our reality is a lie. It's time to fight for our future.

Alexander Calder

Head of the Charris Confederation.

Declaration of War.

Sixteen years ago . . .

The five-year-old boy was led down a battered corridor full of peeling paint. The trouser-cuffs of his blue pyjama suit dragged, his slippers flapped, too big for his tiny feet. It felt like an endless walk.

The strange woman tugging him along peered down at him anxiously. 'Not much further,' she said. She took him to a room, one with a bed, a wonky chair and a child-sized table. A cartoon was playing on an old wall-mounted monitor. 'Spaceman Jo', who breathed hard vacuum and didn't get sucked inside out – lucky Jo.

The boy asked the woman about the background hum, about the coddling scent in the air. He'd never been on a ship before; he didn't know they had a sound and a smell all their own. She told him about engine noise, about the drone of the air-filtration systems, about the floral-scented add-in that killed off any 'nasties' breathed into the air.

'I understand that your name is Jake,' she said. 'But soon the doctor assigned to you will give you a new name.' She smiled a tight smile, rubbing her hands together as if trying to wash them clean. 'If the ship jumps, don't be afraid. It jumps a lot.'

3

Jake knew about jump-gates and the folds in space they created. His father had shown him once, demonstrating with a scrap of paper. 'Folds, you see, folds.'

Jake thought they must be going on a trip. He felt sure that one day soon those folds would take him back to his parents, to his brother, his sister. He'd been playing out in the fields, in the tall reeds; that's the last he could remember of his home.

Later that day, he met the doctor assigned to him. His name was Milo. He looked friendly with his broad face and shiny red cheeks, but even though he smiled and smiled, there was a darkness in his eyes.

'Session always begins on day three,' he said, 'that's when you'll meet Mr Lieberman.'

Jake didn't know what session was. He didn't care about day three. He didn't want to meet Mr Lieberman. He just wanted to go home. He lay in his bed that night as the ship jumped from one place to another and cried, his fingers knotted into the covers. He screamed for his mother until finally Milo came in and touched something cold to his arm. 'Sleep now,' he said. 'Go to sleep.'

The next day Jake had breakfast in the galley with all the other children, the sound of chatter alien to him, as was the closeness of all those other little bodies. He stared around at them, fascinated. He'd never seen so many children in one place. He babbled, excited to be with them all. He learned their names. Their special names: Nespi, Silnen, Lonil, on and on, names he'd never heard before. Names Milo had made up for them, they said. They were Group J-180. Jake liked that. He liked to feel a part of them. They whispered about their *parents fearfully. It wasn't allowed, they told him, to remember your real name or where you came from.*

The ship jumped again that night. Jake screamed, everything around him twisting and buckling, coiling up and flying apart. Home never jumped.

Milo didn't come into his room this time; another man did. He threw the covers off him and grabbed for his arm. 'Damned planet-born brats are all the same,' he snarled before the blackness came.

Jake cried the next day. So full of grief he couldn't stop. He threw his fists at Milo when he came into his room. 'I want to go home,' he yelled. 'Take me home.'

'This is your home,' Milo said, with a set jaw. 'The Bliss is your home now.'

Day three brought his first session. A white room. A man in a white coat, with the palest grey eyes he'd ever seen. He stood with a computer slate, scrawling across it with a stylus. 'Well now,' he said, pausing to offer out his big hand. 'I'm Aeron Lieberman.'

Jake swallowed and held out his hand. 'Please can I go home?' he asked as his hand was swallowed up. The man shook it very gently and smiled.

'Let's do this first, shall we?' he said softly. He moved over to a panel on a long black box. He pressed a switch, and a door swung open. Inside stood a chair; it faced a flat black screen. 'It's a game. That's all. You've played games before, haven't you?'

Jake nodded.

'Well this is a very special game. It makes you remember things. Things you'll never forget.' The man moved to a countertop. He put

5

the slate down. 'But you shouldn't remember anything while you're upset or angry, or even happy, because that does bad things inside your mind.' Lieberman smiled again. 'So we take all those things away and put you in what we call a Passive State. Do you understand?'

Jake didn't. He nodded anyway, wiping a shaking hand over his face, determined not to cry. 'Be a strong little man,' his father always said.

'Come here,' Lieberman beckoned. 'Session one is mathematics. Basic theory. Theory's always a good place to start.'

He couldn't be a strong little man; Jake ran for the door. Milo stepped across his path, holding out his hands to bar his escape.

'No,' he yelled, kicking out as Milo grabbed his arms and held on tight.

'Just sit inside the box for today,' he'd said persuasively. 'Just a little practice. It'll be over really soon. No harm done.'

He might be only five but Jake knew when someone was lying.

His new name arrived. He didn't like it. It was J-Seventeen and a list of numbers and letters. 'I don't want it,' he said, sticking his lip out and crossing his arms. 'My name's Jake after my grandpa.'

'You can choose something simpler,' Milo said, sitting down next to him on his bed. 'Anything you like. We just don't want you to be Jake any more. That's the past. You could be . . . Jeven. That's a good name. The J and the seven all together.'

Jake stuck his lip out a little further. 'Don't want it.'

'If you decide to be Jeven I'll bring you some treats, I promise.' Milo smiled. 'I'll always keep my promises to you. You should keep yours too. That's important. I always want you to do exactly what you say you're going to. Can you do that for me?'

His father had said something similar about the truth and trust, being honest, being a good person.

Jake sniffed and nodded. 'Yes,' he said, wanting to make his father proud. Jeven, he thought, trying it out. Telling himself to always be Jake in his head, no matter what treats Milo brought him.

'Jeven's your adventurer's name,' Milo told him. 'That's what we are here. We're adventurers in the world of science.'

PART ONE
BROKEN PEOPLE

CHAPTER 1

The room was grey. It smelled of sweat, machine oil, the thick stench of cooking grease, as if the last meal he'd eaten had caught in his shirt, his hair. Stokes swallowed, coughed. His throat hurt, his stomach hurt even worse. He lay curled up on a threadbare mattress on a metal bed, staring at grey-on-grey two-tone walls; frowning at the pit-lines that marked a recessed toilet and sink. The buttons to retract them were evident in red, little notices attached he couldn't read: too hazy, too far away.

He flinched; convinced that an avalanche of information was about to bury him up tight and steal all his air away, a flood of memories determined to tell him things he didn't need or care to know. He fought for control and won – just the memories of the last fourteen days. A freighter headed nowhere useful; a captain who gave him a grunt job in the hold, who let him break every transport law in existence for no good reason except that she thought he would end up in her cabin, in her bed. Day thirteen and he'd passed out in the hold, just fainted dead away. Not his fault, the Captain had a punishing schedule, and those not acclimatized to it would suffer. He drew his knees up against the pain of his stomach.

A face appeared at the window – a thick square of composite in a metal door – a face whose edges refused to sharpen. Not hard to guess: the Cap, or one of her crew, come to tell him it was time to get out, get off. They didn't want a sick kid on board – no matter how pretty his face.

'Stokes. Can you hear me?' A fist pounded on the door. 'Stokes. Get your stuff. We're on-planet. You hear me?'

A siren's wail drowned out the words: the all-clear signalling the crew that it was safe to leave the ship. It changed pitch to a low-grade, muted tone, a sound that pulsed in time with the aching cramps of his belly. Its last echo died, but the pain remained. Even so, he made an effort to rise, pushing his palms into the mattress and locking his elbows straight, gasping as he anchored himself there, half up, half down.

He looked at the face at the window again. No doubt about it: the Captain. Blonde hair. Not pretty, not ugly. Miss Average come to visit. Miss Average speaking through the circular vents peppering the window like bullet holes. 'Stokes. You all right.' No inflection, no feeling. A statement.

Stokes breathed hard, angled his legs slowly over and managed to sit on the edge of the bed. He let his head hang, hair falling over his face, looking down at his naked feet, at clothes encrusted with the grit that had caked the cargo bay. His skin looked as grey as the room.

'Stokes?'

He lacked the energy to gather words of his own; he raised his head and looked at the window.

'You feel all right.' Another flat-ended statement. 'You need a drink. There's water in the sink.'

He glanced at the wall recesses, trying again to distinguish toilet from sink, but retracted they were all nothing but lines in the wall. He knew he couldn't reach them, he wouldn't get that far. He coughed again and heard the door slide. 'I want you off, Stokes. You go to a doctor. You go to Disease Control. I don't want my boat off schedule because I've got a sick kid on board. I'll put you out the back hatch, then you make yourself scarce. You hear me?'

He looked up and saw a gun's muzzle.

'Off,' the Cap said.

'I'm not sick.' He tried to make his speech sharp, but the words still escaped in a throaty whisper. 'Let me stay. I just need to rest a day or two while you're unloading. You'll see I'm just worn out. You jumped three times. I can't take that. Please, two days and I'll go if you want me to.'

He knew looks counted for something; a little trick of aesthetics, the way a body was built got returns. She liked the fact that on any Reaches dock she could have him trail her about, walking merchandise that flashed status louder than any piece of jewellery.

'Please . . . Hetta.' He added the familiarity none of the Cap's crew dared to use.

Her eyes flashed over him once, then again more slowly, measuring his worth against her inconvenience. A pretty boy on a ship full of ageing, ugly scum, a little prize she hadn't got her hands around yet. He tilted his head, gave her a tired little-boy-lost look and watched her eat it up. Sex got you something, but you didn't give in too soon, you left them wanting as long as you dared.

'All right. But you get any worse, you're off.'

'I won't get worse. I promise.'

She backed off and let him lie down again; turning the overheads down as if she gave a damn about him personally when he knew all she wanted was his body warming her bed.

*

13

'Stokes?' a whisper across his cheek. 'You feel better?' the Cap's voice. Hours must have passed, he didn't remember: little chinks of dreams all he could recall. The Cap prodded at him, slipped a hand under his shirt, hope in her wandering fingers. 'Hey, Stokes?' Her lips nuzzled his neck, found the sweat on his flesh, the chill.

He shuddered, and she drew away.

'I met somebody today out on the dock,' she said. 'A man looking for a kid by the name of Jones, passing through on a false ID. One with the name Joseph Stokes on it.'

His eyes snapped open, the words getting through where the physical contact had failed.

'The man's name was Pak.'

He pushed his way upright. The Cap had a sour look: downturned mouth, narrowed eyes.

'He says he's been on this kid's trail for eight months. Says the kid's a runaway out of Beta Station. Says his folks want him home. That it was all one big fat misunderstanding.'

He waited. Her pitch. Her rules. He had nothing to offer if Pak had money. He wasn't certain he had the resources to offer her much of anything else either, but she knew that.

'Hetta?'

'Shut up, brat. You know what you're worth. You know it every time you look in the mirror. So you want to deal? I'll keep my mouth shut. I've done it before to fill this damned ship full of scum. You get cleaned up, you move into my cabin and you stay there until I'm bored with you.'

Kudos. She had wrinkles she couldn't afford to fix, age she couldn't defy without a big enough bank balance, but she could gain a little stature among the other captains. Gain a little pet to follow her about. He'd played this game before with far bigger fish. 'That's all you want?'

'No pride, have you, brat.' She lifted a finger; trailed a nail down his face. 'So what are you? An illegal genetic? Your mamma and papa decide they had more money than sense? They'd be so happy knowing you'd rather give yourself to me than go home to them.' He held her gaze as his stomach roiled. 'So I get to keep you, and Pak goes to hell. That okay by you?'

He wanted to laugh but swallowed it back. She'd believed Pak's deceit. That would make things easier. 'Whatever you want, Hetta.'

The familiarity made her smile this time. 'So you're a runaway. Is it that simple? Your parents disappointed in you for some reason? Let me guess, you didn't make the grade. Got the looks, all right, got the charm. So what else were they after? Some scientific prodigy the Government could stick in one of their foundations? Somebody they could make their money back out of, one way or another?'

He nodded, added nothing else.

'Shame they couldn't have sued that illegal gene lab, they'd have made a fortune.'

'What did Pak offer?'

'More than you're worth.'

'Where is he?'

'He's looking for you. You rest now. Tomorrow I want you on your feet, looking and smelling one hell of a lot better than you do now. Tomorrow we'll have some fun. You got that?'

She kissed him on the lips this time, a lingering kiss he forced himself not to recoil from. She was nearing sixty, he guessed, old enough to be his grandmother.

She wiped his lips clean of her lipstick when she was done, smiled at him when his eyes stayed locked fast to her. 'Good kid, aren't you?' she said. 'Such a shame you damn well know it. Tomorrow, Mr Jones.'

He got a queasy sensation as she hesitated at the door, a sense of something being very wrong with her, but he smiled until she left: a fool's smile on a fool's face. Damned fool.

When he got up, dizziness made him feel like the ship was still airborne, still tilting under his feet. He refused to lean into the imaginary sway; he searched the floor for his boots, his jacket. He grabbed both. Looked for the little silver case he kept his things in and snagged that too. He hurried to the doorway and hit the lock.

Cold air streamed down the corridor outside. There had to be an outside hatch open somewhere; unguarded he hoped. A fast exit would suit, straight out onto the dock. A big dock, he reminded himself: Elysian, Omega Quadrant. It would be crawling with people, workers, tourists; lots of places to get lost in. He would need a ship off-planet fast. He'd need another con job, even though he'd had his fill, was sick to his middle with it all. But things were changing out there. He'd best keep moving.

And besides, he'd made a promise and he would keep it.

He moved out into the air-stream, and the chill seeped straight into his bones. He put everything down and shrugged into his jacket, worried by even that small delay: an empty corridor rarely stayed empty for long.

'Stokes!'

He froze; waited for footfalls, uncertain who the voice belonged to.

'Where you going?'

He did a slow about-turn.

It was Dawes, with his ugly twisted face, his jaw turning gum over continuously.

'Cap's cabin.'

'Got that far have you?'

He shrugged. 'Her idea.'

Dawes moved over to the wall com, depressed it, his eyes never leaving his catch. 'Cap? Your little trinket's on the move. That okay?'

'Where's he going?' came back, sharp and edgy.

'Says your cabin. He a little too eager, Cap? You want me to slow him down?'

'No, put him in, lock the door. We're got a bidding war on the unloads, I don't need the distraction. You tell him to take a damned shower, and not to touch my stuff.'

Dawes chewed his gum, took his finger off the link. 'You hear that?' he asked.

'I can go on my own. I don't need an escort.'

'I do what the Cap says, saves me a lot of time and trouble. Move, brat.'

Stokes did as he was told. He picked up his case and walked the corridor without any real clue where the Cap's cabin was. 'You have bidding wars very often?' he asked as Dawes pushed him into the lift. 'I thought you only carried food supplies.'

Dawes grunted. 'Don't ask questions, makes you look like a Downsider when you start being nosy. Spacers don't ask; they do. Downsiders yak, yak, yak.' The lift's door slid to, and the motors came to life, their humming the only noise except for Dawes' chewing.

Stokes got a strange feeling as the lift rose, a tangled knot inside himself. He leaned hard into the metal wall, hugged his case to his chest, swallowed and closed his eyes, tensing as the lift landed and the doors slid open. He managed one word as two of Hetta's crew barrelled inward, hands grabbing for him, the gleam of a hypo flashing closer: 'Pak.'

'Sour-faced bitch' was Frank's first impression of Captain Hetta Combes. The paper she slid over the desk didn't help.

'You want two thousand more? Jones isn't worth that much.'

The Cap raised her brows. 'Had another offer.'

'I thought this was an exclusive arrangement.'

She smiled, the lines about her mouth as deep as knife cuts. 'Nothing's exclusive, Pak.'

Frank added 'liar' to sour-faced bitch. There hadn't been another offer.

'Thinking about keeping the kid. He has good bones. A damned nice attitude,' she said.

Frank frowned: that sounded closer to the truth. Her office stank of cheap perfume; likely she sat drenched in the stuff, likely Jones stank of it too – but the big-time payoffs Frank had lavished on her had so far offset even Jones' obvious charms. Forget following credit chits and fake IDs; if you wanted to find somebody like Jones you hit his main form of transportation – ships like the Cap's that traded right on the edge of what was lawful. Frank picked up the pen on the desk, ringed the two thousand on the note to denote he had no problems with it and slid it back to her. 'If you're looking for a reason to keep the kid, you won't find it here.'

She smiled; he didn't return it.

'So why didn't it go to plan?'

She shrugged. 'It went fine. I fooled him. I didn't even lock him in. He was jump-sick. He was grateful. I played it the way he expected me to, right down to threatening to throw him off.'

'Right up until he tried to leave?'

'Something must have made him antsy. Wasn't me. I admit I played with him a little. Hard not to; not often I get his kind on board. But I had his exits covered and I knew he didn't have a gun stashed anywhere. No licence logged on his chip. No way he was getting one either, not on my boat. We got him cornered, the drugs did the rest.'

'I hope you were careful.'

'I'm always careful with drugs. Don't fret; he's in one piece, he's breathing. And if you play nice, he's all yours. But no transaction on a Rim planet; Customs poke their noses into everything. We'll go further out. We'll do this Reaches style, or not at all.'

You didn't shake hands with freighter caps; you sealed the deal with a nod and an affirmation, nothing else. 'I'm happy to deal.' Frank indicated the note. 'Just as stated. You can call my ship with the details once you've chosen a place, time and date to complete.'

The Cap grunted. 'If I decide to complete, I'll send a messenger. On foot is safer, I don't trust anything to the airwaves around here.' She gave him a predatory look. 'You got any history with this kid besides the job?'

'No.'

Another grunt. The Cap leaned down her side of the desk and pulled out a bottle of bourbon and two glasses. She set the glasses down, poured the bourbon, gliding his over the sheen of the metal. 'Got yourself a nice line of bullshit going on, haven't you? Best you get over it, if you want to finish this.' She took a fast sip from her glass. 'So what the hell am I really carrying, Pak? Not some milksop brat gone AWOL, that's for certain. This kid's a player; says exactly what you want to hear, gives you his puppy-dog look to get where he needs to be. So what is he really?'

Frank picked up his glass, tossing down the cheap bourbon, which soured his throat and made his tongue burn. 'He's a murderer.'

The Cap snorted. 'Not the first one of those I've had on board. Back to my first question – is there some history here? He knows you, you know him.'

'No.'

'You play straight with me, Pak, or I don't play at all.'

Frank straightened in his seat, took a deep breath. 'I took on a job:

a mercenary-type deal on a ship called *The Marabell* – a prison barge out of Eta Quadrant. They had a riot going on on board.' The Government always paid mercenaries to take the first proper look-see. Dead mercenaries looked so much better on the news feeds. 'Coming out of a lift, the man I went in with was killed: headshot. I got hit in the leg. The round went straight through my armour.'

'So sue the manufacturer,' the Cap said helpfully. 'Let me guess: you bought second-hand.'

'I bought what I could afford.'

She smirked at him. 'Cheap gets what it deserves. So what happened?'

'Jones was on board in the transport section. He found me. Helped me.'

'Saved you?' She tagged on a sly little twist of her lips.

'He needed me to get off. Prisoners' IDs are removed; he needed one to access the escape pods. He needed a live one.' Under-the-skin biochips died the moment their owners did; everybody knew that. 'He bandaged me up, got me moving. Got me off that ship.'

'Nice of him.'

'Not nice. He needed me. He deserted me on-planet. He left the pod with nothing but a mask and some oxygen canisters.'

'Left you in agony with no help coming.' The Cap smirked again.

'No – he left me on Almerdia with meds, food, water, and he left the homing beacon running. Search and Rescue found me.' Frank took more bourbon on board while the Cap waited, cold-eyed and rigid.

'Go on.'

'A few days later a man called Clifford Greeley came to see me at the hospital. He's the director of the Dunbar Institution on Beta, the place Jones was being sent back to before he escaped. Greeley told me the kid's been on the run for over two years. He has a list of men he's trying to track down. He's already dealt with two of them. Greeley showed me some holos of the crime scenes. Those men were headshot. Executed.'

'Jones has killed, twice over?'

'Jones plans to kill fifty-seven times over.'

The Cap's eyes widened. 'Doesn't track.'

'It does track. The kid's a killer.'

'Not from what I've seen.'

'You said it yourself: he's a player. You were being played.'

She snorted. 'I don't get played, Pak. How'd he get off Almerdia?'

'He took one of the environmental suits from the pod and walked through twenty miles of desert in a sandstorm to reach a mining dock. He'd have been dodging Search and Rescue and the cops' efforts to find him all the way. Rudimentary, low-tech efforts, granted – but still, you need to be a very determined kind of crazy to face those kinds of odds. He left the planet on a hauler called *The Saxonville*. Greeley called that ship himself; her crew claimed they had no passengers. They claimed they searched their boat, no stowaways. They didn't tell the truth.'

'Why?'

'Because Jones doesn't look like what he is. Because he's a good liar. He tell you any lies? He tell you everything you needed to hear?'

Her mouth tightened, her gaze fixed on the empty sheen of her desktop. 'If he is a killer, he needs a motive.'

'He's deluded. He has a core fantasy dating back years. He's convinced the men he kills have done something evil. He calls what he does justice.'

'So he won't murder just anybody – or he'd have killed you, Pak. He'd had accessed that escape pod then got rid of you the fast way.'

'Which is exactly what Greeley said. His list doesn't change or deviate. His mission is set.'

Her gaze narrowed. 'So why did this Greeley hire you? Why hand a Government problem over to a man he'd just met? You in Investigation?'

'No. Transportation. I used to transport executives out to the Reaches ports.'

That made her laugh. 'I take it that wasn't going too well.'

Frank's turn to squirm. 'No. My ship failed her relicensing application. She needed upgrades. I couldn't get them done and pay my crew. Luck put me in the right place at the right time so I took the job on *The Marabell*. I thought that payoff might give me a little more time to straighten things out. Greeley hired me because he thought I'd made some kind of connection with the kid. Jones has relatives: two aunts on Earth. They want their nephew brought back whole by somebody they can trust. They're worried the cops won't go easy on him, considering what he's done.' Frank unclipped a handheld computer unit from his belt and passed it across the table. 'I'm not supposed to show anybody this, but, if you need proof, this is all the info Greeley gave me. The kid's drugs, his intended victims, his last known contacts.'

The Cap turned the unit about, stabbing a ragged nail at the controls to turn it on.

'Key up Intendeds and you'll get a list of Jones' targets: fifty-seven names, together with locations, marital status and employment details. I've got half the damned things memorized I've checked them over so often.'

'Doctor Vishal Kumar, fifty-three, from Bombay, India, married with one child,' the Cap read off the screen moments later. 'Doctor David Peterson, sixty-eight, from Alfa Station, married, no children. Both dead. Both doctors, one was in Disease Control Research, the other worked in Station Environmentals.' She raised thin, blonde brows. Hit a key. A page flash, and she angled the machine off the desk. Frank saw colours reflected in the metal. There was a picture in the comp's memory: Jones in a group of other kids. A short-haired younger version, standing with his arms slung over the shoulders of his peers, all of them grinning broadly. The rest of the kids wore blue; he wore dark green. His shirt had a logo on the right breast: Beta West Gardens. He must have had a job there some time. Some day-release programme, Frank assumed, one that led to an escape route off station. The kids looked commonplace: a mixed bag of sizes, shapes and colours, maybe twenty all together, looks ranging from the plain ordinary right up to Jones' absurdly good-looking. No names were listed, the pictures headed by the statement 'Seventeenth Birthday Party'. Jones' own, perhaps.

'There a drug this kid won't swallow?' the Cap asked. She'd reached the kid's meds list. An odd mixture of ten drugs, without any of the anti-psychotics you might expect. Instead: vitamins, minerals, decongestants, pain meds, antacids, anti-inflammatories, something to boost the immune system, something for depression perversely right next to a fancy-named stimulant, right next to something to prevent seizures. 'Chemical soup,' the Cap muttered.

A doctor on Almerdia had told Frank the same. It was a dangerously addictive combination too.

Another page flash. 'Known contacts?' the Cap said. 'Let me guess: he's never headed you in the direction of a single one of them?'

Frank shook his head, picked up his glass and downed the rest of his bourbon.

The Cap placed the handheld down and passed it back across the table. 'Your Government man was a little mean with the info, wasn't he? You seriously trust Government?'

'Greeley seems honest enough to me.' Frank retrieved the handheld, turned it off. She was right, the unit contained nothing substantial, and Greeley had never added anything to it. The man – so well dressed, well groomed and well spoken – had been damned unhelpful. There'd been no face-to-face meeting since the initial encounter in the hospital. All Frank had been given was a mailing address if he needed to make contact himself. Every communication since had been sent to and fro scrambled and protected, as if Greeley expected those messages to be intercepted.

Frank didn't feel right about any of it, but he sorely needed Greeley's money. He locked the machine safely back onto his belt.

'I'm not in a hurry to trust anyone with a Government label,' the Cap said.

Frank shrugged. He stayed legal, likely she didn't. He paid the taxes and tariffs he needed to. He tried to be a good citizen; he'd found no reason to be anything else. He reached for the bourbon, pouring himself a fresh glass even though the Cap had hardly touched her own.

'How long have you been looking for this kid?' she asked.

'Eight months and change, ship-time.'

'You ever get this close before?'

'A couple of times, but healthy he's a hard catch. He doesn't quit no matter how hemmed in he gets. He wounded one of my crewmen once to get clear. Shot him in the arm and knocked him out in a bathroom on Zigma Station's shuttle bay. Fried the door lock and left him there. My man was lying there for half an hour before anybody found him.'

'Sounds desperate.' She toyed with her glass, eyeing Frank with no warmth in her gaze.

'Do we have a deal or not?' Frank asked.

'You'll get your kid, Pak, when I'm happy you're not as big a con artist as he is. You don't get a damned thing until I'm satisfied. Understood?'

'So, we're done?'

She almost bared her teeth. 'Not an over-friendly type, are you? Reaches-born ex-military, I'd guess.' She motioned to the scar on Frank's chin. 'Military shows. It shows in all kind of ways. And military goes right along with Government. I'll get somebody to show you off.'

She got rid of him the fast way, handing his exit over to a big slab of a man, all fat, no muscle, ugly as hell too. At the outside lock of the Cap's ship Frank turned back to him. 'How often does your Cap deal straight?'

The man's smile made him uglier still. 'She's old. Nobody's killed her yet. You work out it.' The hatch hissed closed.

Jones, alias Joseph Stokes, alias twenty or so other names, raised his head, realizing that he stood pinned against a wall in a crucifix position. The two men holding his arms shook him.

'Wake up.' The Cap stood in front of him, a stern look on her face.

Jones swallowed, his throat so dry his words became a cough. He guessed where he was: her cabin. A big comp unit was visible, personal effects scattered about on metal shelves. The Cap liked figurines. She liked real books.

'There anything you want to tell me?' she asked sharply. 'Pak's paid a lot to get this far, but that doesn't mean all negotiations are off. There anything you want to say? There anybody you want me to call?'

Call the news stations; he might have choked out. Something's about to happen in the Reaches that'll change everything.

The Cap smiled, coming close in to palm his face in one hand; a controlled move, one that lingered, one she clearly enjoyed. 'I want

25

the truth, Jones. I have Pak's version, now I want yours. Give it to me. Or I'll take it.' She motioned aside to Dawes. Chewing gum as always, he had a hypo set in one fist.

'I take meds.' Jones struggled against the grip of the men who held him.

'I've seen your stash.' The Cap took the hypo and waved Dawes away. 'Let's try again. The truth, then I'll decide how I can profit from it. That's how I do things. I make a profit every which way. I'll take from Pak, from you, from any-damned-body I like.' She touched his face, a languid stroking manoeuvre this time, temple to chin, to lips. 'Take anything I like. You got that straight? Now, you want to tell me your real name or do you want this to get serious?'

He looked her over, piled on the disdain, the contempt, added at the last a knowing smile. 'My real name's Jake,' he said.

CHAPTER 2

Frank stood behind a bluff of rocks at the top of rise, watching a six-limbed lizard scuttle towards him; Frank all too wary of toxins and what a purple and yellow skin might indicate on a creature fast coming into range.

'So we just sit and wait now?' To Frank's left sat one of his crew: Haine. The man glared at the blurred image on the portable monitor of the rain-drenched, empty vista below them. 'This damned planet's an eyesore.'

True. Solkaris, like a lot of Reaches planets, scraped a living, from mining this time around. Frank didn't need the Government's planetary ID logs on his ship to tell him that: the place stank of lubricants even though all the mining went on miles beneath his feet. The fat raindrops left greasy smears in their wake, and if he swallowed one accidentally, it left a slippery, foul-tasting residue on his tongue. No wonder the place had a D-class designation, despite an A-class atmosphere, a low geological risk rating and an advisement that all its native species were 'relatively' benign.

Frank hooked the lizard sideways with the toe of his boot. It rolled, showing flashes of pale abdomen, before it righted itself and ducked under the overhang of a rock. Max Harrison, hugging a rain-slicked boulder, glowered at him for that move. The man held the tiny ultrazoom maxi camera Clifford Greeley had supplied. Next to him, Kady Kincott had charge of the audio mike, another of Greeley's gifts to them, top of the range and beyond anything Frank could afford. Those two members of his crew could easily pass for brother and sister: late twenties, even-featured, blond. The hot looks Kady shot Max every now and again denied that misapprehension.

'Four hours, for Christ's sake. She said two.' Haine, the tallest and broadest of them all, ran a hand across his wide nose. He blew on cold hands, then yanked the hood of his waterproofs down further. In the dimness his dark-eyed, dark-skinned face all but disappeared.

Frank shifted closer to him, not that he wanted the conversation. They had an open-sided shelter up, one that offered little protection from the wind that flapped through it, one they'd need to clean down when they were done. Better it than the greasy rain.

'Just why the hell did you agree to this?' Haine grumbled on. 'Hasn't this brat caused us enough embarrassment? One shot-up arm, one broken tooth, concussion, cuts, bruises, abrasions.' Haine delighted in his list of grievances as if every injury Jones had caused had been to him personally. Frank had taken the broken tooth; the concussion had been Max's. They'd all suffered the cuts, bruises and abrasions, but still Haine took the prize, because he was the man Jones had shot.

'All the time we've wasted on this brat and now here we sit waiting for some woman to deliver him wholesale.'

Frank didn't reply: an answer would encourage more complaints, and he wasn't in the mood. Maybe the rain was the better option. He moved out to the edge of the rocks, squirmed out over one and stared through his binoculars. Nothing to see; below them lay featureless flat land, dotted with puddles. Left to right and back again, zoom in or out, it all looked the same. Solkaris was an eyesore.

'She tunnelling in?' Haine asked him. 'You honestly trust this woman?'

'Her deal, her way,' Frank replied. 'And she's not the type to like an argument.'

'She the type who'll leave us waiting here forever like a bunch of fools?'

'She won't. She took the first instalment. She'll deal straight now for the sake of her reputation.'

'On body traffic. Nice.' That came from Max, Max who'd had a sour look on his face all day.

'We all know what the delay in contacting us was about,' Haine rumbled on. 'She was up for playing with her toy a little longer.'

'She'd have checked Frank out,' Max said, with another lowered-brows look from under his hood. 'His business licences on Beta, maybe even a full check at Central Data.'

Kady pointed eastward. 'Shuttle's coming in.'

'No other ships are allowed anywhere near the drop-off point,' the Cap had said over the com hours earlier. 'No shuttle, no land vehicles, nothing in scan range.'

She'd told them to wait at the top of the hill, then one body was to walk down it. No more, just one man was to make the exchange.

Frank took to the incline, knowing his crew would hear every word. One hint of something amiss and he'd have covering fire if nothing else. Not that it would do him much good; the Cap's ship likely owned enough firepower to wipe out his crew, the incline and half the hillside in seconds.

The incoming shuttle was the mud-brown variety. It came in heavy, hitting so hard the soil gave under Frank's boot soles as he walked towards it. The ship spewed up mud and water as it noisily powered down.

Frank tipped his hood back as the bay doors rose, standing clear as the blonde Cap waved him inside. Frank shook his head: too tight a bay, a large black crate inside it and very little else except muscle. The Cap's crewmen set about the thing on all sides, Frank backing off as it slipped down the ramp-way and made a dent in the dirt. 'What's this?' he asked as the Cap followed it down.

She pointed towards a sky full of dirty grey cloud. 'Never know who's watching. This is the box you paid for, Pak. It looks the same, doesn't it?'

Frank spilled rain off his hood as he shook his head again. 'How the hell should I know?'

'You trust me, that's how you know.' She patted the crate. 'Superior merchandise, all the way from the Inner Rim at hardly a credit's haulage. In perfect condition: no marks, no blemishes. You really want to argue here? You really want another delay?'

Frank glanced back up the hills; looked again at the five-man escort the Cap had at her back. 'I trust you,' he said as if he had a choice. 'But if anything's amiss your second payment goes astray.'

The Cap cackled out a laugh. 'Nothing wrong with this shipment, Pak, it's been tried, tested and approved.' She gave him a smirk, turned and strode back up the ramp-way. The shuttle's door pulled closed.

That simple, that fast an exchange, Frank stood staring at his own reflection in the shiny black sides of the ominous crate she'd left him.

*

Inside the crate Jones' lids flashed burgundy, with a crimson corona. His prison was square rather than oblong, fresh air barely stirring through the breathing holes that circled its lid. He lay nose to his knees, tied and gagged, with no room to move. Worse, the Cap had drugged him. She'd risked mixing her crude concoctions with his meds for the sake of trying to get the truth out of him. She'd done so for days, and for days output from *The Bliss* had tangled with reality: unwanted data, theory, lots and lots of theory, thrown into his mind from nowhere. These days nothing came back straight or with a warning attached. But he hadn't confessed a single thing about Jake. He never did.

He banged one knee into the side of the crate with a thud, the pain stalling it all. He tried to concentrate on sounds, on engine noises and muffled voices, to calm himself, to slow his breathing. But the Cap's drugs slewed every good intention sideways. More of *The Bliss* came back, memories this time, a nauseating surge of them.

Bang went his knees against the crate. More pain to drive it all back and back. Thumps vibrated through the walls, the floor canting beneath his head. He braced his tied hands as it dipped. More thumps, more shifting, and the crate levelled out again. He sniffed, took a deeper breath, the adhesive's vapours of his gag a sour sting in his nostrils. He found another memory: the Cap, her body over his, her breaths short and fast. 'Bad for business.' Her fingers tangled in his hair. 'Beautiful boy, so, so obliging. Now tell me the truth. Tell me where you came from, Jake.' Panic rose, the past, once called, wanting to twist free. The Cap leaned all her weight onto his shoulders, yelling for help, trying to force him down as he struggled.

He strained against his ties, slammed both knees hard into the crate's sides. He squeezed his eyes closed tighter and tighter, the corona flared – as red as blood.

An insurge of fresh air washed over him, accompanied by shouts, curses. Hands dug into his arms and legs.

He didn't fight as he was lifted.

His ankle ties were cut, his feet hitting the ground at odd, tangled angles. He dropped, thumping down onto his shins, the floor beneath him spilling dust into his nostrils. The gag was torn away, jabbing fingers catching at his ribs, trying to free up his wrists. He bawled out his own curses.

'He hurt?' somebody asked.

They prodded him flat, someone pulling his shirt up over his chest in jagged, urgent jerks.

'Jesus, I thought she said no marks.'

'Was she a little rough with you, Jones?' a deep booming voice asked.

They gave him a blanket. He curled himself up in it but found no warmth.

'She must have drugged him.' Another voice: lighter. Kinder. 'It's okay. You're okay now. You're going home.'

He had no idea where that might be. *The Bliss*? He opened his mouth, a hurtled rush of nonsense spilling free. Someone touched his face, and he flinched, striking his head into the crate behind him.

'We should ask for our money back,' the darkest voice said.

'Shut up, Haine, I want to hear what he's saying.'

Tricks, he'd learned those to keep the truth inside, to keep his secrets hidden. He'd confess dead-ends, misdirect if he could. As undone as he was he settled on Milo's name. He let go a string of it, and knew there were tears on his face when he said it. He wanted Milo.

Sixteen years ago . . .

Jake trusted Milo – even when he strapped him into the black box and sprayed something into his veins they called B567. It left him feeling languid, emotionless. He didn't care what they did to him next. It didn't matter. Passive State, they called it. They filled him full of something else they named 1778. Then the door to the box closed, the complete dark, feeling like nothing more than an extension of himself. The screen in front of him lit, colours appeared first, a drift of them. He watched, hypnotized, then numbers and letters started to scroll upwards at such speed he couldn't even recognize their shapes. 'Just lie still, relax and watch,' that's what Milo had told him. 'We're going to make you clever. That's all.'

When the door finally opened again, his eyes stung in the light.

'There, that wasn't so bad, was it?' Milo leaned in to unstrap him. 'How are you feeling?' he asked. 'Good?'

Jake nodded. He tried to stand, but his knees gave way.

Milo picked him up. He carried him through the corridors outside and laid him down on his bed in his little room.

Jake snuggled down, feeling exhausted without knowing why. He closed his eyes.

'Output, in the morning, Jeven,' Milo whispered when he came in to check on him. 'Promise me you'll be a good boy.'

'I promise,' he said.

Output, he discovered, meant sitting at a table in a dim little room and trying to scribble out what he could remember of the information he'd seen the day before. They wanted to match the input to the output. A dark-haired woman sat and questioned him then, asking if he'd understood any of it at all. He hadn't. Med checks came next. Two men scanned his brain and scrawled things on their slates. 'No sign of damage,' one said, sounding surprised, looking at the large screen across the room, the one with layer after layer of brain tissue on it, in violent multi-coloured overlays.

Jake soon settled into the ship's routine. Long weeks, months of sessions. Input. Output. Med scans.

He spent more and more time with the other children. Narie became his best friend: a little red-haired girl, skinny with a big smile. She was always full of fun and devilment.

They sought each other out whenever they could, at mealtimes and playtimes. They'd whisper in corners, exchanging information, trying to decide what was going on: where they were. How big the ship might be, because they'd never seen anything except the same corridors, the same doors. The one marked Bio-hazard, the one marked Key-coded Personnel. The one marked Control Groups. The one marked Species K-900. Keep out. Neither one of them was brave enough to do anything more.

*

At least not until a few months later, when Jake noticed a panel in his room was loose.

Alone one day, he set to work, prising it free, fighting it from its metal lip with a pop of sound. He didn't worry for a second about being caught, far too excited even to consider it.

There were wires behind the panel and a skinny gap of space. It was so narrow he had to wriggle his shoulder in to fit. He edged sideways until the gap grew bigger. Two choices faced him: a ladder in the centre of a pipe leading up and a pathway off to the side. He'd go sideways today, he decided. Up could wait. He squeezed himself along until a grille appeared. He peered through.

The girl in the room was Narie. He didn't recognize the doctor who injected her and settled her inside the black box.

But the other man in the room was Milo.

'How many are you down to now?' the doctor asked.

'Twelve.'

The man hummed. 'Not doing so well on the J series, are we?'

Milo didn't look at him. He stared at the floor.

A shrill piercing scream came from inside the box.

'Dammit.' The man opened the door. Narie tried to burst away from his reaching fingers as he freed her. She beat her fists at him, her mouth yawning wide to let out scream after scream.

'Damn J series.' The man's arms closed like a vice over her shoulders, pinning down her arms. 'Passive State collapse. God knows what she's integrating.' The man hung on, the girl a writhing monster in his arms. 'Get a sedative.'

Milo dashed for a drawer, turned back with a hypo in his fist. Narie collapsed the moment he used it. She lay discarded at their feet.

'We'll watch her for a few days. Monitor the side effects. I doubt she'll last very long. Looks like you'll be down to eleven.'

Jake pressed himself back into the wiring at his back, his breath coming so loudly in gasps he thought they'd hear. The ship felt alive, its pulse thundering through his bones as he held back tears. Milo sobbed as the other man left. He gathered up the little girl's limp body and carried her away.

Jake never saw Narie again. Milo told him she'd gone home.

He didn't want to go back into session. He pretended he was ill, his stomach hurt, his head did. He avoided it for a whole week, then Milo took him to the white room anyway.

The box terrified him, the data, most of all Passive State. He sat shaking when the drugs entered his veins, hoping, begging to find that null time when nothing mattered any more.

His muscles relaxed, he unravelled, feeling each blink grow slower than the last. It was all right. He'd be all right, he persuaded himself. If he just relaxed today would be just like all the hundreds of other days. And it was.

He learned. The Bliss taught him, he was taught no other way. Some of it he understood, some remained beyond him. 'You'll grow into it,' Milo told him. 'It's there ready and waiting for you to grow into. You won't feel it, you'll never know, it'll just be there when you need it.'

He knew now why the The Bliss jumped so often. She was running away. He knew about the Government laws she'd broken; he knew all about the Government now. He knew about Colony directors, station masters, the names of every position you could be elected into. He knew the real power came from the Planetary Heads of State. He knew all their names, the worlds they'd come from, the place they stayed in, their permanent enclave with their families. He knew about war and uprisings. He knew the Government, so closely knit, so determined to resolve every problem amongst themselves, had ended them all. He knew they controlled science, deeming many advancements far too dangerous to be released. Milo said that their caution would kill the future. That The Bliss was the future. She was the future of education, and that freed everybody.

Jake knew The Bliss hadn't freed him.

He secretly searched the ship's duct-ways meaning to escape her, some of the spaces narrowing so badly they scraped the skin from his bones. One day he spilled into a place full of cages. Black-skinned creatures held captive in groups behind great slabs of glass. Half his height, they had taut, sparse bodies and yellow eyes. He stood shaking as they gathered beyond the thick glass, staring at him.

They flared colours.

He blinked. Blinked again, sure he was imagining it as the colours, intermingled, mixed, a huge wash of it hanging over the creatures as if they'd become one giant being.

Was seeing colours one of things he was supposed to grow into? He'd never tell, he vowed. Never.

He didn't hear the footfalls behind him as hands grabbed him and gripped him tightly.

Lieberman.

He pulled away, leaned back on the glass, the creatures behind him baring their teeth at the man. 'What are they?' he gasped.

'They're the source,' Lieberman said. 'They're where it all comes from.'

CHAPTER 3

'Frank?' Max said, his young face full of creases. He stood at Frank's shoulder as Jones, folded within his blanket, finally stilled. 'Did you make sense of any of that?'

Frank grimaced. In his experience you could rely on only two things in life: trouble and confusion. Both came to visit too many times in a lifetime, usually when you didn't want either, usually when things were complicated enough. He'd had his fill of both. The others had drifted back; seated themselves and belted themselves in as the shuttle had begun to move. Max had asked that question because likely as not he'd lost Jones' words over the metal's vibration, over the engine's ardent howl as the ship had begun to pull up. But Frank had the gist of it, the name at the centre of it all as Jones' words had fallen headlong into and over each other. Jones had a list of fifty-seven people, and his life revolved around killing every one of them. Frank had wondered at those names long and hard for eight months; he knew exactly where Milo Horton's details lay on Greeley's handheld. Horton lived on a spit-of-nothing planet in the middle of nowhere, and it sounded like Jones had not only been to visit, he had a long-standing relationship with the man. Something with friendship involved, something with emotion involved. And if that was a fact, something had to be very, very wrong with Greeley's version of the truth.

Jones lost hours to feverish sleep. He thought he ought to still be in the crate when he woke, but no – he found himself in another grey room, listening to not the shuttle's whine, but to a lower-grade hum. The sound of a bigger ship. Frank Pak's ship, *The Nova*.

He knew what he'd done, but even after the stress of being cooped up in the blacked-out crate, even under the influence of the Cap's drugs, he'd only lost one name: Milo, Milo's place, his last stop before he'd found passage on the Cap's freighter. His home literally underground because Milo lived like some animal in a burrow, hidden down deep with his up-link and his computers: Milo listening to the world go by on the buoy up top with all the equipment he needed to unlock every piece of hidden agenda that buoy sent through the black, FTL or otherwise: Milo breaking the law, breaking into encrypted data packets. He sent warning after warning. Stay on Reaches, never stray into the Inner Rim. There are too many people looking for you. Alexander Calder's calling in favours. Things are changing every day now. Power plays are being made. Be careful. You'll get caught.

Jones lifted his head, the door sliding open. His eyes blurred, watered; Frank Pak a gliding shape, a bleary ghost, getting closer and closer.

'You awake? Bad idea; we're going to jump. You have an aversion to that, according to Greeley.' The man took his arm, aiming something at it. 'It's a trank. A nice safe one. Nothing that's going to bother whatever the hell else you're on right now. You hearing me?'

Frank had a colour, it was the lightest blue. It made Jones' insides hurt. After *The Marabell* he'd dearly hoped he'd never see that colour again. He'd hoped he never have to deal with any of the complications that came right along with it.

He didn't have any reason to believe the hypo was anything dangerous; he relaxed and let the man apply the sprayer. He heard the canister deploy, lost the rest.

'Jones?' His name was called later – much, much later perhaps, he had no way to tell. No way to know where the ship had jumped from or where she'd ended up. The drug left him in some lazy, languid place between sleeping and waking, where his body didn't ache, where the bruises on his ribs didn't catch every time he breathed too deeply.

'Why didn't you kill Milo Horton?' Frank's voice sounded a long way away, light years distant. 'He's on your list, same as the other two you put down. But you didn't kill him. You want to go back to Milo, Jones?'

'Go to hell,' the words felt clumsy in his mouth: too big, too awkward.

'You want some info? Does he help you out? You hold a gun to his head while he does that? Did he get your drugs supplied for you? He's a doctor, he could do that. He could get one of those prescription passes logged onto that fake ID chip of yours. Your chip good enough to do that?'

Jones focused on the face that hung over him: salt and pepper hair, dark eyes. The scar that corded Frank's chin· a wide, fat, ugly scar.

'I put a call out to him. I got a reply. I asked him all about you. About how come you didn't kill him like you were supposed to. I got an answer, Jones.'

Jones wanted to laugh. 'He wouldn't have talked to you.'

'Maybe we'll go pay him a visit.'

'You don't know where he is.'

'You're talking like there's some friendship involved, Jones. Where did that come from? You're a head case, a reasonless fanatic on a little seek-and-destroy mission. Isn't that the truth?'

'It's not reasonless.' Jones held his breath to stall the rest. His *Bliss*-damaged mind loved anomalies; it threw up all kinds of twisted challenges. Frank Pak was one of them. 'Steal the rest if you want it so badly. Use some more drugs and steal it,' he blurted. 'Try and fail – the Cap did.'

Nothing happened. There was no fresh assault on his arm to pump more drugs home; instead Frank backed off. Jones heard him on the wall com outside, calling for the case that must have been packed up inside the crate with him.

He lay still and waited.

Frank meant to paw through his possessions for clues, and Frank had an escort all of a sudden: a big black man. Jones knew him: Haine. Haine with an electronic dart gun he held cocked and ready as if he thought his captive might be physically able to make a charge for freedom.

Frank set himself down in the open doorway, opened up Jones' little silver case and slowly began to take pieces of clothing from it: raggedy, end-of-stock clothing because Jones never wasted his money on the good stuff. Clothing Frank searched before he set each piece aside. Old shuttle tickets came next; a snowstorm of paper scraps, some of them dark with scribbled, intricate shapes. Jones wrote in a code all his own. Frank barely even glanced at the pages. At the case's bottom he found Jones' comp unit. He lifted it clear and began hitting keys. 'You leave any secrets behind on here?' he asked it as if he knew the answer already.

The unit was so old it did very little. Jones played games on it to pass the time, to fill the hours of boredom and emptiness he rarely filled with company.

Frank discarded the unit as quickly as he had the rest. He stood up and pulled something else from his pocket. The sight of it made Jones start, made him put up his wrist where the thing ought to be strapped. 'What's this?' Frank asked.

'It's a medical alarm. Press red and the display will tell you when my meds are due.' He was overdue; even full of tranks Jones felt the dip in his attention span, the tremble in his flesh and the tingle in his fingertips. He wiped at a runny nose, rubbed at eyes that wanted to close.

'What's this, Jones?' Frank asked sharply. He'd pulled something else from his pocket, something that must have been taken from Jones' own pocket earlier. Frank held up a little carved wooden bear. Milo's carve-and-lase kit had fashioned it. The kit Jones had taken as a present to a friend with a little artistry in his hands.

'It's a bear.'

'Earth creature, right?' Frank frowned at it. Maybe the man had never seen the animal before. Milo's favourite: a Canadian brown bear, resident of Alfa's zoo. A picture on the man's handheld had become the model for it. When its varnish had finally dried Milo had presented it like the prize it was. 'I made you something. Keep it safe. Keep it with you.'

He'd escaped Greeley's institution and tracked the man down. Milo, who'd stood at the door of his rickety little shack on a faraway world, his face turned ruddy with shock. The past had come to call. His reckoning had come after so many years of guilt. But Jones had no final peace to give him, just demand after demand, Milo so silent, so yielding, so full of remorse.

'Vent it. Vent all of it. None of it's worth a damned thing.'

Whatever Frank had hoped to gain with his little circus of prying, he'd failed. He packed the case back up and gave it to Haine, and Haine carried it away. Frank leaned a shoulder into the door's frame and folded his arms. 'Greeley lied to me. He told me you don't deviate. And you did. Big time.'

'Your problem. Not mine. I need the head. You going to help me use the head, Frank?'

Frank made a huff of sound: amusement or pure disgust, Jones wasn't sure which. The man stepped out and closed the door.

The eight steps to the head set Jones' head throbbing, his vision a sickly rush of edgeless shapes. He needed ten deep breaths before he could focus enough even to find the right button to press to release the head from its drawer-like slot in the wall. His urine was thick, deep yellow and likely full of chemicals. He had very little water in his system right then to help flush them out. Done, he stared hard at the head's little inset stickers: Press once for standard flush, twice for double flush.

Water was precious on a ship, it cost her to carry it and filter it clean over and over again. Jones flushed the head three times for the sake of wasting it.

He pressed the button to slide open the sink, leaned over and drank from the tap. He pressed down both warm and cold taps then but found they were on a timer. He flushed the head again, hitting full flush five times before someone thumped on the window. 'Stop that or I'll lock the damned thing into the wall.'

Frank was back.

Jones went to the door, slumping hard against it for the sake of his wandering balance. Dark-eyed Frank stared at him. 'Kady's getting your pills sorted. You're late, over five hours and counting,' he said.

Not good news, but the drugs the Cap had given him, the drugs Frank had given on top of those, had hidden the worst of the withdrawal. You could fool a body sometimes.

Frank stared, eyes sharp. 'So Milo Horton's your friend now, is he?'

Jones smiled. 'Do you think Greeley hired you because he thought you'd be stupid enough to stand there and ask me questions, Frank? Find a fast way out of this. Head for the far Reaches. Go somewhere quiet and listen to the feeds. Something's about to start, something you don't want any part of.' Sincerity earned him a puzzled frown. Passive State collapse, the Government's this time, their nice steady safe regime was about to go to hell. 'Revolution, Frank. Free the tech. All that dangerous stuff the Government's been hanging onto.'

Frank shook his head, looking half annoyed, half amused. Political peace had bred that lack of concern, lifetimes of it. 'Don't bother playing mind games with me, Jones.' The line of Frank's lips curved as if he wanted to add something with a softer edge, something about *The Marabell* most likely. But Frank was interrupted. 'Kady's here.'

Jones' meds came in a little plastic cup. Fifteen little friends come on home to him. He sat on the bed with the water bottle they came with and swallowed them down, one by one. Food came next: a heat pack carton and a big heat pack drink. He couldn't eat the food but he sipped the drink down slowly, the hot chocolate sweet and sickly. Finished, he lay down and waited, angling his head so he could see the window between his naked feet. Frank appeared. Nice man Frank, visibly still deciding what he dare and dare not ask. His quarry didn't deviate, his quarry killed – Greeley must have hammered that message down hard.

Jones plumped up a pillow and settled his head back down, closed his eyes and drifted, knowing nice man Frank would leave. Frank didn't like the look of the truth. Not today.

Frank took Jones' case up to the galley. It wasn't the best place to sit and brood, with people passing in and out constantly collecting food and drinks, but there he sat, setting all Jones' things out on the galley table.

Jones had him pegged, five hours on *The Marabell* had seen to that: an ex-military grunt, one who knew when to keep his mouth shut, one who knew he'd be a fool to play stupid games with Greeley's truth.

'Did you call Horton?' Kady made her way to the drinks machine.

Frank nodded. 'Yes, but I doubt any computer listing for him is even real if he's involved with Jones. We're not going to get an answer.'

'Are we happy, or sad?'

'Happy . . . I suppose.'

Kady tapped her order into the machine, the bright-red appliance a recent upgrade thanks to Greeley's money. *The Nova* bulged with Greeley upgrades. Kady leaned a hip into the machine's warm side to wait. 'You want to try moping out loud for once? You want to give a little insight into what's going on between you and pretty boy Jones?'

A straight question. The straightest any of his crew had dared recently. Frank squirmed where he sat. He had given them a rough outline of what had happened on board *The Marabell* – at least as much as he'd given Combes and Greeley. He'd missed a lot out, the details, the A to B to C confession. 'Not right now.'

The drinks machine pinged its Ready signal; it was ignored. 'Are you ever going to tell us?'

Frank let his face go rigid; his time in the military had taught him how to do that, desperation had taught him something else. He'd aimed his fists at Jones on *The Marabell*, told him to save himself. Lies, all of it. Jones had seen right through every word, grinning at him, all damned pretty boy: jet-black hair, green, green eyes. Saying in solid reassurance as if his word meant something, *'I'm going to help you, Mr Pak. I swear to you, I'm going to help you.'*

'He needed me to get off that ship, that's all you need to know.' He gave his standard reply, used his standard glower to go with it. 'And Jones broke my damned tooth. We forgetting that? We forgetting he shot Haine? Jones doesn't go easy on anyone.'

That shut Kady down – for a whole ten seconds. 'Still, can't blame the Cap for wanting to hang on to him as long as she did.' She grinned, clearly heading the conversation in that direction to needle him. 'Joking. I'm allowed to joke, aren't I? We've all gotten so serious lately anyone cracks a smile I think I ought to vid it.' She finally collected her drink and sidled over, settling herself down opposite him. 'What's that?' She picked up the bear from the mess on the table. 'Nice. Where'd he get that, you suppose?'

Frank shook his head. 'He told me to vent it . . . along with the rest.'

'Well, there's not much here to hang on to, is there?' She passed a hand over the clothes pile. 'Not exactly *très chic*, is he? Looks more like he was going for the dock tramp look, all long hair and dirt. Still, he got by. He had a pocket stuffed full of station credits.' She sighed. 'Still, not enough clues here to explain that fake ID. That would have cost him – Joseph's a nice name. I could go for a Joseph.'

'But you'd be joking.'

Pink painted lips curved upwards. 'He's too young for me. A little out of my league, too.'

'A serial killer is out of your league?'

Her smile widened. 'I was thinking more in the looks department. Nice trophy though, I can seriously see the Cap's angle.
Obviously the serial killer part puts him down my to-do list a
little.'

Frank plucked the bear carving from her fingers and put it back
inside the box. He leafed through the ticket stubs and the notes he
couldn't read.

Kady cocked her head, watching him. 'You think there's something more here, don't you?' she said, her voice low and wary. 'You
think if this kid went to all that trouble on *The Marabell* he can't be
all that bad. That if Greeley told one lie, he might have told a dozen.'

Frank glared up from under his brows, but this time his standard
glower didn't work. She kept right on going.

'You're thinking this kid got some help somewhere along the
line, too. Not just from this Milo character either, a big mess of
help from somebody with money. Help that might come after us if
they get to know pretty boy's locked up in a cell.'

'You done?'

'If you're allowed to mope your way through this thing you can't
blame the rest of us for doing the same.'

Frank leaned back in his seat. 'You the spokesperson? Has there
been some talk going on between you all I ought to know about?'

'I'm an independent operator, you know that. I don't need anybody shoving me in any kind of direction, thank you.'

'Fine . . . you hate me doing this alone, you keep on going.'

Kady wrinkled her nose, narrowed hazel-coloured eyes. 'Okay,
how about the pill stash? Who takes fifteen of those damned things
a day these days? You telling me some doc somewhere couldn't go
in and fix some of those neurological problems he's supposed to
have? I checked those pills on the med comp; they're highly addictive even on the low-dose versions Jones takes. The point is, pills

can make people crazy just as easily as they can cure them. Pills can be used to control a person, make them dependent on you. Make them afraid not to behave. Afraid to leave.'

'But he found a supplier, and he must have done that soon after he escaped.'

Kady nodded. 'Horton, most likely. Jones had intel before he left the station, must have.' She frowned. 'Why didn't Greeley just put a tracker tag in the little bastard? That would have slowed him down.'

Frank pressed a nail into the side of the case where the thing had taken a dent. 'Sounds like a lot of unanswered questions to me. You want me to give the kid a few more drugs; we could get the whole damned truth that way? You think I ought to do that? Because Greeley's not talking, and he's Government, and Government attention we can well do without.'

Kady pursed her lips. 'You signed stuff before you joined the military, didn't you? You're a military man, holding secrets just like old helmsman Foley, right?'

'That's different, that's just a general sign-off. I wasn't in Ops or Security, I never saw any military secrets worth a damn. This is bigger. Worse. Nothing about this thing feels right.'

'Except the money?'

'That was the biggest red flag of all.'

'So, back to the pretty boy on *The Marabell*?' Kady suggested.

'There's no debt there.'

'Yet, the boss refuses to do anything but bullet points when it comes to that ship. He goes off on his own to mope about it all the time instead. Are you confused, Boss? Because the rest of us are.' Kady's face was grave. 'What exactly are we supposed to think about this kid the boss says he owes nothing to?'

Frank made a point of reaching across the table's width and catching at her sleeve. 'Don't let the looks fool you, or the attitude.

Jones can do charm. He'll say any damned thing you need to hear if he thinks he'll gain from it. You be careful around him, you hear me?'

Kady nodded. Twenty-eight years old and she did what she chose to, when she chose to, but she knew her limits.

Lord, Frank hoped that was the truth.

CHAPTER 4

'A Colony director's son, aren't you, Mr Max? You into politics? Costran, isn't it, out on the Reaches?' Jones rested against the composite of his cell door and stared right at Maxwell Harrison. Max had been a cop on Gamma Station. He looked the earnest, innocent type, all wide cornflower-blue eyes, blond hair and capsule-tanned skin. 'All your brothers and sisters live together in one place, don't they, like they're afraid of catching something.' He kept his voice airily light, just like a politician. 'Does Daddy know if anybody's doing anything behind the Government's back? There any dissent?'

Max stared at him as if he'd lost his mind. Max knew where to find a revolution; he'd look it up in a digital library. 'Frank said you were talking crazy. He told me to ignore you.'

'You're not concerned? Tell me, are any of your siblings acting strangely?' Jones let out troubled sigh. 'Damn, I forgot, you haven't been home in over a year.' He hooked a finger through one of the precision-cut Os in the composite window. 'So, why did you do it?'

'Do what?'

'Take that bribe they kicked you out of the cops for.'

Max's face stilled, every sharp plane and angle evening out.

'That's one hell of a face, Mr Max. Did your respectable Colony director father break the law to get a good-looking son? You know the Government propaganda about those gene ships. They're illegal and dangerous. You could drop down dead any second.'

'I'm not an illegal,' Max said curtly. 'And my life isn't any of your business.'

'Well, you're right into my business, Mr Max.'

'Your business is our job, or did that pass you by?'

So Max did sarcasm; cops liked that. He had a cop's haircut too: a regulation buzz cut the man was obviously fond of, though it did him few favours – unless that was the point.

'Did your family throw you out?' Jones asked.

'They didn't throw me out.'

'You throw yourself out? My info says you did.'

Max's eyes narrowed. 'Your what?'

'I've got lots of info, Mr Max. It says you went on a three-day drunk before you decided to take a long trip Inner Rim to a friend on Earth. Did he throw you out, by any chance?'

Max's mouth opened; closed. No fast retort appeared. Cop slow to react; he'd obviously rather shut up than mess up.

'So, my info's right?'

Max edged a little closer, the crease between his eyebrows like the three-pronged imprint of a bird's claw. 'I don't give a damn about your info. I'm not here to make conversation. I'm here because that damned fool Cap filled you full of drugs. Somebody has to watch you. I'm not here to talk, or to listen. You understand?'

'Fine. I'll just ramble on to myself; you don't have to listen. Your friend threw you out, so you went to Beta Station and found a dumb job you knew your father would hate. Being a cop's one thing, it comes with lots of kudos. Daddy could stare down his nose and say, "Hell, law enforcement's as good as charity work." But finding out your son is being paid to ferry businessmen around is like finding out he has no brains, no civil conscience and worst of all no intention of redeeming himself. That has to hurt. But you want to hurt him. You spent long enough trying to please the old bastard, time for a little payback.'

No reaction. It seemed you could prod at Max all day and he wouldn't react. He'd just stare at you with his soft blue eyes and his good-looking face and sigh a little.

'Daddy treated you like dirt. The precious family name had taken a beating. Director Harrison wouldn't like that. He's far too far up the Government's backside these days.'

Max shook his head. 'You want to rile me, find something else. I'm over this.'

Jones leaned closer to the window, his words a mist of condensation between the grid of Os. 'The men who wanted you to take that bribe took you down into the bowels of Gamma Station. They hung you off a gantry rail by your ankles with maybe a fifty-foot drop below you. I'd be scared – how scared were you? But they threatened more than just you, didn't they? They threatened your sister.' Finally he got a reaction: a tiny involuntary flinch. 'Little sister Judy. Fourteen years old, on station in school, living with you. They drugged her senseless, tied her wrists, spread her legs wide apart. Put their dirty hands all over her, right up until you yelled, "No".'

'Shut up, Jones.'

Jones stared straight into cornflower-blue eyes. 'You caved. You did whatever they asked. They wanted the cop codes, didn't they? The codes that gave them access to a high-security section of station's rat runs. Antiques theft, wasn't it? All that for a few pieces of old Earth wood. They upped your bank balance to make you look like an accomplice, then they got off station and told you to stay quiet. And you stayed quiet for months because you were sure they'd left somebody behind to watch you. Somebody who might decide to finish off what they'd started with you and your sister.'

'I said, shut up, Jones.'

'Then, for her sake, you told somebody what had happened, so you could get her off the station. Somebody you thought you could trust, who would help you work it all out without getting the cops involved. Director Harrison, the man with all the power, all the influence. But Daddy's a real politician, so he called the authorities and sent your life all the way to hell.'

Max banged on the composite. Shoved his palm against it. Leaned towards the lock.

'Max,' a barked call came from behind him. Max shoved off and turned around. 'What's going on?' Frank's question, Frank coming in like a fire blanket.

Max glared at Jones. 'He's done some digging. He knows things about me. About my time on Gamma. Details.' He paused for breath before adding sourly: 'And he was yammering about a rebellion again.'

'That's getting old,' Frank landed a hand on Max's shoulder, whispering something to him Jones couldn't catch before raising his voice again as he towed the man clear and set him on his way. 'Go down to the hold, get those prison reg clothes out of stores for our guest here.'

Jones, propped against the door, calmed the angry pound of his heart. A close call, very close, he'd had more to use, too – Milo knew how to dig and dig into people's lives. He could have added lies to the truth, lies about that father Max loved so much and hated just the same. Get a man off balance; he'd do a hundred stupid things.

'So you have some info, do you?' Frank hooked his fingers into the Os at the composite's sides, spread his body across the width of the window and hung there, all threat, his face close in and stern.

Jones smiled at the posturing. 'You want to hear?'

Frank gave a quick, hard nod.

'Frank Pak, forty-two, son of a mining-sloop helmsman. Single. No kids. Joined the military at seventeen and became a grunt on *The Monterey*. Got out aged thirty-one after his dad was killed in a mining-rig accident. The insurance settlement was big time. It bought him a ship, *The Nova*: an old ship. He hired a helmsman called Foley he'd known on *The Monterey* and set himself up a company doing haulage for five years. Then he bought a military-grade belly gun. The big corps like those, and the ex-military types who can pass the psych tests to keep on using them. And you keep on doing just that, don't you, Frank, because you're not prone to temper, or to panic. Such a shame you failed every advancement test you applied for in the military. No rank advancement. Not academically bright. But that's all the dull part, isn't it? You want to talk about your childhood? Your mother? You were ten years old when she walked out. She took your brother with her, but she left you behind. Was there something wrong with you, Frank? Something she didn't like?'

Frank didn't scowl at that announcement, he smiled. 'That's very good, but I hope you didn't pay too much for it because it's worthless.'

'Is it? Yet it all fits in so neatly. You never married, you bar-crawl for friends. You save them from their own messed-up lives by employing them because that way they're less likely to desert you – or worse, be disappointed in you. You risked your life on *The Marabell* to keep all those grateful people around you. They won't make you feel worthless the way your mother did. All your rejects and discards wouldn't dare. They're all so predictable, so safe, but they're all broken, Frank. Almost as broken as you are.'

'So who glued you whole, Jones?' Frank pulled his fingers clear of the window, backing a step before sighing, long and deep. 'You really think trying to rile us is going to get you something?'

'I know you. That'll get me something.'

Frank cackled out a stiff, strained laugh. 'It'll get you a shower and some fresh clothes right now, not much else.'

'I'd rather have some food. Right now.'

'Three hours on *The Marabell* and I know you too, Jones. You want anything from me, from now on I'm going to make you say "please".'

Jones laughed himself, a well-practised easy roll of it, he turned it into a smile; the brightest one he owned. 'Is that all you've got to threaten me with? "Please". Fine. I'd like some food, please, Frank.' He won another cold, intense study for that.

'Kady's in charge of you, med- and meals-wise. All your intake has to be logged, according to Greeley. I'll send her down to sort you out.'

'Can't wait.' Jones added a smirk to that, pointing off down the corridor. 'So what's down there?'

'You doing recon, now? Don't you know the ship as well as you know us, or do you just want to keep the conversation going?'

Jones shrugged. 'You decide. You're the one in charge, Frank.'

Frank narrowed his eyes but still motioned ahead. 'Lift to A deck, or down to C.'

'A deck?'

'Helm, living quarters, the galley.'

'This is B deck?'

'Holding. Greeley sent word that he wanted all three guest quarters stripped down and made into holding cells. You think he's expecting company?'

'I don't know, is he?'

'Leave Kady alone, there's a lot there to pick at.'

'Then you'd better warn her.'

'Don't worry, Jones, I'll be warning everybody.'

Kady Kincott had a hard-eyed look. The dark teardrop of a birthmark marred her left cheekbone, her hair was a vivid mix of red and pale blonde. She appeared ten minutes after Frank's exit and she'd clearly been tipped off. 'Heard you're doing life stories now. You want to do mine? You want me to start you off? Orphanage ship, *The Milan*, out of Cappa Station. A good girl right up until they abandoned me at eighteen on station with a hundred credits and a job slip. Go to office C, pick up form two-two-one. Get a sleepover pass for a fortnight. After that, go to hell.'

Jones, at the window, said nothing. He dropped his attention down to the selection of cartons she'd brought along on a tray: soup, drinks. No bread, no biscuits, not a sniff of anything sweet, and he craved that.

'You want me to go on revealing myself, Pretty Boy, or do you want feeding? I know, let's get me all stripped naked and out in the open first.' Her brows lifted on the beat of stripped naked, blush-pink-painted lips becoming a crescent. 'Almost raped at nineteen. You want to get into that like you did with Max and his sister? You want to go over that in some detail?'

A cough caught Jones by surprise, turning his reply into a spluttered-out breath. His next clear in-breath sent a stab of pain across his ribs. He bent half over, wincing.

Kady cocked an eyebrow. 'Sounds nasty. You after some sympathy?'

Jones coughed again. Coughed until his head ached with pressure, the surge of pain intensifying across his ribs until he was forced to sink down beneath the window. He sat there panting hard, feeling the weight of Kady's stare on the crown of his head.

'You still waiting for sympathy? Sympathy's not stupid enough to come in there alone, so we might as well get back to me. Almost raped at nineteen coming out of one of those dive bars in Cappa's bowels, one of those here-one-night-gone-the-next places. I took the fast way down one of the service-bots' maintenance tube-ways and hey presto – a two-man hunting party. Lucky for them there were two of them. I knifed one in the thigh, got the other across the face. Got me a little scar, too, across the breast. You want to look?'

Jones let his head sag, wishing she'd shut up for ten seconds.

'Hey, you okay?'

The door flap behind his back pinged a warning as it slid open.

'Try the juice if your throat's playing up. It's chock full of sugar. It'll stick.'

Some boxes were pushed through, the flap closed. Jones scooted them round in front of him, his free hand curled up middle chest where the congestion still sat like a lump of gristle. He read the Day-Glo colours of the juice labels: orange, pineapple, an alien fruit called *hallash*. The soups were chicken, beef, a bird called a *gnasheer*. 'You have any chocolate?' He peered up at the window but he couldn't see Kady. 'The dark kind?'

'I don't know.' Kady leaned back into view. 'Not sure anybody eats the dark kind. Might be something in stores down below. The stuff Frank feeds the executives.'

'Could you look?'

'Damn cold down there.'

'Max is down there, isn't he? Couldn't you ask him to look?'

Kady puffed out a grunt. 'Sounds like you're asking for a favour.'

'I saved your boss, didn't I? That's worth a favour. I got you all a well-paid job when he was going out of business.'

'Lord, Jones, are you employing me now?' That made her laugh. 'Fine, I'll go down myself. I'll go visit Max. I'll go warm him up some, he'll like that.' The suggestion was breathy, as if she meant to warm Max up the fast way. Sex down in the cold, all wrapped up tight with handsome Mr Harrison. She was the type and she wouldn't be bashful of the fact either. Jones heard her on the wall com calling for reinforcements. He opened a drinks packet meantime and got a slug of tepid orange juice down. Full to the brim with added glucose, it eased a thousand hurts.

'Time to go, Pretty Boy.' Kady leaned back into view over the rim of the door. 'Thanks for saving the boss. Must be a comfort knowing you've done at least one good thing in your miserable, twisted little life.'

He forgot himself, frowned, then hurriedly plastered on a smile to cover it. 'You spend any time warming him up?' It was the truth, had to be. Frank and Kady, Max and Kady, anything with a pulse and Kady.

Kady just shrugged at him. 'Takes something cheap to know its own kind, kiddo. How cheap were you with the Cap?'

'Very damned cheap,' he sent back. She grinned down at him, a little twinkle softening her eyes. She'd take everything he threw at her, he knew it, and she'd smile, and she'd shrug.

'Got to go, Jones. Don't wear yourself out.'

'You neither.'

With her gone he clawed his way upright. He placed his palm flat to the door's lock and took a deep breath. *The Bliss* had taught him to do more than see colours. She'd taught him lots of secret things he'd never confessed to anyone. Sometimes he could push his thoughts right into circuit boards. Sometimes things exploded. He winced and let out a frustrated breath. Not this time.

Big man Haine appeared next. He looked like a volcano on the edge of blowing apart. He stood outside the window, brows set into a downturned V, eyes jet-black and fixed. Jones saw a flash of colour. The man's aura. Purple, black, brown. Not pretty, but then neither was Haine.

Jones stood with a drinks carton, steadying his cough and himself with a prop of glucose. He had a tremble now that refused to settle, a flush of heat rising over his body that brought sweat to his forehead. Likely he'd been given something extra during their last trip through a jump-gate's nauseating folding exercise.

'Foley's got something on the scan up top,' Haine said in a voice as deep and dark as his stare. 'Some ship's vectoring in without broadcasting an ID signature. You got any idea who it might be? This ship's got one hell of a belly full of armament. Whoever it is, they just might find themselves in pieces if they're not careful.'

The news, unlike the sweetness of the orange juice, didn't sit well. Jones frowned. 'No ID? Sounds like a pirate.'

'You know any pirates, Jones? Or are you only interested in revolutions?'

Jones smiled at that sneering attack, forcing the expression to stay put even when he noticed the sheen of sweat on his forearms as he leaned hard into the cold window. He was getting a little backwash of dizziness every time he dared to move in his head now too. 'Pirates? They're not my problem.'

'No. That's right, our problem. Cops don't like debris. Military don't either. We'll be in all kinds of trouble if we leave anything behind us in little pieces. You want to warn anybody?'

'It's a pirate. Or it's nobody. Ships glitch.'

Haine's wide nostrils flared. 'Fine.' He went to the wall com, went on it to ask what was going on up top.

'Got an ID now,' an unfamiliar voice returned. 'It's a little pleasure sloop. *The Valdese*. Nothing to worry about.'

'Got it, Foley.' Haine turned back to the door. 'You were lucky this time. The boss might have needed that info, and I might have decided to take it.'

Jones made sure the smile he wore this time was small and smug. 'The boss might not have been too pleased with that.'

'The boss would get over it.'

'Has the boss been playing fast and loose with my meds? Has he dosed me with something extra? Damn fool if he has.'

'You think the boss is after your bones the way the Cap was?'

'That a no, or a maybe? Because I don't know how the boss is inclined. Do you? The boss nearly got himself killed to pay your wages. So he must love you. He must really love you, Haine.'

Haine grunted. 'Heard you've been playing a few games down here. So did you get to the transparent section of your repertoire? Why don't you try yelling, "Let me out. Let me out." That'd be about as subtle.'

'So, "Let me out."' Jones mimicked the man's deep, dark rumble perfectly. 'You know you want to. I've given you enough excuses: insulting your crew, getting into their lives. And didn't I put a hole in you somewhere? On Zigma, wasn't it? Why not take a little revenge? You want a few more reasons to get some payback – off an orphanage ship, weren't you, just like shy little Kady? Worked in every job going. Don't you get along with people, Haine?'

Haine snorted. 'Why not just get to the best part?'

'Your choice. So, let's start with Lisa. You shot her dead. One murderer to another, how did that feel?'

'You tell me.'

'But you loved her. That makes a difference. Drugged up out of her skull, firing a gun into the furniture, then at you. You took fire, didn't you? Shot in the shoulder, grazed across the stomach. And then you shot the woman you loved. When isn't love enough, Haine? Well, you know that answer now.'

Haine gave a deep, throaty laugh. 'Oh, you really want to play, don't you, brat?'

'Like you said, the boss will get over it. The boss will forgive just about anything, won't he?'

Haine narrowed his eyes. 'How about I leave the guns in the corridor? How would that be? How about I slap you around a little just to make myself feel better?'

Jones put his juice carton down on the floor. 'Deal. You opening the door now or are you going to keep on jabbering at me?'

Haine showed teeth, his smile more of a snarl, his gaze suddenly very bright. He unclipped both weapons from his belt – the real gun to his right, the dart gun to his left – making a show of holding up both before he chose a spot on the far side of the corridor to lay them down. He turned back around. 'You want to change your mind? I come in there I do payback in spades. Like you said, the boss does forgiveness.'

Jones backed up three steps to give himself some room as Haine keyed the door open.

The man loomed in the doorway, his hands raised a little but not yet fisted: big hands, muscular arms and neck, on a body only going soft across its middle. Haine used the ship's gym all right but he clearly ate to soothe the pain. He probably drank too; he had enough reason to. He'd come home one night and found his wife in a drugged-up frenzy, shooting pink flamingos on her new Vulmara flooring. Imaginary pink flamingos with big dirty feet. He'd killed her. All his choices gone because she hadn't felt the first bullet, or the second, or the third; only the fourth to her brain had stilled her. Haine went half crazy himself then, until Frank Pak found him passed out in a bar one night. Frank really did bar-crawl for friends. One act of mercy Frank might regret if Haine was habitually this unpredictable, this extreme.

Jones backed up another three steps.

'You running away?' Haine asked. 'You're not scared of a few bruises, are you, brat?' He'd left the door ajar. Jones sidestepped, needing more of an angle to see the guns the man had left behind. He guessed it would come down to a scramble, plus a few bone-jarring thumps before he laid hands on either. He'd faced trickier odds; he'd dodged the faster Max and Frank a time or two.

He waited as long as he dared then moved hard and fast to Haine's left. Haine swung at him, and he ducked back then tried to slip by, but Haine's clumsy punch proved to be a ploy. Haine lunged and snared a fistful of shirt. He hung on, pulled hard, and they both went down. Flesh hit, bones smacked into metal, and Jones' world of greyness turned a shade darker. He tried to wriggle free, took a thump across the cheek, another on the other side that scraped across his chin. Then Haine wheezed a breath. 'You want some more?' He threw a punch that set Jones' nose streaming blood. Jones balled himself up, flashpoints of pain racing from point to point across his face.

Guns in the corridor.

He kicked out, connected, got a grunt out of the man followed by a flat-handed slap across the skull that set his ears ringing.

'You want to get out of here so bad? I'll take you out.'

Jones fought every handhold; his shirt tore, nails scraping his back. He took another blow low to the stomach and doubled up again. Haine leaned over him, his lips curling around a torrent of curses. Jones yelled, his ankle caught, pain ripping through his insides as Haine wrenched him straight and dragged him across the shine of the plating and out through the open doorway.

Guns in the corridor.

His stretching fingertips brushed the grip of one weapon, the gun spinning half around. He made a stretch and a grab, but still his fingers fell short. It was as if Haine had measured that distance. 'Let up,' he gasped through fresh agony, his injured stomach spasming as he was jolted along. 'Let up.' He kicked out with his free foot and lost that too, his ankle caught in Haine's other fist.

He stopped fighting. Hc lct himself be towed along, feeling the blood drip from his face, the knot of the bruises on his chin and cheek. He twisted about to try to get a hold on the plating, but it had no gaps, no joins, his soiled fingers doing nothing but leaving streaks of blood ribboning across the shine of the floor.

The guns were now two dark smudges in the distance.

The sliding stopped, something hissed, a door opening to his left. He took the chance and grabbed at the rim of its frame. Haine prised at his fingers. 'You were a damned fool to start this,' the man ground out, jawbone rigid, eyes disappearing into the deepening cross of his brows. He kneed at Jones' ribs. 'You want worse you fight me some more.'

Jones guessed where he was heading. He knew he'd lost this one, misjudged and mistimed it. But if you were smart every plan you made had a counter-plan. He let go of the doorframe and let the man prod him into the gleaming metal cylinder beyond. The door slid closed. 'You ready, brat?' Haine yelled from outside. 'Got to warn you, this is going to be just about as cold as anything gets.'

Jones swallowed down coppery blood. He tucked down, his muscles tensing moment by moment. A rush of sound and he was drenched in frigid coldness, water shooting from the room's cylindrical sides. He bit down hard on a cry of pain. Hair slapped into his eyes, his injured face cleaved by a thousand icy needlepoints. He wore watertight V-seal clothing, but his shirt leaked at the neck, runnels of bitter wetness chasing down his chest and back. He dipped his head to his knees, trembling, deafened by the water's drumming on the metal tray underneath him.

Minutes passed and heaviness gathered in his chest, his forehead. He sputtered out bloody water, staring at toes that were steadily turning blue. His fingers wouldn't flex, flesh and sinew rigid against his bones. His body so numb, so brittle now, he felt sure it would shatter. Let it, he thought. Just let it. He was alone. He'd always be alone.

Eleven years ago . . .

Milo told Jake the dark-skinned creatures were called Species K followed by a list of other numbers, a Government designation, with a Government warning not to interact with them. To leave them be on their home world. The Bliss never let anything be.

Jake wanted to meet one of them. He asked Milo. He asked Lieberman. He begged, he cried. He knew there was no reason for anybody to say yes. He was watched closely now, his days of escaping into the ship's skin long gone.

His medical tests returned one day after session, Lieberman staring at them with a deep frown. He scrawled notes on his computer slate. 'I think you should meet one of them,' he said abruptly.

Milo looked horrified. 'No,' he said. 'My God, what are you thinking? It's just a childish whim. He doesn't know what he's asking for.'

Lieberman walked the room's width with the slate. Handed it over, pointed to the things on it and stared Milo in the eyes.

'No,' Milo repeated.

'It's an experiment.' Lieberman said forcefully. 'That's what we do here. We know they're sentient. It might be interesting.'

'They're violent.'

Lieberman stabbed at the slate again. 'Do we have much to lose?' he asked starkly. 'At this point in time why are we even arguing? He's the last of the J series. He's been remarkably resilient, but it's time . . .' he glanced at Jake. 'It's time he went home.'

Home didn't mean home, Jake knew that. No one who'd vanished like Narie had ever gone home. He knew he was changing day by day in ways Lieberman couldn't even imagine. He knew something had gone wrong inside his head.

'Tomorrow,' Lieberman said.

Milo stood shaking his head. 'This is going too far. You're making a spectacle out of him. A sport.'

'Don't argue with me,' Lieberman said. 'Unless you want to go home too?'

Milo spun about. Stormed out. The door slammed.

'This is too much,' Milo whispered to Jake the next day, checking the sensors they'd attached to his skull. Milo's face stark white. He crouched down, slipping a knife into Jake's fingers. 'Hide it.'

'The damage in my head,' he whispered, slipping the knife up into his sleeve. 'Can't it be fixed?'

'They won't do that here,' Milo whispered. 'Side effects have to be monitored, never altered.'

He still trusted Milo. His word. The promises they made to each other. There was so much pain in his eyes these days. He didn't think Milo wanted to be on the ship either, not any more. He'd had a dream of creating something wonderful, and it had turned into something ugly neither of them could escape.

They stood in the room with the glass cages where Species K was held. They had an audience. All the personnel on board seemed to *have turned up to watch. There must be over fifty standing in the corridor.*

'Put him in,' Lieberman appeared, monitor in hand. 'No delay, Milo. Let's get this done.'

Milo pulled Jake close, held him tight. 'I'm so sorry.'

The creature inside the glass box had sensors gummed to its skull too. The interior of the box had a smell, deep, pungent, musky, it made Jake's nose itch. He wiped at it. He had knowledge in his head about all manner of animals, big and small, from all kinds of worlds. Threat posture was this; submission was that; it all mingled in his mind as he stood there waiting, but he knew nothing about these creatures.

The beast bared its teeth, creeping forwards, its gait a knuckle-to-the-floor skulk. Jake glanced back; he couldn't hear any noise from beyond the glass. He could see the bleak faces. The more squeamish had glanced away, expecting bloodshed. When he looked back the creature had a yellow flare. An aura.

He stood still, trying not to tremble.

It blinked, he mirrored it. Three blinks, four. Did that mean something? Did the way it moved – so slowly, cautiously, teeth bared, showing fangs, flicking out a violet tongue. Should he mirror that?

The yellowness still hung about it like a cloud. Changing, adding blue tints.

He didn't dare move. He barely dare breathe. It drew closer on sinewy legs, its knees on the wrong side. Hands with six fingers, two thumbs. A flat face, two nostrils that flared. Huge yellow eyes sliced down the middle with black irises. He swayed where he stood. It was half his height, half his weight, but he was soft flesh and it was hard muscle and claws.

His knees gave way; he sank down, slowly, slowly to its level to wait for it. Not looking at it now.

He swallowed hard, closed his eyes, and reached a hand towards it. Felt its hard finger brush his. A flash of colour. Bright white light. A flash of pain, a burning in his head so swift and so violent he barely had time to scream before he felt himself drop. His body jerked, jerked again, every nerve ending firing. White light in his head. White bright and hot. Something burrowing inside his mind. The creature. Looking for him. Searching him out. Trying to know what it couldn't comprehend. An angry creature, full of rage.

'Milo, no!' Lieberman yelled. He heard a shot. The burning stopped; after it came a tumble of images. The knife he'd never thought to use slipped free from his sleeve as he was lifted. 'Dammit, Milo. This is your last chance. I swear.'

'I didn't kill it,' came Milo's bitter angry retort. 'I'll leave the killing to the real monsters.'

He woke, blinking up into the overheads in his room. He tried to speak, but his thoughts refused to gel, his legs wouldn't move.

Milo sat on the edge of the bed. He laid a hand on his arm. He could barely feel the weight of it.

'The data's still being analysed.' Lieberman's voice. He couldn't see the man. He didn't know where in the room he stood. 'The paralysis is likely shock.'

'You don't know what the hell you're doing,' Milo said sharply.

'I know this is the end of the J series. I'll do it tomorrow in session. He won't feel it. I want to map his brain as it happens. It might be useful. You'll continue with the new group in the new section. You need to put all this behind you. We learn from our mistakes and we

move on. Our investors won't stay patient forever. We need solid results. Tangible applications.'

'All you have is a God-awful mess. I'd wish I'd never come here,' Milo hissed. 'I thought this would be the future, but it's nothing but barbarity.'

Jake moved, he twitched. Milo gathered up his fingers, held them tight. 'Go to sleep,' he said. 'Just go to sleep now. It's just the shock. You'll feel better in the morning.'

Promise? He wanted to ask. Knowing it was all a lie.

The creature had burned images into his mind. Things he could still see. Images of its home. Where it came from. Where it wanted to be. A rocky landscape, a dry wind in his face that smelled of salty water. Other creatures, young and old, gathered around it in a tight little group, all thinking the same images, the same colours. Connected. Always connected. Sharing it all. It had sensed something in him, some kinship. His vulnerability, perhaps. His desolation. It had spoken to him in its way before Milo had intervened. It had said, with its images of family: You're not alone. But he was, he was completely alone. The last of his kind.

CHAPTER 5

'Haine?' Frank's voice barked from outside the shower cubicle. 'What's going on?'

The water jets died, the silence left behind punctuated by the rattle of Jones' shivers against the walls. He stared at the hazy reflection of himself in the metal, at white skin and startling flashes of scarlet. He closed his eyes, heard the door hiss open, heard, as warmer air piled in from the corridor, Frank's shocked 'Oh, Jesus.'

Frank might do forgiveness but he clearly wasn't in the mood to do it today. He started yelling, bellowing at the 'damn fool' that was Haine, ordering him to go call Kady on the com and get her to fetch a painkilling shot out of Greeley's stock, to call Max up because he might need some help and he damned well didn't want it from Haine. After that Haine was told to go up to helm and stay there, Frank adding threats about cut pay and a loss of dock privileges. In the middle of it all Frank configured the shower's dryers, starting at a low setting then slowly building up the heat. Jones got a slow warm-through, his hair flying this way and that as he battled to get a straight breath down.

'Is your nose broken?' Frank asked. He crouched by the stall's side, one hand on the doorframe, one resting on the dart gun he carried on his hip.

Jones lifted a hand to his face, stirring to life a burning sting across the bridge of his nose. He wiped blood away from his lips, his fingers suddenly gloved red and sticky. He shook his head.

'How about your cheekbone?' Frank asked.

Jones touched it, the rising heat of the blowers bringing in more pain, a deep-seated marrow-gnawing stampede of it. 'No.'

Kady came into view beyond the doorway. 'Hell,' she said with a grimace.

'He needs a painkiller,' Frank told her. 'Then we'll move him up to the med bay. Max,' he yelled towards the lift. 'Get up here.'

Footsteps sounded that broke into a run.

Jones coughed, the harsh brittleness of it hurting his chest, his head, the sting across his nose. He squinted upwards. All three of them stood over him in the gap of the doorway now, a little sympathy evident.

'What happened?' Max asked.

'Haine happened,' Frank returned dourly.

'Is he okay – apart from the obvious?' Max asked. 'Kady mentioned something about a coughing fit earlier.'

Kady kneeled down in the stall and gave Jones a shot. She offered him med wipes for his nose, cleaned off other parts of his face for him he didn't even realize were cut.

'Let's move him.' Frank was the next in, pushing around Jones in the narrowness of the stall before dipping back into a crouch. 'Don't fight me, all right?' he said, pulling Jones' left arm over his shoulder. 'You hang on and don't damn well fight me.'

Max edged in and took Jones' other side. And there Jones hung, refusing to help, his hands swinging limply over both men's shoulders. They pulled him up, gave him a moment for his head to settle then eased him out into the corridor. He coughed there, Frank resting a palm on his chest as if he wanted to feel from just how deep down those coughs were coming. 'Take a rest,' he said, more edge than concern in his voice.

They walked the corridor when Jones said he was ready, entering a lift at its end. A bland grey-painted lift with a panel that indicated three levels and no more. A little ship, Jones reminded himself. Little people with little lives on a little ship. The metal of the back wall touched his shoulders, and he leaned into it, easing his weight off Max and Frank to test his balance. He had to get back to work now, get back to his main occupation lately: escape. He had to know the spaces the ship owned if he wanted to know the ship herself. He searched the lift panel again, looking high and low for serial numbers, for ship design and refit codes, for anything Milo's information might have left out. He had to make the effort or plan B would fail as miserably as plan A.

He tried to keep his head up coming out onto A deck. He saw lights up ahead, the steady flash of monitors shifting over numbers and images: helm. Helm nothing but a dim little room right at the corridor's end, her doors locked wide open.

He passed other doors by left and right as they walked. Crew's quarters, stores, a shower, a head, all of it painted a muddy beige. The same colour stopped all of a sudden halfway down the corridor as if his capture had disturbed an attempt at redecorating a ship whose original basecoat was mid-shade grey. He saw a galley, a drinks machine in the far corner together with a big refrigeration unit. The long sweep of a metal-topped table took up the other wall, bordered on two sides by a high-backed bench. Grey in there too but for a piece of art. A yellow oblong was screwed to the wall. Watered-down sunshine it looked like. Crew psychology: a happy colour amidst the gloom to keep a crew smiling merrily away. It clearly hadn't worked any magic on Haine.

His human crutches tugged him into more greyness: a med bay, waist-high drawers and cabinets on three sides. Kady was in charge of a slide-out cot, one which owned a thick plastic-covered mattress that looked friendlier than the one he'd left behind in holding. She set two big, soft pillows at its end. Comfort meant something when every bone in your body ached. Jones sat down on the bed's edge and let his head hang, nursing his nose with one hand while staring at the plating beneath his feet. There was a rug bolted there, some landscape he couldn't make out: strange twisted trees, a bird or perhaps not, to the foreground. He leaned down lower to look.

'You feeling all right?' Frank asked, and Jones glanced up. He sniffed and swallowed down blood in a sickly coppery rush.

'Going to give you another shot,' Kady said. 'One of Greeley's anti-bacterial boosters.'

'When did you last visit Disease Control, Jones?' Frank asked.

Jones, so fascinated by the rug, didn't answer.

'Would that fake chip he has be up to holding that info?' Kady asked. She motioned Max over to a portable chip reader set on a one of the countertops. 'It would have to be, wouldn't it? He took shuttles. They wouldn't let him on board unless the medical stats were up to date on his chip.' The Government loved their ID chips. Bio hardware, powered by your own heartbeat, they never died until you did.

'His chip has his drugs stash logged,' Max said, holding the reader up in range of the chip that sat lodged under the skin at the back of Jones' neck. 'The Cap visited Boveron, didn't she, before Elysian? According to his chip he never visited either planet.'

'So Combes let him forgo Disease Control,' Frank said. 'That was a damned fool thing to do considering the amount of meds he's on.'

'Like she cared about that,' Kady said. 'She was drugging him so she could have a little fun. One contraindication and she could have killed him.' She sounded genuinely angry. 'Same kind of problem if he'd gone to Disease Control. They'd want to get into all the interactions their drugs might cause with his meds. He'd hit a delay every time. That's if that med count didn't make them decide to go in and get a deep read off his chip. Then he'd really have been in trouble, wouldn't he? So, go to Disease Control only when you're forced to, otherwise avoid it. I bet that's the same reason he didn't dare carry a gun. One wrong check-in on an Inner Rim port and he'd be in trouble. That's when he used that ID at all. Pay in credits and look for anybody who doesn't mind keeping you off the ship's log. That's your preferred option, right Jones?' Jones blinked at her, nodded belatedly, watching her use her thumbprint to get a drawer to glide open. 'You know he shouldn't really be travelling at all with the meds he takes,' she said to Frank. 'The healthy travel, the sick stay home. Last I heard Disease Control can make it illegal for you to travel if you're a risk. You'd need a doctor and a lawyer to get you clear of that one.'

Jones looked down to the alien planet rug again, examining the tufts of blue-green stalks that might be grass, at the trees with branch ends that looked like clenched fists. 'It's Artisell-One,' he muttered to himself. A buzzing sensation started behind his eyes, the shivers that came along with it raising every hair on his body. Trouble was imminent if he didn't damp it down. More *Bliss* output, a whole raft of pointless information about 'Sell-One pushing its way into his head. He beat one hand into the side of the bed so hard the metal clanged.

'Jones?'

'Sell-One wanted out in a blinding rush, every detail: planetary stats, native creatures, flora, fauna, even local Government residential applications for land appropriations. Utterly pointless, useless information, ten years out of date. Jones thumped at the bed again, watching dislodged blood droplets slap onto his lap, trying to rescue himself, trying to shove his thoughts off track for just one single precious second. 'Jones?' He felt a grip on his shoulder; urgent fingers digging in. 'Dammit, he's going to pass out.'

Frank thought he'd seen a ghost during his military days on *The Monterey*. Down one of the tight little corridors that joined the gunnery bays to the crew's quarters something not quite real had passed right through him, he was sure of it. Twenty years old, naive and scared as hell, he'd sunk down onto his knees; feeling at his chest as if he thought it ought to have left a hole behind it. He had a similar feeling all of sudden now, sure and then not sure he'd seen a flash of his home world. More precisely he'd seen a flash of 'Sell-One's main city in computer-mapped topography. Her land various shades of brown as it rose and fell, her buildings picked out in grey, the blue of a lake complete with all its recorded depth readings. There and gone. He checked over to Kady, to Max, both of them hanging onto Jones as they tried to get him down flat on the cot. 'Did you see something?' he asked.

'Did I see what?' Max asked, as Kady shook her head.

'Nothing,' Frank excused in a rush. 'Nothing.' It was stress most likely, he told himself. He'd had far too many doses of that lately.

He helped to roll Jones over; Jones sucking in tight gulps of air through his mouth, his flesh slippery with sweat, heat beneath it, his arm moving as if even half-conscious he wanted to beat this fist into something. Frank caught him by the wrist and held on tight. 'It's all right, Jones. You're going to be all right.' He thought he owed the sympathy, he thought he could spare Jones that much.

Nearly twenty years of combat training; monthly exercises on alien worlds, men firing dart rounds at each other while ships screamed down from the heavens, then screamed right back up there again hadn't meant a thing on board *The Marabell*. Frank's kind of soldier had never seen a war. The troop carriers had been set up to guard against alien attack, but no aliens had ever showed. Now the regular military was touted as a career opportunity for Reaches brats. Special Ops and Government Security set up to handle any real emergencies.

The Marabell had felt like a war. Back to that one admission Frank hated most of all. He'd needed Jones in the worst way possible.

'You coming back?' Kady stood leaning down, her face close to Jones'. 'You see me? You okay?' She glanced up to Frank, her frown a mirror of his own. 'I think you might need to mope over something else soon,' she said quietly. 'There's more going on here than a bloody nose and a beating.'

Frank nodded, nothing to say. Sometimes decisions made themselves.

Jones lost all sense of time, he kept sliding right back into the black in the seconds between one breath and the next, and those breaths were getting harder and harder to take. Something was clogging up his insides, something Disease Control probably knew all about on one planet or another he'd visited. He'd been a fool to miss out on those visits. It was illegal too; everything supposed to be logged onto your chip. And Kady had been right; with his pill count he shouldn't be travelling. He shouldn't be taking trips through jump-gate vortices that might kill him. He had all kinds of internal flaws that might, in the in-between, mean an embolism or a fit, or a heart attack. Lots of body stresses could kill the healthy in the in-between, let alone the physically flawed.

'Jones, can you hear me? We're going to jump in five.'

He thought sometime in the past they'd given him his meds to take. He thought he'd had a drink and visited the head but with whose help he didn't know. He had a recollection of helm, all her monitors aglow, a silver-haired, grey-eyed man's gaze raking over him, his head shaking. 'Kid's a mess. Kid's an all-out disaster, Frank.'

'Hey, Jones.' Someone kneaded at his shoulder, their fingers like a cat's endless pawing. 'Jones, you hear me. Jump-gate. We're going to jump. We're heading into Delta. We going to get you some help, then get you home.'

Comfort, whoever stood by his side was trying to offer some comfort, but all it contained was a promise of confinement. *The Bliss* was over, gone, gone forever. He had to think of his future now, that's what Greeley had told him. He had – he'd lied, cheated, stolen, hidden a myriad of talents that grew and grew year on year. Now he travelled through life like a rat to get where he needed to be, to do what he needed to do. He shrugged off the hand on his shoulder, murmuring, 'How long have I been here?'

'Two days.'

It couldn't be that long. He coughed, and pain gripped his sides, squeezing hard into his ribcage. He curled up where he lay, jerking at one wrist that wouldn't come free. They'd tethered him to the metal side of the bed.

'You have some passengers, Jones. Something we can't treat safely because Greeley didn't supply all the right meds. We can't give you anything he didn't sanction, it's too risky.'

Plan C, Jones thought groggily. It wasn't a plan he wanted to use. It would take him right back into the worst trouble he could imagine. Rebellion, revolution, all those words the Government had put away.

The hand touched his head, stroked at his hair. A small, light hand.

'Kady?'

'Just hang on.' A rattle came then, the ship's vibrations growing more and more intense as she closed towards the gate. 'I'm going to put you out for jump. Safe trank, okay. Safe.'

Jones held his breath, hearing the med canister's hiss. The world blurred, went black.

Eleven years ago . . .

Lieberman had expected the creature to kill him, Jake knew that. He knew the days after Milo's rescue were gifts Milo fought to give him. He realized those gifts would end.

Milo came for him one morning, his face white, the hand that reached for his shaking. 'One more session,' he said.

Jake didn't argue. Too tired now. Too defeated. His head lolled as he sat in the box. Lieberman sprayed drugs into his arm and Passive State overwhelmed him. More drugs: T778, a huge canister of it. He knew Lieberman's plan – push him to his limit, overdose him on drugs and information, map the death of his damaged brain on their monitors. He'd be an experiment right to the end.

He heard Milo outside the box protesting. He listened, unable to care, the argument growing heated until footsteps hurried out of the room.

Nothing outside the box mattered as the data started to stream. More information than he'd ever seen before: maps, schematics, planetary statistics, Government policies, human history, information about The Bliss, *the experiments . . . the failures. The successes.*

The information buried itself deep into his mind, the logic of it lost to him. Pain began to build behind his eyes, his overburdened senses fighting for comprehension, for equilibrium. Still he watched the data stream. He started to shake, his heart pounding then fluttering out of rhythm, his overloaded brain beginning to shut down. The blackness wanted him. He welcomed it in, consciousness drifting as the walls of the box started to vibrate.

A booming noise thundered beyond the box's sides. A siren wailed, an announcement over the ship's com yelling, 'Government. Government frigate. Protocol one. Repeat protocol one. Destroy all evidence. Destroy all evidence.'

The box opened. Light poured in. Lieberman stood flaring colours in a fast overlay, as fast as the data he'd just seen. Jake searched the room for Milo, but Milo wasn't there. Lieberman pressed another hypo to his skin. His heart surged again. Pounded.

'Adrenaline,' Lieberman said, hurriedly releasing his restraints and pulling him out of the box. The man wild-eyed as the voice yelled over the com. 'Boarding imminent. Boarding imminent.'

'Stay alive.' Lieberman shook him. 'Find somewhere to hide. Somewhere dark. Let the data settle. Stay quiet. When you see the Government troops go to them. They'll protect you. Stay alive, you hear me. Keep it alive. One day I'll find you.' He was shoved away.

Shot full of adrenaline, flight or fight reflex fighting to destroy Passive State, he scrambled out of the door. In the corridor gunshots echoed as screams, horrible fear-filled screams, sounded. The Bliss was killing herself.

He had to find Milo. He had to. He cannoned into a locked door, beat at it with his fist, yelled at the lock. Surging with drugs, information, his damaged mind was busy making external connections with the world. The door opened. He stared hard at it, with no real idea what he'd done or how he'd done it. He might have felt shock if he'd had the resources left for it.

He kept on running, trying to stay away from the noise, from the shouts and the screams, from the gunfire that popped loudly left and right as the corridors intersected. He ran through places he'd never been before, down long corridors that dripped water, across floors full of dirt and litter, by walls full of holes that gaped like mouths. The heart of The Bliss broken down and crumbling. Noise up ahead, a man's yells, a child's high-pitched begging. He veered left, barrelling into a darkened room, one with a huge window that overlooked the ship's vast belly.

The spin of flesh moved beyond it, lifeless black bodies with thin sinewy limbs floated and spun. His fingers strangled the hand-grab beneath the window. His stomach knotted, recoiled, his knees gave way. He couldn't vomit, he couldn't move, he just sat on the cold, cold floor as a blistering rage rose into his throat. All the things they were killing, and had killed in the past, the atrocities they'd committed. These murderers were the ones who deserved to die.

The thought jammed, refused to move: Passive State collapse. The Bliss shaped emotions, fears became obsessions. He knew the utter madness those emotions created. The data told him so. He had to find a way to survive them. Lock them away; hide them in a box in his head.

Forget. He told himself. Forget it all, or you'll go mad.

Forget. Forget it all.

His heart thundered, sweat broke out across his body. He lay down right where he was, closed his eyes and forced Passive State to take hold again, allowing the languidness to take to his bones. He told himself to forget over and over until like the data his mind integrated the thought and he forgot the burning rage, the absolute need for vengeance.

He made his mind a black empty space.

'It's all right,' the soldier who shook him awake had red hair just like Narie. Soft blue eyes, just like hers. He wore a black uniform, a logo across the breast that said Medic. 'I'm here to help you. No one's going to hurt you. I'm from the Government. Do you know what that is?'

He nodded.

Grim-faced soldiers took him to another ship, to a room, to silence and quiet, to doctors who came and went. They asked him questions, but he could only nod or shake his head. He was mute. He'd forced himself to forget far too much. They took scans of his brain and muttered things. He'd need drugs, they said. They'd try to stabilize him. They'd try, before he became prone to seizures and blackouts.

An aristocratic-looking man came to visit him a week later. He sat on his bedside, smiled and said in a soft mellow voice, 'My name's Clifford Greeley. I'll be taking care of you from now on. We have a very special place for you to live where you'll be safe.'

Jake moved his tongue around his mouth, tried to make sounds but he still couldn't speak. He wanted to ask about the The Bliss's last day. He didn't know why he couldn't remember it. He wanted to ask where Milo was and Lieberman. He wanted to ask if any of the creatures had survived. But what he really, really wanted to know was if the Government was any better than The Bliss.

PART TWO
IDENTITY CRISIS

CHAPTER 6

Stations didn't like people; people ruined the calc. Entrances, exits, whether through travel or births and deaths, they all threw off the calc. Frank imagined stations as huge computers doing endless measurements to ensure the smooth supply of oxygen and heat; the efficient recycling of human waste and water; the uninterrupted import of food and goods a station didn't make or grow – and those were plenty. Delta, just like all the rest, forced to play endless games with the calc its citizens messed up on a day-by-day basis. Recalibrations made to balance their whims against station output. Upwards of five million lives on board, and smoke had to be coming out of the rear end of that comp unit.

Frank sat up at helm, Foley by his side, the man grunting at a display on his control boards. *The Nova* glided down Delta Station's dock on an allocated lane, a red guidance buoy on a steady flight path ahead of her.

'Negative time lag is a very comfortable three hours and change. Just don't ask me what day it is,' Foley said before he hit a key. 'Looks like berth F two-two is way out on the western edge.' He started to whistle between his teeth as he checked his monitors.

Someone had yet to invent a composite that could reliably stand up to every rigour of space travel; retractable cameras mounted every which way in the ship's hull served Foley instead. Monitors rose up before him, five across, five high, without a visible join to separate them, Foley or the ship's comp integrating or dividing them as needs be. How the man snatched up all the info he needed from the rapidly changing images and data streams, Frank didn't know. From outside views to navigational information to buoy guidance readings, the information was a flash on Frank's retina, a non-event in his head, and then it all moved on.

Twenty minutes earlier they'd received a red light inside one of the station's one hundred and twenty air locks; a warning of decontamination protocols, followed by express air and gravity readjustments. *The Nova* was guided into the tight space of the lock then secured into place by safety grapples. Her screens had flashed warnings while alarms buzzed. Foley, swiping at his sweat-beaded brow, having nothing to do but watch the automatic pilot's display. One miscalculation by the comp running those grapple arms and they might have slammed into the lock's walls. They hadn't, of course; they were sedately following their guidance buoy. Its image took up three of the monitors dead ahead; its one-six-two designation flaking, its sides severely dented. No one had ever had a major accident on Delta, that fast-track route to notoriety still waited for some poor soul, but often enough a buoy got thrown off course by some hazard or another and took a glancing blow off the station's walls, hence poor one-six-two's battered red backside.

Foley's whistling stopped. 'Company at the berth by the looks. And it looks like more than just Disease Control.'

Stations might dislike people but they loved bureaucracy. They loved to immure staff in ship safety checks, ID checks, customs checks. In or outbound you had to abide by stations' requests to examine your goods, property or licences. If you were sensible you cooperated, you stayed polite, and you made damned sure all your paperwork was clean and up to date. You didn't smuggle one ounce of anything you shouldn't and you didn't get upset over the delays those suits might cost you. Blacklisted for being antsy or smart-mouthed and you'd get ten times worse the next time around. On station you didn't dare bribe anyone, you saved your money for the Reaches, where it would get you a few favours. Here you'd find yourself arrested – because you could be sure the Government had another suit ready to check up on the moral fibre of the suit checking up on you.

Foley's cameras picked out three white-clad station officials and another man wearing charcoal standing in the yellow safety zone of berth F two-two. No surprise to Frank they had people waiting for them. He'd put a call in to Delta's Disease Control Centre, another to Health Service Admin, one to the Dock Master's Office and one to the cops, just to be certain all Station Control's protocols were satisfied. Frank had nothing to hide.

Foley sat hitting switches left and right on his board of controls, his face starting to relax. 'Coming down. Likely you'll feel the bump.'

Frank didn't feel a thing, Foley settling the ship down softly in the safe area of the berth where the vents beneath the landing grills could suck up all her spent gases and neutralize them. Foley switched back to autopilot, *The Nova* then occupied with her own shut-down routines. He keyed another switch to set the ramp-way unfolding from her hide then played with a camera control to get a close-up of the waiting men. They had even more company now. A med car had turned up; it sat parked up next to Disease Control's grey vehicle. Two med-techs climbed out and spoke to the three men in white coveralls from the DDC, all of them waiting to be waved through by the dock jockeys: those men dressed in orange whose job it was to maintain the safety of the dock. Not such a problem on a planet where a dock could spread itself out; here space cost money, so station crammed as many ships in as it could before safety became an issue.

Foley got a severe close-up of a man dressed in a high-necked charcoal suit, so close Frank could see nostril hair. 'That a cop?' Foley asked. 'Did we ask for a cop?'

'Did we have a choice? It's just routine.'

'Hate routine. Ramp's locked. Company's just got a wave-through. You've got half a minute if you've got anything needs saying to the cargo.' A knowing look followed that and a glance to the corridor and the med bay.

Frank got out of his seat.

Lately their cargo only moved to cough and to use the head, otherwise Jones didn't trouble himself. Kady, the ship's med-tech, had done what she could. She'd found evidence of a little trespasser in his bloodstream. Jones had an infestation: some form of parasite had settled into his lungs. Disease Control wouldn't let that happen ordinarily; they didn't like diseases getting passed on from one dock to the next. Kady had been hamstrung by Jones' other meds, unable to treat him properly, able only to mop up bloodstained mucus, keep him fed and watered, and give him nothing but Greeley-approved non-specific anti-parasitics and anti-bacterials, hoping to stave off complications.

Frank waved Kady out of the bay. 'Give me a minute,' he said as she went by. He keyed the door closed then went to the trouble of hitting the lock. He'd make a speech, he decided. He'd hammer home the fact they'd be watching their cargo every single second. 'Jones?'

No movement and no answer. Frank moved to the cot's side and watched Jones' eyes roll beneath his lids. He reached out – touched Jones and gasped . . . *shreds of material, blankets, that rolled and spun far out in the distant darkness of space.*

Something else, less clear, an oval the colour of flesh, hazy, as if it were being reflected in the dark gloss of a window.

Surely it was a face.

Not space. He was looking into a cargo hold, and there was a window, a huge composite pane in front of him. Blood droplets; he could see blood droplets pass beyond it. Outside the window in the massive hold he saw the ship's doors crank ajar, just a crack, and everything in there hurtled towards the gap.

He stared harder and harder trying to make sense of it . . . and jumped, his nerves getting a jolt; the door to the med bay being pounded at.

Frank filled his lungs, shuddered, then found it hard to stop; he was hallucinating. Jones had surely infected him with something. He focused on the cot. Jones sat up now, his green eyes a bright contrast to the dark bruises around his nose and cheekbone. Frank half expected him to say something, but Jones just carried on staring.

Frank had to clear his throat. 'We're in. We're on dock. Disease Control is inbound.'

The door took another hit, and his frayed nerves jumped again. 'Frank?' Haine bellowed. 'DDC wants in.'

Frank hurried to the door, keyed it open, then stood waiting for the influx of people. He wiped his mouth, his forehead, the memory of the image like a crackle in his mind. A feeling of presence was overwhelming. Crowded mess-hall presence like on *The Monterey*. People crushed elbow to elbow in an echoing tight space, the overwhelming sense of being a very tiny part of a huge, huge mechanism.

Disease Control appeared with their cases, and their masks, and their endless precautions. He vaguely heard the voices of the doctors, while he sidelined one of the techs to ask for a few tests himself, only to be told that was standard practice. All he had to do was wait his turn.

You're going insane, Frank thought bleakly as the DDC finally finished their tests on him and the rest of the crew, pulled down their masks and quit, asking questions about the ship's water, waste and air filtration.

Nothing to worry about, they said. Just a minor E-grade infestation, and a comp model needed to sort out what ought to be administered to Jones, after taking into consideration the drugs list Kady had supplied. A list that got frowned at, wondered at, and a kid who started making defensive little bleats. Jones clearly worried they might start messing with the chaos he was taking.

Frank heard a cough, one Jones would have been proud of, and turned about.

'Detective Pike. Western Delta Division. The cop's jacket had a left-sided bulge. Station cops never wore visible weaponry, that just wouldn't be civilized. 'You're Mr Pak?'

'That's right.' The cop readjusted his earpiece before he took Frank's offered hand, Frank receiving a dry, efficient handshake from a man who looked ten years his junior.

'We need to talk. Somewhere private.'

Frank indicated the galley doorway opposite. Inside, Pike closed the door, locked it and didn't make a move to sit down. 'We have a problem, Mr Pak. A rather large one.'

'Oh.' Frank decided to sit. He decided to place his hands flat on the table too, where the cop could see them.

'Your report about Jeven Jones having a fake chip . . .'

'Yes.'

'According to Central Data it isn't a fake. Joseph Stokes exists. My colleague has just confirmed his chip's given a perfectly legitimate surface read and it matches the info Central has on file. The kid's father's been trailing you since you captured him. Michael Stokes' ship is logged as . . .' The cop checked a handheld, making it hum a low note, as he got the info he needed. '*The Valdese.*'

A belly-churning moment, one that caused a mental hiccup, Frank just stared at the man.

'You reported Jones as a listed fugitive,' Pike went on. 'Did you see the complete police listing?'

Frank shook his head. 'No. I never saw it at all. I assumed . . .' He stuttered to a halt, in that place again, with that sense of *presence*, that sense of being overwhelmed by the deadening weight of a crush. 'Are you telling me it doesn't exist?'

'We have no record of it. As a result we don't have an ID code for Jeven Jones to trace through Central Data.'

'That isn't impossible.' Frank sounded as bewildered as he felt. 'What about Clifford Greeley and the Institution? They'd have bio-details. They'd have Jones' ID code too.'

'The Institution has a P140 Directive Designation.'

'A *what*?'

'Anyone under their care is a protected citizen. Their files aren't kept at Central. I'm afraid the Institution by law isn't allowed to confirm or deny that Jones exists. I'd need to apply to the Government itself to get that information released. And I'd need the Stokes chip to prove to be a fake to have any reason to do that.'

'Clifford Greeley exists. He's employing me. I have the damned contract. He got me the right licences so I could legally track down Jones in the first place. You want to go ask him some questions?'

Pike frowned. 'Mr Greeley is also a protected citizen. The Institution refused to confirm or deny—'

'What the hell kind of crazy set-up is this?' Frank couldn't stop his voice from rising. 'Are you telling me somebody who doesn't exist employed me to go catch somebody else who doesn't?'

'They do exist, Mr Pak,' Pike assured him, 'just not openly on record. Not at Central, where anyone's allowed to do a search on a person's ID code.'

'But these P140s are legally responsible?'

'Yes.'

'So Greeley pays taxes, he can get arrested, you just can't investigate him without the Government's say-so. Is that it? The Government can warn you off?'

'I must stress, Mr Pak, I'll only be interested in pursuing Mr Greeley for questioning if this turns into a full-scale fraud investigation.'

Frank scrubbed both hands across his face, trying to calm himself down. 'A legitimate surface read doesn't prove that that chip's real.'

'The info matches Central records,' Pike reminded him.

'Which could be done. Nothing's impossible, right? It could still be a fake?'

'I've never heard of anybody managing to do it before, Mr Pak.' The cop gave him a pitying look.

Another thought struck. 'I have data on the kid. I have the data Greeley gave me. Wait here.' Not a good idea pushing by a cop, but that's precisely what Frank did. He hurried down to crew's quarters and snatched up Greeley's handheld, another idea making him hang a right into the med bay on his way back. There was another cop in there now, on standby by the bed with the DDC. Frank ignored them all. He snatched a bottle of Jones' pills from a drawer and read the label. A long number in red took the place of a patient's name. There was a doctor listed, an official-looking gold stamp half obscuring the print. Frank kneaded the tension from his forehead. He'd heard of people having their names changed, their IDs altered, witnesses mostly, people at risk from reprisals, but he'd never in his entire life heard of a P140.

He felt the weight of someone's gaze on his back and glanced around, expecting it to be Jones. Jones smiling at him, the kid knew naked panic when he saw it. But Jones wasn't looking at him. Nobody was. He pocketed the bottle and returned to the galley. Inside he turned on Greeley's little machine and handed it over.

Pike fiddled with the expensive little unit for ten seconds then held it out as if it were dirty. 'There's nothing on here.'

Frank snatched the thing back and stabbed at its controls. He got a 'no data listed' message flashing up on every page he tried. Not possible. Not damn well possible. It had wiped itself. Frank barely resisted the urge to throw it at the nearest wall. He held his temper, trying to work it out. Cops wore locator tags; they continually emitted an 'on-duty' signal. That had to be it. That signal in close proximity had caused an auto-wipe. Damned non-existent Greeley didn't want that info getting out.

Frank handed over the pill bottle. 'Jones' meds. There's a Government stamp and a doctor listed on every bottle we have on board. That's legal. We're C class only; we couldn't carry those fancy drugs otherwise. I bet Joseph Stokes takes the same meds. The exact same drugs as Jones.'

Pike grimaced. 'That may be true, but even if I can contact the doctor involved there will still be the P140 to get around.'

Frank huffed out his disgust. 'Fine, try this for proof. The kid has two relatives on Earth. Two aunts. That's proof right there that he is who I say he is.'

'Do you know his aunts' names?'

Frank hissed out a breath, feeling his face flush. 'No. No. *Dammit*, their names weren't listed.' He did throw the handheld this time. It smacked into the wall with a satisfying thud and dropped to the floor. 'Why did I expect anything to go my way here?'

'We still need to do a standard read on the kid's chip, Mr Pak,' Pike said, looking bemused.

Of course, a standard read would follow the cursory surface read. The cop was clearly trying to reassure him. Fake chips always glitched on that deeper read; it involved years of collected data. Why worry, why work so hard to find other ways to prove who Jones was? The chip was a fake; it would glitch. The Government trusted those things to the nth degree, so why shouldn't he?

'I do have to warn you, Mr Pak, Joseph Stokes' father is heading into station. Real or not, he's seems to be a man with money and plenty of influence behind him. He's already talking about a civil case if my department decides not to charge you with kidnapping. I'm afraid he has a lawyer on dock making all kinds of threats.'

Frank stood sweating, heat still seeping up into his hairline. 'Stokes isn't this kid's father. Let me guess: you can't test DNA on that score.'

Pike shook his head. 'No, and I wouldn't at this stage. Besides, there's no point: according to the data we do have the boy's adopted. There's an orphanage listed, I'll be checking their records.' Pike gave Frank a sterner look. 'Are you absolutely certain there's no chance you made a simple mistake. You locked up the wrong person?'

'No,' Frank bit a hole in the word. 'I know Jones personally. We spent time together on a boat called *The Marabell*.' He explained it all as briefly as he always did when it came to *The Marabell*.

'We can check the logs of that barge.' Pike's tone gained a few rounder edges when he'd finished. The expression he wore far more sympathetic.

Frank took a breath. 'If by some miracle that chip does pass that standard read I hear you can go one better. A deep read, right down to the metal? You can test a citizen's chip by law, can't you?'

Pike frowned. 'My department wouldn't sanction it, not on your insistence he's Jeven Jones and nothing else.'

'Then either wait and get his info from the Government – or hell, call it a drill. A test case.' Frank's voice grew breathless and fast, the idea suddenly gaining so much momentum it felt unstoppable. 'Some kind of internal assessment of your own procedures for chip fraud? You do those, right? Nothing insidious about one of those, nothing for a fake father to get mad about when he's got nothing to hide.'

'I'd still rather have grounds. It might look like harassment.' Pike looked thoughtful, Frank holding off to give the man time to think. One long study and Pike let out a belly-deep sigh. 'Look, I can't make any promises, but your record's clean, and,' Pike hushed the rest up, 'I'm a Reaches brat. I did some carrier time myself when I was a kid.'

An angle Frank hadn't even thought to pursue. A friend for no other reason than they'd both joined the military, both of them trying to make enough money to get a foothold Inner Rim, where the real opportunities were.

'If the kid's chip clears its next read, I'll talk to my superiors and see what they say,' Pike offered. 'They might let me run with it, who knows.'

Frank wrung his hands together to stop himself from slapping the man on the back. He smiled his relief, getting an understanding little smile in return from Pike.

Frank sobered. 'I need a favour. I need to speak to Jones before he leaves.'

'I did notice your passenger has a few bruises, Mr Pak.'

'My passenger attacked one of the crew.' Half a lie, but Frank couldn't muster up any guilt over it, not now. 'I swear to you, I never touched him. I'd be a fool to start now with you here, wouldn't I?'

Pike gave him another stern little look. 'All right, once the DDC are through in there you can have five minutes. Just five, and I'll be right outside the door.'

The DDC left the med bay finally. Inside on the bed, Jones sat with his hair adrift, his face drained and pallid. Frank waited for the men to get clear then keyed the door closed.

The image echoed. He was certain now he'd seen a face in the window of what must have been the cargo master's observation port. A boy's face: black hair, green eyes. A boy standing where he shouldn't be, in a little room full of comp gear and control panels. A boy who clung to an emergency hand-grab under the window because shock had stolen all his strength away.

There were bodies in the hold, a vast twisting swarm of tiny bodies. Bodies that didn't look human: black, wiry little demons from somewhere.

On the bed Jones coughed into an open palm. Same black hair and green eyes. A young man's face where a child's had been, Jones clearly confused by the lingering silence. 'Did you get some bad news, Frank? You look like today's been all bad news.'

Frank reached out to the countertop and anchored himself to it, fixing himself firmly to the present.

'Didn't they tell you? Seems you've conjured yourself up a daddy now.' He got a tight little shrug for that piece of information. 'Your chip will glitch, then that rich fake daddy of yours will get himself arrested. How'd you set this one up, Jones? How'd you get that chip logged at Central? How much damned help do you have out there?'

Jones smiled, he gave another shrug, rocking with the effort of breathing through infected lungs. 'How the hell did you get like this?' Too much naked frustration evident, too much emotion feeding off the shock of the chip debacle and the impact of the image, and he hauled the rest back.

Jones coughed, said nothing. No advantages to fight for, and Frank knew he wouldn't waste his breath. The silence made the decision for him; he keyed the door open and stepped out. Pike, standing guard out there, closed it for him. Frank didn't say a word to the man. He retreated up to helm, needing to curl his fingers around the rim of Foley's boards for the sake of having something else to anchor his body to.

Foley dragged a hand through grey hair, his brow wrinkling. 'I'm guessing by the look of you that we have a problem?'

Frank grunted. 'Jones has a problem. Greeley does.' He found the centre of it all with that statement. None of it was his damned problem.

Station procedures always took time, Disease Control snail slow over signing their patient out to the hospital techs. Ten minutes into the wait and Foley took a call. The ship trailing them had come in, the cops informing *The Nova* they'd had her set down at the dock's eastern edge. Five minutes after that the two hospital techs finally ambled up the ramp-way and went straight to the med bay. Jones insisted he didn't need a chair or a stretcher, that he was happy to walk down to the dockside, which meant more paperwork to cover the techs' backsides in case of an accident. Legalese always got tangled up and it always took time.

With everything signed by Jones – using the name Joseph Stokes – and the techs and countersigned by Officer Pike, Jones moved out. He went wearing orange detainee clothes and non-slip hospital slippers, his shoulders wrapped up in a grey hospital blanket. And he went coughing all the way, walking the slope of the outside ramp with Frank and his crew at his back without a glance or a single word spoken to any of them.

Frank watched the dock warily, knowing something might be coming in fast from that trailing vessel. No one stood waiting below except a dock tramp: large hooked nose, long listless hair. The man stood with his hands in the pockets of a long coat that looked to be covered in grease or dirt. A dusty bird, Frank thought. A curious, big, ugly, dusty bird had come to see what was going on.

The hospital entourage pulled level with the tramp, and Jones shied back, shaking his head. A negative to whatever question the tramp had launched: maybe asking for money, maybe being nosy.

Frank pulled level himself as the med-techs reached the hospital car and started to load their patient. 'You waiting for something?' he asked the tramp.

The man's paper-white skin lay taut over blade-sharp cheekbones, his deep-set brown eyes giving Frank a slow examination: brow to boot soles and back again. He gave an exaggerated shrug.

'Get the hell out of here,' Frank snapped.

The tramp sank down as if slapped. He skulked away, backing off between a row of transport cans, his attention locked to Jones and the hospital car.

'Max,' Frank called. 'Get that hospital location. I want you watching that kid every second. Take Haine with you.'

Max moved away, clearly keen to get an address before the hospital car pulled out.

Frank turned and headed back up the ship's ramp, hesitating at the doorway as Foley appeared. 'How much do they charge here for a priority call?'

'Depends on the time of day and the call traffic.' Foley gazed off over the dock. The hospital car as it drove off gathered up an escort: a cop car. Another stayed where it was on guard. A ship down the bay had an angry father on board, Frank reminded himself. It seemed Foley was thinking the same thing. 'The kid's daddy might come visiting, Frank.'

'The kid doesn't have a daddy.' Frank pushed by angrily. 'I'm sending Greeley a message.'

Direct Delta to Beta communication meant FTL relay connections, time lag and inherent mechanical glitches; far better to forget a direct call and send a one-way encrypted message to the mailing address Greeley had supplied. They'd used the thing plenty of times before, it worked well enough, and Greeley always answered as promptly as the set-up allowed.

Frank settled himself down at helm, using two fingers on the alphabetized portion of Foley's boards, he slowly typed a message out: *Nova on board Delta > Jones sick > ID discrepancy > Counter-claim of Joseph Stokes > Michael Stokes (father?) on station > Have requested complete chip analysis> Handheld wiped itself? > Need Jones' ID verification urgently > Pak.*

Happy with it, he encrypted it and sent it out to Station Control's computer, which would duly dispatch it via one of the station's thirteen signal buoys as soon as a suitable slot became available. As a carrier grunt Frank had grown used to waiting his turn, but on station turns had price tickets attached. The more you paid the faster your turn came up, messages nothing but a bidding war if you weren't a cop or in the military. Frank had paid plenty but still he knew he'd likely be sitting there for hours waiting for a reply.

A board light lit, a caller's number flashed up and Frank hit the com control 'Yes, Max. Where are you?'

'On a station tube connection going to G sector.' A background mechanical drone almost drowned Max out. 'It shouldn't take long.'

'Okay. Call me when you get to the hospital.' Frank hit the off button then reconfigured the comp to get a call through to Station Dock Control. 'Station, this is *The Nova*, berth F two-two, ship's owner/occupier Frank Pak calling. Can you give me a ship's berth number for *The Valdese*?'

'Negative, *Nova*.' The station tech on the other end was station polite, trained to talk in bland inflectionless station-speak. 'We have a D7 on that ship.'

'Sorry, a what?'

'A D7, sir. A Protected Information Article. I can't tell you where that ship is.'

Frank snorted. It seemed a day for protection orders. 'But I could walk the dock and find it?'

'Yes, sir, you could, but I can tell you it's in the secure sector, so you'll need a security pass to reach it.'

'Do you have an owner/occupier listed for it?'

'Calder. Christian MacKay. Out of Alpha, sir.'

'And that information isn't protected by that D7?'

'No, sir.'

'But the ship's in the secure bay. The rich people's bay, right?'

'Yes, sir.'

Frank hunted for another question. 'There an age listed for that OO?'

'Thirty-five years. Standard Earth calc.'

'There any listing on that info for a Michael Stokes?'

'Yes, sir. He's on the ship's passenger list.'

Same ship, same OO as the pleasure sloop that had trailed them.

Ships dumped their flight record data into the station's main comp automatically when they came close enough. This one hadn't changed ID or OO – it would have been illegal if it had. But Stokes didn't own that boat, he was a passenger – which posed all manner of questions about Stokes when enough questions about him had stacked up already.

'Do you wish to place a call?' the tech asked.

Frank seriously thought about it: ask the man why he'd trailed them; ask why he hadn't confronted them with the truth if they had his son on board. 'Negative, station. You've given me all I need. Thanks.' He cut the com, had one more idea and paid for a connection to Station Web. He typed in Christian MacKay Calder and waited.

No specific hit came up, just a list of Calders. There was an Aldine Calder, a Bordern Calder, a Candial Calder – who laughingly turned out to be a pure-bred shih-tzu dog.

No Christian MacKay.

Way down the list Frank got snarled up reading about a Martha Delaware Calder. A woman who gave copious amounts to Alpha's Eden projects. There might be a family connection between all the listed Calders – except the dog – but if that were true Frank couldn't find it.

He glanced to helm's door and the empty corridor outside it before he started looking for anything else. Then he tapped in, visions and telepathy. The Government scientists were eager and verbose in their insistence that neither existed. He watched the words flicker, reading definitions then, not from scientists but from kooks and fans of the out-and-out peculiar. He stabbed at a key and killed the screen, Foley coming into helm carrying two strong black coffees. Frank sat back and tried to look relaxed.

'Thought you could use the shoring up,' Foley said handing one cup over. 'So what's the plan?'

'I'm doing the plan. Waiting is the plan.'

Another com light lit again, Max's call number flashing up. Frank hit receive.

'We're at the hospital,' Max said over the link. 'The place is huge. We're walking through right now trying to find admissions.' He stopped talking, Frank able to hear a buzz of background noise: muttered conversations, hospital com announcements, a baby's plaintive wail and, somewhere far away, soft, soothing music.

'Keep going, Max. Leave your link open.' Frank sipped at his coffee, burned his tongue and let a string of curses go.

Foley raised his brows. 'Aren't we in a colourful mood today.'

An old jibe, not an unwelcome one, but Frank couldn't find a smile. 'Any idea what it would take to make a perfect chip?'

'How about a miracle.' Foley eased himself into the helmsman's seat. 'That's an A1 watertight piece of tech, last I heard. And they're upgraded batch on batch. My chip isn't yours, yours isn't Max's, and so on. Only Central Data and the cops really know the difference. Jones doesn't have a legitimate chip, it's a fake, it'll scream on the tests. They won't have to yank the thing to tell, they'll ask it for the kid's DNA code and it'll spit out the Cannon Trophy water polo results.'

'That'd be nice.'

'We've nothing to fret over regarding that chip. We ought to fret over the delay instead. This kid's slippery, we know that. The cops get careless he'll be on his way.'

'That's still a better option than a real chip.'

'It's not a real chip, Frank. It can't be. The Government depends on those thing to keep things neat.'

Frank nodded, he didn't argue. He settled again, sipping down hot coffee, listening to the background hum coming over the speakers. Max's voice was audible now, Max lying through his teeth. 'What the hell's he doing?' He couldn't make out the words of the reply Max got to his inquiry, but the voice responding sounded high and melodic: young and female definitely. He waited for Max to get clear, the background noise falling away, Frank hearing water: a fountain. The place must have a residents' garden.

'Frank, you there?' Max asked eventually.

'Dammit, ease back. All we want is the kid's room number.'

'Don't worry, I'm just being friendly. Jones is in room eight-zero-two North Diagnostic. The Contagious Disease Research team have just left. Do you want me to send Haine to go and stand outside his door? There are plenty of cops there according to the desk, at least three uniforms.'

'Why do I need to send Haine?'

'There's a nurse here taking an interest. I want to work on her, see if I can find out if there's anything else going on here we ought to know about.'

Frank gritted his teeth. 'Max, ease off, you hear me? We don't want any more complications heading our way.'

'Understood. I'll be careful. Just trust me a while, okay. I told her I was a cop, and she didn't ask for an ID. Look the part, act the part – I can do this.'

Max was smart enough not to wait for an argument; he shut the com down, leaving Frank with dead air. 'Dammit,' he snapped.

'Look the part, act the part?' Foley repeated dolefully.

'Dammed fool was barely a cop: twelve months' duty time. And what if what he's doing gets back to a real cop?'

'So call the fool in,' Foley said, with a familiar little brow hitch that meant the exact opposite. 'We're not curious, are we? We don't want to find out what the hell's going on here.'

Frank curled his lip and scowled. He knew he wouldn't be making that call. He sat back and drank his coffee, deciding to revert back to his original plan. Waiting.

Two hours in and the com came alive, a number ID Frank didn't recognize lighting up one screen. '*Nova* here. Frank Pak speaking,' he said into the open link.

'Mr Pak. It's Officer Pike, just a call to keep you up to date. The logs from the Penal Corp for *The Marabell*'s last voyage don't list a Jeven Jones, but they do list three P140s on route to Beta. I'm afraid there's no information on who boarded the P140s or exactly where they were heading to on station.'

'Hell.'

'There's more bad news, I'm afraid. The Stokes chip passed its standard read.'

'Say again?'

'It passed a standard read.'

'It couldn't have.'

'I'm afraid it did. It read perfectly. It spat back an entire twenty-one-year history. It's the right shape and the exact design configuration of a Government chip for the time period and planetary zone of the kid's birth, and it's in perfect working order. The good news is we're yanking it. My department's ordered a thorough look; right down to the materials it's made of. It's being called a departmental training exercise – officially, at least. I'll give you another call as soon as I know how long this thing is going to take.'

The com light went off.

'I damned well knew that was going to happen,' Frank muttered just as a left-hand monitor started to warn of a buoy message being routed to them. The flash of a countdown as the comp unscrambled it, then Greeley's reply flashed up: *Nova, standby > Sending liaison > Bernard Aubrey.*

Frank's resulting frown couldn't get any deeper. 'Bernard Aubrey? Who the hell is Bernard Aubrey?'

CHAPTER 7

In his hospital room Jones fought to stay awake. He knew he'd been drifting in and out for hours. He knew a group of doctors had mused over his drugs, mumbling about comp models and contraindications, and how a duplicate model might be best to make sure. He'd had a shot finally – half a cure. After it, a warning that there'd be follow-up meds, several types of them, as if the doctors thought he'd care about swallowing a few more pills.

'Are you awake?' Another white-coated doctor stood over his bedside, wearing that indifferent yet concerned expression only those in the medical profession seemed able to master. He spoke slowly and softly as if he were speaking to a simpleton. 'Can you hear me?'

Jones slurred a word, blinked languidly. He remembered the hospital room; one of those tiny station types painted in that dusky blue the psych people decided calmed patients down the most. He'd lost track of time for certain. The very last thing he remembered was a nurse piling speed-healing gel on his face while a suit from DDC had paced the room and fired questions at him about food contaminants. Where had he been and what precisely had he eaten there? Could anything have been contaminated by faecal matter? A pleasant thought. It was all something to do with livestock-spread sucking worms, prevalent on Distal. Egg to lava to full-grown worm, the man from DDC had explained it all. Sucking worms could kill a human if left untreated, he'd stressed. A large fine would be heading his way, he'd been told, one to encourage him never again to miss out on a trip to Disease Control. A lecture had followed about how he owed it to the entire human race not to break rules when it came to contaminants.

Jones didn't remember any of his replies, but he knew he would have lied, and done it well. He very rarely did it badly. He recalled that one of the doctors had tabled a full work-up request then. They wanted a full in-depth study of his brain. They wanted to figure him out, to investigate a fifteen-pill-a-day habit that made no medical sense. He'd refused; he remembered that. Then the cops had arrived to do their chip read: a standard read. No refusal allowed. He'd rolled onto to his side and tucked his chin down so they got a clear shot with a data reader at the back of his neck. Hums and buzzes from the machine had followed, together with little tuts from human lips. Jones began to drift, remembering it all, too bone-weary to concentrate.

'Mr Jones?' The doctor said. He tried again with a name change. 'Mr Stokes? Joseph?'

Best he react to that. Jones stirred, making a show of trying to wake up.

'Joseph. The police are going to remove your chip.'

'What?' He said it as sharply as he could. 'Remove it? Why?'

'They want further checks of its validity.'

'Its validity? Why do they need to check it again? It just passed a standard read, didn't it?'

'It did.' The doctor, a round-faced thirty-something, glanced aside to the other man in the room. Detective Pike stood there in his high-necked grey suit, last season's fashion, but for a cop that was remarkably up to date.

'Mr Stokes,' Pike said as if the name carried no validity at all. 'Mr Pak's ID checked out, all his licences are clean, he has no criminal record. He claims you're Jeven Jones. So far we're had no verification to prove that's the truth, but even so my office has decided to carry out a complete check of your identification chip.'

Jones flailed weakened limbs, making a pantomime out of trying to sit up. 'I told you, Pak kidnapped me. He bought me off a blasted freighter captain. I told him who I was. I told him the truth, and he ignored me. Is my father here? You said he was on station. Where is he?'

'I'm sorry, your father can't see you yet,' Pike said. 'Procedure states we have to class you as an *unknown* at this point. You can't have visitors. You can't employ a lawyer to act on your behalf. You can't refuse to have your chip examined. Until your chip reads cleanly or does not, you are, in effect, in limbo.' Pike sounded astounded by his own words. Evidently procedure had been written on a comp somewhere and had been soundly ignored until now. This had to be a first for Delta.

'You're telling me I don't exist even though my chip just scanned perfectly?'

'I'm sorry, you'll be Joseph Stokes only when we can positively verify your ID down to your chip's internal mechanics. It's within the law's right to demand the ID verification of any citizen.' Pike folded his arms.

'You've really nothing to worry about,' the doctor soothed, his attempt at sincerity as convincing as his concern. 'As soon as your chip passes its tests you can go back to your family.'

Jones threw back a little spoiled brat upset: he sucked at his lip, wiped at watery eyes. 'Fine, but the truth is I'm a rich kid, and Pike's a Reaches brat. He prefers good old straightforward ex-military Pak. Pak wanted the test, so he's got the test. This isn't procedure, this is straightforward prejudice. Take my chip, detective, do whatever tests on it you want. I'm Joseph Stokes and I'll expect a full apology when this is over.'

'I'm afraid that isn't authorized according to procedure.' Pike didn't even attempt to hide his self-satisfied little smirk. 'I need to make a call then I'll get my technical staff organized, Mr *Stokes*.'

Pike's call went straight to *The Nova* and Frank at helm. 'It's happening right now, Mr Pak,' he said over the link.

'How long will it take?' Frank asked.

'The techs can't put an exact estimate. They've never done this before. Ten to twenty-four hours is their best guess.'

'Okay . . . that's fine. We're in no hurry. Look, I called Greeley, he's sending somebody to speak to us. A Bernard Aubrey.'

Pike hummed. 'If you want to send him over to me, that's fine. If I can speak to Mr Greeley through him, that's fine too, but so far it's not looking good as regards the Stokes chip. To be honest this whole thing's becoming a little disturbing. It's beginning to have far too many overtones. Do you understand what I mean by overtones, Mr Pak?'

It was a warning. It was, Frank realized, an out-and-out yell that something on Pike's end of things didn't feel quite right. And it clearly might come down to outside threats if he pursued it. A *Max* situation caused by Calder, or worse a Government mess still unravelling. 'Are you all right, Pike?' he asked in a low voice. 'I don't want anybody to get hurt over this thing.'

'Caution's always best. There's no point in overstepping our boundaries. I'll give you call once this thing's settled.'

The link went dead, and Frank shifted in his seat, not daring to glance aside at Foley. 'How deep do you think *we're* in to all those overtones?'

Foley huffed. 'Right now, we're nothing but Greeley's cab company. Let's hope it stays that way.'

The com came alive again, Frank checking the call's source before hitting the panel's receive button with far more force than necessary. 'Where the hell have you been?'

'I had to dodge a real cop for a while.'

Foley sat shaking his head.

'I told you, Max, I don't want any more trouble here,' Frank said over the link.

'You'll want to hear this, believe me. And don't worry, it's just a little scrap of info I got out of the nurse, that's all.'

'This patient confidentiality kind of info we want broadcast over an unprotected link?' Foley asked.

'It's obvious info we should have had if we'd had a med scanner on board,' Max sounded annoyed abruptly. 'The rest is info Jones himself is spreading to every doctor and nurse who'll listen.'

'Fine, tell us what you've got and be done with it,' Frank said.

'Jones has suppressed immunity, and those meds he takes aren't the whole reason why. He's missing a few things – things like his spleen and left kidney. And you can add to that mystery evidence of internal scarring. Trauma most likely caused by a gunshot wound. Jones has a whole story concocted to explain it. He says it was a hunting accident, followed by a quick exit after a family spat. An unsuitable girlfriend, an angry father, you name it, it's in there. And Joseph is a handful by his own way of telling of it, refusing anything but rudimentary treatment just to rile his old man. That's his explanation for the pills too. No neurological fixes allowed because Joseph hates his daddy, and Joseph likes to take his vengeance out on his own body. The kid likes his games and he's playing them all right. The docs have treated him for the infection. Daddy's around, but the cops won't let him through. The man has a lot of security with him. I've seen it: seriously well-muscled, well-armed security.'

'Nice,' Foley muttered. 'Daddy's brought an army with him.'

'Max, the kid's chip just cleared a standard read,' Frank said. 'A whole twenty-one-year history in a chip with all the right specs. And I just got warned by a cop about damned overtones.'

A long length of silence came back.

'You think we've got the wrong kid?' Frank pressed.

'I'm backing off, okay.' Max sounded nervous instantly. 'You want that yelled over this link? I'm backing way off. Do you want me and Haine to come back in?'

'No. No, stay put for now, but stop asking questions. Just watch. Stay quiet and watch.' Frank cut the link.

'Government,' Foley said as if the word tasted rancid on his tongue. 'Damned Government's hiding something.' He pointed to the second screen along. 'That look like an Aubrey to you, Frank?'

On the monitor a tall white-blond man was striding up *The Nova*'s ramp-way.

'You watch your step. You say please and thank you,' Foley warned as Frank headed for the door. 'You hear me?'

Half a minute later Frank stood hauling the outside hatch along its running tracks. With the door only ajar the man standing on the ramp-way stuck out his hand and left it there for Frank to stare at. 'Bernard Aubrey, Mr Pak. Mr Greeley sent me.'

'That was fast.' Frank didn't take the offered hand. 'I take it you've heard we've had some ID problems.'

'I heard. I'm from Delta CI, Mr Pak.'

'Criminal Intelligence?' Frank bit back a scornful *Oh really*. 'So what's going on?'

Aubrey avoided eye contact, studying the dock at his back from the ramp's height before pulling a palm-sized metal box from his pocket. He flipped a switch.

'Is somebody listening to us, Mr Aubrey?'

Aubrey eyed a maintenance crew, grey-clad engineers moving in a rolling gantry so they could climb high enough to repair a tear in a big hauler's skin two bays down the dockside. 'I couldn't say. I'd like to make one thing clear: I'm here because Clifford Greeley sent me, not because I'm on the Joseph Stokes case in any official capacity. I have made Mr Greeley aware of the developing situation.'

Frank narrowed his eyes. 'I'm guessing you're not considering talking to the cops on our behalf? I'm guessing no ID stats for Jones are about to turn up?'

For the first time the man's eyes settled firmly onto Frank. His irises were almost indistinguishable from his pupils, his swarthy skin a sharp contrast to his white-blond hair. A cosmetic fix, for sure. 'I have fresh instructions for you. Stay quiet and stay clear. You let this play out any way it has a mind to. You don't interfere. You're a legitimate businessman, behaving in a professional manner.'

'Did Greeley expect me to be something else?'

Aubrey smiled. 'From what I've been told Jones has a history of procuring help, a way of bending people's loyalties one way or another. I hope you're exactly as I've stated: a legitimate businessman following his employer's instructions.'

'If Greeley lied to me about this kid and about himself, do you seriously think I'm interested in why he did it? Or who or what the hell Jones really is? All I'm interested in is getting my crew out of the mess I've made here the quickest way possible.'

Aubrey pursed his lips and glanced at his little machine, speaking to it rather than to Frank. 'I'm glad you know your limitations. Don't push them. If Jones' chip clears and the cops don't charge you, get off the station and return to Beta. You'll be paid. Well paid. For now, lie low. You're too conspicuous at the moment. Do you understand?'

'I'm beginning to.'

'Good. If Jones' chip proves to be a fake—'

'Then I'm still the cab company?' Frank tilted his head, raised his brows.

Aubrey nodded. 'It's been nice speaking to you.' He offered his hand again, and again Frank ignored it. Aubrey made no comment, he turned about and walked down the ramp-way, his attention locked to his little machine.

Frank let a breath go, leaned inside the ship and hit the com panel. 'Foley, we need bug killer. The best there is.'

'Bug killer?' Foley echoed.

'Somebody's listening to us. Call Haine and get him onto it. No delay. Get it done, right now.'

The TV in Jones' room hung from the wall, the monitor surrounded by an out-of-place ornate silver frame that looked antique but most probably wasn't. A station network broadcast was airing a round-up of all the local on-site news. A body had been found in the lowest station level, crammed between a nest of utility pipes. A body sectioned up into a hundred pieces in a collection of Mr Hungry Devils Hamburger cartons. A body meant to be collected up for future digestion by some fanatical fast-food cannibal, a flaccid-faced cop was suggesting. The ID-less corpse dominated this news cycle. It, and pictures of a man running through the main retail concourse stark naked, who, when interviewed, confessed he'd done it to protest against the rigidity of station laws regarding the keeping of poisonous white-backed Ovaciant tree lizards. The cop's technical division had taken Jones' ID chip over eighteen hours ago now. He had healing gel smeared on the tiny wound at the back of his neck, and, of all things, a receipt for his missing chip on his bedside cabinet. Even nonentities needed paperwork, it seemed. The cops had also taken his fingerprints and computer mapped his iris. They hadn't mentioned his blood. DDC had a sample; Jones presumed they'd share it if the cops wanted his DNA.

'Three,' Jones said to the TV, and the channel flipped to Station News Three, where a dockworkers' walkout was verbally being beaten to death by two opposing teams of political commentators. Station Three was the sombre channel, devoted to the upcoming station master election, share dealing and industry news. Jones had no access to anything but the hospital-supplied Delta broadcasts: no outside news, no entertainment channels, nothing at all coming in off the buoys from Earth or her sister Inner Rim worlds. He was bone-numbingly bored; nothing was of interest any more but a bowl of ice cream a nurse had supplied to ease his painful throat. Real ice cream, with real-life unaltered cream, and delicate slices of bona fide fruit inside it, the supply of which, together with the appearance of the ornate TV, suggested a high-level subordinate sent by Christian MacKay Calder had found their way into the hospital administrator's office. Somebody had been bought. The same somebody who likely had been instructed to keep his media interests small and well contained. Good food because he was sick, no 'real' TV because Christian knew he constantly hunted for clues, constantly searched for faces he might remember from long ago even on TV news bulletins. Christian knew things he didn't, he was sure of it, and he'd clearly deemed Delta a safe area. No one he wanted to find had ended up anywhere near this station, or he wouldn't have been allowed those station broadcasts either.

He sighed, staring into his bowl at the pale, red-flecked mound of melting ice cream. He sat concentrating long and hard on every mouthful. He knew how to time-fill – he'd done enough of it over the years. And besides, it stopped him from thinking about what waited for him outside the hospital walls, and the plan C he'd never wanted to use. The plan he'd known was available the moment *The Valdese* had turned up on Frank Pak's tail.

The door pinged a warning before it slid open. The familiar cop appeared. Pike had been sucking hard on something sour by the looks of him. 'It cleared,' he said, his words downbeat and dour. 'Right down to the metal.'

Jones bit his lip. He wanted to say a lot of things: rile the cop for the sake of it, add some acerbic sarcastic remarks for the sake of it. But he was Joseph now. He had to be Joseph. 'I told you,' he said, making sure he sounded childishly sullen and angry.

'It's police policy to be ruthless with ID discrepancies,' Pike said.

Jones smiled at that lie. He took another mouthful of ice cream and let it ooze slowly over his tongue.

Lip curl, almost a snarl, and Pike turned for the door. 'I'll send your father in.'

Five minutes, and the door pinged again. This time his 'father' walked in. Jones didn't recognize the man; nevertheless, he ordered the TV silent, pushed aside his ice cream bowl and, with an air of wounded juvenile pride, slipped his arms around his father's shoulders as the man leaned over the bed. A rib-crushing hug followed, completed by Michael Stokes' choked little sob of relief, all for the benefit of a nurse who flitted about, tidying the room. Stokes pulled up a chair, his security team settling themselves into every vulnerable space in the room. With eight men watching her every twitch, the nurse licked dry lips, made her excuses and left.

Stokes moved a finger to his mouth, saying nothing until one of his security team set a machine on the bed's end, a little scanner/jammer device used to kill any audio or visual signals going outward. 'You'll be out as soon as you get your chip back,' he said in a low, firm voice. 'You'll be taken to an apartment. Christian is waiting there. You will behave yourself. You won't try to escape. Do you understand?' He stared at Jones hard-eyed. Stokes doubtless another high-level Calder subordinate with a fake name and a fake past. Christian's interventions these days could contain a million layers of deceit.

'Yes,' Jones said.

'The doctors said you shouldn't travel, not yet. Your lungs are still inflamed, they need time to heal. You're prone to infections? All the same we need to get you off this station by tomorrow at the latest.'

'I can manage that.'

The man's heavy brows dipped. 'When we leave you'll play your part. The machine will take care of verbal audio, but don't say anything out of turn, there may be people out there who can lip-read.'

Jones nodded. 'I understand.'

The man leaned back in his chair and let a sigh go. 'So, have you seen the news today?'

The Stokes chip came back with security of its own: two cops and a doctor. The doctor wanted him to sign something, some legalese Stokes refused to let Jones touch until he'd had a lawyer take a look at it. The papers got sidelined into the hands of one of Stokes' guards. Then another man came in with clothes; not simply something to change into, a vast array of designer labels to choose from. Jones picked at random and got dressed. The effort made him cough, made the blue-hued walls sway, the sombre faces of the security men surrounding him blurring out of focus. He didn't complain; he didn't say a word. He was put in a wheelchair then. Stokes himself pushing him along the hospital's busy corridors. Jones kept his head low, seeing feet and legs passing by and little else. Only the harsh 'ha-hum' of someone clearing their throat finally made him glance up. Max stood by a water cooler, his face unshaven, dark circles under his eyes. Clearly a man who hadn't slept; clearly one who wanted his attention.

Jones opened his mouth, but Stokes' hand landed on his shoulder, his fingers pinching into skin. 'Don't. Don't say a word.'

Stokes glared at Max, and Max glared back. Stokes pushed the chair by, and Jones craned his head around. Max didn't make a move to follow them, he leaned into the cooler with the casual air of somebody who didn't give a damn instead, calmly watching them getting further and further away.

Even when they reached the outside doorway Jones still watched Max, worried some of Stokes' security might drop back to deal with him. None did, but hands had drifted into jacket bulges where guns were kept, one man wagging a finger in warning at the now distant figure of Max down the corridor.

Max still didn't move.

As the outside door slid closed behind them, Stokes pulled the chair to a halt.

'We'll have to take the tube, station refused to authorize a vehicle.' Station's prerogative: fuel in whatever form took up storage or tapped power station refused to spare. 'We can borrow the chair – or would you rather walk?'

Jones stood up for an answer, forced to lean into Stokes as his balance went astray. Stokes didn't let go as he steadied himself, the man holding him jarringly tight. 'Slow and steady,' the man said as they moved off.

The tube station was crowded; with little independent traffic allowed, they always were busy no matter what the time of day. Jones shuffled out onto the platform trailed by black-suited security, Stokes pulling him to a standstill as a train glided down the track-way and drew to a silent halt.

As the carriage doors opened and people piled out Jones saw Max again: Max being forcibly pushed back across the platform by two of Stokes' men. 'Don't hurt him. He's nobody; there's no need to hurt him.'

Stokes signalled to the men on the platform, making an aggressive gesture that made Jones even edgier. He tried to get by to see what was happening, but Stokes pulled him forward, shoving him through the tide of still-exiting passengers to get him into the carriage and down into a seat.

'No trouble,' Stokes reminded. He glanced aside with menace enough to make the passengers taking seats nearby look furtively away. 'Sit still and be quiet,' he added loudly, suggesting he meant everybody close enough to hear him.

Jones stared at the adverts piling across the tube-way's electronic boards inside and outside the carriage. No point in yelling to a bunch of people already wary of Stokes and his darkly suited entourage. No point in trying to strike up conversation with Stokes or his men either, they'd nod maybe, or shake their heads, nothing else. There were no soft underbellies on show here, Christian knew him too well. The man had learned by experience how he found his escape routes.

The train pulled to a halt as it reached the next platform over.

Stokes leaned in, placing a hand under Jones' elbow to get him moving again. 'Ten-minute walk,' he said.

They took a route directly down the shopping concourse, where the trees grew in troughs under the plating, where the squirrels ran across the shoppers' paths and the multi-coloured birds flocked, hunting for food.

Jones caught flashes of himself in the reflective surfaces: a pale-faced kid, his head lolling, coughing now and again on air thick here with the scents of lavender and grass. Station policy: keep the shoppers' noses happy, remind them of Earth, a world most of them would never pass the security evaluations even to visit. The Government was there in permanent residence.

Jones stopped moving, McKintock's Genuine Spirits a flash of fierce yellow over a shop frontage. Sensory overload, and his feet stopped hearing from his brain.

'Joseph?' Stokes' voice rose a notch. 'Banis, help him,' he ordered, and Jones was instantly shored up on his free side.

Weakness. Show them how fragile he was, then make a break for a crowd. Look for a service hatch, maybe something the cleaning bots used. He promised himself one bloody-minded attempt at escape. But the weakness wasn't an act: his knees wouldn't hold, his thoughts refused to gel.

He saw another flash of a colour, a red squirrel darting out and frightening one of the gatherings of fancy birds, the resulting up-surge a shimmering burst of red and blue plumage. More station homage to the mother world: a concourse full of Earth originals.

'Joseph?'

Jones saw his own face's reflection again: cheekbones too sharp, eyes too shrunken. Saw behind him in the shadow of a tree a big black man: Haine. Damn fool Haine was following them.

They turned a corner, entered a building, walked across a wide lobby that smelled of new carpet. Deeply piled, blood-red carpet all that Jones could see. He couldn't lift his head. Wouldn't.

They entered a lift, and his two-man escort leaned him bodily into the wall.

'Jones, are you feeling all right?' Someone cupped his face, and he reacted in mindless affront. He kicked out, toe-punting someone with his brand-new designer boots, someone who swore bloody murder at him.

'Stop it,' Stokes snapped at him.

When the lift doors opened they got him moving again, down a corridor, down to the doors at its end, the carved doors of a luxury suite. Calder trappings stood in full view: a two-man guard with shoulder-slung rifles. Plainly visible live rounds on station in a civil area. Christian could do that. He might not have pushed to circumnavigate station's traffic laws but he was a Calder, and nothing would stop him demanding properly attired security.

The heavy wooden doors drew silently open.

'He's not doing too well, sir,' Stokes reported.

'Jeven?'

The name made him shudder. It didn't belong here; it belonged to another time, another place, a different set of people. The anxious timbre of that all too familiar voice belonged to another time too, one full of pain, a burning sensation in his side as a bullet meant for a Calder had sent the day dark. The same frightened voice had yelled for help then, down in the dark of Alfa Station, where the pipework crisscrossed overhead, where the rats scurried, where other human vermin sold drugs to bored, rich fools.

'Jeven, can you hear me?'

A touch on his chin, and Jones cringed back, squinting hard at the face before him. Lank brown hair, a hooked nose: Christian in his dock tramp disguise. His rich man's version of poor: clean fingernails, gold rings, designer dust sprinkled on designer wear-and-tear clothes. 'Bring him inside. Sit him down. Stokes, fetch some water.'

Moments later Jones sat staring through the pinnacle of wealth: a viewing window that framed the black. Stars watched, light years distant. Jones felt their pull, he set himself adrift to meet them. 'Jeven?' Christian's call again, the man pulling the water glass from Jones' deadened fingers. 'Do you hear me? Are you all right? Stokes, do we have all his meds for the infection?'

'Someone's collecting them from the hospital pharmacy now, sir.'

'Did he ask to walk?'

'Yes, sir. I didn't argue, as instructed. I was careful. One intercept by Pak's crew was dealt with. We persuaded the man to go home. Another crewman tailed us but he kept his distance.'

'Good. Good.' Christian's voice dropped. 'Any word on the other matter?'

'I've heard it's being dealt with. Everything's in place for the authorities to tie everything up neatly and cleanly.'

Jones frowned, hardly hearing, hardly understanding. 'What other matter?'

'It's none of your concern,' Christian told him as warm hands wrapped around his cold fingers. 'An accountant was trying to cheat my uncle. It's nothing to do with me, honestly. It's all right. You're safe. Do you need to lie down? Do you need to rest?'

Jones knuckled his chest, his heart fluttering out of rhythm. Two fast beats, one elongated pause and it steadied. 'Are you lying? Have you killed somebody, Christian? Are you planning to? Are you going to kill Pak?'

'No. No.'

Jones swayed where he sat, peering at Christian sitting next to him, not sure if that was the truth. He pulled his hands clear of the man's clutching fingers.

'Do you want to call his ship?' Christian asked. 'He hasn't been hurt. No one from that ship has. No one will be.'

'Then what's happening?'

'I've told you, it's my uncle's mess. It's nothing to do with me.'

Was that half the truth or none of it? Jones searched Christian's face, looking for deceit, realizing those TV broadcasts had forewarned him. The Mr Hungry Devils Hamburger killer was a Calder fabrication; somebody in the family had definitely removed a human annoyance. They did that kind of thing all the time. 'I need to know how far things have gone. You have to tell me about the revolution, right now.'

CHAPTER 8

Jones had done a very stupid thing in a bar on Alfa. He'd seen a rich man, one whose eyes had locked onto his. Who'd shown an interest, as well he might. Jones had had his hair trimmed, he'd bought the latest fashion, he'd pretended to be drunk, lurching all over the bar staff demanding booze, patting himself down for credits he couldn't find. Playing the rich man for the man's contacts, his money, a little influence. He hadn't checked with Milo. No, a background check on the man would have been far too sensible. He'd rather play the odds. He'd had no clear idea what he was attaching himself to when Christian had come over and offered a little help. Jones had reeled back, wagged an accusing finger. 'Sorry,' he'd slurred. 'Not that way inclined.' Then he'd held the man's gaze for far too long, signalling a maybe, a 'You want me, you better be prepared to work damn hard to get me.'

A very dangerous game with a Calder. Milo had yelled when he'd heard that name. They were everywhere, they'd spread like a disease, he'd said. An entire extended family of aunts and uncles and cousins all working around the hub of Alexander, Christian's father. A man definitely involved in illegal tech. Gene tech.

127

Life-expansion technology. He likely owned half the ships hiding out in the black.

'Get off that station,' Milo had warned. 'He'll want to know who you are. You can never let that man find out about *The Bliss*. He'll want every part of it.'

He'd fled for the dock right then and there, trailed all the way by security types trying hard to look nonchalant. Crossing one of the shopping concourses a young woman had walked smack into him, a gun's muzzle catching him under the ribs. 'No trouble,' she'd said, as if describing what an easy catch he'd been. How much trouble dare he be on a station, with no chip back then, with no real ID.

They'd escorted him to a hotel room, pumped him full of drugs and asked him who he really was. He was Jake, Jeven, J-seventeen, of course, from *The Bliss*, later from Greeley's Intuition, a murderer now and then. He'd hung on to it all, hung on and hung on for hours, days. He'd uttered finally the name *The Bliss*. That was all. That was all it took for a man like Alexander to start looking for information he could use. Alexander who'd stared at him with such admiration, astounded by his bloody-minded determination to hang on to his secrets. 'I'll kill you if I carry on,' he said. 'I'll find you out another way. You're different, I know that much.'

In the apartment, Christian settled himself on the chair opposite him, took a slow breath and paused. He was about to talk about a revolution; such things took a few mental adjustments.

Keep the people a long way apart, they were easier to control that way, that was one of Alexander's theories about the Government. Feed the Inner Rim and bleed the Reaches, there was another. Years ago he'd worked in Secret Ops and military security details. He'd developed an insight into the workings of the Heads of State, far, far too deep an insight. He'd theorized that the Government had lied about the technology it endlessly rebuked: this was dangerous, that was untested, that would likely kill you. Alexander had developed a liking for tech. He surrounded himself with it. Milo was damned sure he owned many of the gene tech ships that flitted about on the edges of known space surrounded by spotter ships. Always moving, always looking for Government intervention, though nothing on board would ever be traced back to their financier. Alexander paid patsies to take every fall, according to Milo.

Alexander had certainly developed a way to make perfect ID chips, his supporters now logging them at Central. His biggest triumph yet. A sure way to undermine the Government's rigid population controls and an easy way to infiltrate high-level postings with false personnel. He'd tracked down The Bliss. Now his ambitions included it and every piece of tech generated by it that had ever existed. He wanted Lieberman most of all.

Christian still hadn't said a word, he sat pale-faced. Calder faces were always thin and lugubrious even when they changed, and they often did. Calders changed names too. Jones often wondered if they changed sex on a whim. 'Christian,' he prompted.

Christian spoke at last, looking mournfully sorry as if it were all his fault. Now it seemed Alexander had plans for military carriers. He had sleeper agents on board, admirals in control of highly armed ships. 'He's gathering it all around the most well-developed planet the Reaches owns,' Christian said. 'Charris. The Charris Confederation.'

Jones swallowed, feeling heartily sick.

'He doesn't know I'm here,' Christian said in a rush. 'I'll protect you.'

Jones put a hand on his chest, his heart pitching out of rhythm again. He wished he'd never been to that bar. He wished he'd never looked into the man's sad eyes and thought that here was some weak fool he could use. 'I'm involved in this because of you,' he snapped, sounding like a spite-filled brat. 'You as good as gave me to him. You knew what he was doing and you gave him *The Bliss*.'

His strange lapses had caused the man's betrayal, Jones knew it. Christian had told his father of his odd new friend who would zone out for minutes at a time or worse collapse in a dead faint. A brain disease, a tumour; Christian must have wanted checks and he'd wanted the best men to do them. His father could provide those, his father could provide so many reassurances. But when Alexander had tried to trace the false name he'd used back then he'd come up empty.

Jones sucked in an angry breath, staring at the stars outside the observation window, the vastness of space, the distances jump-gates swallowed up in hours. Out there were people he had to find for reasons he couldn't, wouldn't put aside.

Fingers brushed against this own. 'I'll keep you safe,' Christian whispered, settling down close beside him. 'It'll be all right.'

Jones pulled himself clear, palmed his forehead, felt the sweat there, the chill. 'I need a drink. A "real" drink.' He didn't mean one drink either; he meant an oblivion of drinks.

'A small brandy,' Christian said, worriedly. 'Just one.'

Jones downed his brandy in three gulps. He coughed hard then, teary-eyed as he sat watching a room full of expensive Earth wood and deep-piled fabrics pull further and further out of focus. Brandy normally liked his meds well enough. He didn't overly much care if it didn't right then, he knew he'd fall asleep eventually, just pass out where he sat in a room full of security in front of a man who sought to own him. Who did just then. He sighed, breathing in the vapours of the brandy dregs in the glass he held tight to his chest. Christian's voice was a continuous backdrop drone. Everything he knew he confessed – that was Christian. 'I have clean IDs we can use. We'll hide in the Reaches. Life will be basic, at least until my aunt can secure something more permanent, more secure. Martha's on my side, she's prepared to help us.'

'Where is she?'

'Inner Rim. Negotiating some deal or other.'

'Same hair, same eyes?'

'Dark-red hair, lilac eyes now. Too gaudy both of them. She's had a recent cosmetic fix, too. Illegal of course. She wanted to look older this time. Age equates with authority, she said.'

'Where's Alexander?'

'I don't know – not precisely. I've lied to him, agreed with his plans, so he'll stay in contact.'

'Red hair, lilac eyes?'

Christian smiled his saddest smile. 'No, he's the same as ever.'

'Gaunt, wiry, bad tempered?' Alexander Calder had deep-set eyes, thinking eyes that scrutinized then pulled people apart. Stand too long in front of him and he picked you down to the bone. 'Has he found Lieberman?'

'He refused to tell me.' Christian glanced away. He didn't lie well.

'Does he have anyone else?'

'I don't know.'

Jones stared into his empty glass, knowing that was a lie too. 'I'd like another drink.'

'You've had enough.'

'Of thinking. Yes, more than enough. So stop me.'

That appeal won him another brandy. He drank it down the fast way, everything growing indistinct, everything wallowing and pitching even with his eyes firmly closed. Drinking on top of meds really was a bad idea. He felt the weight of Christian's hand on his shoulder. 'You need to rest. I'll have you taken into the other room.'

He squirmed, security on all sides helping him up, one man snatching the brandy glass clear before his limp fingers let it go. They tugged him along, led him to a bedroom, laid him out on the bed, taking off his boots and draping blankets over him.

A fingertip stroked hair off his forehead. 'You're safe, I promise.'

Jones shifted, blinked. He forced his scattered thoughts back together and pushed himself to a sit, shoving thick pillows into a wedge behind him. The blinds were closed in the bedroom, but he knew there would be another star field on view beyond them, another rich man's show of wealth.

There were no security men present now; only a stuffed owl watched them with wide, glassy eyes. In russet plumage it swooped across one wall. The bird was an illegal import possibly, or something ancient. Another stuffed bird stood on a table before the blinds, a humming bird stuck mid-hover in front of a wide pink flower. No hotel bought such expensive and illegal curiosities. 'Does this place belong to Martha?'

'Yes.' Christian busied himself supplying a heavy cut-glass tumbler full of water. He perched on the bed's edge again while Jones drank down what he could. 'She's terrified that what my father's doing is going to split the family apart. She thinks at some point we'll be at war with ourselves. I've told her I don't want any part of it. All I want is . . .' his words petered out, his lips tightening.

'Your lost little pet?' Jones suggested lowly, bitterly.

Christian smiled, one of those sad, lost smiles Christian did so well. 'I'm here to protect you. To help you.'

'To save me from myself?'

'As you saved me. Have you forgotten that? My debt.'

'Your nonsense.'

'Would you like me to list your own collection of nonsenses? I know all your games, all your lies.'

Jones laughed. 'You don't know anything at all.'

Christian drew a ragged breath. 'Even so,' he said firmly.' It all ends here. You have to learn to live another life.'

'With another name, in another cage.'

Another ragged breath, and Christian refused eye contact. 'We'll be leaving in the morning. My ship's timeslot out is already booked. We'll have to triple jump. You'll be tranked of course, but even so it's a risk.'

Jones shrugged, receiving another look: bafflement.

'Don't pretend you don't care if you live or die.'

'What have you left me to live for?'

A distressed look then, one Jones placidly stared right through.

'More games. More lies,' Christian said.

'You hope. You presume – I'd like another drink. Another brandy.'

'No.'

'You'll never make me happy saying no.'

Christian's face stilled into a stone-hard mask. 'One more brandy. One more damn brandy.'

Drinking down his third brandy Jones realized he had no clear idea when he'd had his second. Time as meaningless a concept as when he'd been on *The Nova* or in his hospital room. He watched Christian stalk back and forth across the bedroom, his long coat throwing off palls of fake dust on each aggravated turn. 'Is tramp still the latest fashion?'

'Is drunk?'

'Do the Calder perfumers concoct a scent for you? Odour of tramp: garbage and rat faeces. I want another brandy.'

'Absolutely not.' Christian's voice quailed. He always fought to be stiff-backed, impassive, he always failed. He'd need a miracle to win against the man he tried to mirror: his father. Christian's efforts made Jones laugh. It made him laugh until his stomach hurt. 'What's so funny?' Christian asked sourly.

'You are. This is, all of it.' He couldn't stop the laughter; it bubbled up out of his chest and refused to stop.

'Drink and drugs don't mix. You need to sleep it off.' Christian, coat flapping, whirled towards the doorway.

Such a shame you couldn't slam doors that swished to and fro so silently.

Jones spied the brandy bottle across the room. An oversight, Christian made those often. Christian had always been a riot of badly concealed emotions and naive ideas: a thirty-five-year-old teenager. That made Jones laugh too, a soft rise and fall of it breaking free as he padded over to a skinny-legged little side table and the elegant crystal decanter balanced on its top. He took the brandy back to bed, wrapped his fingers tight about it and inelegantly seduced it.

He slept finally in a brandy-soaked heaven; long and deep where nothing intervened, no data, no memories. He woke with a yelp of shock to more darkness, coarse folds of cloth trapped about his face. He twisted around, thrashed out, his wrists and ankles caught and held fast. 'Christian,' he yelled out in panic, his own brandy-scented words fuming up his nostrils. He threw his head back, trying to get some air between himself and suffocating fabric. 'Christian,' he yelled.

The voice that answered him wasn't Christian's. 'Quiet down

now, you'll spoil your Calder boyfriend's surprise. Lieberman
wants you, Jones. So he'll have you.'

The kid's chip had cleared right down to the metal. The news was
hours old and it still hung around *The Nova*'s corridors like the
worst of bad smells. Frank warned his crew if they spoke one word
on the subject he'd do murder. He had his reasons. Max hadn't
followed orders, then, when he'd run into trouble, he'd called
Haine in to intercept Jones' party on the concourse to find out
where they were heading. And Haine had come home with an
address: the Latitude Hotel, private apartment seventeen C.

So his crew were curious; Frank didn't blame them for that. He
did blame them for being visible, for showing their faces where
they shouldn't have been, for acting like idiots to a man. And now
damned fool Foley was up at his boards calling in favours from all
over the station to try to find out all he could about the Calder at
the heart of Michael Stokes' lie. All because that damned chip had
cleared, something that should have been straight-down-the-line
impossible.

On the plus side – there was one – Stokes' lawyer had stopped
making threats, and the cops had let the whole matter drop. Frank
had been free to book a timeslot for undock from the Dock
Master's Office, receiving one for midnight-zero-three. After that
he'd placed a call to Bernard Aubrey, receiving nothing but a
comp's 'not available' message for a reply. Damn the man – but
they were already following instructions; they were getting off the
station. Frank considered taking a walk down to the Delta CI
offices if Aubrey didn't call back. If Aubrey wasn't available in
person then double damn the man, Frank wasn't going to wait for
him to appear, and he wasn't going to leave another message.

With everything neat and tidy he had time to waste. He paced up between the galley and the lift right up until an impatient Foley waved him into the galley. Foley had compiled a list; it lay scrawled in black ink on a big piece of paper on the galley table.

'That's all you got?' Frank sat down, leaned over and spun the paper about. He read the notes, squinting at Foley's handwriting. And snorted: Alexander Calder, Christian MacKay's father, wasn't just rich, he was obscenely rich. Foley had scribbled down a list of companies he was involved with.

Christian MacKay Calder. Alexander's sixth son. Frank snorted again. Alexander had a lot of kids, an improbable number. Frank wondered how he found time to do much else except breed. He gawped at what he read next. 'So this Christian's a party boy with a pretty-boy fetish. That's not Jones' style, is it?'

'Help with unlimited funds attached sounds like Jones' style to me.' Foley slotted himself into the seat opposite. 'They're a cagey lot too, that'd help. Info's hard to find about them even on Station Web. I did get one little snippet from a news reporter I know over on Station Three. He remembered fronting a piece that aired a year or so back about someone who saved Christian's life down in the pipe-ways under Alfa. That's drug territory according to my source. Three security types didn't leave the scene alive. Damn shame is my source couldn't recall all the details, and the file's been deleted – obviously.'

Frank tried to disguise his shock and failed, he guessed, judging by the Foley's little under-the-brows look of sympathy. 'Jones saved Calder.'

Foley shrugged 'His "saving people" habit seems almost as bad as his "murdering" habit.'

Frank frowned. A run-in with some rough types down in the boondocks would explain a few missing organs. A fast fix would have likely been followed by a wait in a tissue lab while some high-priced doctors got set for a slow-grow. Jones must have started to get twitchy in the meantime. Maybe the help was becoming more of a hindrance. 'So how come this Calder didn't find him first?' he asked. 'He has to have had more resources than we do. How come we beat him to it?'

Foley hummed. 'I thought about that one. I came up the answer. It's called dumb luck. Right time, right freighter cap adds up to dumb stupid luck in my head.'

Frank leaned back and crossed his arms. 'What about the chip? Did Jones' rich party boy supply that too? You know how screwed up that chip is?'

Foley nodded gravely. 'Might be a good idea to ask Greeley about that one.'

Frank smiled. 'Seriously – is this all you've got?'

'I got more than you did, Mr Five-minutes-and-my-backside-needs-an-airing.' Foley yanked his piece of paper off the table and shoved it into his pocket.

'So now we have it, what do we do with it?' Frank asked. 'The kid's chip cleared right down to the metalwork. Legally he's Joseph Stokes.'

Foley raised grey brows. 'Greeley's going to want details. He gets details, we get paid. We don't want to look sloppy here. We have Calder's address, we have a head count on what security he has.'

'Cab company,' Frank leaned across the table. 'Remember us, we're the cab company. We don't want to get in too deep. And Greeley was the sloppy one; he should have made sure they removed that chip on *The Marabell*.'

Foley shrugged. 'Oversight or prison authority incompetence, or Greeley didn't believe that chip was anything but a bog-standard fake. Why assume he'd believe anything else?'

'Cab company,' Frank said again more sharply. 'And likely not even that any more.'

Foley grabbed for sleeve as Frank got up to leave. 'I'm not done. The cops found a body down in the pipe-ways today, no ID and it was chopped down to the size of mincemeat.'

'You've lost me.'

'A signature death: a warning or a message. Drug barons do similar. Death encourages good behaviour. You do it a certain way, everybody who needs to know knows who did it. It might well be a warning for Jones' sake, to keep him safe, to warn people to keep their mouths shut.'

'You're guessing, Foley.' Frank tried to tug himself free. 'An ongoing investigation would have locked the station down.'

'Then they've already caught somebody. Nothing bad ever lands in money's lap. That's what I'm saying. Money has a habit too of circumnavigating Government.'

Frank found it funny suddenly, smiling in spite of the grim expression on Foley's face. 'Are you seriously telling me Jones is with a power-crazed, murdering party boy who had somebody hacked to pieces for the sake of making a point?'

'I'm not saying it's true, I'm saying it's possible.' Foley added a stern little glare to that. 'The more we know about who's out there the more trouble we can avoid.'

'Trouble's gone right by us, Foley.'

'So we'll be grateful, take our info and leave. We pass on what we can to Greeley and we ask for a backdoor out of this. Right?' Foley jutted out his chin. 'Right?'

Frank hauled in a steadying breath. 'What the hell else do you think I'm going to do?'

The hand on Frank's sleeve tightened. 'I think you're going to find Aubrey. I think you want to leave us out of the loop again; you want your info straight from him without us hearing a word of it. You think you owe Jones something.'

'Not true.'

'Frank, you haven't been flying straight since you met that kid. So prove me wrong because I'm thinking it'd be sensible if we all stayed on board, just in case somebody out there is making examples out of corpses.'

Frank yanked himself free. 'If I want out onto that dock, I'm going out. You want to follow me? You want to do that?' Frank got a white-hot glare for that. Foley had been in the tight confines of a ship for so long even the open spaces of a station scared the hell out of him. And you never pointed it out, you never dared even hint at it unless you wanted a week of frigid looks and cold silences.

'Take somebody with you,' Foley growled out. 'Or take a gun. Keep it hidden.'

Frank wavered. Now he'd riled Foley up to boiling point he thought he at least owed himself a dramatic exit.

He pushed by and headed back towards helm; the armoury sat right outside its double doors. 'I'll be back in an half an hour: one half-hour. If I don't appear right on the dot, call the cops.' He meant to placate the man with that statement but when he turned back he met another heated, frustrated stare, Foley's grey-stubbled chin working as if he'd decided chewing on his words right then would be just about as useful as spitting them out.

After two tube rides, and a walk through Station West Botanical Gardens, he didn't find Aubrey. The formal woman on the desk accompanied by two security men told him that Mr Aubrey was unavailable today and for the rest of the week.

So that was that. A pointless little exercise for no good reason

Frank could think of, except maybe he had thought of throwing a few extra questions Aubrey's way about their errant cargo.

He had a feeling as he walked back under the palm trees of the botanical gardens that he'd picked up a tail. He glanced back, his gaze roving over a hook-nosed woman, then a tall man in a black suit, then a little elderly woman with a pet dove balanced on her shoulder.

They all looked eerily familiar. He touched the gun under his jacket, wondering just what the hell Foley expected him to do with it on station. Shoot somebody in the middle of civilization; that'd be a good idea.

He wandered into the Latitude Hotel, taking a quick look round, just for the pure hell of it. He walked the blood-red carpet, found apartment seventeen C, saw the scarred faces of the security men outside the doors. Did he expect to hear Jones yelling for help? The kid was exactly where he'd wanted to be, with his rich, helpful, smitten Calder. 'Go home, you idiot,' Frank told himself firmly. 'Go the hell home.'

Home, when he reached it, turned out to be overflowing with awkward little silences. He stowed his gun back in the armoury, went and sat in the galley, eating his dinner facing a crew whose faces were poker straight.

Foley sat hunched over his food with an expression of pure disgust on his face as if every mouthful he chewed tasted like something solid out of the waste pipes. He was clearly still working on forgiving Frank for daring to leave the ship alone – and judging by the atmosphere in the galley he'd expressed his misgivings to everyone on board, which made Frank wonder if the tail he thought he'd picked up earlier had, in fact, been nothing but his own crew making sure he got back in one piece. He didn't dare ask that to be confirmed or denied, likely it would only start an argument which might well lead to another discussion of how straight he'd been 'flying' lately.

As day wore into evening he went into crew's quarters. He settled onto his bunk, staring sullenly up at the underside of Max's bunk above him. Maybe when they got home there'd be an executive transport job waiting. A fast turn-about from under Greeley's nose would be nice. Greeley wasn't going to be too happy, no cargo to deliver and only eight months completed out of a twelve-month contract, ship time. That meant a deal had to be struck somehow. But the job, Frank reminded himself, was very, very over. He closed his eyes, deciding he had one option left right then: sleep.

'Your friend's turned up.' Foley nudged him awake none too gently hours later.

Frank rolled over, found his arm half asleep under him and shifted again to let the blood flow back into it.

'Hey, dopey,' Foley said. 'You getting up, or do you want me to go tell Aubrey where he can go wedge himself?'

'I'm coming,' Frank replied, rubbing at his numbed fingers. 'Dammit Foley, I'm halfway there already.'

Frank had half an arm by the time he ambled out into the corridor. He went straight up to the outside hatch, he didn't open it, he turned on the com by the door instead with his still-tingling fingers. 'Pak here. What can I do for you?'

A delay followed, likely caused by Aubrey working out whether he needed to press anything on *The Nova*'s ancient com board to reply. 'I have some new instructions for you from Mr Greeley,' came back finally.

'We're getting off station regardless. I have a midnight slot booked. I called you and got your machine. I left a message then I went to Delta CI to find you. I was told you weren't available.'

'Yes . . . yes I know all that. Please, Mr Pak, can I speak to you inside? It's station night out here. It's freezing.'

Frank cursed, rubbing at his arm, then at his prickling fingers before he hit the right switch to open the hatch. The door made a grinding sound, the old mechanism in need of a Greeley upgrade or two. Ice-cold air rushed in as it gaped open, Frank shuddering at the influx. Station nights were always miserable, half-lit, frosty affairs. He sucked a breath down, but not for the sake of the cold: Aubrey held a gun tight in his fist.

Heavy footsteps sounded on the ramp-way, a dark outline getting closer, one that bawled, 'Get inside, you fool!' so loudly at Aubrey he jumped. Aubrey stepped in, Frank backing up in a hurry, bumping the corridor wall behind him as Aubrey pressed the gun he held into his chest.

'What the hell is this?' Frank asked. 'Am I under arrest or something?'

A silver-haired, square-faced stranger followed Aubrey in, aiming his own gun at Frank. 'Hands up and clear, Pak.' The stranger's voice was low and grating, a thin red scar circling his throat from ear to ear a wide smiling explanation for it.

Frank raised his hands. 'I'm not armed.' He forced eye contact with Aubrey. 'Are you going to explain this?'

Behind Aubrey the other man raised a com-link to his lips. 'Durham, you're clear to move. Do it just as rehearsed. Speak to no one unless they engage. Understood?'

'Understood,' a young voice with an audible tremor within it responded.

The stranger motioned to the wall com. 'Call your crew up here, Pak. No guns. No trouble.'

Frank kept his hands visible as he moved. The thumb he used to depress the switch on the com going white to the quick. There was no prickling in his fingers now, there was too much adrenaline flooding his system to allow it. 'I want everyone to come up to the access corridor. Come up unarmed with your hands above your heads. I've got some trouble up here. Call in to confirm.'

Foley came on first, sounding breathless. 'What kind of trouble?'

'The kind that carries guns and doesn't answer questions. It's a little edgy up here. Slow and easy rounding the corner to the hatch, okay?'

'I'm heading down.'

Max came on next from holding. 'What's happening?'

'Just come up unarmed, Max. And slowly. It's going to get crowded down here and I don't want any misunderstandings. Are Kady and Haine still down there with you?'

'Yes.'

'All of you behave, you hear me? There are live rounds up here.'

'We'll be careful,' Max said before the link went dead.

Foley appeared first, coming round the corner to the access-way with his hands well above his head. Max, Kady and Haine crowded in minutes later, the tiny corridor that led to the hatch fast becoming a bottleneck.

'What's going on?' Foley asked.

No answer from either of their visitors, but Frank closest to the open doorway could see more shadows on the ramp-way.

'Get up,' a young voice pitched into the gloom of station night.

Frank stared harder. There were three figures down there, one being dragged, one whose feet refused to fall flat, whose head lolled, his body sliding downward even as his escort fought to right him.

'Oh Jesus,' Frank hissed out. He glared at Aubrey. 'His ID's

143

clean. This is kidnapping. Stokes isn't going to sit for this and neither is Calder.'

'They're cooperating,' the square-faced stranger replied.

'Is station? What did your people do? Blindfold everybody they passed by on the way in. The cops are bound to hear about this.'

The square-faced stranger just smiled. 'Station saw a drunk being rescued from a dive by a couple of his friends. It happens. If anyone saw I doubt they cared. The cops won't get called.'

'Forever?' Frank asked.

'For long enough.'

'And who the hell are you?'

'Patrick Nash.' The overheads shone off a grey-white crew-cut, Nash's mouth hangdog, his deeply set grey eyes darting from one to the next of Frank's crew. 'We have need of a ride, Mr Pak, and you're it.'

Two young men stepped through the hatchway with their burden. Nash hit the lock, the door sliding closed as the young men settled their senseless charge down onto the floor. Jones' arms looked bruised, his hands lying clawed and dirt streaked. His shirt was wet, the stench of booze rising off his body as if he'd been lying in a vat of it.

'I want this crew settled,' Nash said. 'Holding for all of them save the helmsman and—' he pointed with his gun, 'her.' Kady visibly flinched, Max pushing his way forward. 'You want to argue? Harrison, isn't it?' Kady pushed Max back, shaking her head at Nash, who smiled again. 'Hodge, Durham, get them settled. Aubrey, take the other two up to helm. Pak and I will deal with Jones.'

On the floor Jones blinked up at Frank. '*Marabell*,' he muttered faintly as if the name of that ship meant something wholly terrible to him. '*Marabell*.'

Eight months sixteen days ago . . .

Jones had been called Joshua the day he had been caught by Greeley's Government agent. He did have a liking for oblivion. He'd been shamelessly drunk in a little sleepery behind a tavern in a dusty little port at the back end of nowhere. He'd barely even been able to focus on the rat-faced stranger charging in his door with a raised dart gun. He'd laughed a lot then too, but that was drink and meds for you. Oblivion had a price, and he kept on paying it. He'd been cuffed and dragged out, transported to Eta Station and held in a cell until secure transport could be arranged. His ticket to Beta included a trip aboard a prison ship, The Marabell, *a huge ugly lump of scrap heading for decommission. Not a secure ship at all, considering how many inmates got loose. Perhaps he'd helped a little with that. He did have a peculiar talent for opening locked doors. Just a little confusion was all he'd been after so he could head for the life-pods or the shuttle bay. He hadn't planned on a full-scale riot.*

The place reeked of blood as he walked it, guilt turning his stomach over. Knowledge wasn't experience; he made mistakes. The corridors lay littered with bodies dressed in orange prison reg

145

clothing; the inmates had turned on each other in a massive struggle for power. The sound, the feel of the place, caused memories to echo. He bit his lip, drawing blood, swallowing it down as he stepped around dead men. His fault, he reasoned shakily. All his fault. A big, big mistake letting anyone out – as big a mistake as getting drunk, as getting caught.

'Help me.' It was such pitiful plea it made him shiver. 'Please. Help me.' A man sat propped up by the lift doors up ahead. A battle-armoured man stripped of his weaponry, he sat squarely in a pool of blood. He batted blood-stained lids, needing a shallow pant before he could plead again. 'Please. Help me.'

It looked a hopeless task. Too cruel and pointless to drag this poor man to his feet, to cause him more agony just so he could die some-where else, some other corridor, some other room.

'Please.' Another rasped appeal.

Jones edged closer warily, saw no gun, no weapons at all. He crouched in the man's blood, leaning in to try to track down the wound lost in all the gore – a nicked artery surely in the man's left thigh. The man's attempts to stop the bleeding had done little to help. Knowledge streamed into his head. He winced. Understanding wasn't doing. He'd already had a day full of mistakes.

The man grabbed his wrist, hung on despite Jones' flinch away. 'My name's Frank Pak,' he gasped in a rush. 'I have people out there. I want them to know what happened to me.'

Friends, he meant.

'Please . . .' Pak gasped, pushing himself back against the wall, his body all tension and pain. 'Please just tell them this was my fault. I just wanted to keep my ship running. Keep things together. Money. I needed money.' His eyes closed. He relaxed little by little, stilling. Leaving.

Going home.

Jones gritted his teeth. He could sit by and utter a few useless words of sympathy. That's what a normal person would do. One who'd never been on The Bliss.

He shuddered. He'd pushed his thoughts into circuit boards and machines for years. Things had disintegrated before now, smoke had poured out of circuits. He'd always made plans to cover his failures, plans on top of plans. This wasn't a plan. This was either curiosity or desperation or a merging of the two. Play the odds, why not? He'd either save this stranger or kill him – and this sad soul was already dead.

He gathered up the man's wrist, hung on and pushed inward, inward, feeling resistance. A blue man. Blue aura. Going damn, damn deep, catching fading memories: a boy running through fields chasing cows on a world where the trees looked like fists. A boy who stood in a dark little metal house with a twisted hurt feeling in his chest as his mother looked at him with disdain. Not her favourite son. Oh no. Not at all. A mistake she wished she hadn't made. The boy had run away one day, lugging a big case to a shuttle port, his lip trembling, tears in his eyes. 'I'll show you I'm worth a damn.' A boy who'd grown into a man in the tight grey confines of a military carrier, his buddies all around him making jokes about him. Cautious Frank. Careful Frank. Steady old Frank. Forty since the day he was born. A man who felt worthless and incomplete. A man who wanted to be somebody, who just didn't know how to do it.

He delved deep. Too deep.

And liked the man, found something in him, a mirror of himself from so long ago. A Reaches world. A family. An ordinary life.

You're not alone, Frank.

And you're not going home. Not today.

The man sucked a shattered breath. Hung on to it. Exhaled.

Breathing when he surely shouldn't be, more blood on the floor now than inside his body.

'Live,' Jones willed it.

Nothing was impossible if you wanted it enough. He hung on to Frank Pak, held on to his memories, held on tight to every piece of who he was, leaned down, took hold and started to drag his body towards a med bay. He'd fix him. He'd try. He'd set this right because it had been all his fault.

In the med bay he forced Bliss input out of his head. He tied off then repaired the artery, his fingers inept and shaky. He searched for artificial blood and transfused it. Gunshots came from the corridors outside, so close by that he went and dragged furniture across the doorway to keep them safe. The air coming through the vents suddenly stank of smoke.

He sat at Frank Pak's side for an hour, two, one hand permanently fixed to his wrist to feel his pulse grow stronger and stronger. Stealing from the man, his past, all the little stupid things he'd done, was ashamed off, the things he loved, the people. He found inside him an endless sense of disappointment. Frank didn't like Frank very much. Such a sad thing, to feel this man eating away at himself when there was nothing wrong with him at all. Nothing Jones' broken mind could find.

Frank woke finally, shrugged back, fearful of him. Blinking as the sounds from outside reached him.

Jones smiled, beamed like an idiot, offering a water bottle and a chocolate bar. 'I'm going to help you, Mr Pak. I swear to you I'm going to help you.'

Frank hitched a breath, tears came, embarrassed, awkward tears, hidden behind one hand. Relief and terror. Jones nudged the water and the chocolate his way and sat back, giving him room to unravel as Frank's aura flared in calm solid blues.

'I thought I was dead,' Frank sniffed hard, wiping at his face self-consciously. He hauled a deep breath down, taking a worried look then at the pristine white layers of bandage wrapped around his leg. 'How did you do this?'

'I know a lot of doctors.' Jones got a deep, deep frown for that remark. 'I know a lot of med theory,' he added. It wasn't a lie: The Bliss had filled his head to the brim with theory. Maybe he looked a little wobbly himself, a little strung out.

'Are you okay?' Frank asked him. 'You're from transport, right? Blue coveralls.'

'That's me. Transport.' Half a beat he sat there, Frank peering at him as if he must be lying about something. 'Psych section,' he added with a shrug; he might as well admit to being insane.

'Just do as I tell you too, all right?'

Frank really thought he ought to be in charge. Filled up to his eyeballs with painkillers and he was all ready to get moving. 'We need an exit into the cargo bay. That's where the military are.'

Jones shook his head. 'I think we're closer to the escape pods. We could get off that way clear and clean.'

Frank didn't argue. Frank was attacking the chocolate and the water, gathering his strength. Finished with those, he held out his hand. 'Help me up.' Frank leaned hard into Jones' shoulder as he limped through corridors filled with smoke and bodies. 'They'll all be heading for helm,' Frank said. 'That's up. Lower corridors should be clear,' he gasped, the painkillers' grip already wearing thin. He lost his footing and went down with a grunt of agony.

Jones dipped down to help him just as Frank caught him by the collar and pulled him close.

'You should leave me,' he said raggedly. 'I'm too slow. If anyone comes back this way . . . we don't have a gun.'

Jones shook his head, grinned again, knowing the man. Knowing where those words came from. Frank needed to prove to himself he was brave, strong, all those words men wanted to be. Die an honourable death. Never be a coward.

'You hear me. You have to leave me.' A sharper tone because Jones still stood there smiling – far too blasé a reaction for the middle of a riot. A thump on his chest then as if Frank wanted to beat those words home.

'You're not a coward,' Jones said out of nowhere. 'You're a good man. A better one than I'll ever be.' Perhaps the giddiness of saving the man had made him say that. Another mistake, Frank heaved a breath, looking at him as if he'd slapped his face.

He wished then he could tell Frank Pak everything, every moment of his life, Share himself too, The Bliss, the creatures, all of it. Every little thing he could do. He ached for it. He could trust this man. He knew him through and through.

'The escape pods,' he said firmly, prising Frank's fingers from his collar. 'We'll be fine. I won't let you die, I promise.'

I can never meet this man again, he thought. Never. Just in case I've done a very stupid thing. Just in case the link I've made can never ever be severed. I have no idea what I've done, what I am, or what I'm turning into. And I just keep on making mistakes.

PART THREE
REBELLION

CHAPTER 9

Coldness on his forehead, coldness on his chest. Jones reached out, snatching at something, something that cursed and pulled away. 'Quit it,' snapped a voice he knew, one that didn't belong in his dreams or in Christian's apartment. A man he hoped he'd seen the last of. Frank stood over him with a dripping wet towel in his hands. 'Nash's orders: clean up the cargo. We don't want to disappoint the man, do we?'

'Nash?' The name refused to register, refused to generate a face. Jones pushed himself upright. He recognized the grey little cell and the feel of the mean little mattress underneath a body fast getting the shakes.

'Are you drunk, Jones? You bathing in booze these days?' Frank asked sharply, offering the towel.

Grit cracked between Jones' teeth, the white fluff of cobwebs on his arms, his shirt wet and sticky about the neck. 'Oh God.' A bolt of shock, and every hair on his body reacted. He remembered sounds, Christian's warning shouts, hands tightening around his wrists and ankles as his own yells drowned out everything else. 'Nash?'

'With Aubrey. They took my damned ship, as good as hijacked it. Greeley's taking some damned risks here.'

'Greeley? Greeley didn't do this.' Jones looked over to the door. They were locked up tight, judging by the lock indicator. 'Nash isn't with Greeley.'

'Aubrey is.'

'Aubrey? Who's Aubrey?'

Frank backed up a step, dipping to the floor to gather up a pile of clothes. 'Get cleaned up. Whatever lies you're making up right now, keep them to yourself.' He threw the clothes on the bed's end, added the towel, then turned and walked as far away as he could get.

'Frank?' Haine called – from the next cell, it sounded like.

'He's awake,' Frank called back. 'He looks like hell, but he's awake.'

Jones yanked at the neck of his dirty shirt, trapping his fingers and making a clumsy mess of trying to get it up over his head. He pulled the clean one on with the same jerky movements. Too many drugs in his system for certain. His blood felt too thick, his head throbbed, his heart labouring so hard he gripped at his chest and hung on. 'Who's Aubrey?'

'Delta CI,' Frank said. 'Greeley sent him to warn us off, to tell us to sit on the dock on a wait and see. Your chip cleared. Congratulations. Nice job. I ordered a timeslot off; when we got close to it Nash and Aubrey appeared.'

'What time was the slot?'

'*Is* the slot. Midnight-zero-three.'

'We're still on the station?'

'Yes.'

More memory wanted in, lost pieces of time that needed to make themselves heard. 'Nash couldn't get his ship bumped up the lists. He was waiting for a favour, it never showed, and he couldn't wait.'

Frank moved closer, listening now, showing interest. 'Why?'

'Because they broke into the Calder apartment through the walls, through the utility crawl-ways. That's why. They got me out the same way. They have to make a clean, fast exit. They have to let Christian go because they're not here to kill him. They wouldn't dare.'

'They? Who the hell are they?'

'The Charris Confederation.'

Frank frowned at him. 'The what?'

Jones dropped his feet onto the chill of the plating and stood up. He leaned into the bed, saving his wavering balance, realizing he'd have to explain it all for Frank's benefit and for the benefit of his crew next door. He had to make it clear just how far Alexander Calder's ambitions stretched. He almost told it all, only almost. Details always had a little extra value, he kept those to himself. Frank's expression shifted from amusement to bemusement and all the way back again.

'You hearing this?' Frank finally pitched at the walls.

'It's bullshit,' came back in Haine's dark rumble.

Frank moved three paces closer. 'What you're saying isn't possible.'

'Why? Why isn't it possible? Because it hasn't happened in a long long time? Nash is military. I think his help was the same. Masked, gloved help that had to have come from Delta's military attachment.'

Jones shivered. Input wanted in. Memories. Data. Any inconvenient moment would do. The room refused to hold steady, images bled, Frank just a flash of blue aura drawing closer. Jones held out one hand, not sure if he intended to stop, not sure if the man wasn't about to bounce him off a few walls. 'Don't.' He pushed his palm into the man's chest and held him away, other things tugging at him, stray senses that coalesced. More of those extra senses *The Bliss* liked to send in entire battalions. 'Somebody's coming.'

Frank's brows knitted, he stepped back, his attention settling onto the door. Seconds passed. Five, ten, fifteen long seconds, and footsteps sounded, Nash finally standing framed by the window. 'How are we?' His voice contained a harsh throaty rattle that Jones recognized far more clearly than his face: Nash yelling at him to shut up, Nash leaning close to say, 'Let's have a little talk, shall we? Let's discuss just how we're going to treat each other over the next few hours while we wait for this thing to pan out.'

'The kid just told me you're a revolutionary,' Frank said blithely.

Nash spluttered out a laugh. 'A what? Is that the lie he's come up with to explain this – a revolution? Well, I'm sorry to disappoint him. I'm not quite up to a revolution this trip.'

Frank moved over and stood right in front of the door as if he needed to see the man's every twitch. 'So Greeley sent you?'

'He did.'

'So why didn't he warn us you were coming?'

'Because to begin with you weren't part of the plan. Things went awry. I had time restraints, people let me down, your ship was the only option left. We'll be on route to Beta once we're up and out. Meantime your crew will stay under guard until I'm certain they're trustworthy. I'm in charge now, Greeley's order. I hope that isn't a problem?'

Frank made an open-handed gesture. 'No problem to me. Are my crew up at helm okay?'

He received another wide smile, one that still didn't touch Nash's eyes. 'Your timeslot's nearly up, I'll need your codes for undock. Why don't I prove to you that your crew are fine and take you up to helm?' He keyed the door open, sending his hollow smile Jones' way. 'I'm glad to see you're looking better. Sorry about the booze and the trank, but I didn't want you yelling all over the station. My people didn't hurt you, did they?' It sounded more like a declaration than a question.

'Who's Aubrey?' Jones sent back. 'Is he one of your infiltrators? Greeley will find out what's happening soon and he'll start asking questions. Greeley's Government all the way through. Do you have any idea what that really means, Nash?'

Nash's smile didn't waver. 'Very good, very dramatic – but we're busy right now. You'll have to save the rest of the show until later.'

'You think I won't tell them the rest?'

'I think if I were you I'd pick my lies very carefully.' Nash's voice dropped a notch. 'Misunderstandings might prove a little hazardous to you health. Now if you'll excuse us, we need to get off this station.'

You could see military in a man sometimes, the way he moved, the way his eyes never settled but just kept on moving. Inside the lift Frank stood furtively watching Nash. And Nash watched him. Military for certain, but that didn't mean anything. It didn't mean Jones had been telling the truth. Greeley headed up a Government institution; there was no reason to suppose he couldn't wield a little power, especially if circumstances merited it.

'Don't listen to Jones,' Nash said as the lift landed. 'It would be a mistake. He could make Fairyland sound like it's real, and you are, of course, looking for discrepancies right now.'

'All I want is a quiet way out of this for my crew.'

'Don't worry, they'll get it. And they'll be well paid for all these extra little inconveniences, too. Believe me, there's nothing to be concerned about.'

Frank forced a swallow down. Concerned wasn't quite the right word for it.

Up in the cramped space of helm he found one of Nash's young underlings covering Foley and Kady with a gun. Foley normally lounged bonelessly in his chair at the boards, now he sat ramrod straight.

'*Nova*, berth F two-two, please prepare for undock,' a Delta Station tech advised over the open com.

Foley began to hit keys, Frank moved closer to get a better look at Kady, who had the second chair. She sat white-faced, her hands crossed in her lap.

'Are we okay in here?' Frank asked, purposely getting in the way of the young crew-cut with the gun.

'Give the man some room, Durham,' Nash ordered. 'Sorry about the weaponry, Mr Pak. Precautions, I'd still rather take those. Durham, move I said.'

Durham shifted back, tight-lipped and grim-faced.

Kady's hand found Frank's and squeezed down hard. 'Did I miss anything,' Frank whispered.

Kady shook her head.

'Nothing to report,' Foley glanced back, straight down the barrel of the repositioned Durham's gun. 'We're just getting acquainted aren't we, son?'

Sour-faced Durham didn't even twitch.

'Request OO scan,' came over the com, the station's undocking protocols swinging into action.

Frank leaned in and pressed the scan button on the console. One piece of equipment he knew well; incorruptible tech, one Customs checked and checked again. Station owned security aboard every ship that had a licence to dock.

'Retinal confirm,' station ordered. Station always liked to double-check everything.

Frank hesitated.

'Is there a problem?' Nash asked.

A problem? No, there wasn't a problem; there were lots of problems. He didn't like Nash, he didn't trust Aubrey, he had a kid in holding who was legally Joseph Stokes. This was kidnapping and hijack. He didn't even want to think about a damned revolution. Yes, there were lots and lots of problems.

'Mr Pak?' Nash prompted.

Frank leaned forward between Foley's and Kady's chairs hit the Read key on the scanner's console and stared dead ahead while that same piece of Government kit scanned his retina then sent a scrambled and encrypted visual station's way.

'Scan confirmed,' the same bored tech over at Station Dock said. 'Thank you, Mr Pak. Please stand by.'

The Nova's owner/occupier details came up on the centre monitor in front of Frank, next to a display showing a sky-high pulse rate, one that station had measured through his eyeball. Frank's attention snapped to the message in red beneath it: *Buoy number 102 on amber.*

'Requesting a voice confirm,' the tech came back on. Station normally stopped at the retinal, that pulse rate must have hit Station Dock and caused some screen or other to flash a warning.

Frank forced himself to calm down. 'Frank Pak. Beta Station. Residential prefix: 80127387044556/BFC. West.' He cited his details without a hitch. They'd check his voice pattern, they had one, stations were manic when it came to ships like *The Nova*. A high-grade missile carrier; if she aimed those weapons at the station the death toll might easily hit the million mark.

One screen over stood blank; Frank could see Nash reflected in it, the man's hound-dog mouth couldn't turn any further south.

'Voice confirmed,' came over the com. 'You're free to depart *Nova* at midnight-ten. We're running a few adrift. We have a safety crew on your perimeter. Please look out for your assigned buoy. Thank you, *Nova*, have a safe flight.'

A countdown came up on the screen directly in front of Foley, Foley's hands flying over the controls. 'Going to warm us up,' he said.

For a split second Frank wanted to do something rash, hit the com and yell to that bored station tech that his ship had been taken.

'I'd best get you seated, Mr Pak,' Nash said as the plating began to dance beneath Frank's boot soles. 'Essential systems aren't live, I don't want you rattling around during undock. We'll sit it out in the galley with Mr Aubrey, if that's all right by you?'

Frank obediently went galley-ward. He sat down on the bench inside and strapped himself into his seat. All the while the ship's walls vibrated around him, *The Nova* moaning and groaning her way through undock. He prayed Nash had everything else locked down, including his crew; right then the ship was nothing but an aircraft exiting a tight, difficult space: prone to sudden moves, prone to throwing her occupants clean off their feet.

Frank glanced to Aubrey opposite him. The man was taking quick rapid-fire breaths, sweat beading on his pale brow, his fingers a tightly knitted bundle on the tabletop. Aubrey refused to look at him; he sat watching Nash's every move instead. Now there was something else it might not be best to think about.

The Nova pitched and settled, pitched and settled. Nash took no notice, the man chattered on in an eager fashion that collided jarringly with his stiff, inflexible mannerisms. He talked about the stricter ship licensing laws; the new medical legislations; the new dock feed collars brought in to prevent wastage due to leaks. He asked Frank about the upgrades he'd fitted and those he planned to. Nash constantly switched subjects in a fast round, as if he'd rehearsed it all in case he ever got lost for words at a party. He moved onto *The Nova*'s age, her plating and whether or not a bullet could hole it, taking calibre and range into account. One hell of a leap of subject matter, and one Frank didn't appreciate.

The wall com crackled finally, Nash caught mid-sentence. 'We've cleared the lock,' Foley said over the link. 'Safety systems will be online in six minutes. Do I get a jump-gate heading?'

Nash unbuckled himself, went over to the galley console and depressed the switch. 'I'm coming up.' He left, thumping his palm into the door panel's control to keep the doors locked open.

Frank counted down seconds. It ought to take no more than fifteen to reach helm. He counted to twenty, slipped out of his seat, hurried over and hit the panel. The door slid closed. He rounded on Aubrey. 'You came up my ramp-way with a jammer device, Aubrey. You want to reassure me, here? You're from Greeley. You both are. You want to tell me all this is exactly as stated.'

Aubrey's lips drew into a hard fast line. 'You'll let this play out, Pak.'

'Let what play out?'

Aubrey unbuckled his safety harness, got out of his seat and went over to the drinks machine. He pressed buttons, ordering one black coffee. No cream. No sugar. Instantly he added what he'd just cancelled, as if he'd suddenly struck a dietary what-the-hell.

'Aubrey.' Frank shifted over to his side. 'Who's on my ship? Who are the hell are you?'

'We're from Greeley,' Aubrey said impatiently.

'Do you have any proof of that?'

Aubrey watched the machine, drumming his finger into its side as if he could urge it to go faster.

'Is the Charris Confederation real?'

Aubrey gave the door a long, wary study before giving Frank the same. He leaned closer and said in a half voice 'You'll let this play out. I didn't get myself this far into this mess just to see you ruin it. I *am* from Greeley. Nash isn't.'

'Are you telling me he's a revolutionary? Do you know how absurd that sounds?'

'This revolution may well have links to the military, Pak. Do you understand the implications of that, how widespread that is, how dangerous? Nash believes I'm a legitimate sympathizer. He trusts me.'

'Does Greeley know what's happening here?'

Aubrey shifted closer still before he whispered, 'We're not sure who we can trust at this point; we have to be careful what information we share and with whom.'

'You don't *trust* Greeley?'

'I don't trust all of his associates. We have to be very careful. At some point I'll report to my superiors.'

Frank sucked a breath. 'At *some* point?' he snapped.

'Keep your voice down. Nash came to my apartment in the middle of the night, I didn't have time to call my office. He wanted help getting off the dock. I sidelined him here instead.'

'You brought him *here*?'

'I'm in control of this situation, Mr Pak.' Aubrey stood white-faced and sweating. He didn't look like he could control a sneeze. 'I will take action at the appropriate time, but for now you need to let me continue with my work. You're ex-military, I believe. You know how to follow orders.' Aubrey plucked his drink from the machine and took a slow sip, his dark eyes flickering back across the room. He visibly flinched as the door swished open.

'Is everything all right?' Nash asked from the doorway.

'Everything's fine,' Aubrey replied woodenly.

'You closed the door?'

'The lock glitches sometimes. It needs an upgrade.' Frank winced at his own feeble excuse. He sidestepped Aubrey to get to the drinks machine himself. He hit keys: coffee, black, no sugar. His mouth tasted like ash.

More talk around the table followed. Nash wanted to know about Artisell-One, about Frank's childhood out on the Reaches, the agriculture, the livestock. He added his knowledge of Frank's parents' messy divorce with a glint in his eye. No clue to where he'd got his info from, but he used it Jones fashion. Frank shifted uncomfortably in his seat and changed the subject. He asked about their heading.

'A small Inner Rim port,' Nash replied. 'Greeley intends to meet us there himself. He doesn't want any more surprises.' Nash looked like he was enjoying himself.

Frank tried not to twitch, tried not to look edgy or to frown at Aubrey, who seemed stuck fast in place. The man was a terrible actor; he wasn't behaving like somebody used to working covertly ought to act at all.

Frank needed another drink. He shifted back over to the machine and ordered another coffee, wishing the damned thing could add a shot of pure alcohol to the mix. He plucked the cup from the machine's innards just as a clap of sound cut through the muttered conversation behind him. Frank spilled his coffee, burned his hand. He spun about just in time to see Aubrey drop backwards from the bench to the plating. Blood stained his chest.

Is that why Nash wanted to talk about ship's plating and bullets?

Nash calmly leaned back in his seat; his gun lay cocked over sideways on the tabletop, its barrel aimed squarely at Frank's middle. He pulled a handkerchief from his pocket and loudly blew his nose. 'A chest shot is less risky than a headshot, don't you think? I hate headshots. Blood, skin, hair, brain matter, bone. If the skull shatters it goes everywhere. You aim for the chest, the bullet's likely to ricochet internally, that'll kill a man fast enough. Blood, yes, but less chance of a *real* mess in the end.' He chuckled and blew his nose again. 'It makes my nose run even when I do it with my bare hands. Some subconscious reaction, do you think?' Nash's brows rose as if he really did expect a nice conversation about murder and runny noses. 'You really ought to put that coffee down now, Pak. Put it down.'

Frank didn't turn his back. He edged himself over to the countertop, bruising his spine into the metal as he put his coffee cup down. He wiped his stinging hand down the front of his shirt as Nash strangled his handkerchief getting it back into his pocket. 'How much did he tell you?'

'Nothing. He didn't tell me anything.'

'You asked, he told you. The Charris Confederation. Revolution.' Nash stroked a finger delicately down one side of the scar that circled his throat. 'He proved a very amusing diversion for a while. No experience – I'm sure you noticed.'

On the deck, inexperienced Aubrey groaned, his wide terrified eyes staring right into Frank's. His fingers splayed across the deck, reaching out to him.

'He said his office knows all about you. Who you are, exactly what you're doing,' Frank said.

Nash laughed. 'It's too late. They're lagging so, so far behind it all.'

'Then why shoot him?'

Nash stepped around the table, his foot nudging at that reaching hand of Aubrey's. 'I have plans, Pak. Plans regarding him, plans regarding you.' He kicked Aubrey's hand aside and kept on moving.

Frank shrank back on reflex. He raised his hands. 'All I want is a quiet way out of this for my crew. Take the ship; take the kid. Go where you need to be, just leave my crew out of this.'

'You make it sound like you don't care if you live or die, Pak. Just so long as your crew are fine.' Nash used his gun like a club, slamming it inwards to catch Frank under the ribs. Frank bent double, cringed away, hit the room's corner and lifted his hands up further still, refusing to defend himself against anything else incoming. Nash's gun levelled off at his temple. Nash didn't like headshots, Frank stayed motionless, praying that was the truth.

By the table's side Aubrey gurgled out a protest. He began to shift, his fingers flat on the plating now as he tried to haul his body towards them. Aubrey might be green but he was damned brave with it.

Nash turned half about and raised his gun.

'No,' Frank yelled.

Another silenced gunshot clapped across the galley. Before the shot's echo died Nash turned the gun back round, settling it chest-high in front of Frank. 'Seems I've made something of a mess after all.' He grabbed up the front of Frank's shirt and shoved him towards the doorway. 'Get down to the lift before I decide to make another one.'

From inside the lift car Frank could see right through the ship, all the way down the corridor into helm. Even with the gun's silencer engaged Foley and Kady must have heard those shots.

The lift doors closed.

Frank shifted his gaze to the lift's panel's display, telling himself to take deeper breaths. 'Are you military?'

Nash's reflection in the metalwork gave a twisted smirk. 'I've been in the service since I was eighteen. Calram company, off *The Salvatore*. On compassionate leave – my mother died, poor soul. I was on Delta on something of a recruitment drive.'

'Are you following orders here, Nash? Or are you trying to get noticed?'

Nash's expression hardened. 'Alexander Calder has a family. A huge extended enclave. Those ties are slowing us down. He protected Jones for his son's sake. Cosseted him. Damned embarrassing. That's why I decided to take him.'

'Take him where?'

'To where they're reconstructing *The Bliss* tech. Once Jones is on board that ship, Alexander will see reason. Jones isn't anything special, he's just another piece of the puzzle.'

'*The Bliss* tech?'

Nash cold grey eyes filled with amusement. 'Play a game with Jones some time, start a list, say planets, and see what happens.' He snorted at Frank's confused frown. 'They put things in his head on a ship called *The Bliss* over sixteen years ago: diagrams, lists, endless reams of useless data. Drugs created from alien life formed chemical changes in the brain that laid down perfect memory, the non-fade, non-degradable variety. You say the right word and all that crap spills back into Jones' head, and if it spills too fast, from what I've heard, he goes over like a tree in a windstorm.'

Frank swallowed, cold to his middle. 'Sixteen years ago?'

'That's right. That's where the scientists decided to start their experiments. On little kids, that's where teaching starts after all. If we can perfect that tech, the applications are endless.'

'God almighty,' Frank said as another thought struck. 'The scientists, the doctors Jones murdered – they all came from that ship.'

'Things got a little violent the day the Government sent in Special Ops to down that boat,' Nash said. 'Those scientists had secrets to guard and financiers to protect. They tried to kill everything on board.'

The images came back, Frank shuddering where he stood. Vented dark bodies in the hold, Jones staring at them with no feeling in his legs.

'We'll be rendezvousing with a carrier: *The Mistral*,' Nash added, before he let out a smug little laugh. 'You've just had a day full of shocks, haven't you, Pak? That carrier's ours. Grunts follow orders; they go anywhere you point them so long as the man in charge has the right stripe on his uniform.'

The lift landed. Nash hit the panel, the lift doors opening to reveal holding and one of his young subordinates, a red-haired youth whose wide eyes brimmed with naked unease. 'Is everything quiet, Hodge?' The youth nodded. 'Good. Get Pak settled. When you're done I need you in the galley. You have a mess to clean up.'

In holding Frank got Max and Haine for company this time and thanked God for it. He sank down by the foot of the door as soon as Nash locked it, a quiver in his bones, both body and mind playing catch-up. He deep-breathed, lifting a hand to ward Max off. 'I'm okay,' he said, sounding just the opposite. He explained then everything they hadn't heard, confirmation of everything no one in their right mind would want to hear. Both Max and Haine ended up sitting close, faces stark and stilled.

Frank ran a hand through sweaty hair, feeling his skull under it, wondering what else Jones might be able to force through skin and bone. Frank hadn't confessed that part of it; he doubted he'd ever dare.

Haine's dark eyes flashed; a grumbling tirade following about the revolution and the Government and where he'd like to stick them both. Meanwhile Max sat tight-faced, his thoughts turning in another direction. 'How come Nash only has a couple of kids with him?' he asked. 'It doesn't make sense.'

Frank shook his head. It didn't. Nash's people had gone through Delta's walls to get Jones out. They had enough manpower to do that, and they'd need access codes to those rat runs to do it too. 'They must still want to keep things quiet. That has to be where the manpower issues come from. They're not ready.'

'A couple of green kids won't be hard to fool,' Haine said in a dark undertone.

'Foley and Kady are still up in helm,' Frank reminded him. 'Nash split us up for a reason.' He stalled Haine's reply with a wave of his hand as the com in the corridor outside came alive.

'This is helm,' Foley said, his every syllable clipped. 'We're going to jump in ten. Be warned we're going in from a nasty little gate that isn't Government-sanctioned. I'll sound another warning ten seconds out. Hold tight.'

And now they were using illegal jump-gates. Those cheap setups the smugglers and the illegal tech ships scattered about like bull's-eyes for the miltary to fire at.

'Man sounds rattled,' Haine murmured.

They all sounded rattled. Frank went to the window and peered both ways down the corridor. Hodge would still be occupied helping Nash move Aubrey, and Durham had to be watching helm. 'Jones,' he yelled. 'Can you hear me?' He waited, counting down ten seconds. 'Are you listening to us? Do you know about Aubrey?

Aubrey's dead, Jones. Nash shot him. I believe you, all right. There is a Charris Confederation. I know who you are. I know everything.'

Silence.

'I tried calling earlier. He didn't answer,' Max said. 'Maybe he's out of it, better for him if he is if we're heading for jump. 'So what do we do now?' he asked, knuckling his hands together.

'We wait,' Frank replied with a grimace. 'We wait for a chance.'

CHAPTER 10

The Nova jumped without any sign of Nash, Hodge, or Durham, without a sound out of Jones next door. She jumped from a chancy out-point, her computer plying out automated warnings over the com in the corridor, Foley telling them to ignore the shakes, the jars and the rattles and worry about anything going pop or bang instead. A ship in the middle of the vortex might lose her grav plating, or her shields, she might rip her skin and send you hurtling towards the gap – that was if your own body didn't decide to fail you first. The bed was the only solid thing in holding, Frank, Haine and Max used it to anchor themselves while the metal around them screamed.

Thirty minutes in and the final all-clear sounded.

Foley reported they were safe: no intercepts on their in-point, no ships or rocks heading their way. No report followed on where they were, just a final 'we're fine up here', and the com went dead.

'So that's that,' Haine said, letting go of the bed's metal side.

Max pushed himself over to the wall and leaned against it. 'More waiting?'

'More waiting,' Frank echoed.

The waiting was punctuated by a supply of food and cold drinks, and more importantly by Kady's reappearance. Frank shouted questions to her, but she had no information to offer, Frank sending far more back than he received. But she was whole, untouched, just far too far away for Frank's liking.

He tried Jones again and got nothing.

Hours passed, the clock in the corridor outside visible through the composite. They'd left the station at midnight-ten Delta time, but the ship's clock had never been set to receive station time on her lower decks. *The Nova* still marked her own slightly adrift version, insisting it was zero-three-twenty-five. Frank stood a while watching the numbers tick over, shot nerves and hours of boredom leaving him weary and dull-witted. He gave up finally, sank down, leaned his head back against the door and allowed himself to drift. He lost another hour that way, coming awake to a solid vibration and a booming sound that set his teeth on edge. 'What the hell?' He blinked, his chest tightening, his breathing growing short and fast.

When the boom's echo died he heard a familiar voice. 'You can't play games with my stuff. I need my stuff. You stupid, stupid—'

Boom.

Frank scrambled up to the window. 'Jones?'

'Stupid . . . Stupid,' Jones yelled in a voice that rose then cracked apart. Something hit the metal again with another explosive crash.

'Stop it!' Frank strained to see through the composite, moving from one side of it to the other to try to see into the corridor outside. 'Jones, there's no one down here. They're all up top. They can't hear you.'

Boom: a sickening collision as if a body had fallen from the wall to the floor with a bone-shattering smack. Then quiet; utter unbroken silence.

Frank watched his own breath steam up the window.

'Damn lab rat's losing what's left of his mind,' Haine said acidly from his seat on the plating.

Boom.

Frank slammed his fist into the door. 'Jones, listen to me.'

Boom.

'Jones, for God's sake, there's nobody down here.'

Boom. And silence.

'Jones?'

'Somebody's coming.' Jones' words were a fierce, impatient hiss. 'Somebody's coming. Always mix the pink pill, with the blue pill, with the red pill, with the yellow pill, with the—'

Boom.

'Stop that.' A new voice, one Frank thought he recognized: the red-haired kid, the worrier. He positioned himself at the window's furthest edge, from there able to see the youth's outline outside holding one.

'Give me my damned pills.' Jones' holler ended in sucked breaths. 'I swear I'll break bones in here until I get my stuff. You tell Nash I'm doing damage. You tell him the cargo knows what he's worth.' The bang, bang, bang of a fist against metal followed, then a halt and then more and worse, as if Jones had decided to sit down and use his feet.

Nash's kid disappeared from Frank's view. He glanced about to Haine and Max. 'I think he's planning something.'

'*I* think he's insane,' Haine raised his voice over the din of Jones' pounding.

'Jones,' Frank called. 'Shut it down and listen to me.' And Jones did just that, leaving Frank nothing but that eerie hollowed-out silence again. 'Are you tracking? Do you know what you're doing?'

'Get off my floor, you dirty birds,' Jones cried out, using Haine's wife's death to maximum effect. 'Get off my damned floor. Going to shoot Daddy when Daddy gets home.'

'Son of a bitch thinks that's funny.' It was Haine's turn to bang on the metal. 'Shut it down, you crazy son of a bitch.' He thumped, and Jones whacked a reply. The red-haired kid, Hodge, barrelling back into twice the noise he'd left behind.

'Quiet,' he ordered, in a voice hardly loud enough to carry over the clamour. 'Nash says you can have your stuff. I've got your pills. Look. Look, they're right here. Jones, do you see? They're coming.'

Frank watched the half of Hodge he could see hunker down to the service hatch at the bottom of Jones' door. He heard metal slide and guessed the pill cup was being slipped through.

'No . . . get it off . . . Get it off the damned floor.'

Frank heard the plastic cup ricochet; saw pills spinning past his doorway and across the corridor outside. 'Good,' he whispered, sure all the noise and Haine-baiting had to be a ploy. 'Good kid.'

'If he gets past Hodge,' Max hissed lowly, 'do you seriously think he's going to let us out?'

In the corridor Hodge chased down pills; cherry-cheeked and hard-jawed. 'Need some help?' Frank asked him. Hodge held up his hand, a small device lay in it, a panic button or the like, something that could call help with one swift depression.

'I've called the Captain down,' Hodge's voice had an audible tremor. He spilled pills back into their plastic cup.

'The Captain?' Haine echoed. 'Where you come from, Hodge? You from a carrier? You military?' He didn't get a reply, Hodge just battened his mouth closed, his blush reaching his hairline.

'Pink pill, blue pill, take two, you don't get ill,' Jones rambled from next door. 'Pitter-patter, pitter-patter, don't take your pills, your mind will shatter. Somebody's coming . . . Somebody's coming.'

Hodge stood up, good and straight too. He faced left – lift-ward.

Somebody was coming all right. 'Jones threw his meds out, sir.' Hodge held out the offending cup. 'I don't think he'll take them. I think he's crazy, sir.'

Haine nudged Frank's arm and leaned close. 'You think Jones' plan includes Nash?'

Frank didn't answer; Nash stood staring hard at him. 'Hodge, put Pak inside with Jones. *He* can persuade him to take his meds. If Jones isn't dosed up in twenty minutes I'll shoot Pak and leave his body behind for the kid to mull over for a while. How's that suit you, Pak?'

Haine put a clenched fist right on the lip of the window, hanging it there to signal his own thoughts on the matter. Behind him Frank could see Max moving closer to the door.

'He'll take his pills,' Frank said levelly. He glanced behind him; caught Max's tight expression, the expectation within Haine's dark-cyed glower. 'And you two will behave,' he added under his breath. 'You won't do anything stupid.'

Max didn't step back, Haine didn't move.

In the corridor, Nash's eyes drew into slits.

Frank gave Max a shove to get him moving then did the same to Haine, making sure both stood well clear before he dared turn back to the door.

Hodge stood sweating, the pill cup rattling its contents, his other hand constantly readjusting itself on the butt of his gun.

'Everything's fine, Hodge,' Frank soothed. 'There's nothing to worry about.' Hodge barely blinked as Frank eased his way out into the corridor. He handed over the pill cup while Nash offered a water bottle. The man was smiling again. 'Don't damage my cargo, Pak. You do, you're dead anyway.'

*

'Looking good, Jones,' Frank said as he got his first look inside holding one. Soup cartons, drinks packets; it looked like everything that Jones had been brought to eat or drink had ended up being thrown at the walls. And some of those cartons had broken apart, leaving wide ribbons of greasy stains behind them.

Jones himself sat in the narrow gap between the bed and the wall, his knees tucked up, his head resting on the bedside.

Frank heard the door close, he turned to see Nash peering in. 'I'm not going to leave any marks on him, Nash. But I will get him to take his stuff.' Frank took another look at the smeared grease on the walls 'Maybe you ought to send some more food down. I might be able to persuade him not to redecorate with it this time.'

Nash gave another of his twisted little smiles. 'Hodge, see to it. Call me down if you need me. I'll be in helm.'

Frank waited for the man to leave then nudged a drink pack sideways with his toe, clearing his way to the bed. 'You feeling okay, Jones? You been having a little fit in here?' Frank perched on the bed's far side, offering the pills and the water bottle over the rucked-up blanket on its top. 'Or were you thinking more about getting out?' he added quietly. 'You want to stop playing now and get your head wired up straight again. Hodge has a panic button: he presses it, and Nash comes running. And Hodge is too much of a baby to do anything without Nash hanging over his shoulder.' He added the rest then, everything he'd found out, everything he'd told his crew next door that Jones might or might not have already heard through the walls.

As he finished Jones' head came up. 'You're light blue,' he said around a cough. 'The colour of the sky,' he tacked on as if that should explain that strange assessment perfectly.

'Okay—'

'Nash is like . . . a bruise. Bruised colour. Bad colour.' If he hadn't been drunk when he been dragged on board Jones sounded it now; his words wouldn't hold steady, some were slurred, some got half lost.

'Did you understand anything I just told you?' Frank asked softly. 'Do you understand what's happening here? Why don't you take your pills then eat something? Then we'll talk about anything, any colours you like, all right? Take your pills.'

'Why?' A little head tilt came with that, the flesh on Frank's arms tingling: too sharp an examination, too much cunning suddenly in Jones' gaze.

'You'll get sick – sicker,' Frank corrected.

'I shoot people in the head. How much sicker can I get?'

Frank pushed himself over the bed; dropping off its far side into a crouch. He leaned close to Jones ear and whispered. 'If it comes down to me ramming your pills down your throat I'll do it. I will hurt you; and I can do it without leaving a single mark. If you don't behave Nash is going to kill me, and that's not going to happen.'

Jones leaned away, pressing his back against the wall. He held out his hand and flattened his palm. An immediate surrender.

Frank started to hand out pills in groups of three, giving up the water bottle just as something came through the hatch at the door's bottom. 'Food,' Hodge yelled.

'Hodge is yellow,' Jones murmured.

'I never doubted it.' Frank handed over three more pills.

'Durham is red, so's Kady. Not the same shade, darker. It doesn't mean the same.'

'I'm sure it doesn't.'

Jones swallowed pills, adding nothing to explain his little colour wheel. Finished, he leaned into the side of the bed again.

'You're not done,' Frank said. 'Food next. You behave, you do whatever I tell you to.'

'You have a purple edge now,' Jones said on an expelled breath. 'Purple, with a hint of red.' After he'd drunk down half a carton of soup from the heat pack, Jones leaned over into the bed's side, beached there unmoving. Frank let him be; he went over and tidied what he could in the room, piling drink and food cartons into one corner and making a fast pass over the stains with the wipes he requested from the watching Hodge.

Done with all that, he went back to Jones. With thoughts of floating debris churning in his head, he picked up one wrist and checked Jones' pulse. Rapid, but maybe rapid was normal after downing fifteen multi-coloured pills. There was no fever, not much warmth to feel in Jones' flesh at all. He snagged the blanket from the bed, wrapped it up over Jones' knees and chest then sat back down himself.

He'd met his deadline easily enough. He wasn't going to die just yet.

Maybe three hours went by before Jones stirred, and then it was with a ragged, fast breath and a sudden jerk of his body. He straightened up; face stark and still as if a bomb had gone off in his head.

'Morning,' Frank said, stretching the shoulder he had propped up against the chill of wall behind him. 'I'm blue. What colour are you?'

Jones screwed up his face, hugging his fist to his chest. 'I didn't say that. You're lying. I wouldn't say that.'

'Okay – somebody said it, and it wasn't you.' He got a very worried look for that; one of the most troubled he'd ever seen out of Jones. 'We've got to get out of here, Jones. We have to get this ship back.'

'We?'

'You weren't planning to escape? I'd make a plan if I were you. Last I heard this revolution was planning to stick you on a ship and dissect you.'

'A ship?'

'*The Bliss*, or the resurrected version.'

Jones went a few shades paler. He blinked hard, saying nothing, as if he'd needed a moment to clear the dust out of his head. 'Fine. I'll help you. I'll even promise to do it, but on the other side of this you have to let me go.'

'You're going to promise to help me, that's nice.'

'I don't lie about those.'

'Well, I'm not in a very trusting mood right now. Greeley lied to me. So did Nash. So did Aubrey.'

'I won't.' Jones swiped dirty fingers over eyes that looked heavy-lidded and shrunken.

'Because?'

'Because . . .' Jones repeated, a pained look on his face. 'Because—'

'Because I'm a *good* man?' Frank suggested, lowering his voice to the barest whisper. 'Like on *The Marabell*?' Another agonized look. '*This Bliss*. This ship full of kids, what was she precisely? What build?'

Jones sat in his little gap between bed and wall, frowning at him. 'I don't know. She was old, that's all I know.'

A beat-up old cargo vessel, Frank supposed, like one of the illegal gene ships. Stripped out, full of supplies and med-tech, flitting from jump to jump for evermore. Order your baby at one end maybe ten jumps later and a few close calls with the military, trying to fry your baby, your baby would be ready to be implanted – if you could find your gene ship again. 'So where did the money come from? They weren't selling anything, were they? No goods in, no goods out?'

Jones sagged. Jones looked like he wished Frank were stone-cold dead right about then. 'I don't know that either. You ever find out, let me know.'

'So how many of you left this little experiment of theirs?'

Another white-hot look: maybe Jones would rather weld him to the plating. 'Thirteen. None from my section. Are you done?'

'You don't want me asking you questions.'

'No.'

'Why not?'

'Because . . .' another stall, another angry look. Jones dropped his voice to a whisper again so no one next door would catch a word. 'Because I don't know everything. And because what I do know wouldn't make any sense to you. It doesn't always make much sense to me.'

Frank snorted. 'Well that's damned illuminating.'

'I don't think the way you do.' Another drop in volume, and Frank had to strain to catch every word. 'I don't think the way any-body does any more . . . and you're blue, Frank. And you *are* a good man . . . but I can't help you this time unless you make a deal. I have other things I need to do.'

'Other things like murder?' Frank suggested.

'It'd be better if you don't ask me questions. You know all you need to. I told it to you, and believe me, it's the truth. If you don't want to make a deal then we're done with each other. We're done.'

It had to rate as one the oddest conversations Frank had ever had sober. But if Jones really had come from a ship that flitted from jump to jump while they stuffed his head full of junk, maybe he'd be optimistic to expect much else. 'Do you know where you come from?' He chanced. 'I mean originally. You had to have had a family somewhere, a mother at least – a womb. Did you come from a gene-ship yourself? Did they just implant you . . . somewhere?'

Jones could move pretty fast considering the state he was in. He could get a solid grip too. He hauled Frank up, hands white-knuckled around his jacket, glaring right at him with dilated pupils. Blisteringly angry for no reason Frank could fathom.

'Shut the hell up and stay away from me. Get away from me as fast as you can.' Jones shifted one shaking hand to his head; with such an agonized look Frank half expected his forehead to explode. 'You have to stop asking me questions.' His knees went out from under him. Frank was forced to grab for him, grab and wince as something flashed into his head. Data, damned data. He let go and let Jones drop, backing a giant step to get clear. He retreated to the room's far side, far, far happier when he stood that far away.

'Frank?' came from next door. Haine's voice. 'You all right? He gets antsy, hit him. Hit him a lot.'

'I'll do that, Haine,' he sent back. Antsy, he'd have preferred that. There really, really was an awful lot of mess in Jones' head, and he wished like hell Jones would be considerate enough to keep it there.

The door flap opened, a tray slid halfway across the floor. The water bottle on its top wobbled; a pill cup spilled its contents. Pills rolled away. 'Meds,' Hodge yelled. And Lord you could measure time with that: a whole twenty-four hours gone by.

Frank looked over to Jones on the bed. He'd woken up finally He'd eaten, used the head. He'd ignored Frank, and Frank had ignored him. He slept deeply now, there'd hardly been a move out of him for hours.

'Jones,' Frank bellowed. 'Your stuff.'

Jones didn't move.

Frank shifted over to the bedside, leaning down to peer into a face gone slack. 'Hey.' He nudged warily at Jones' shoulder, a shoulder that yielded and rocked back. 'Your stuff's here. Take your stuff.'

Frank pressed two fingers onto Jones' forehead just as cautiously: a clammy, sticky forehead. He shifted his hand down to Jones' chest, settled it and knuckled his fist hard into bone – *and saw blackness, solid and immovable, as if blackness had become a physical thing. Not a darkness he shifted through, a darkness he could place his hands against, his fingertips tickling over its smooth, rigid surface.*

Frank heard himself cry out, heard his own boot soles beat a retreat. A thud at his back, and air whooshed out of his lungs, his hands finding first the scratch of the stubble on his own cheek then the wall he'd just cannoned into.

The room around him was holding, grey not black.

He became aware of his every breath, the air rushing down, then out; his every blink, the brush of his lashes against each other. 'God almighty.' Did Jones have an off switch?

Frank shoved himself off the wall. He went to the door and banged his fist against it. 'Hodge. Get Nash down here. Tell him there's something wrong with Jones.'

Hodge appeared at the window. He peered at Jones then at Frank, suspiciously.

'Call Nash down here,' Frank said more slowly, more firmly. 'Don't make a decision for him, Hodge. He's not to the type to forgive a mistake.'

Hodge shot him another distrustful look then went over to the wall com and made the call up top.

'Yes, sir,' Hodge said at the end of his call. He cut the com and moved back to the window. 'You're to kneel in the far corner with your hands on the wall. Any trouble and . . .' he tailed off. Whatever instructions Nash had given him they hadn't settled well, they'd left Hodge with all manner of facial tics.

Frank did as he'd been ordered. He sat on his knees, his back to the bed, his palms flat to the cold metal as Nash came in. His entrance covered by the armed and sweating Hodge.

'I can't wake him up,' Frank said, the blackness haunting him, the huge solid mass of it that owned Jones. He held his breath, forcing the memory back as he twisted half about to watch Nash lean over the bed.

'Damned sickly milksop brat,' Nash stood canted over, trying the same knuckle-to-the-chest manoeuvre Frank had tried. 'Jones?' He called without a trace of urgency. He started doing other checks. 'No fever. Breathing rate is steady. Pulse is within limits. A little fast.' He backed up two steps, paused. 'He's playing us, Pak.'

'No, no he isn't. This isn't a trick. There's something really wrong with him. He's . . .' Frank very nearly said 'off'.

Nash glared at him. 'He wants up to the med bay. He wants to get closer to helm.' Nash headed for the door.

'No, he needs help. Look at him. He couldn't fake that.'

The door closed on Frank's protests. He turned about on his knees and set his back to the wall. The blackness was still a part of him; he didn't have to shut his eyes to see it. 'Jones,' Frank shouted as if Jones could rescue him.

He heaved in air, held it, letting it loose with a flurry of words. 'No personnel shall leave any item unsecured. No unauthorized personnel shall enter a designated amber area during an alert. No personnel shall leave their quarters after jump until the safety klaxon sounds. No personnel shall bring unauthorized goods or persons on board during dock.' Frank resorted to the familiar regulations from *The Monterey* to keep the blackness at bay. The regs every grunt had to know by heart.

He repeated regs on and on, his voice growing worn and tattered until finally the solid blackness lost its solidity and drifted away like smoke. Frank rested his head against the wall then, shaking, swearing to everything holy, whether he believed in it or not, that he'd never ever touch Jones again.

A little mental push, that's all it took. Door locks were code-based; most things comp-reliant depended on codes. All you needed were the right ones and you could fool a door into thinking the unlock panel had been depressed. Key codes, number codes, bank codes. Codes let you into all kinds of things – and out of them.

Jones leaned into the door – cold, cold door – setting his hand onto the gap between it and the wall. Codes were simple, uncomplicated, and locks were willing, always willing if luck was on your side. Just a little shove into their circuits and they gave up everything.

'Jones?' Air came with the word, as if someone stood blowing them right into his lungs. 'Jones, can you hear me? Wake up.'

Jones batted his lids, focused. No door, no metal, an expanse of grey ceiling and overheads instead, the flicker of a shape obscuring one light and then the next. A long, long backlog of thoughts followed, an internal shuffling of memories, past, present, today? Not today. Another lock, some willing lock from long ago allowing him access to the dark hold of a ship.

Jones opened his eyes and raised his head.

'God almighty.' Frank looked scared, a sunken-cheeked, wide-eyed scared. 'You were out, just gone.'

'Out?'

'Off,' Frank corrected, sounding frustrated by the word.

'Off?' Jones echoed. Not asleep, no, something else, something deeper. Some new alignment in his head, or something breaking free, something that shut him down completely as it tried to surface. 'It's all right. That happens.'

'It happens?' Frank echoed, sounding even more frustrated.

'The lock.' Jones pushed himself off the bed, setting himself against gravity when his bones seemed barely able to feel the tug of it. He pitched forward. He would have fallen, but Frank grabbed him and held him up.

'Dammit,' the man snarled.

Jones slid one foot forward, slowly this time.

'No. Lie down. Lie down.'

Jones ignored the man; he let his other foot shift. He moved; he walked, heading for the lock, everything else swirling. The walls wouldn't hold still, the floor buckled and twisted, but his thoughts stayed solid. The lock. The lock. The lock. With each advancing step, the thought gained weight until he pressed his fingers against the metal door. A push of his thoughts, his imagination, and it would work. This time it would work. It wouldn't all jink sideways and disappear.

They'd get out. He'd get away. He'd find *The Bliss*.

He jolted back, blinked hard, tried to focus and couldn't. He hadn't fooled the lock, but the door was opening. It pulled wide, a body coming inward.

'When did he wake up?'

'Just now. He's out of it. I don't think he knows where he is.'

A grunt of breath. 'Jones, can you see me?'

Jones shied back again, something pushing against his shoulder, pressure on his arm.

'He needs his meds,' Frank said.

'Do you expect me to pick them up off the floor, Pak? I've got resupply incoming. Take him back to the bed.'

Jones fought the move, finally feeling gravity's pull beneath his boot soles he let his bones cleave to it. Not moving this time, staying close to the lock, close to the door.

'Jones,' Frank said, 'Turn around. You need to sit down. Your meds are late. You need your stuff now.'

Jones didn't move. Two rough palms grabbed around his chin, a face shifted into view, lips snaking around teeth. 'It's me. It's Nash.' Nash showed him the gun he was holding. 'Do as you're told before I decide to put a few holes in Pak. Move.'

Jones moved as quickly as his ailing body would allow and he didn't stop.

Frank flinched. He'd cornered Jones enough times to know if you got within striking distance you were in trouble. Nash's head jerked back violently, thumping into the wall, his body contorting as he wheezed and gagged for air. His fingers clawed at his throat where Jones' jabbed fist had landed. The gun Nash held rose shakily.

Jones flashed forwards to knock it off target, his free hand aiming a strike towards Nash's eyes. He dug into the soft flesh under Nash's eye sockets. The man roared in pain, blood welling on both cheeks as Jones yanked at the gun in his hand. Nash swung it upwards hard and fast, catching Jones under the chin with an audible crack. He pitched back, hit the wall and slid down it.

'Stay there,' Nash bellowed, pulling the other gun he carried – the dart gun, tracking him with it as Jones hauled his way upright. He edged himself over, trying to shield Frank from the live round in Nash's other fist.

'You stupid son of a bitch. You think this is a game? You want a lesson in how to behave.' The gun aimed at Frank rose a notch.

Nash squeezed the trigger, Jones yelled. Frank ducked; but the shot went high, holing one of the overheads with a pop and a shower of glass. 'The next time's not for show,' Nash snarled out. 'Hodge,' he yelled. 'Get in here.'

Frank licked dry lips, wondering if he ought to get a grip on Jones before Nash lost his patience. Jones would play ridiculous odds and he wasn't the one about to get shot. He took a step forward. 'Jones, back off. Back off now.'

Too damned late. Jones threw himself forwards, twisting aside as Nash's dart gun discharged with a hiss and a whine. The missile hissed passed his arm, hissed passed Frank too, its delicate prongs and electronics flattening into the opposite wall. Jones barrelled into Nash's chest, both of them falling in a tangle of arms and legs into the gap between the bed and the wall. Jones fought to pin both guns down, his efforts discouraged by a barrage of vicious kicks from Nash.

Hodge ran in, looking shocked, clearly having no idea who he should aim his gun at first.

'Shoot Pak,' Nash yelled.

Hodge aimed a live round at Frank, his eyes blinking furiously.

'Hodge is yellow. Hodge won't fire.' Jones' yell was harsh and airless. Nash straddled his middle, Jones trying to hold off both of the man's captured wrists. Nash swore at him, leaning his weight down as Jones' strength started to fade. Too close: Jones freed one hand and aimed another upward strike towards the damaged flesh under Nash's eyes. He dug in and clawed downwards. Nash bawled out in pain, the guns dropped. Jones fumbled the live round clear. It skittered across the floor and came to a halt in the bed's shadow. 'Hodge won't fire,' Jones shouted again.

Frank stood eye to eye with the kid, watching a string of nervous tics and twitches cross his ashen face.

Play the damned odds, Frank told himself. He twisted to his

right and went down, stretching underneath the bed for the gun. He snatched it up just as Nash powered in a fast jab. Jones' head snapped back, his every limb shuddering then going slack.

'Get off him.' Frank lurched forward, aiming the live round at Nash's head. 'Get off him. Now. Give me your gun.'

Nash ground his teeth in disgust and threw the thing aside. Blood seeped down his cheeks, the flesh torn and already dark with bruising. Chest heaving, he calmly stood up, pulled the familiar handkerchief from his pocket and wiped at the worst of his wounds. Then he waved the bloodied cloth at Hodge. 'Kill him.'

Hodge's mouth unhinged

'You tell him that again, I'll shoot him,' Frank snapped.

Nash laughed. He turned his back on Frank, gathered up Jones by the ankles and slid him clear of the gap. 'So was this the plan all along, this tired little charade? Jones is sick?' Nash laughed again. 'Damn fool me for being careful with him, Pak. Damn fool me for not shooting him when he started this. You know I can't kill him, but after this little performance I will do him some damage. You want me to start breaking bones? An ex-military grunt, aren't you? Let's see just how tough you are.'

'I'll shoot you.'

'I think doing that might galvanize even the reluctant Mr Hodge into putting a hole in you somewhere.'

At Nash's feet Jones shifted, shuddering back to life with a fit of choking. 'Hodge won't fire,' he gasped out, slithering sideways down the wall.

'Aren't you done yet?' Nash grabbed for his wrist. 'You right- or left-handed?' Jones aimed his free fist at the man. A weak strike Nash caught and held. 'No fight left in you now, is there?' Nash dropped Jones' hand, flashing a backhanded fist around towards Jones' jaw.

Frank turned and aimed his gun squarely at Hodge as Hodge tried to step closer to Nash. 'Put your gun down. Do it, or I'm going to fire.'

Hodge's eyes snaked to Nash.

'Hodge,' Nash said calmly. 'Aim your gun at Pak and keep it there. This is why you're here, to fight, to stand by me. You let me down with Aubrey, you won't do that twice. You've got to do better. A lot better. The revolution doesn't tolerate cowards. Squeeze off a round into Pak.'

Hodge baulked. He shook his head, his jaw starting to tremble. 'I can't do that, sir. I can't.'

Frank took a step closer to Hodge; gun to gun he forced eye contact. Held it as he watched sweat drip down Hodge's forehead. 'Ten seconds from now I'm going to shoot you, Hodge. Stand and wait, or put your gun down.'

'Shoot Pak,' Nash yelled. 'Do it, Hodge. You hear me. Do it.'

Hodge wailed, spun in a rush, clearly deciding on a third option. He fled, charging through the doorway, his footfalls as he ran down the corridor outside accompanied by hoarse broken sobs.

CHAPTER 11

'Steady, Pak. Take a second to think about this.' Nash lifted up his open palms as Frank swung his gun back to him. 'We can still make a deal here. I can get you and your crew out of this whole mess free and clear.' He took three unsteady paces towards Frank and kept on coming.

Frank loosened his grip, relaxing to take the gun's kick. 'I've no reasons left not to shoot you, Nash.'

Nash stopped moving.

Frank swallowed, took a solid breath and waited it out, just to make certain Nash wasn't going to push the issue. Then he edged right to get a clear look at Jones. 'Jones, get up. Get out of here. Haine, Max, Kady,' he yelled. 'Jones is coming to let you out.'

Jones clawed his way to his feet, moving in fits and starts, his balance so far gone he needed the wall's support. He stood canted against it, white to his lips.

Nash turned his way, inclining his head as if he were talking to a child. 'You still thinking straight? I've a little info for you. *The Bliss* is back, Jones. Do you want to know where she is? Do you want to go visit all those nice people who tortured you?'

'Shut up, Nash,' Frank snapped. 'Get out of his way.'

Nash retreated one step but kept on talking. 'You're going need to think now, aren't you, Jones. You're going have to think how to get clear of this the best way possible considering your condition.' He turned his thin-lipped evil little grin Frank's way. It spread as Jones noticed the pills scattered across the plating. 'The help's a little distracted, Pak.'

'Jones. Move out,' Frank said sharply.

Jones didn't hear; he dipped down. Fifteen scattered pills on the floor, and he started to take inventory, slowly and deliberately tracking them down. Frank got a look when he was finished; a narrow-eyed look he fought to read. Regret? Was Jones standing there thinking he'd made a mistake?

'Move. Now. Let my people out.' Frank let his gun's muzzle track Jones' exit before swinging it back to Nash. He started to back up, slowly and steadily, collecting up the dart gun as he went, hoping Jones had done what he'd asked, realizing he'd best be damn careful making his exit in case Jones hadn't. Then he heard thumps against the corridor walls and Max's ardent protests. He could guess what had happened. 'Haine, leave him alone,' he yelled. 'You leave him the hell alone.'

Jones sat where Haine had dumped him, opposite the door of holding two, thinking vaguely that he needed his sanity right then – and there it lay safely sheltered in his fist. Fifteen little capsules of pure sanity. A cough rattled free of his chest, his ears full of the hum of voices. Haine, Max and Kady were free now. Nash disarmed and locked up, Frank needing to destroy the door's lock completely to get it done. Jones shuddered. He'd overlooked something important, something Nash had reminded him of about his *condition*. He took his pills in careful, slothful rations of three, his body starting to hurt, too little adrenaline left now to mask the pain. Above him Frank passed the dart gun to Kady with a muttered 'See if you can get this damned thing working.'

'Did Hodge go up to helm?' Max asked.

'Locked in tight with Durham by now, I'd imagine,' Frank replied as Haine nudged at Jones with the toe of his boot.

'We don't need the cargo out here, Frank. We should lock him back up before he causes us the same kind of problems he just caused Nash.'

'You want to go sit in a cell, Jones?' Frank asked, wearing a 'one-wrong-word expression' Jones didn't dare challenge.

'I just helped you escape. I'll help you until you find a clear jump-gate out of this.'

Frank frowned, hesitated. 'Because?' Hard emphasis on that word and a little headshake with it.

You're a good man.

'I'll help you,' Jones repeated firmly. 'I promise. You can trust my word.'

Haine snorted. 'Course we can – any trouble, brat, and you get vented.'

'Gun's had it, its circuits are blown.' Kady slipped in between them all, nudging Haine out of her way with the barrel of the dart gun. 'So we're down to one weapon. Any suggestions what we do with it?'

'We take helm,' Haine glanced around. 'Anybody got any clue where we're heading?' He stared at Kady; she'd been the last one down from A deck.

Her eyes widened. 'I don't know.'

'You didn't overhear anything, see anything? A star map, a planet? You didn't hear a buoy's Nav signal?'

Kady shook her head.

'We jumped,' Frank said. 'We could be anywhere, heading anywhere. That carrier Nash said we'd be rendezvousing with could be out there right now, and we wouldn't know it. Everybody agree recon might be a good idea?' He got nods for a reply. 'The med bay computer links up to helm, I'll go up and take a look at it, find out where we are and if that boat's inbound.'

'I need my meds.' Jones struggled to keep his tone low-key. 'There should be some extra stuff up there as well. Meds from the hospital.'

Frank hesitated, his lips drawing tight as if he too had realized he'd overlooked something important. 'I'll look,' he said. 'Haine, come up with me. The rest of you stay here.'

Frank started to sweat in the lift, the old cage rocking in its housing while making unhappy grinding noises. Nash's two kids could be waiting up above in the corridor all set to start a fire-fight as soon as the lift's door slid open: familiar territory. When the lift doors had cranked open on *The Marabell* bullets had come storming through the gap. So the military's reconnaissance unit been wrong, or the inmates had tampered with those observation bots somehow.

Frank licked dry lips, hearing the echo of those shots pounding inward. Five shots right, one shot left; living and dying measured by the width of the lift's walls. Agony in his leg then, one shot piercing armour it shouldn't have. Blankness had followed, not unconsciousness, a null time where the pain wasn't. Then the pain had come charging back.

Frank tightened his grip on Nash's gun. Things had happened on that ship he couldn't remember. He'd lain in the corridor trying to stop the bleeding. He had enough medical training to know it was already far too late.

Then Jones had appeared. Insane Jones from *The Bliss*, who'd done the impossible.

The Nova's lift landed. The doors opened, Frank taking aim, the familiar contours of his ship suddenly full of shadows and threats.

No one fired.

No one waited to.

Haine motioned up the corridor to helm. Its doors stood fast shut, its lock indicator flashing red to signify an internal lockout: the door would no longer respond to the external panel. Every lock on board could be overridden from helm. Nash had locked Foley out of the system; otherwise Foley would have hit the right keys long, long ago and caused havoc.

Frank moved out, Haine at his heel. They checked each room as they went, checking for ambushes, checking for booby traps, their progress painfully slow but thorough. Foley had a camera on the corridor, Durham and Hodge at helm probably sat engrossed by their every move.

Finally Frank keyed open the med bay doors. He found it as empty as the rest. He surrendered the gun to Haine then went over and woke up the computer. It sat in the bay's furthest corner, wall-mounted, with a touch screen. Frank pawed at it to get Nav up on the screen. He requested a Nav guide image, a map of where they were, then waited for the machine's other inset opening – the print bay – to spit out a hard copy. It took its time, Frank wondering for an uneasy moment if Foley had been locked out of that system as well. But the copy arrived: a jet-black sheet with numbered circles of white dots. A star map Frank hadn't the brains to read. He went back to the keys and typed in Basic Mode. Basic, designed for even the most navigationally illiterate, spelled out in plain English the shipping lanes and the shipping within them.

'We're not on a main lane,' he told Haine, the man stood by the door, watching helm. 'The nearest doesn't have a name, just a number designation. No known planets close either, just more number designations. This is going to be meaningless to us.'

Haine huffed. 'You want me to yell to the expert? Knowing Foley, he'll answer just for the hell of it.'

Frank peered at the screen, waiting for the display to change to inform him of the local shipping and its location, all that info coming off the nearest buoy. 'All jump-gates are logged as clear.'

The nearest subspace ship's Intel came up next, and again he got a list of useless numbers. He keyed up Specifications and the machine blipped and retyped the list on the screen. 'Oh hell.'

Haine swung about 'What?'

'There is a carrier out there.'

'*The Mistral*?'

'No – *The Nelson*.'

'A different carrier? What the hell does that mean?'

'I've no idea.' Frank decided to make copies of every relevant Nav guidance statistic the computer had. He folded them all up with the star map when he was done, leaving them by the computer's side while he searched the bay's drawers and cupboards. Things spilled: instrument trays, bandage packs and boxes of hypo canisters showering the floor, all of it getting toed sideways as Frank assaulted another cupboard. He eventually found a box full of meds, set it on the med bay table, flipped the lid and rifled through the bottles inside; looking for a hospital logo, looking for the right date. 'The kid's hospital meds aren't here.'

'So?'

'So a sick Jones is more useful than a healthy one when you're undermanned. A sick Jones is collateral.' Likely Nash knew Jones' infection inside out. Likely he was playing games with Alexander

Calder too, point-scoring against him with other portions of his damned revolution.

Haine looked like he had bellyache.

'We still have the anti-bacterials Greeley's docs prescribed down in the hold.' Frank said, certain Nash would have left those behind. He added C-class meds to the box, anti-bacs and anything else that looked like it might help, making a pile that teetered over the box's lip.

Haine's brows dipped. 'Tell me we're not going to contact that carrier for the sake of that damned brat, Frank. Tell me that's not going to happen.'

Frank didn't tell him anything. He retrieved the papers, tucked them under his arm, picked up the box and left.

No one could read the stats or the star map; back down in holding, the papers were passed from Frank to Max to Kady to Haine and back to Frank again. They ended up with Jones on the deck; he sat smoothing the last remaining creases out of the uppermost page. 'It looks like we're in Omega Section Seventeen. I think *The Nelson*'s admiral is Burrows.' Jones nestled a palm against his chest; a spate of dry coughs getting in the way of the rest. Afterwards his words sounded brittle. 'But this isn't his sector. He's Zigma.'

'Right,' Haine growled. 'You can read those damned things, and you know admirals, and we should just swallow all your crap down without a squeak.'

'I can read them and I do know admirals.' Jones shoved the papers aside, busying himself with the overflowing box of pills, taking inventory just as Frank had done. Frank shifted his feet; the stores in the hold had yielded nothing, he'd already explained there were no pills from the hospital, no follow-up meds for the sucking worms or the chaos they had left behind. Jones had waved him off as if he didn't give a damn. 'Burrows was born on Cappol-One,' Jones said '*The Nelson*'s a little piece of nothing out on the Reaches. The Government classed her as non-viable and stopped subsidizing her mining operations. After that the colony's infrastructure collapsed. I think Burrows still has family there.'

'You're making this up,' Haine said. 'That boat could still belong to the Government.'

'Are you sure you want to be stuck out here with this?' Jones shrugged up tight, wrapping his arms around his knees.

'We have Nash; maybe his kids will negotiate for him,' Max suggested as Haine shoved by him and started to pace.

'They must have had instructions from their Cap in case of emergencies,' Haine grumbled out. 'They're inexperienced, they'll be scared, they'll cling to whatever he gave them, and I bet he said no deals. We need to get to the armoury so we can blow the door lock.'

The armoury sat right outside helm's doors with a camera over it for company.

'Foley's in helm,' Frank reminded him.

'They won't kill the helmsman. Rules are you never kill the helmsman unless you can fly the damn boat yourself,' Haine returned. 'You telling me you think one of those kids can handle this boat?'

'No bombs, Haine. No grenades,' Frank said firmly. 'We need something else. We need to scare those kids without tipping them right over the edge.'

Jones' head came up, tilted, more than a little arrogance in the look Frank received. 'Why don't you just cut off their air?'

'Can't do it,' Haine snapped. 'Air supply and filtration runs ship-wide, we cut off their air we'll all suffocate.'

'You can do it,' Jones insisted, gaining a sharp-eyed look. 'You can isolate helm, A6 through A12 on the environmental computer's display. Cut and suck. Cut A6 to A8, leave A9 to A12 filtration inlets running. And cut off the oxygen supply to the emergency masks while you're at it. It's an old ship; it's not an incorruptible system. It'll be in the critical procedures protocol. It's all on the comp, iconed, listed. Just click on the No box, the ship does the rest. Then pray your helmsman's smart enough not to ruin it all by plugging back into what you've just plugged him out of.' Jones checked over to Max. 'Are there any other breather masks in helm – the cylinder kind?'

Max headed up stores and equipment and Jones clearly knew it. Max shook his head. 'No, they're all stored in emergency casements outside in the corridor.'

'Fine. So cut off their air.'

'It makes sense,' Frank said.

'It still leaves Foley trapped,' Kady said sharply.

'Hodge didn't fire at Frank,' Max said.

'From what I saw of Durham he might not be so fussy,' Kady countered. 'And if he gets scared he's not going to worry about who's going to fly the ship.'

'If things go badly Foley can get the air back up and running. Right?' Max directed that at Jones. He received a nodded affirmation.

'A6 to A12 – how'd you know that?' Haine stepped in front of Jones. 'How do you know the air's not on an incorruptible system?'

This time the look on Jones' face wasn't arrogance, it was a cocky, keen challenge. 'The Bliss. This is C-class G18X built, what, forty years ago? So A6 to A12.'

'Damn lab rat,' Haine sneered. 'So we get helm, then what?'

A banging noise interrupted, the window to holding one getting a solid battering. A pasty-faced Nash peered out. Sweat glistened across his top lip, drying blood thick under both swollen eyes. 'Pak, take me up to helm, let me call *The Nelson*. I can get you out of this.' One bruised palm pressed against the composite, Nash seemingly completely unconcerned by the appearance of the wrong carrier. His pale eyes flickered from one person to the next in the corridor. 'On my word, I can get you all clear of this. Come on board *The Nelson*, hear all of it, hear our objectives before you dismiss them. The Government's rotten to its core. Give me the opportunity to prove that. Let me call that ship.'

It seemed the murderer of unarmed Aubrey, the man who'd ordered Hodge to shoot Frank down, had run out of threats.

Frank glanced about; his crew wan-faced. 'Anyone happy to do that?' His gaze settled on the most reasonable, most level-headed person available. 'Max?'

'No,' Max said immediately. An uneasy glance to Jones followed, one that turned into a deep frown.

'Don't ask me to give a damn about what happens to that stupid kid,' Haine spat out, glaring full-force at Jones.

'Yes or no, Haine?' Frank said calmly.

'Dammit, no,' Haine snarled out. 'The man's going to kill us.'

'Kady?' Frank prompted.

Kady shook her head. 'I heard him yelling at Hodge when the kid broke down moving Aubrey. He's as cold as they come. Foley would say the same.'

Frank nodded, 'Seems our opinion of you is unanimous, Nash.'

Nash stared down at Jones. 'Then factor this in then or dismiss it, Pak: you delay this thing too long and your cargo's dead.'

Haine laughed. Spittle landed on the composite, the big man leaning close to Nash behind it. 'No hospital meds on board and nothing Greeley prescribed. Do you see us panicking?'

'Those parasites are still active,' Nash settled his gaze onto Frank.

'You have a time limit here; those things are going to mature, they'll move around his body to lay their eggs. They'll block blood vessels. They get into his heart or his brain and they will kill him.'

'Don't force them into caring, Nash.' Jones down on the floor gave a loose little relieved smile that made Nash's eyes narrow.

'Don't you dare sit there and talk them into killing you,' he hissed.

'I think dead's the better option for all of us, don't you, Nash?'

Frank rubbed tension from his forehead, checking about to gauge his crew's reactions to that statement. He got a nervous looks from Max, from Kady, while Haine looked nothing but sour-faced. He didn't dare glance down to Jones again; that was one hell of a wide suicidal smile he'd chosen to wear.

'I vote we take helm,' Jones said, clearly deciding it was time to get them all moving again. 'Max, do you think you can handle the environmental computer controls?'

'I think so,' Max didn't sound confident. The computer sat down on C deck, in the cold bowels of the ship.

'The computer's display will walk you through it,' Jones raised his brows at Frank, and that smile made a reappearance. It seemed Jones had decided to make all their decisions for them, and so far nobody was arguing. He palmed another bout of pained coughs.

'Frank . . .' finally a note of concern from Kady. 'If those parasites are active . . .'

'Then he's decided to take the consequences,' Frank said firmly. Jones saved people when he wasn't killing them, he'd worked that out. He didn't dare look at Jones again, he swung about. 'Max, do it, go down to the hold, deal with the computer. I'm going up to the med bay with Haine to see if we can bully those kids out of helm.'

*

Jones smiled at Kady when they were finally all alone. She was armed with nothing but the broken dart gun she had lodged in her fist. She frowned at him, uncertainty in her eyes. 'You think I couldn't take you, the state you're in?' she said. 'You're a fool if you think I can't handle myself.'

In response Jones heaved himself upright.

'What are you doing?'

'Well . . . if we're going to fight.'

'That's funny, Jones. So you're funny too, who'd have guessed?' She stepped back, aiming the gun she couldn't use.

'Are you going to shoot me with your broken gun?'

'The gun's metal, Jones. So far as I know your head isn't.'

He laughed at that and sidestepped her, Kady tense and wary as he went across the corridor and pitched his weight into Nash's door.

The waiting Nash moistened his lips. 'Is it time to play a few more games, Jones? You'd be better off telling them to call that carrier. You're going to die.'

'If I'm going to die there's not point in asking for any information, is there? No point in making any deals.' Jones turned around.

'Wait,' Nash snapped.

Jones turned back. 'Do I have a little longer than I thought?'

Nash's attention slid over to Kady. 'Do you want to do this with an audience?'

Kady stood holding her broken gun, her expression stuck somewhere between confusion and all-out rage.

'What do you want me to do with her?' Jones asked as if she wasn't even there.

Nash smiled. 'You could kill her.'

Jones leaned closer to the window. 'Give me a reason.'

'The kids you left behind. Chishen, Tambie, Mittal, little Domal?

The Bliss really didn't want anybody to be reminded of any real people with those names did they? Do you think they're still in the institution?'

'Alexander doesn't have them.'

Nash raised his brows. 'No?'

'I know where they are.'

'No, you only *think* you know. You've been out of the loop for almost three years now.' Nash's gaze sharpened 'So, let's deal for dead bodies. Kill the girl first then I'll tell you where they are. After that, if you get really busy, I'll tell you about all the people Alexander's collected together. I'll even tell you where *The Bliss* is. I'll tell you what she is now. Her make. Her weaponry. Oh yes, Jones, they armed her this time around.' He paused, Jones having to fight to keep his expression dispassionate.

'Jones,' Kady said tightly, she'd heard all of that. He glanced back, and she readjusted her grip on the gun, swapping it about to turn it into the club it really was now. 'Step away from him.' She stood with her feet apart, braced to dart left or right. He imagined she'd fight like a demon when it came to it.

'I promised to behave,' he said levelly. 'I keep my word.'

She didn't relax, not for a second. He moved, she moved back. He held up his hands, settling down onto the floor by the side of Nash's door. She still didn't relax.

'Change your mind, Jones,' Nash said sharply from above his head. 'Kill her. Kill them all. You know they're dead anyway.'

Frank stood in the med bay, listening to the long-drawn-out silence coming at him from the helm's com.

'We don't know how long we can waste on this thing.' Haine stood at the bay's doors covering helm's entrance with Nash's gun.

'You want to get a few new Nav guide stats. You want to see how far out that carrier is now?'

Frank shrugged a negative and reconfigured the com. 'Max, are you ready?'

'Environmental computer is set,' came back, a shiver in Max's voice. 'It all worked out just like Jones said it would. Tell me you want me to do this thing before I freeze down here.'

'Not yet. I'm still trying to talk to helm out of it.'

That got a grunt out of Haine. 'Except helm isn't talking. Helm has a dummy stuck between its teeth.'

'Best find yourself a coat, Max, and stand by.' Frank cut the link, hitting keys to reconfigure it once again.

'The Nav stats might tell us how long we have,' Haine rumbled out. 'Because the cargo never mentioned it.'

Frank trapped his tongue between his teeth. They were missing things in the rush, no one had thought to ask how much time they had. The carrier on the Nav image had looked a long way out, but it was all relative, and Frank couldn't make sense of the numbers, none of them knew how to except Foley – and Jones, it seemed. 'That carrier won't do a thing until she knows the situation over here is secure.' He hit com keys again. 'Helm?' His third try to get a reply out of helm, and his irritation was audible. 'This is Frank Pak – Durham, Hodge, you're on a secure link, nobody else can hear us.'

Another wait. Frank sure he could hear Haine by the doorway grinding his teeth down to nubs.

'We understand.' Finally, a growled, impatient, equally irritated reply. Durham's voice, Frank was sure. 'We have a carrier on intercept, and we are holding your helmsman hostage. We will hurt him if you threaten us.'

'You need our helmsman in one piece, Durham. That carrier's

not going to be too impressed if you fly straight into her. I'm guessing neither one of you has the vaguest notion of how to handle this ship.'

Hush over the open link. Not a breath.

'Hodge?' Frank changed tack. 'Nash isn't happy with you, Hodge. Do you understand the kind of unhappiness I mean? The kind that got Aubrey killed. Nash doesn't seem to have much of a conscience, does he?'

No answer, and this time the com light turned to red. They'd cut the link. Durham and Hodge clearly wanted some private time to talk things over. Likely as not Foley would add a comment or two, he'd proved very adept at dealing with callow juveniles, Frank himself could testify to that, having been one himself a long time ago. But he wasn't at all certain how much Foley knew about their ongoing situation, or even if he might be able to add something new to it. Worse, Durham and Hodge could be sitting at the boards grinning at each other, knowing Nash's plans to the last dot and dash.

'Are either of you military, Hodge?'

The com light turned green. 'No, sir.'

'Then you're civilians?' Frank frowned. Civilians who slipped into calling the enemy sir felt like a big clue. 'Were you originally from an orphanage? One of the Government ships or a charity foundation?' Silence again. 'Come on, Hodge, talk to me. Tell me we're not all being played for fools here.'

'We support the Charris Confederation,' the churlish Durham returned. 'We will free the colonies and the tech. Cold-blooded murder may well be a part of that. Anyone who doesn't understand that is a fool.'

A protest from Hodge; one that got short shrift from Durham, and the com cut out again.

Frank took a breath. 'Damn mess.' And Lord, it was a monster of a mess. A war, massive ships firing at planets over the vast distances of space, one hell of a fiery end to the whistle-and-bang variety of conflict the grunts were used to.

He hit the com again, knowing a light up in helm would be blinking for attention. The com panel's light flashed green again. 'Durham, Hodge, surrender helm. This is the last time I'm going to ask.'

'We support the Charris Confederation,' Durham said, pride in every syllable. 'We will not surrender.'

'Durham, Hodge, in ten seconds I'm going to cut off your air.' Frank shut up, he waited, he didn't expect a reply. At his count-down's end he reconfigured the com. 'Max, do it.' Frank cut the com, ran a hand over his brow then glanced about, straight into Haine's glare.

'You want to tell me what we're supposed to do if those kids decide to open those doors and start firing?' he asked.

'If they start firing I'll fire back.' Frank went over and nudged Haine's arm, signalling for him to give up the gun. Haine passed it over happily enough. Frank settled it into a two-handed grip before he crouched down by the foot of the door. Helm's doors had no half lock; if they opened they'd have to go back all the way. Frank trusted his aim, his own self-control at that moment. Just when Haine cranked up into a round of agitated doubts he calmed right down. They had to let it ride out now; they didn't have any choice.

Time passed, and he started noticing tiny details around him: a line of dirt on the wall across from him, the dust bunny in the corner outside helm in a spot the brushes of the mop-bot always found hard to reach, a long scratch across helm's doors he didn't recall.

Haine moved back into the bay. 'I'm going to open the com. You happy to yell from there?'

Frank nodded. 'Pak here,' he said seconds later, raising his voice so the unit the room's width away would pick him up clearly. Helm's doors were strong but not thick, the kids probably had him in stereo. 'How's the air in there, helm?'

'It's hard to breathe,' Hodge returned over the link, every nervous word interspaced by a little pant.

'Air's fine out here, Hodge,' Frank replied.

'They're not going to kill us if we surrender,' Hodge hissed, clearly forgetting the link was open.

'We're not giving up,' Durham snapped.

'I can't get this damned air down,' came far more loudly in another voice: Foley, the first Frank had heard out of him, Foley playing up by the sound of him.

'I want you to try to call *The Nelson* again,' Durham instructed.

'I told you, they've cut my boards,' Foley returned. 'I can't call out any more.'

Frank smiled; Foley was helping out, it seemed, by throwing a few lies into the mix. 'Durham,' he said. 'Surrender helm. You can't win this one.'

'Durham, please, we're running out of air,' Hodge pleaded breathlessly over the link. 'The carrier will deal with them. That's Burrows, Admiral Burrows. You think he'll just let them go.'

'It'll look better if we still have helm.'

'Lying dead over the boards,' Foley snorted. 'Yes, son, that'll impress the Admiral, all right.'

'Why don't you shut up?'

'Why don't you see sense? Pak is military trained the same as Nash. You think you're messing with a civilian here. You think he won't push this to the limit. Soon as we turn blue in here he'll have those doors forced open. He takes too long doing that and we're all dead.'

'He won't kill you,' Durham returned. 'I'm not that stupid.'

'Rules are if you sacrifice one life to save four crewmen you shrug your shoulders and tell yourself you did a good job. Pak can fly this boat just as well as I can – he doesn't need me. You think he needs you two?' Foley's lies just got bigger and bigger.

'Durham,' Hodge's voice dropped another notch. 'We're not military, we don't have to do this.'

'We're not leaving helm,' Durham snapped. 'We'd rather die at helm.'

'That what you want, Hodge?' Foley asked calmly. 'Because you're holding a gun, just the same as he is.'

A thump followed, a thump and a yell.

'Frank. Door,' Foley bawled. Frank shot up from his crouch, helm's door indicator cycling to green. The doors began to open, Frank slipping through the gap as soon as he had enough room. The shadow to his right was Foley at the door control; the figure to his fore happened to be Hodge, red-faced and panting. Durham lay flat out on the deck, reaching for the gun Hodge must have prised away from him.

'No.' Frank stamped at the kid's fingers then hooked the gun clear.

Haine rushed in. He shoved Hodge over to the wall, Hodge more than happy to surrender his own weapon. He stood bowed over then, sucking in great gusts of the fresh air streaming in from the corridor.

'Damned stupid kids.' Foley stood breathless and ruby-cheeked himself. He returned to his boards, punching keys rapidly. 'Foley here, helm is secure. I'm turning my blasted air back on.'

Frank motioned Durham up. The sour-faced juvenile's nostrils flaring as he glared at Foley. 'That's right, my boards are just fine, you are that stupid,' Foley said.

Hodge stood by quietly. Haine covered him with Hodge's own gun, telling him to put his hands on his head now his breathing had levelled out. Hodge's raw-boned face had turned a sickly white. He did was he was told. 'Please, sir, we can't help you,' he said in a rush.

'Help us?' Frank queried.

'With *The Nelson*, sir. We can't help get you. Captain Nash gave us strict instructions and we've already—'

'There's no we,' Durham spluttered out. 'You, Hodge. You did this.'

Hodge's head went down, his lips quivering, consequences starting to swamp him.

'Hodge, you're both clear of this now, my word on it,' Frank said. 'Just tell me what they expect. Does *The Nelson* expect to dock or just to escort this ship someplace else?'

Hodge looked up, set his jaw and took a deep lungful of air. 'They expect to dock, sir.'

He wasn't lying, not by Frank's reckoning; he hadn't the resources left to conjure one. 'Haine, take them down to holding.'

Haine sniggered. 'Babysitting, my favourite. Move, babies.' Haine used his gun to prod both his charges into the corridor. 'Don't make me scare you, we don't want any more wet nappies this trip.'

CHAPTER 12

Frank stood at Foley's boards, his gaze sweeping across monitor after monitor, Frank spellbound by their forward aspect. *The Nelson* sailed in; a deadly black mass, angular, huge; fore and aft, and every space between, bristling with armament. Her bay doors gaped, all set to release unmanned attack drones; she could deploy those, or manned fighters, at a moment's notice, if she wasn't content with simply using a missile to blast them off her forward view screens.

'You okay?' Frank asked, sliding into the chair next to Foley.

'Peachy,' Foley returned. 'I had a ball, suffocating in here with two jumpy kids. Nice idea – one of yours?'

'One of the cargo's.'

'The cargo? The cargo's allowed to pitch ideas now, is he? You care to fast-track through the whole of what the hell is going on here.'

Frank did so, his attention held by *The Nelson*, while Foley huffed and puffed his way through the truth as Frank saw it, not entirely happy when he'd finished. 'So what the hell do we do now?' he asked.

'We negotiate.'

'For what, a brain to share between us? A revolution. Hell, even I'm too damned young to remember the last one of those. That Government enclave was supposed to have killed this kind of political crap stone dead.'

'This started with a civilian, not a politician, Foley, and he's seeding it right through the military.' Frank paused to get a few deep breaths down of helm's newly circulated air. 'We have Nash, their cargo; that carrier has something to lose here.'

Foley grimaced. 'Armament, that's what she's got to lose. We're in the middle of a bad deal, thanks to Greeley, thanks to his damned antsy brat.'

'Damned antsy brat can hear you,' came Kady's fast retort.

Frank spun his chair about. Their cargo was inbound, trailed by Kady, who still had no working weapon to hold on her charge. She shrugged as she held up the broken dart gun.

'Go open up the armoury and pick something out that'll work,' Frank told her. A concession to caution that got a shrewd little smile out of their cargo.

'So the antsy brat's allowed up to helm, now is he?' Foley said.

Pasty-faced and graceless, the antsy brat in question cocked his head and allowed his smile to spread. 'They'll shoot Foley, Foley will suffocate – it seems neither option came true.'

Foley grunted. 'You after applause? If you're staying, by the looks of you, you'd better sit down.'

Frank slipped out of his seat, getting clear so Jones could take his place. Settled, Jones leaned forward, squinting at the systems screens under the main monitors.

'No stations,' Foley told him. 'No habitable planets. No signal buoys. No passing ships. No witnesses. Bye, bye, little ship. Boom.'

'I take it you're the resident optimist?' Jones leaned both hands on the control boards, propping himself upright. 'Has *The Nelson* started transmitting a systems alert yet?'

After hitting several keys, Foley snorted. 'Wonderful. Yes, she has. She's warning us she's running on Amber. All her weapons systems are now live.'

Jones stifled a shuddering cough and swallowed hard. 'Did Nash's kids speak to her?'

'The boys said they had a situation developing.'

'And what did *The Nelson* say?'

'Deal with it.'

Jones stared hard at a monitor. 'Are we holding position?'

'Nash's boys told me to, and they had the guns.' Foley hit another key, checked a display. 'We are presently rock solid. Auto is compensating for drift.' Foley turned his chair about a little, raising an eyebrow at Frank. 'Anything the boss would like to throw in, or is the boss comfortable with his helmsman being grilled by his cargo?'

Jones strained to see another display, not bothering to check around to Frank himself. 'You want me to shut up, *Boss*?'

Challenge in that; Jones who'd got them all out of holding, Jones who'd given his word to help them out, who sat there looking like he might just have a plan. 'Let him run with it,' Frank said. 'For now.'

'The cargo would like to know if that carrier knows we've retaken helm,' Jones said. 'Did those kids give them any clues?'

Foley shook his head. 'I cut the com when you cut the air. Those kids were sending nowhere after that and they wanted to. They were getting frustrated and bleating at me, but they couldn't tell a com board from a galley sandwich, so it wasn't much of a poker game.'

'So *The Nelson* still thinks everything's relatively fine over here?'

'And if she does, what does that get us? We don't have much to play with here, do we.'

'We have Durham and Hodge. We could try to bluff our way out of this.'

'*The Nelson* expects us to dock,' Frank said, adding something Jones hadn't asked or heard about. 'And we can't use those kids, I promised them I'd leave them out of this.'

Jones frowned round at him. 'You promised?'

'Yes, I promised.'

Jones clearly thought that deserved an even bigger grin. 'Dangerous things, Frank. They can get you into all kinds of trouble – I suppose we all agree Nash won't be much help.'

'So what do we have left?' Foley asked.

'The truth, plus a few well-chosen lies.' A cough got in the way, Jones leaning back in his chair afterwards and panting hard and deep.

Foley sent a dipped-brow gaze Frank's way. 'By the sounds of it the cargo's not doing too well. So why the promise to help us?'

'I think we were the easier option,' Frank admitted.

'Easy?' Foley chuckled. 'Long damned time since anybody called me easy.' A light flashed on the com board, and he sobered instantly. 'That'll be *The Nelson* calling.' He opened up the link.

'This is *The Nelson*,' a deep, gruff voice said. 'Respond. We are still waiting for clarification of your situation, helm.'

Foley grimaced and cut the link. 'I'm not sure just how much longer she's going to wait for that if her weapons are live.'

Jones leaned in to press the send key, Frank darting forward to snatch his wrist clear. 'What the hell are you doing? I said you could help, I didn't say you could take over.'

Jones' head tilted, every plane and angle of his face caught in the brightness of the overheads. Jones carved out of stone: no panic, no fear, poor callow Hodge's opposite in every detail. 'Don't you trust me?' The wrist Frank held wrenched free.

'This is my ship, my people. I have a lot to lose here,' Frank said sharply.

'And I don't? I offered to help and I'm keeping my word. I know how to get you out of this, but I need to do it in my own time, in my own way. You say "no" to me, Frank, and I'm gone. I'm back in holding.'

Adrenaline pumped into Frank's bloodstream, pushing into all the places where the fear lay. He needed a fast decision and he wasn't good at those – but Jones had a keen-eyed look he recognized from all those times Jones had slipped away from them when good sense told them it was impossible. Jones didn't quit no matter what the odds, and now Jones was on *their* side. Frank bit his lip, backed up a step, giving Jones room to turn his attention back to the boards.

'Dammit,' Foley muttered under his breath. 'Damned boss better know what the hell he's doing.'

Jones reached out and hit Send. 'This is helm responding. Please tell Admiral Burrows, the J-Seventeen needs his attention.'

Frank glanced to Foley, Foley shrugging to mark his own confusion.

'I repeat. This is the J-Seventeen,' Jones said calmly. 'I need to speak to your Admiral.'

'Stand by,' the voice on the other end of the link instructed. Jones hit the off key and shut down the link.

'That won't happen. You won't get the Admiral. You won't get a negotiation with the brass,' Foley said. 'Maybe we'd be better off turning ourselves into a moving target.'

'With all that armament she has pointed at us I really can't see the point,' Jones replied. 'Besides, now they know the J-Seventeen is in charge of this thing, that carrier won't dare fire.'

'And this J-Seventeen reference is what, exactly?' Foley asked, wiping the sweat from his forehead.

'A code, for identification purposes.'

'Is that supposed to reassure us? If you're so sure that ship won't fire, why the hell aren't we running?'

'Trust me,' Jones said firmly. 'If they know the crazed J-Seventeen is in charge everything they try will be slow and careful. The J-Seventeen isn't predictable; the information trail would have told Burrows that.'

That got a troubled look out of Foley. 'J-Seventeen or not, you still won't get the Admiral. You'll get some underling speaking for him. He's not going to let some kid on a little sloop walk all over him, no matter what colour your version of crazy comes up on a scan, or how valuable they think you are.'

The com light interrupted again, Foley opening up the link. 'This is Com Officer Morrow.' Foley turned a little sarcastic smirk Jones' way. 'J-Seventeen, do you have a more complete code I can verify?'

'J-180-D10-89-3ZXH. What else do you need? *The Bliss*. Section G. B deck. Experiment I-dent code JG7771-9. The last of the J series. I repeat; I want to speak to your Admiral.' Jones set his hand in his lap, leaving the com wide open.

Kady shuffled in at Frank's back; he turned, pressing a finger to his lips before he waved to the boards to signal the live two-way link. Kady had gained the gun she'd craved, she held it up: a dart gun. Frank pointed to the corner, setting her into a position where she could get a clear shot at Jones if needs be. There was no point in being wholly stupid.

'Stand by,' the com officer said over the link.

A ten-second wait. 'This is Admiral Burrows,' a placid, mellow voice said then. 'J-Seventeen, I'm listening.'

Frank shifted uncomfortably; carrier brass talked to no one but carrier brass, during sixteen years of service he'd never spoken one word to *The Monterey*'s Admiral.

'Burrows, where the hell have you been?' Jones asked acidly. 'I have Nash, his crew and this ship's crew, and I want you off my view screens.'

'That won't be happening,' came back.

'Were you supplied with my psych file?'

'I know who and what you are. So why don't we both be polite and reasonable about this. May I call you Jeven?' The name, the way Borrows said it, carried so much weight it made Frank start.

Jeven? J-Seventeen? You didn't have to work too hard to see the connection.

Jones hissed air between his teeth, 'I don't give a damn what you call me, Burrows. I have Nash in holding. Is he of any consequence?'

'Yes, he is.'

'Are you going to let me kill him?' Jones said it like a kid asking for candy.

'Of course not.'

'So you would prefer it if I killed somebody else? I have a man called Banks. Is he of any consequence?'

'Yes, he is,' Burrows returned.

That got a swift nod out of Jones. The Admiral had, it seemed, swallowed one lie down neatly. The information trail clearly had a few gaps in it.

'Is it really necessary to kill anyone?' Burrows asked.

'I have a Banks, a Hodge and a Durham on Nash's side of things. A Pak, a Foley, a Haine, a Harrison and a Kincott from *The Nova*. Make a choice.' Jones shut the link down again hurriedly and gave a long-drawn-out cough. The com light flashed, but he sat back, breathing hard and waiting.

'We getting anywhere?' Foley asked quietly.

'The Admiral doesn't like killing people. Nash does,' Frank said as Jones pitched forward and stabbed at the boards.

'Your file indicates you have a list,' the Admiral went on calmly, undisturbed, it seemed, by the delay. 'Are any of those names from *The Bliss*?'

'Are you telling me what I can and can't do?' Jones asked sharply. 'Are you telling me the rules? Do you want me to get a pen and start adding names to my list; you think that's the way it's done? You think I have principles? I executed two men. One of them had a two-year-old daughter; she was sleeping in the next-door room when I killed her father. Don't you dare doubt my intentions, Burrows. Don't you dare doubt just how far I'm about to push this thing.'

'There's no need to kill anybody.' Burrows sounded rattled.

'There is if I need to make a point. Are you going to tell me that's not necessary? Are you going to tell me I can fire up this ship's engines and leave?'

Muffled words came over the link, one comment standing clear above the rest. *Are you certain we're secure?*

'Are you and yours still in hiding, Burrows?' Jones asked over the sound of more muffled background conversation. 'Don't all your shipmates know you're a revolutionary?'

'I control my ship,' came back tightly.

'And I control mine. I'm going to stop talking now; I have to go kill Banks. I'll send him over. After Banks you'll get Hodge and Durham. Last of all you'll get Nash. Nash in little pieces.'

'There's no need to kill any—' Jones cut the com, gripped the seat armrests, leaned his head back and breathed.

'Now what?' Frank asked.

'Now we need a little luck.'

The Nova's freezer was little more than a box room with shelves where the ship's perishables were locked up tight. Frank hadn't asked for help from Nash or his kids, but he'd still found what he was looking for.

'Is he there?' Max's voice echoed across the expanse of the hold beyond the doorway.

'Yes.'

Aubrey's body lay like some huge dormant pupa, his body, swathed in plastic wrap, dumped right at the rear of freezer unit. Frank leaned down, got a grip on the hard, cold ankles poking out from below the white plastic and pulled, dragging the body out into the chill air outside as the plastic rustled and crackled in protest.

Max, washed pale by the brightness of the overheads, wrung his hands together. 'We'll have to unwrap him.'

Frank blew out a plume of curses and fumbled for the end of the wrap, giving it an experimental tug to judge its strength. 'We'll have to roll him free.' He checked up to Max; the man thin-lipped and transfixed. 'You here to watch, or to help? You've seen a body before, right?'

Max edged in, balled up a handful of wrap, timing his pulls at the plastic with Frank's own. Aubrey rolled, elbows and knees thumping into the metal. The last turn of the sheeting exploded a shower of frozen blood onto the plating, blood that spun away and kept on sliding, some of it bouncing back off the walls. So damned much blood Aubrey could hardly have any left inside his body.

'Oh God,' Max said.

Frank cleared his throat. 'Don't say it, I don't want to hear it.' He crunched ice underfoot, moving over to kneel by Aubrey's side. Not pretty: Aubrey's arms lay fast by his sides, his knees slightly bent, the loosest thing on him his white-blond hair. Hair now coated in scarlet ice crystals – but then most of Aubrey lay coated in either red or yellow ice, his V-seal clothing not designed to soak up either blood or urine.

Frank dared a lightning-fast glance at Aubrey's face, hearing Max's own exhalation of shock. 'He looks terrified,' Max said, which didn't help Frank's mood at all. 'How long do you think he lay there bleeding—'

'I said, don't say it.'

Alone and bleeding to death: because Nash hadn't made a tidy job of killing Aubrey at all.

Frank drew the wrap clear, piling it back into the freezer, closing the door hurriedly on its attempts to unravel itself right back into the bay.

'Frank, he's almost frozen solid,' Max said behind him. 'This isn't going to work. Vacuum does things to a body. Burrows will get a close-up of Aubrey's exit. He'll know a fresh body from a frozen one. Blood boils in vacuum, all bodily fluids do. After that the trapped water vapour causes all the tissues to swell.'

Frank snorted, and Max self-consciously dipped his head.

'We got two seconds of advice in the military,' Frank said. 'If you hit hard vacuum without a suit shut your eyes, exhale and try to save yourself. That was it. So Aubrey's a comet, right?'

Max nodded. 'Burrows will most likely sit with his guns over us until he can examine Aubrey's body in detail. He'll do an ID check with Central Data – and that'll only take hours on a military priority call.' There Max stood thinking just like a cop. 'Do you think Jones is factoring all this in? Do you think he expected us to find Aubrey in the freezer?'

'God knows.'

'So what do we do?'

'What choice do we have? We load Aubrey, we vent him, we pretend he's some figment of Jones' imagination called Banks.' Frank sucked down a frigid lungful of air and hauled at icy shoulders, his hands slipping on cloth rapidly thawing out under the heat of his fingers. Both he and Max shuffled sideways towards the open doors of the gun bay with their load. Frank knocked on the switch that levered the gun out of their way with his foot, Max peering down into the deep dark well beneath it.

'Are we just going to drop him?'

The gun below was always on standby; its motors hummed constantly, its rhythmical thump a continuous throb of pressure in Frank's already pounding head. A ladder accessed the bay; there was no other way down, no way to cart a frozen corpse down that wouldn't bend in its middle. 'Hell,' he snarled out. 'Yes, we *are* just going to drop him. On three . . .'

On one they started to swing Aubrey over the gap, on two he was gaining momentum, on three they let him go. Frank didn't watch him fall, the resounding clang of the man's frozen corpse crashing into the metal door below felt like insult enough.

'You think he had a family on Delta?' Max asked.

'I think it's very, very likely.' Frank toe-punted the gun's control then backed to the wall and hit a switch. The bay doors hissed closed, Frank waiting for the seal light to come on. He didn't look over to Max again. Whatever Max felt lately it lay naked and exposed on his face. Likely Frank's own feelings had started to leak out in exactly the same way. He was scared, he was frustrated, and he was trusting in a plan he'd contributed nothing to. And Jones' plans weren't reliable; they depended too much on variables, and chance, and dumb stupid luck.

The seal light came on.

'Let's get up to helm,' Frank said. He followed Max to the lift, crunching ice under his boot soles all the way. There was no time to clean up the mess, and he knew there be a far worse one waiting to greet them when they came back down. All that red ice would thaw.

The lift doors closed. Max hit the panel. The car moaned, rattling slightly as it came to life. Frank screwed his fingers into his palms, fingers that felt filthy right down to their nail-beds. No time to clean those up either. Pure instinct told him he was making a mistake: a big one. Anger rose, the knot of it so hard and heavy in his throat he could barely shift air around it. The image still mocked him, so did that terrifying immeasurable blackness. And there had still been no confessions from his crew that they'd seen anything at all coming from Jones.

He sneaked a glance over to Max. In the middle of madness would a little more hurt?

Max, I've seen things – data streams, images – and I'm sure they came from Jones. He was raving about colours earlier, I'm starting to think they mean something. Something so real to him he's based his whole life around them.

'You okay?' Max hushed the question up.

Frank could see his own expression in the lift walls. He looked like a man about to blow up or break down. He didn't blame Max for that inquiry. 'Bad day,' he returned, hardly opening his mouth to say it. The rest of it stayed knotted up inside his chest.

'We found him in the damn freezer, there's no way he going to look like a fresh kill,' he sent the words barrelling across helm as soon as he reached it. His checks started to burn, his body started to tremble. He got a worried look from Kady still on standby with her gun, another from Haine. Helm brimmed with anxious faces.

Jones up at the boards turned his chair around. 'But we *do* have him.'

Frank took ten mindless steps forward, Max's hand snaking around his arm. 'Are you missing the point on purpose? It's not going to look like some crazy's just killed the man if he hits the cold already frozen solid. This isn't going to work. Burrow's isn't going to fall for this. A five-year-old wouldn't fall for this.' Frank hauled his arm free, looking at the screens again, every one now filled with *The Nelson*'s massive black mass.

'We only have one body,' Jones said. 'This is *all* the plan we have.'

'You have.'

'And you're trusting me.' Jones made solid eye contract. 'And I play the odds. I play whatever comes at me; you know that. You want to play instead, Frank, the game's yours.' An open-handed gesture followed: an offer.

Frank's knees shook under him, black spots in front of his eyes, the rush of his blood a fear-filled hiss in his ears. He was acting like a fool, he knew it, but he'd reached his limit; panic had set in: you didn't face down a carrier and not panic. Yet there Jones sat, so calm, so collected, Jones, rock solid in the middle of madness. *I'm going to help you, Mr Pak. I swear to you, I'm going to help you* – and hell, Jones would try his damnedest.

Jones waited, watched him, watched his hands clench, watched them finally uncurl as Frank swallowed, tasting his own salt-sweat on this lips. 'Final orders are mine,' he said firmly. 'You got that?'

'Yes.'

'Foley, vent Aubrey's body.'

*

Jones leaned back in his seat, sucked at his bottom lip; watching Frank gather himself back together, watching the man look about to his crew as if he thought they needed to know he was fine, he was in control. Jones turned his chair around, snapping a glance back to the monitors, to *The Nelson*, wondering how far he might have to go to get away from her. He felt the weight of Foley's gaze, the man's calm steel-grey eyes trying to pick him apart. 'Venting,' the man said. 'Gun bay doors activated. Amber light . . . Red . . . Doors are opening.' He leaned a little into Jones' portion of the boards to pitch every camera mount possible towards the gun-bay doors. 'Body is venting.' Foley wrinkled his nose. 'Coming into view just north of the forward thrusters. It's rattling off the hull a little. Going to have to give it a shove.' Foley hit keys, re-adjusting one of *The Nova*'s thrusters. His throat clicked. 'Sorry, Aubrey.'

Aubrey's body spun end over end across the camera banks' lower casement; aft cameras giving it up to the forward banks seconds after that blast of encouragement from the ship. That blast had removed something from the man's corpse, something Jones couldn't identify and didn't want to. It made its own dance towards the carrier in a tighter spin, shedding pieces of itself into the black.

Jones stared at the wall, examined the utility tray on the side of his chair, checked over to the gunnery section to his right, where the belly gun's own monitors sat, dark and quiet. He looked at the track in the floor the chair he sat on would slide along to reach those controls. The gun wouldn't solve this problem. He dipped his head, brushed sweat from overburdened lashes and coughed, one of those he held back on until it almost choked him. His chest felt so tight now every breath was a conscious push of diaphragm and ribcage. 'Do we have a jump-gate?'

Foley sat busily hitting keys. 'Comp's got one all picked out for us. Not Government sanctioned.'

Jones sucked at his lip again, caught himself doing it and stopped. Foley kept on sneaking sharp little glances his way. The man was a military vet; he'd won medals for valour, one for pulling a troop transporter clear of an imminent collision with half a mountainside. Foley didn't panic in a crisis, and Foley was visibly searching for signs right then to the integrity of his cargo. 'We'll have to take our chances,' Jones said.

'I guessed that,' Foley returned in a quieter tone.

The com light flashed, and Jones opened up the link.

'What's this?' It was Burrows.

'This?'

'This frozen carcass.'

'The frozen carcass' name was Jenkins. Did I forget to mention him? I don't know who or what he was, but Nash called him sir. He didn't like me; I didn't like him. It was an easy kill. You ready for a fresh one? I've decided on Nash. Nash because out of them all, he's the one I want to kill the most.' Jones paused; shallow breathing. 'I hope I'm worth all this effort, Burrows, considering the mess you're sitting in over there.' He closed the link.

'You hoping to get us something with that?' Foley asked. 'You working on a theory here?'

'I don't think that's a Charris ship,' Jones said. 'Not yet. Burrows wasn't expecting to be pushed this hard, this fast. I'm guessing a little delegation off a hauler was all he was expecting; a few prisoners under Nash's control. A fast trip into system and a fast out is all he can handle. He can't afford to be seen here, not with us, and not with that body if he wants a clean exit.'

'There are three marked jump-points in the immediate vicinity,' Foley told him. 'An inbound ship is a risk – just not a huge one.'

'It doesn't have to be a huge risk, just enough of one to make Burrows edgy. Make him uncomfortable enough he might just decide he's done for the day.' Jones dared to look into those calm grey eyes again. 'How far are we off from that gate?'

Foley checked his boards. 'Depends on how hard and fast you'd like me to head for it.'

'Then make a move. Hit the mains.'

'Before Burrow calls us?'

'Yes.'

'Won't work. Nice try, but it won't work.'

'It'll work. The worst thing we can do is give Burrows time to think this through.'

Foley's wiped a hand across his mouth, gave a little headshake then turned to look at Frank. 'Are we doing this?'

A pause, a long one, Jones could see Frank shifting from foot to foot out of the corner of his eye. Then Frank said tightly. 'Yes, we are.'

Foley stabbed at more keys, monitors lighting up with fresh displays. 'Hitting the mains. All systems are not live; watch yourselves until auto kicks in. Vectoring towards our out-point.' Foley noticed the flashing com light and flicked the link open.

'*Nova*, hold your position.' it wasn't Burrows, it was the young com officer.

'I like fast decisions,' Jones sent back. 'I don't do thinking time. I'm going to jump right out from under your nose, Burrows. You launch anything after me I'm venting bodies. You want that? You want to have a trail of bodies across the black? Are you running silent? How about your ship's logs, are you tampering with those? How many lies will you need to tell at the back end of all of this?'

'We're running silent,' returned: Burrows this time.

'You've isolated helm, haven't you?' Jones said. 'You've shut down the ship's com and all external viewing screens on the rest of your ship. What are you calling it – an exercise?'

Foley motioned, pointing to a monitor. Safety Systems Online flashed, next to a jump countdown, next to a jump-gate the ship had red flagged in triplicate.

Jones hauled in a breath. 'That's our gate?' A major hazard, a jump you might take and never return from, a piece of illegal tech plying out mechanical moans and groans – a dying gate for certain. Jones turned off the com and turned half about. 'Are we seriously going to use that out-point?' Frank blinked at him. His decision, his alone, and Frank baulked. Frank rubbed at a forehead slick with sweat.

'Jump-gate is sound,' Foley said.

'A triple flag isn't sound,' Jones sent back. 'A triple flag will kill you.'

'Not this trip,' Foley said. 'Knowledge gets passed around by those that need it. We might get spun out of the vortex but so long as we don't hit anything we'll be fine.'

Frank still stood kneading at his forehead.

'Trust me,' Foley added more reassurances. 'I can get us out clean.' He sent the rest Jones' way. 'I can work through jump. I can play the odds just as well as any snot-nosed sickly brat.'

'Do it,' Frank said in a rush. 'For God's sake, Foley, just do it.'

Jones snagged another breath down, watching that jump-gate indicator flash in aggravated silence. More numbers appeared, a fast overlay he couldn't keep up with. The com light flashed, and he keyed it open.

'Hold your position, *Nova*. This is your final warning.'

'You'd better be thankful Nash didn't get on board, Burrows, because he was out to make a big noise and he was going to use your ship to do it. He's running under Alexander's radar right now. He's not following orders. Maybe he's not even on your side.' Jones rechecked the screens, catching sight of movement cutting clear of *The Nelson*'s bulk.

'Dammit,' Foley snapped. 'She's launched drones.'

Jones looked back to the com. 'You best hold them back, Burrows, or I'm launching something of my own.'

Burrows cut the link.

Jump countdown flashed in a fiery red as they headed towards their gate. A convoy of silver-hulled drones streaking across the black towards them.

The com light flashed, and Jones snapped it open.

'I don't believe you. I know Nash. I served with Nash.'

'Why were you sent here? Nash said *The Mistral* was inbound. Did somebody else get too nervous to revolt? One hell of a revolution, full of skulking cowards or people like Nash, so ambitious they can't follow orders. Is it all going to fall to pieces before it even starts?' Jones' vision blurred on the countdown's swift plunge of numbers. 'Tell me you didn't get a late call in. Nash called someone on *The Mistral* and he didn't get the answer he was expecting. A fast jump into system, wasn't it, and Nash told you to lock down your crew and isolate yourself at helm.'

Silence on the com now, silence as those drones tracked them. Jones cut the link and leaned back, yanking at his shirt, pulling the clammy, cleaving chill of it clear of his chest.

'They're not slowing down,' Foley said.

Jones checked the monitors, getting lost in a fresh slew of numbers. He started to shake, seeking out a darker monitor where *The Nelson* lurked. He could see reflected faces looking back at him: Max, Kady, Haine. Frank at his shoulder sounded winded, his fear locked up behind a blank, stoic expression. Jones was running out of points to make. He was running out of ideas.

Kill Nash?

He pitched up out his seat and turned for the door. Frank barred his way, his hands raised. 'What are you doing?'

Kill Nash; murder a man. How far would he have to go to keep his word this time? Nash wasn't innocent, he was as bad as bad could get. But could he do it right then, right there, without that urge, that itch for revenge driving him forward? Frank started to lean his weight into his opposing shove. 'Burrows isn't going to let us go. We need to make another point.' He tried to push by, Max and Haine moving forward to stand at Frank's back. Both men looked anxious, but did they intend to help Frank or pull him out of the way?

'Drones are slowing,' Foley said behind him.

Jones twisted about, hurriedly finding the right monitor, the right figures. Foley snaked out a fist to haul him back into his seat. 'They're slowing,' he repeated.

All the outside views died, the ship's camera banks retracting into the protection of her hull, Foley locking his attention down hard to his board displays. 'Out in ten . . . nine . . . eight . . . seven . . .'

Jones dug his nails into his seat's armrests. A hazardous gate, a triple-flagged out and no trank, nowhere to hide.

'Six . . . five . . . four . . . three . . .'

What colour remained under helm's lights intermingled, bled, became an eddy Jones couldn't look at. He shut it out, hiding closed eyes behind his palms to make the darkness of his lids blacker still. The ship howled, she screamed, his seat itself seeming to resonate with every rise and fall of pitch. He held his breath, thoughts scattering in a mind that couldn't cope with the between: too much flux, too much uncertainty. He pitched forward, fighting with senses that longed to cut loose.

Jump tore some people in two, it drove them insane, it killed them; best not to look at it, best to hide anyway if you could. Jones wasn't certain he was still breathing, he wasn't certain he still had any blood left in his brain.

Death felt close, mercifully close.

Pain came back. Pain behind his closed lids that spread into the roots of his teeth. A cutting pain across his chest, a suffocating pain. Jones moaned, his fingers looking for what his eyes daren't. The belt of the seat had activated; he probed for the off switch, pressed it, the belt retracting with a soft whirl of sound. Jones balled a fist to his heart, sucking down great whooshes of air.

Not dead. Not yet.

He dared to look; assaulted by light so bright his eyes leaked stinging tears. He swiped them clear, staring at the monitors: a star field, nothing to pinpoint, nothing really to stare at. But they were out of the gate. Out whole.

'We got slewed, spat right out. Ship doesn't know where we are,' Foley was saying. 'Still got nothing from Nav, it's still trying to catch up. Comp's still swearing at me for the override.' Foley turned his head. 'Cargo's awake, Frank.' Foley's grey-eyed stare had gained a twinkle. 'Looks like we got right out from under a damned carrier, Jones. Look like we did it free and clear too, no complications.'

Pain overrode relief, Jones gripping his chest. Frank kneeled by his chair, catching up his wrist, taking his pulse the crude way. 'Sit still, breathe and stay calm.' Jones leaned over the tightening throb of his heart, heat rising over his body. 'Take deeper breaths. Deep and slow.' Jones nodded, tightness inside as he forced his lungs to work. The shallow little breaths he could manage making his head spin.

'Can we head for Beta?' Haine's shadow spilled over helm's boards.

Foley glanced up to him. '*The Nelson* knows our specs.'

'So you'd rather we hide out here while a war kicks off?'

'I doubt Beta's a safe port.' Frank lifted a hand to try to push Haine back. Haine didn't budge.

'Fine, we'll head back to Delta.'

'Think, Haine. Nowhere is going to be a safe port for us now.'

'So where the hell are we supposed to go?' Haine's words punched against helm's walls. 'What the hell are we supposed to do?'

'We have to stay calm. We have to think this out.'

'Final word is Frank's,' Foley reminded firmly. 'You got that? You argue and you'll be the one in holding.'

Haine didn't argue, not just then. He took a big stride backwards instead. Frank searched the array of monitors. 'Foley, find out where the hell we are.'

Time shattered, Jones losing pieces of it as he sat there trying to get his heart rate settled. He focused on the ceiling, focused hard to steady his still-clambering pulse. He saw a spider, balled up tight in one corner. Spiders had escaped Earth, they travelled, they made jump, they ate whatever tiny alien things fell into their webs, if that alien thing didn't eat them first. The filters added poisons to kill them and anything else; you weren't supposed to take insects for little trips from jump to jump to jump. You weren't supposed to do anything you didn't have a Government licence for. The spider was either sleeping or dead, it didn't move, nothing at helm did except for Foley's swift fingers across his boards.

'Got a buoy's signal. Have a position. We're not on a shipping lane. We're not anywhere we're going to be disturbed.'

Jones' throat spasmed; he coughed, his heart at odds with his chest's heave, his body's aversion to jump leaving a queasy, greasy whirlwind caught inside his stomach. *Kill Nash*: that kept coming back. Kill Nash to get out from under it all. The thought brought a shiver with it, memories of a room that smelled of lavender and copper, curling red splotches staining two photographs on a table-top: a girl's chubby-faced smile beside a bride's white-laced form under an arc of pink roses. Both images soiled with shards of flesh, lost coils of white-grey hair, flecks of bone.

Guilt came with doubt, and he had none. Abused children still smiled, foolish women married men who beat them, women who stood under rose petals with blank, emotionless faces. He'd done the right thing. He'd killed the right people for the right reasons. He always would.

'Jones?'

'He still with us?'

'Jones?'

Jones batted heavy eyelids, thinking of another room, a wide white room, subtly lit. Thinking of a man who lived in a well of his own depravity, pictures on his walls of death. Murder disguised as art, twisted faces full of terror disguised as sculpture. Stink of blood, a pool of it beneath his feet and an endless sense of being sullied, unclean. Evil had a colour, a deep upwelling of brown and grey and black that streamed over a man's being. A dark cloud of absolute truth.

Frank touched his chin, tilted his head up, and Frank was the colour of the sky. 'Blue,' Jones whispered.

Label the man; place a tag on him. Judge him.

'I'm taking you over to the med bay.'

Jones stood, staring hard at all views of the star fields on the monitors, waiting to see if anything came into his head, waiting to see if any *Bliss* input fell into his mind from long ago.

Nothing did.

He turned about to face *The Nova*'s crew: Max, Kad and Haine standing across the width of the room. No relief on their faces: relief had to play catch-up; a collection of anxious expressions faced him instead. Even Haine stood subdued and silent for once.

'Med bay,' Frank reminded, placing a guiding hand under his elbow. 'You're done. We're grateful, but you're done.'

Jones allowed himself to be led. He kept his eyes on the deck, on his own footfalls. He didn't care if they were grateful.

In the med bay Frank handed over a blanket, some water, made his excuses and left. Closing and locking the door behind him.

Frank brushed by his crew as he re-entered helm, brushed by them all without a glance, impatiently heading for the seat Jones had vacated. 'Haine, I want you to go down to holding and keep an eye on Nash and his kids. Kady: med bay. Max, go with her. Watch Jones.' Frank didn't look round, he stared at his fingertips held across the lip of the boards, at Aubrey's blood staining his nails.

'What are we going to do?' Haine asked again.

'I've got that covered,' Frank said. 'Now clear helm. All of you.'

Minutes later he stood speaking into the com mike, Recording flashing on the monitor right in front of him as he explained it all, from end to end, missing out only the parts he guessed he always would leave well alone. He pinched the flesh between his eyes and hit the pause key. 'You sure this can get through without being traced?' he asked Foley.

'We have safeguards. We still have *his* codes; we can encrypt it. It'll be fine.'

'And a spoken message is better?'

'Tactically,' Foley shrugged. 'You hear panic, you react to it.'

'And I sound panicked?' A rhetorical question, one Foley aimed another shrug at. Frank's gaze swept across the other monitors. It was still too easy to imagine. *The Nelson*'s dark brooding mass there, Aubrey's figure spinning and tumbling towards it.

Who bluffed a carrier, who the hell dared?

Frank gave helm's door a worried glance: Jones was locked up; Jones couldn't hear them. He looked back to the com and hit the record key. 'I know this is one hell of a favour. I know how much trouble we'll be bringing down on you but I promise to pay you back – only legally. No more seeping crates, no more backwater meetings with people I don't know a damn thing about. I'm done with all of that. I've told you everything I can think of; I'm going to shut up now. We're not transmitting our ID; we're about to move to a position that'll give us a few more destination options. You say "no", we'll clear out and leave you be.' Frank turned the link off, watching the monitor as the comp dealt with the message and dispatched it. 'You know this might be a mistake.' He drummed his fingers on the console. 'A Reaches planet might not be a good idea right now.'

'Can you think of anyone else we know who can come close to handling this?'

'A double jump if we get a "yes",' Frank reminded. 'You think Jones will make that?'

'He'll make it. He'll be tranked. He'll be fine.'

'He's sick, Foley. He could be very, very sick.'

'He'll make it,' Foley repeated firmly. 'He did us a favour, you think he's going to waste the chance to crow over that by dying now?' Foley pointed to a monitor. 'Looks like we got a fast answer.'

Jones flung himself free of the bed, surged upwards, hands clawing at nothing. His mind whirling, no idea where he was or how he'd got there. Frank grabbed for his wrists, the man's face now shadowed with stubble. He'd lost time, he didn't know how much. He coughed, struggling to get up, get away, but the man held him still. 'Listen to me. We have a destination. We have a safe port but we need to double jump.'

Jones pulled away; fought to be free.

'Stop it,' Frank yelled at him. Blueness washed over him, blue and calm and familiar, his damaged mind reaching out to it. The blueness was safe, you could trust it, you could let it in. He fought the impulse, fought it away. 'Kill me,' he blurted at the tattered edge of desperation. 'Kill me.'

'For God's sake,' came back at him.

You're not alone: he was sure he heard it. He was certain Frank had said it.

'Kill me,' he yelled urgently. 'Kill me.'

He heard a hypo hiss, heard Frank whisper, 'Go to sleep.' Just the way Milo used to say it a lifetime ago. 'Just go to sleep.'

Eight months ago . . .

Jones sat in Milo's tiny galley with his head in his hands. With The Marabell *over with, a sense of foreboding had overcome him. He'd needed to retreat for a while. He'd arrived at Milo's door like a battered stray. Returning to Milo, who understood about half of what he was. He'd sat and explained Frank Pak, his rescue, missing out great chunks of it, as always with a hollow feeling in his chest. His secrets, the things he refused to share with anyone, a weight he carried with him.*

Milo, as Milo would, investigated names, places, delving as deeply as he could. He'd developed a network of contacts he trusted as much as you could anyone you paid for information. Milo who sat down with him now and said in a subdued voice, 'Greeley's hired Pak. I hacked into Pak's account. There's a deposit. He's having refits done to his ship already. There are licence applications going through. Greeley's as good as turned the man into a bounty hunter. He'll be coming after you.'

The news left him swallowing down anguish. Pak, the man he never wanted to see again.

Milo's home was always a dim little place. The man hated bright light as if worried somehow Jones might see something terrible in his face or his eyes. 'It's time for you to stop this. There's no reason why you can't disappear. Get a new name, one you keep forever, and go and live a life somewhere far away.'

'I can't stop.'

'Why not?' Milo hadn't aged well. He couldn't have been more than fifty but he looked sixty, his face full of careworn lines and creases. He'd been given a Government job after The Bliss. He'd been tagged, followed around electronically all day and night. Five years along and the Government had loosened its grip a little. Milo had escaped, craving solitude, obscurity. No family, No ties. Not any more. 'Why not?' he repeated forcefully.

An old question, one that always caused a surge of resentment to rise. How dare the man ask him that, knowing what they'd done, seeing what they'd done? 'Why not? Listen to yourself. Why stop? That's the question you ought to ask. Why stop?'

'Because it's killing you.'

'They've killed me anyway,' Jones said sullenly.

'That's not true.'

No neurological fixes without massive reconstruction, that's what the man had explained. To fix him, they'd have to destroy his personality completely. That's if they could fix him at all. Milo wanted to start a fund, had wanted to ship him off to an illegal medical ship as fast as possible. Milo had no idea of all the things he was about to destroy. 'I'd rather hunt down The Bliss than live forever.'

Milo grabbed his wrist, hissed a frustrated sigh. 'For God's sake, just stop. Stay here. Stay with me. We'll keep moving, we'll travel around all the Reaches worlds. We could find your parents. Your family. You must want that.'

Must he? He sat back, sat away, seeking a little distance. He used the man for information, for the drugs Milo was still licensed to prescribe. He returned to him to rest when it all became too much to bear. Yet even so disillusioned he still kept going, always shifting forwards, always looking. The urge always came back tenfold. Only Milo knew how far he had come, only he knew what he was creating. He hadn't killed everybody from The Bliss, just as he hadn't killed Milo. Some had been added to Milo's tight little network of contacts, all of them ready and willing to seek a little forgiveness in whatever form that might take.

Jones' shoulders slumped. 'You need to find out about Pak's crew,' he said. 'I want to know everything about them. Anything I can use if I need to.' These days he always looked for exits long before he was even caged. He realized he'd always make mistakes but he'd grown into so much knowledge it terrified him. Combat, guns, weaponry, tactics. Not a soldier, no, someone more insidious and predatory. Everything he was was imperfect and fragmented because the science had been too new, too fresh. Sometimes it was there for him and sometimes not. Sometimes he was just a kid with nothing but fear in his head, a great gaping hole where the past he'd never had ought to be.

'Find out about Pak's crew,' he repeated, never adding that he already knew Pak himself through and through. Never adding anything at all about what he really was. Milo nodded, mournful, silent. Already judged, sentenced to this, to helping him unravel it all and set it right.

Jones went outside finally, sat in the decaying tractor shed, knowing Milo would leave this place soon. Move on. It was always safer to keep moving.

They crept out of the darkness just like they always did when he was near. Sniffing the air. Black-skinned, hard-bodied, he joined the wash of colour that hung over them, joining with the pack, ceasing to exist just for a little while, adopted, not alike, not akin. The dangerous violent pets Milo had found for him all the family he could bear.

PART FOUR
BLUE SKIES

CHAPTER 13

Things made no sense, none at all. The oversized bed made no sense, the glitter of the walls was a mystery, and the hum was missing. Ships hummed constantly, heating, ventilation, when they weren't moaning and groaning through jump. But this place was silent; save for *it*; for *its* grunts; for the soft little cooing noises *it* made. *It* hissed sweet-smelling breaths across his face as it leaned over him, its hands heaving his torso up to change his clothes, its fingers pushing his hair flat in clumsy little pats when it was done. *It* shaved his face with the chemicals that stank of antiseptic. But everything around him stank of antiseptic now. *It* did.

He thought *it* ought to be small, black-skinned and yellow-eyed, but no. He saw *it* clearly sometimes, in rare lucid moments between the numbness of sleep. He saw *its* long muzzle, *its* huge eyes, milky third eyelid snaking over now and again. Saw *its* fingers; the sparse thick hairs that grew between the grey skin of *its* knuckles.

One day he'd make sense of *it*. One day when he wasn't hitting his elbows into hard rock, when he wasn't scratching his flesh across walls that glittered, when he wasn't screaming, the darkness of shapes overhead, shapes that hurt him over and over and yelled for him to stop. He was on *The Bliss* surely, the resurrected *Bliss*. The men and women he wanted to find had found him first, their auras flaring ugly colours. The bruised colour of evil. He lashed out, and *it* screamed at him, flaring soft lilacs. *It* wasn't evil.

The chest of drawers was large, nut-brown and very, very shiny. Its drawers owned old-fashioned handles; hard to grasp, hard to pull, but *it* helped him. He'd learned *its* name was Tangle. He'd read it on the nametag on its collar. Tangle yanked open the last drawer down then leaned over its lip to watch him hunt through its contents.

Across the room under the foot of a huge, carved warrior of a door lay his abandoned food tray next to the pile of dirty clothes Tangle had insisted he shed as soon as he'd woken up. Tangle always bought him fresh clothing from this chest, so this chest was of particular interest. It was full of clothes, plastic wrapped and brand new, manufacturers' labels all across the bags. Designer gear: Pacy's, The Devil in Black, Form and Body Weaves.

In the next drawer up he found even more clothes, more expensive labels. Clothes in all sizes but one singular colour: black. Tangle always dressed him like a villain. He started to pull out the third drawer then paused, alerted by the sound of a key settling into a lock. A click, and the door opened, an equally darkly dressed man pushing it open just far enough to slip inside.

No need to panic, Jones told himself. This isn't *The Bliss* – no ship sounds, no ventilation fans, no hum. You're somewhere else.

The man bent down, bagging the dirty clothes into a clear plastic sack while at the same time sliding the empty food tray out through the open doorway with his foot. Done, he stared about the room for ten drawn-out seconds, a predatory, feral look on his face.

'Taking inventory again, are you? You going to do the bathroom next?' He gave a frosty smile. 'I'll call the doc and tell him you're moving around. Let's see what kind of foul mood you're in today.' He stepped out, the door closed, the key rattling again in the old-fashioned lock.

Jones stretched a finger up to touch the furrows in his brow. It was all very, very odd.

'Bathroom?' The other door in the room was smaller, less ornate, and stood close to the head of the bed. Jones held out his arm for Tangle to take. 'Bathroom, Tangle.'

Inside the bathroom, he turned to shut the creature out. He got a poke in the belly for his trouble, the creature's lips curling to show off pink gums and the threat of long, pointed canines. 'Not alone.' Jones rubbed at his middle. 'Nothing alone. I remember that part. I remember.' He looked around. The bathroom's walls were covered in the same glowing brick as the bedroom. A head and a sink lay in two of its corners, a shower stall owned a third.

No bathtub. That was significant. If only he could remember why.

Above the sink there was a wooden cabinet. He padded over to it and opened it up. No soap, no deodorant, no towels; there were no supplies inside at all – but he'd known that. He closed the cabinet and stared into its mirrored door, peering hard into his own hugely dilated eyes, at skin so sallow it looked paper white, at cheekbones stained with murky splotches.

Very damned attractive.

He shot a hand out, bracing himself on the sink's edge, vertigo like a sudden strong push of wind against his back. The little creature dashed in and held him upright, had the nerve even to reach up one long arm and stroke his unruly hair flat. Jones closed his eyes, the blackness before his lids seeming to swill back and forth.

He lost minutes resting there, shored up by alien hands. He'd been sick, he remembered that much. *The Nova* came back, the sparseness of her, her fawn-painted corridors turning battleship-grey where the paint had run out. He thought he ought to still be on board her, not *The Bliss* at all. Instead he had a blue sparkling bedroom full of lavish wood with a mosaic floor, drawers full of expensive clothes and, oddly, a very frugal bathroom with no bathtub.

A body of water was too dangerous, the notion came to him abruptly – a second-hand thought, an old thought. You could drown yourself; you could, if, all in all, you'd decided you'd be better off dead. If you could brace the door closed somehow, even if you were being watched by hidden optics, you might just have enough time to kill yourself. Unhappy people did such things, frightened people.

Something else niggled, a worm-like thought. No windows. Neither room owned a single one. So the room had been designed to be a cell from the get-go.

Jones held still, locking his muscles out so completely he felt rocklike, immovable. He could hear noises outside.

'Mr Jones?' Someone called him politely. 'Mr Jones, would you come out here, please.'

Jones shuffled back to the door, Tangle pulling it wide. People stood in his bedroom: the tall, feral-faced man from earlier stood waiting with a shorter man. A man who wore long robes of vivid crisp greens, his grizzled angular face expressionless. Next to him, wearing a badly cut mud-coloured suit, stood a rotund man with heavy, flaccid jowls.

Jones dared to take three steps back into his bedroom.

'There you are. How are you feeling today?' the rotund man asked.

Foreboding came with the question, apprehension. Jones backed up again, almost tripping over the creature at his heel. 'What *day*? I don't know what day it is.'

'Well, now,' the rotund man said. 'Let's see. If you prefer to use standard Earth calc and not the local variation, it's Tuesday.'

'Month?'

'January.'

Jones shook his head. 'I don't know who you are.'

'I'm Doctor Meeks. I've been looking after you. Why don't you sit down for me, so I can take a look at you.'

Jones took three more steps into the room and wavered. Through the out-leading doorway he could see daylight, golden daylight steaming downward onto an expanse of blue-and-white mosaic tiles. Expensive gilt-edged furniture stood out there, set in clusters. Art lined more glistening blue-brick walls. He checked back to the dour, grizzled man in the green silk: rich man's clothes, a rich man's house.

The doctor waited. 'Please,' he motioned to the bed. 'You're having some memory lapses. They're only temporary; once all the extra meds have cleared your system you'll be fine. You've been on the equivalent of a seven-day drunk, Mr Jones, or at least something very much like it.' The doctor smiled.

Was that funny, should he laugh? Jones smiled instead, his muscles straining to hold it.

The doctor stepped towards him.

Jones shied back and drew his hands into fists. 'No. No. No.' Meeks raised his palms in surrender. 'Please, there's no need for that. You know where you are. You know you're safe. You're reacting instead of thinking. Too much adrenaline's getting in the way.'

He'd bolted before, Jones knew it, and he'd done some damage too, certainly to himself.

'You've been very, very ill,' Meeks added. 'Do you remember? Do you remember landing here?'

The sound of an engine came back, shouts across the darkness of a dock; a big house above on the crest of a rise, lit from below so its walls loomed heavy and ominous. Lots of men with guns strapped to their hips flashed by, com-links in their ears. The air smelled of damp greenery and salt, and there was a rushing sound as the engine's howl died: the sound of an ocean. 'Yes.'

'Then you *must* remember me?'

Meeks' eyes hid themselves amongst the folds of his podgy face. A face that had watched him, lips making humming noises at comp units, thick fingers adjusting drips with translucent tails. 'Yes.'

'Then please – will you sit?' Meeks gestured to the bed again and smiled, his piggy eyes all but disappearing. 'Please.'

Jones edged back to the bed. He sank down slowly. He heard the rich man sigh, heard the doctor set his case down, heard it click as the lock gave. All the time he stared through the open door into that magical sunlight. There was a huge, transparent dome in the centre of the ceiling out there; through it he could see the faded rips of clouds scudding across blue skies. Something from *The Bliss* latched on to that image. Data tumbled into his head, followed by a flash of stats. Theory he could find the middle of. Blue skies were blue because—

'Jones?' A hand fell across his wrist; Frank crouching down close by his side.

Only *this* Frank didn't look the same as the one Jones remembered. This Frank had been scrubbed clean: his skin tanned, his hair neatly trimmed. And this Frank mouthed words as if he couldn't stop himself, words mirroring *The Bliss*'s implanted knowledge.

Blue skies: white light scattered by dirt in the atmosphere, blue light scattering the most— More wanted out, the detail, the mechanics, but Jones lurched back, his own shock shattering *The Bliss*'s input.

'Settle down.' This Frank said firmly as if this Frank knew exactly what had made him recoil. 'Settle,' he repeated. He rose up. 'Doctor, have you got that scanner working? He's more confused than bad-tempered today. He's going to behave.'

Meeks busied himself; pulling a portable med scanning unit from his case and attaching it to a monitor he set down on the bedside table. He waved the scanner's wand slowly over Jones' chest. The man making all too familiar humming noises as Jones' body lit up the screen in vivid colours, slices of his lungs depicted in graduated shades of green, red and blue. Meeks thumbed the wand's controls, making its scan delve deeper and deeper, its internal comp searching for anomalies.

Not a pleasant experience to see your own insides examined slice after tiny slice. Jones screwed up his face in disgust and looked away.

'The sucking worms are still active,' the doctor said. 'They have four stages of development but unfortunately are only vulnerable to drug therapy during two. You miss your meds, you're at risk.' Meeks made a tsking sound. 'Please, try to stay calm.' His piggy-paw landed on Jones' shoulder; Jones' heart now a thundering mass of aggravated muscle on the monitor. 'How much do you remember of the last few days?'

'Bits. Pieces.' Jones motioned to the creature, now settled into the far corner of the room, 'The– ' he floundered.

'It's called a himmer,' the doctor said helpfully. 'Him. Her. Apparently it's hard to tell the difference, externally at least. Best to call it an *it*. They're native to Corrella, where I believe they're a popular pet. Exporting them without a licence is illegal but I believe most stations have a few in residence. You've never seen one before?'

'No. Never . . . I have other pets.'

Meeks leaned in, Jones recoiling as the man's thick fingers darted from flesh to scanner to realign the machine and back again. Meeks brushed one finger far more leisurely over Jones' forehead close to where a bruise sat, and Jones tensed, an ardent sense of anxiety twisting up inside his belly.

Meeks' palm raised his chin, two fingers sliding across his cheekbone. 'Is there any discomfort here? Any sinus pain.'

Jones jerked back. Meeks flared a colour, an ugly brown-yellow haze drifting off his clothes. Meeks touched his face again, and Jones surged to his feet.

'Don't,' Frank barked out.

'It's all right.' Meeks patted at the air and backed hurriedly away. 'I'm done. I'm all done.' He stepped clear, turned off the wand, turned off the scanner and began to stow his equipment back into its case.

'Sit down,' Frank ordered shortly, barring Jones' way forward. 'Sit down. Now.'

Jones frowned, unsettled all over again by *this* Frank. He sank back down, staring at the wall, not at Meeks leaking colour, not at Frank, whose calm blues seeped a red angry glow.

'Do you think he'll be able to travel?' Frank asked as Meeks clicked his case closed.

'With precautions. I wouldn't take him through jump conscious, but a deep trank ought to be fine if he's monitored closely. He's still not well. The fact is I doubt he'll ever be entirely healthy considering his other problems. He does seem more alert; perhaps you ought to try speaking to him again.'

People left, the doctor, the rich man, the techs. Not the himmer:

it remained in its corner. Once the door closed Frank pulled a chair over. He perched on its edge and leaned forward. 'How are you feeling?'

Too confusing a question. Jones blinked, counting each: one, two, three blinks. 'I'm fine.'

'Good.' Frank's face muscles stiffened, the man seemingly intent on trying to hang on to one unvarying expression. 'Do you know where we are?'

Jones shook his head. 'Not exactly.'

'We're on a planet called Telemar. We're safe. Mallin is an old friend if mine.'

The word Telemar caused more information to tumble through Jones' head, a useless list of stats lying in wait. He grimaced, digging his nails into his palms to push it away. 'The rich man?'

'Yes, the rich man. He has a large set-up here, a lot of security. His house is fortified. This is a Reaches planet. Reaches mentality: if you don't guard it, somebody will steal it. Is all this getting through loud and clear?'

Jones nodded, trying to stay focused, worrying about *blue skies*, about Frank mouthing the stats in his head, but a conversation about blue skies didn't seem likely. There was nothing in Frank's attitude to suggest one might appear.

Ignore it. It'll go away. It'll go away when I do. That would be sensible and that would be Frank.

'You stay civil, you don't rile the techs,' Frank went on sternly. 'You don't collect any more bruises. There's a tech on guard out side your door at all times. There are more on every out-leading door and others scattered all over the island. That's where we are, on an island. It's in sight of the mainland, but I wouldn't recommend the swim: the water's full of nasties, and I don't mean bacteria. I mean big things that bite.'

'Your friend's a body trader. A slaver,' Jones said faintly, all those little clues adding up just then: the windowless room, no bathtub, the himmer, all the techs on guard, the fact that here was a rich, rich man, living out in the middle of nowhere. 'A bad man.' His cheeks started to burn. That wasn't a new thought, just residue from conversations he could no longer clearly recall. Jones shook his head, rubbed a palm across his forehead 'I've said that before?'

'Yes. Yes, you have. So you already know my answer. I didn't have a lot of choice when it came to the help.'

'But you don't *like* the help?' He got a harsh look for that, Frank's eyes flickering over the walls. 'Is he listening to us, watching us?' Frank shook his head, but his fingers throttled the arms of his chair. Jones frowned. 'What happened to Nash?'

'He's below. Mallin has holding facilities.'

'Are Durham and Hodge all right?'

'Yes.'

'Is there a war going on?'

A pause before Frank answered. 'There's been nothing on the news feeds.'

'And we've been here for over a week?'

'Yes.'

'So you must be in contact with Greeley by now.'

'We're on a wait-and-see.' Frank eased himself stiffly back into the chair's thick maroon cushions, uncurling his fingers from around the chair's wooden arms, his attempt at looking at ease, looking anything but. 'I need to know something, Jones. Do you know the specific names of the carriers and frigates this revolution intends to target?'

'Doesn't Nash know that?

'No.'

'Have you tried all the chemical ways of asking him? Did you try that with me, is that why I can't remember everything? Did your friend want to try? He is what this is all about, isn't he? You don't want to know, he does? Has he tried asking me without your knowledge? Did he ask Meeks to help? Meeks who's just a little odd, wouldn't you say? A little too happy to paw his patients.' No shock appeared on Frank's face, not a jot of it. 'Are you going to tell me if Meeks is a friend of yours too?'

'We never left you alone with him.'

Jones frowned, he glanced to the himmer.

'We never left you alone,' Frank repeated. 'You attacked the man twice while you where half out of your head . . .' He trailed off. 'Do you think I'm too stupid to work this out? People are colours. I'm blue, right? So tell me, Jones, what the hell kind of colour is Meeks?'

Blue skies echoed, clear and loud, blood roaring through Jones' ears, his vision narrowing right down, his body spiralling through a rush of pure shock as Frank sat in his chair and calmly watched.

What colour was Meeks? An evil, ugly bruised colour. The colour he'd shot dead twice over.

He kept his mouth closed, time sliding by, Frank's steady gaze unwavering. So he'd ignore *blue skies* if Frank couldn't. He'd deny it all. He'd sit in perfect silence until it decided to go the hell away.

'Nash doesn't know anything,' Frank said finally. 'He was asked, he doesn't know. His kids don't know. All I'm asking is what you know. My friend has ships heading into Alfa; all he really needs to know is which shipping lanes might be in danger.'

Jones hunched his toes into the cold of the tiles beneath his feet, concentrating on the chill to keep his expression dispassionate. 'There are three ships patrolling Alfa with Reaches-born admirals: *The Saint Claude, The Galmont* and *The Sierra*. Out here you have *The Amity* and *The Burbank*.'

Jones peered suspiciously at the walls. 'Does your friend import to Alfa? How would he do that? How come he doesn't get caught?'

'That's enough.' Frank shifted awkwardly in his chair.

'Who does he know? Who's he connected to?' Jones clenched his fists and took a fast breath. 'Do you trust your friend? Your Reaches friend?'

A gun on Frank's hip, but no boots on his feet, soft shoes instead. He wore a loose shirt and trousers. Not his clothes: too expensive, too modern. Frank, it seemed, was accepting all kinds of favours.

Frank rose out of his seat in a rush, tipping a cushion off it he didn't bother to retrieve. 'I trust him. I've known him since I was a kid. My ship's on resupply. We're planning an exit here – do you understand that? We can't go home. Even when we get rid of you, we can't go home. We won't make it that far; the damned revolution will target my ship. I'll be calling in favours everywhere I can. My crew will be doing the same. Any help we can get we're going to take.'

'Greeley will fix it,' Jones returned levelly. 'That's what he does. He fixes things. He'll get you home, if that's where you want to go.'

'Really?' Frank said with a disgusted huff. 'I can't wait to see how he intends to do that.' He headed for the door.

Blue skies echoed, but Jones didn't say a word. He gripped the bed linen in two tight fists. The door's lock clicked over, and he lost a shattered breath. Too much, too fast: not on a ship, days on a planet and in a place he didn't trust. Tangle pushed one downy paw into his fist and held his hand, the creature standing by him like some giant breathing teddy bear wanting nothing but to give him comfort. Jones unravelled its fingers and patted Tangle's head. 'It's all right, you don't have to do that. That's a lie they taught you. You don't have to lie to me.'

CHAPTER 14

It might help if you stopped thinking like a sane person, Frank told himself as he walked across the hallway outside. Stop trying to make solid sense of it, stop trying to make it neat and clean. It isn't. Jones isn't like anybody else, by his own admission; don't expect anything around him to be – including yourself.

He'd become a part of *The Bliss* experiment, he'd worked that out in the week he'd had to consider it. He'd become part of the side effects the revolution surely wanted to tease out of Jones' head, all the faults and flaws and downright lunacy. Telepathy, visions and a whole lot of other bizarre mental tricks he didn't even want to consider.

So think like a lunatic but still concentrate on the only two important things left, he told himself: getting paid and getting clear of the whole damned mess.

He called Greeley daily from the little comp room he headed towards now. He always asked the man on duty inside to leave – as if he thought his privacy actually meant something. Mallin definitely possessed more than one comp room, Frank was certain of it. He was also certain Mallin knew second by second what was happening in every room of his house. Comp tech filled this particular room, cameras were pitched on every hill and valley of an island you could walk in a day if you chose to – and Frank had twice over, trying to think a way clear of the mess he'd found himself in.

Today he found the room empty. He sat down at the boards, tapping at the keys, sending a brief encrypted message Greeley's way as was his habit. *Kid's health's still improving*, the bare bones of this one.

With his message sent, he reconfigured the com. 'Foley?'

Humming returned over the link. Usually he got a tuneless whistle, but today Foley was in a humming mood. 'Yes?'

'How's the ship?'

'Last time I checked she's still under me.' More humming. 'Yes, just checked again. Still there. Nice view of a planet, pretty to begin with, a little boring now.' More humming, the painfully tuneless kind.

'How's Kady?'

'Checking everything over for the four-hundredth time. Being on planet was fun, she said, but checking everything is infinitely more fascinating. How's Jones?'

'Better. A lot better.'

'I hope he hit the doctor.'

'Not this time.'

'Shame. Did you ask the question?'

'Yes. Five ships are likely.'

A sharp out-breath followed. 'God Almighty.'

'Agreed.' Frank blew out a breath himself and swiped a hand through his hair.

'You still there?' Foley asked.

'Yes.'

'Just relax. Everything's fine.' Odd how Foley didn't sound either relaxed or fine himself. Everything might be falling apart, but why worry about it? Just hum and play make-believe.

'I just sent another message Greeley's way. No reply to the last three yet.'

'Give it time. There's no point in panicking over silence.' A pause, and Foley lowered his voice as if he thought that somehow might stop them from being overheard. 'Remember the ship's ready, Frank. We can exit. Boards are clean of Nash's lockout codes; door locks are working. Stores are logged, and the place is clean. It's nice knowing people who can clean a boat right down to the forensic level.'

Frank let out a derisive little snort. 'Seems we came to the right place.'

'Yes, we did,' Foley said firmly. 'Tell me when you get an ETA from Greeley. I've already picked out plenty of places we can go to lie low for a while.'

'You're repeating yourself.' He was, Frank was too, their conversations were always echoes of themselves, day after day the same fears expressed as simply as possible.

'I'm only repeating myself to make sure you're hearing me.'

Frank smiled grimly. 'I'm hearing you. You want me to start calling this thing a *holiday*.' He paused and glanced to the door. 'I've got company, I'll call you again later.' He keyed the link closed and swung his chair about. He forced a wider smile, Mallin coming in and leaning into the boards. You didn't get much time alone at Mallin's; you got trailed, you got tracked.

'I've got that info you wanted about those military boats,' Frank said, getting into it all even though Mallin had likely already heard every word out of Jones' mouth. Mallin, who had one of those faces smiles didn't like, settled into one of the other seats in front of the monitors, fidgeting with the green silk robes about his legs as he listened. During their last encounter, years past on Beta Station, he'd worn a modern, up-to-date suit. Before that, as a cereal farmer Mallin on 'Sell had worn threadbare trousers and ragged, cuffless shirts.

How did the man import illegals onto Alfa, where the checks were triple-fold? Was that a clue to just how far down the line the Calders' revolution had secretly spread, right onto station, right into Admin, right into the suits checking on the suits.

'I'll inform my people of the specific risks,' Mallin said, his expression turning thoughtful. He fiddled with keys then, tapping at them absently with his manicured nails to change the displays on the screens. He didn't say another word. They did silences, great swathes of them while both of them twitched. Frank scratched his head and self-consciously fiddled with keys himself. He changed a monitor's view. Now it showed a clearing where native broad-leafed trees dipped low over a pond of blue water. Telemar was a good-looking planet, a D-class due to a mess of tectonic plates all merrily rubbing against each other. Low buildings and farming only, thank you. The revolution might call that a lie – no earthquakes, just the Government trying to keep places like Telemar sparsely populated.

Frank hit another key. Now the monitor showed a stand of different, taller, needle-leaved trees, which swayed back and forth close to the flat, dark circle of the landing dock. No shuttles sat on the dockside today. Traffic passed back and forth frequently, but Frank had no idea whose ships they were: Mallin's, a contact's? Things were loaded for certain: small boxes, small crates, illegal something or others certainly.

One more key strike and on the monitor a boat bobbed lazily next to a landing jetty. No pleasure vessel, this boat had a gun turret and a missile launcher very visibly attached.

THE NEMESIS LIST

'I'm waiting for a reply from Greeley.' Frank forced the words into the depth of silence. 'We should be out of your way soon. Sorry I keep throwing your man out, I need some privacy.' That felt like a dangerous admission, and a rather pointless one.

Mallin smiled. 'I told you the house was yours when you arrived,' he returned smoothly. 'I meant it.'

'Of course,' Frank returned in the same easy tone. 'Jones' info might be sound. He seemed a lot better today. No fighting, no heading for the exit.'

'Yes, I saw that for myself.'

They did those too: curt little answers whenever they came close to who owed what to whom. In days gone by Mallin's crates had seeped all over *The Nova*'s hold. Frank had been lied to years and years ago about what he'd been carrying but he'd known the man since childhood and he'd forgiven him. He'd said so sincerely enough. He'd known Mallin was heading into deep, dark places, but only a fool threw those kinds of friends away. The sensible just stayed well clear of them until the day they ran out of choices.

Frank cleared his throat. In front of him a screen died then flickered back to life, the comp taking over to flash up a warning. There was an encrypted message coming in from a C. Greeley.

Greeley never gave any clues of his location; his messages over the last few days had grown more and more infrequent, containing little but acknowledgements that Frank's own communications had been received. This message had Frank rising from his chair even before he'd read it to its end. He looked to Mallin, hoping again that all the man's affectations were false, that somewhere beneath them all was the man he'd known long, long ago.

'I don't run,' Mallin said levelly. 'I built this place so I'd never have to run.'

259

'I need to get my crew out,' Frank returned, glancing back to the screen again. 'This thing may be too big to fight.'

Jones uncurled, his feet getting wound up in discarded, rumpled bed linen. 'Dammit. Dammit.' He kicked out, kicked himself free, staring up at the glitter of the ceiling under the wash of amber wall lights, his body wound tight and aggravated.

Noise intruded: thumps and bangs from beyond the thick door, interspersed with muffled voices.

He sat up, listening harder, watching the himmer hurry over to the door. It gave two quick slaps on the wood – its usual signal to the tech on duty that it wanted out. Then it stood back and waited. And waited.

More noise from outside, clearer words shouted out. *Half-hour wait on the weather.*

Jones slid down the bed's length, the himmer hurrying over to help him as soon as he stood up. He didn't slap on the door when he reached it, he pounded on it with his fist – and that hurt, hurt him all the way down to his backbone. 'Your damned teddy bear wants out,' he yelled, and that hurt too: pain stabbed across his temples, seared across his cheekbones. He rattled the door handle. 'Can't you hear me?'

No reply. The door didn't shift, no key rattled in the lock. And there was silence outside now: no thuds, no voices. Jones fretted, worried he might have dreamed it. His senses were screwed up, screwed with; his sense of reality was floundering, his sense of time didn't exist. There were no clocks in his luxurious cell, no window views to judge the time of day from.

Tangle banged on the door with both fists, chattering now and starting to panic. Jones fought the urge to panic himself. Maybe the creature was off duty, maybe there was a second himmer waiting to take over. Maybe it was something that mundane, that everyday. Or maybe it was something wholly terrible.

Jones hit the door again; for twenty seconds two sets of fists pounding away at the wood. Tangle grew frantic, Jones matching the creature's rising frenzy.

At last the lock clicked, the door started to open. Tangle rushed through the widening gap, startling the man on duty. The gaunt-faced tech lost his grip on the door, and it swung wide. Jones squinted out into the hallway, blinded by the glare of bright white light. Men dressed in hooded rain gear stood in groups, dripping water onto the blue mosaic. Men wiping mud and water off equipment with wadded handfuls of white paper towel. Black, shiny crates stood end to end mid-floor, their lids pitched open. Other smaller boxes stood stacked close by them, cables trailing out of their sides like a chaos of escaping snakes.

'What's happening?'

The tech pulled at the door for an answer. Jones stuck his foot in the way – not a smart move with naked toes, not smart leaning into a door being pulled closed either. He stepped forward, stuck his whole body in the way and got an ill-tempered glower out of the already irritated tech. The even grumpier-looking men outside glanced their way. Maybe twenty stood out there, four to a piece of gear, some checking up to the dome every now and then. A dome with a torrent of water flooding down its seamless curves.

'Mr Harrison,' the door tech called.

Max appeared out of the throng. He stood hooded and soaking wet, a smudge of mud dark across his nose. 'Get back inside, Jones. Now.'

'What's going on?'

'Nothing's going on, all right?' Max, it seemed, had cloned Frank's expression, that impenetrable non-event of an expression.

There had been a discussion some time, Jones felt sure, some agreements made on just how to treat the cargo if you ever had the misfortune to meet him again. His sullenness got loose: confused childish emotions making him cross his arms and pitch his weight into the doorframe. 'No, it's not *all right*. So why don't you take some time and explain—' Max didn't bother; he grabbed two fistfuls of shirt and heaved Jones backwards, shunting him roughly into the room. The door pulled closed with a heavy slam right in front of his nose.

His childish rage ran riot then. It was the drugs and the isolation; Jones knew it. He wasn't whole; he wasn't in control. For ten long seconds he stood there pulling himself back together, getting himself back in order, sorting through the anger and knowing none of it was real. None of it was worth a damn.

The himmer rushed back in, the door slamming closed after it too. It rattled a pill cup up at him urgently. 'For God's sake,' Jones snapped, snatching the cup. 'Was that it? Was that what all the fuss was about?' The creature didn't like being yelled at, it cowered, its bottom lip juddering and shaking. 'So you're upset. Hard luck. Hard damned luck on you.' Jones doubted it understood every word he said, he was damned sure it couldn't speak. Dumb and mute, it did have an uncanny way of making him feel instantly guilty. He quietened down. He sat on the bed's edge and took his meds. He rubbed at the himmer's head then, apologizing to it silently with each slow stroke as it sat on the floor by his side. Tangle began to coo happily; and Tangle, it seemed, had a very apt name: tangles aplenty in its thick brown coat, an odd thing considering it always reeked of antiseptic. Jones bit his lip and sat forward, working at one of the tight little knots in the creature's coat with his fingernails, his actions growing intense. Groom it yourself, care for it, bond with it. It was pure manipulation.

More noises intruded from outside: yells and door slams. Twenty-minute wait on the weather, Jones recalled. He crawled across the bed, grabbed a pillow and cradled it under his head. A house full of techs out there, and he hadn't even the energy left to try to find out what the hell they were doing.

'Jones', the word was urgent, the shake at his shoulder the same. 'Jones?'

Jones snapped his eyes open. More time lost, and every time he woke up his mind raced to catch up again. 'What . . . what is it?'

Frank loomed over him. 'Greeley's ship just entered the system. We've got maybe half an hour before he sets down. I want you up and ready. You got that?'

Frank dropped news like a bomb, Frank who stood there with a long bloody gash dripping blood down his cheek. A gash Jones sat up and peered hard at. 'What the hell have you been doing?'

Frank shifted uneasily. 'Greeley's ship was attacked before he reached his out-point. I doubt he got tracked through the gate but likely he's being looked for. I've had a few precautions set in case my crew needs a fast exit. That's all you need to know. Now get up and get ready.'

Jones did just that. The himmer helped, finding him a jacket and some boots while an increasingly agitated and curt Frank harried it along. 'It's time. Move,' he said finally.

The himmer dashed over, its little furry shoulder braced under his hand as Jones moved again, feet slewing, strength coming and going in waves as he made his way through the door.

'Corner of the hallway to your right,' curt Frank said.

Jones turned that way, glanced up to the sky beyond the ceiling dome and saw darkness.

Across the mosaic in the further corner an ornate games table stood surrounded by chairs. Frank motioned to the seats. 'You sit there,' he said. 'You stay quiet.'

He sat down; the himmer fussed, bringing him a cushion to set behind his back before it sank down to the floor by his side. To his other side a dark shape loomed: Haine. 'You move and I'll flatten you,' he said as Frank headed towards another off-leading door. 'You got that, lab rat?' The himmer glared up at the man, bared its teeth and growled. 'Same to you,' Haine growled back.

Jones heaved down a steadying breath and slid his hand down the himmer's head, stroking at fur that wasn't so full of tangles any more. 'We'll just sit,' he said more to it than to Haine. 'We'll just sit and be quiet.'

CHAPTER 15

The Greeley Frank had first met on Almerdia had possessed a wide, wide smile and jovial brown eyes. He'd been dressed in expensive clothes: classic, simple fashion draped over a tall, sparse frame. He'd always had a laugh in his voice; his hands flying about in effusive open gestures. Greeley casting himself as your favourite uncle, every move he made saying *trust me*.

The Greeley on Mallin's monitors in the comp room still appeared tall and well dressed but not quite so elegant. Every step he made now was an awkward brace of his weight against a long black cane.

As soon as the man's shuttle had touched down, lights on Mallin's comp boards had flashed red, a complement of extra cameras splitting one of the main screens. A myriad of views of Greeley's shuttle had appeared, followed by images of the man's black-uniformed security techs who had exited then surrounded the vessel on all sides. Now Greeley himself was making his appearance; plus limp, plus cane, plus, in his free hand, a small silver case that swung to and fro with his every clumsy footfall.

Frank ground his teeth, listening to the cackle over his earpiece.

Mallin sat next to him, speaking into the com, sending instructions to the techs on the monitors and those concealed elsewhere. Mallin's techs' response to a crisis was a well-rehearsed routine. They talked in low, calm voices, now and again breaking into streams of garbled code even though the com's broadcasts were already encrypted.

'Are we going to let him bring that case up here?' Max, standing at Frank's shoulder, leaned in to magnify Greeley and his ominous little container.

'He wouldn't bring anything up here that'll risk his cargo,' Frank replied.

The running commentary of Greeley's progress by Mallin's tech remained detailed even though the cameras captured his every stride up the sloping walkway towards the house. He was passing Marker One, Marker Two. Frank had no idea where those markers lay or what they signified. He must have passed them by a dozen times and never known it.

More garbled code came over the com.

'Ten paces away, Frank,' Mallin said. 'You'd better get moving.'

Frank hurried out into the hallway. He stood mid-floor as Greeley entered. The man paused and gave him a perfunctory nod in greeting. Greeley's cheeks appeared hollow, ruddy, his forehead dotted with bruises. A white bandage lay wrapped around the wrist holding the case; streaks of dirt caking the arms and cuffs of his long pale-grey coat. No warm smile was evident today; no jovial brown eyes either, just a grim, tight mouth and sharp, precise little glances that took in the wide room. The armed men Mallin had stationed close to every out-leading doorway of particular interest.

'What's in the case, Greeley?' Frank asked.

Greeley's attention locked onto Jones in his dark little niche. 'Take it. There's nothing dangerous inside it.' Greeley had a mid-timbre voice, never hard, never soft; there wasn't a trace of unease within it. He surrendered the case over to a tech without a care.

The tech took the case outside, the door closing with a soft thump behind Greeley's back. 'My cargo – you said he was fit to travel?'

'He's set when you are.'

'Is Bernard Aubrey here? You didn't mention him in your messages.'

'That's because he's dead.'

'He's dead?' No alarm lifted Greeley's voice.

'You lied to me,' Frank added bitterly.

Greeley nodded slowly. 'Yes, I did. Now tell me everything's that's happened and let me see how much of the truth you've gathered up.'

The man had changed; it wasn't Frank's imagination, Greeley now reserved, pulled in tight physically and emotionally. He wanted his cargo moved to the seat across the table from him. No expression crossing his face as he stared at the crown of Jones' head. Jones kept his head down, mesmerized, it seemed, by the sheen of the tabletop. Greeley felt around blindly for a switch on his cane. It folded automatically, its handle retracting, one length of it sliding neatly into the other. He set the shortened version on the tabletop, absently beginning to rattle it back and forth between his fingertips. Still he looked only at Jones, apparently waiting for his cargo to dare to lift his head and look him in the eye.

Frank settled himself to the man's right; Mallin's voice a loud distraction in his earpiece. 'The dock's settled. There shouldn't be any interruptions. There are no explosives in the case. We're taking inventory.'

Frank waited for Greeley's attention to shift back to him. Still the man's expression didn't alter: no emotion, no relief. Frank cleared his throat. 'I'll start with the day we picked your cargo – special delivery from Captain Hetta Combes.'

He told the barest bones of it all, leaving out details, wondering all the time how much Greeley really knew about Jones. Thinking it might have been sensible to have added a few details about all the kid's little add-ons as a forewarning. That's if Greeley could have found a way to make the improbable sound convincing

Frank added his knowledge of *The Bliss*. He missed out visions of data, of dark bodies dying in an airless hold. Only halfway done, curiosity took hold. He leaned back in his chair and said blithely. 'So, what colour are you?'

'Sorry?' Greeley said, blank-faced.

'There anything you left out about your cargo, Greeley? Anything you need to add?' Another mystified expression.

Jones shook his head, his face so stricken Frank huffed a breath. So there the truth was. Jones had lied or buried it all somehow. With all those tricks he could do, maybe that hadn't been too hard a task.

'None of my damned business,' he said tartly in Jones' direction. He wanted no part in it. Any of it. Greeley had lied; he didn't owe the man the truth. He doubted he'd be able to get it all out straight even if he wanted to tell it. He kept talking, adding on Nash's intervention and Aubrey's demise.

Greeley passed him a grave look. 'I had no idea how deeply Aubrey was involved,' he said, those mid-timbre tones gaining a harder edge.

'But you knew what was happening?' Frank said. 'That's why you hired us?'

'I'd heard rumours, yes. I heard there was an investigation going on into Alexander Calder. I was told to look for inconsistencies in my associates.' Greeley took a slow deep breath. 'But all of that's immaterial now. We have to deal with the present situation and we need to do it quickly.' Lord, he really did sound like one of the Government suits on the news feeds just then, the affectations, the inflections. Vote for me, I'll keep you safe.

'Who attacked your ship?' Frank asked.

'The Confederation. I would guess. It was dealt with. It's of no concern now,' The man's restlessness said otherwise.

'Is there anything else inbound?'

'I wouldn't dare to guess.' Greeley held Frank's gaze for a very firm five seconds. 'I think it's time you checked the status of your bank account. I've made a money transfer. I need you to verify everything's as it should be before we continue.' He paused; across the hallway the door had opened, the tech and the case returning.

'It's full of ID chips, an ID insertion machine,' the tech reported, walking across the hallway. He set the case down on the tabletop. 'Highly illegal tech.'

'For safety's sake,' Greeley said. 'You and your crew are too well known now to be able to travel anywhere without drawing attention to yourselves.'

Frank glanced to Jones, Jones who had told him Greeley knew how to fix things, *really* fix things.

'For the sake of clarity, Mr Pak.' Greeley said firmly. 'I'd like you to check the status of your bank account, right away.'

Frank returned to Mallin's little comp room. Max and Haine waited for him inside, com-links in their ears. They'd heard everything. They already had his bank logo on the comp: a pyramid, corner set, in blue and black. Frank leaned in, allowing the console's reader to gather up his transmitted ID code. If the bank hadn't caught up with his multi-global, multi-station wanderings an estimated wait signal would flash up, telling him how long he might have to starve to death or to run from his creditors. Banking updates flashed back and forth constantly, but still whole packets of data often got mislaid for days. Not today: *Standby* flashed up.

'So how much did we make?' Haine leaned in too, his face glowing. He'd obviously decided today was going to be about as good as a day got. 'This mess better have paid us some decent compensation.'

Frank checked the monitor and heard his own throat click around a dry, dry swallow. Zeros marched before his eyes, zeros that ought to have little smirks attached, that ought to be making rude gestures and calling him an utter fool. His next thought was that they were in serious trouble; his thought after that was that Haine was about to do something very, very stupid. 'I'll deal with this,' he said, making sure he said it without a trace of panic.

Greeley had men on the dock, he had a ship in orbit, he could do damage and he was Government, and Mallin, his old, good friend, might well have Confederation contacts for all he knew. The two of them might just start a war between themselves.

He backed up. 'Max, I need you to check this. It must be some kind of error. Those transfers are never reliable.' He backed right into the open door with a thud of his boot heel. Very together, very damned calm and collected. He raised his hands to both men when they moved to follow him. 'I want you to stay here,' he aimed that at Max, who nodded, blue eyes overly wide and bright.

Max folded a hand around Haine's arm. 'We'll check with the bank, we'll find out what happened.'

Frank made sure he closed the door behind him when he left. He walked back across the hallway.

Please God, let it be an error.

'I'm bankrupt,' he pitched across the room. All heads snapped his way. 'I think it might be a mistake. The bank's messed up.'

'I'm afraid it hasn't,' Greeley said calmly.

Frank pressed his tongue to the roof of his mouth. No outbursts, no rages, he warned himself, not with Haine in the comp room, not with Mallin listening to every word they said.

For once Greeley wore an earnest, almost apologetic expression. 'I need you to continue to carry my cargo. It's likely I'll be kidnapped or killed returning to Beta. It'll be safest for Jeven if he disappears with you. I'm about to make you a far less visible target than I'll ever be.'

Frank's attention slid over to Jones. He sat white-faced, silent, staring at the tabletop again. Kill me, he'd yelled before they jumped, as if he known for certain that would be the easiest option for them all.

'I have a computer tech with me,' Greeley went on. 'He'll need access to your ship immediately. He'll alter your ship's ID codes and all your transport and shipping records. The ship's discs will list you and the boy as the ship's owner/occupiers. I have new identities for you and your crew. You will no longer exist at Central Data. You will no longer exist at all.'

A full fix, he meant. A Joseph Stokes-sized fix with no chance of bio-data being cross-referenced. That's how much he wanted Jones to disappear. Frank's nails bit into his palms.

'All your details will be on handhelds, but you will have to remember some data of course – who you are, where you've been for the past year at least, just in case you're ever asked any questions by Customs. You'll be a short-hauler from Alfa, out to expand into system-wide trips into the Reaches. Jeven is your nephew. You'll keep him safe if you ever want to get your lives back.'

'And you can get our lives back if you're dead or you've been kidnapped?' Frank managed to get out in a level tone.

'I have subordinates. I've left instructions with them,' Greeley said firmly. 'I'll supply you with a contact code. Don't trust anybody who doesn't have it.'

'That's desperate,' Frank returned. 'This is all pretty desperate, isn't it?'

'It's the best I could manage at short notice.'

Frank almost laughed

'I will get you home, Mr Pak, one day, with compensation attached. I promise you.'

That really, really was comforting. Frank dropped into a seat, his knees felt weak, a definite tremor working through him as adrenaline surged, fight or flight reflex and he couldn't do either.

Greeley pulled a com-link from his pocket and keyed it open. 'Helm, get Granger over to *The Nova*. I want a Confirm as soon as he has her IDs changed.' He looked back to Frank. 'Now, I need to speak to my cargo. Somewhere private.'

Five minutes later and Frank edged his backside into the corner of Jones' room in an attempt to stay out of the way. He had a hypo full of trank in his pocket in case of emergencies. Greeley had an expensive-looking jammer unit working, its flashing light an endless distraction. Jones sat on the bedside, all pout and hard, hooded eyes as he tapped one booted toe impatiently on the tiles. Odd to see him with that little kid's glower on his face, odd after all he'd done to see him looking so much like a kid anticipating getting his backside spanked.

Greeley limped back and forth, the man working through a list of grievances. 'Six months on station on open release making your plans,' he snapped. 'No electronic tag, nothing but a daily call-in to the institution.'

News to Frank: information laid out neatly for his benefit, he was certain. He wiped his chin over, felt the pull of stubble against his palm. His other hand lay flexed around the hypo in his pocket. He doubted he'd need it now, Jones seemed set to go the other way, no defensive outrage, weary resignation instead – or at least the appearance of it. Greeley in contrast sounded like he was chipping teeth on every syllable. 'We had so many hopes for you. That you'd make a real life for yourself: a real home, real friends.'

A tiny reaction escaped Jones on the beat of *friends*, one unguarded clear-eyed look of anxiety beneath all his brooding insolence. Greeley had to be hunting for those pressure points. He pulled a chair over and set it down squarely in front of his charge. He set his cane down, freeing his hands so he could catch up Jones' wrist, measuring him by the thump of his pulse because he clearly couldn't rely on anything else.

Jones stood the contact for two seconds then prised himself free. He retreated to the ancient dresser in the opposite corner to Frank, leaning his weight over it to shore himself up.

'How did you find Milo Horton?' Greeley asked.

Silence from Jones, a gathering weight of it. Greeley shook his head at angrily. 'The man kept his name. They all did. That should never have been sanctioned.' More information for Frank's benefit. 'Still, it must have taken time and persistence to track him down. Six months of it?' Greeley went on. 'The six months you spent free on Beta? So you had three names – is that all? What else have you been doing out there?' Jones ran his finger over the gloss of the dresser's lid; drawing an imaginary animal it looked like, something with tentacles maybe, something with a long, long tail. 'Are you going to answer me?' Greeley asked sharply.

273

Jones carried on doodling.

'What was so special about Horton?' Greeley pressed. 'Why didn't you kill him?' Jones shrugged down, resting his forehead on his crossed wrists, tousled dark hair falling across his face. 'Murder isn't justice, Jeven. You can't judge people when you don't know the truth, the whole truth of what they did or why they did it.'

Frank got a glance from Jones then, a penetrating look as if Jones wanted to see his reaction to that statement rather than Greeley's.

Greeley paused, wearily rubbing a hand over his eyes. Getting nowhere. He limped over and took a grip on Jones' arm. 'Sit down. Please. Don't argue.'

Jones allowed himself to be towed away from the dresser and back towards the bed. He sat down; Greeley pulling his chair so close this time they were knee to knee. He took up Jones' wrist, out to measure him again.

'We need to make a deal,' Greeley said on a slow out-breath. 'We need to make some concessions, some solid promises to each other. I hope to God I can still trust those from you?'

Another glance to Frank, a raking worried look, and Jones gave a swift nod. He drew back his hand and crossed his arms.

Nash had two young men with him, didn't he? What were their names: Durham and Hodge? Two innocents, by Pak's account. Do you want to help them out of this thing? What about the little creature you had with you outside – the himmer. Do you want it in the deal? It could be sent home. It could be set free.'

The blood left Jones face, a muscle spasming above his jaw line.

'The men you killed, one of them had a daughter, she's five years old now. Do you want me to help her? Her name is—'

Jones surged towards the door, Greeley fast enough to get in his way and pull him off course. 'You'll do it. You'll make *promises* to me, ones I can trust. You all lived on promises on *The Bliss*. I know that. Currency in little deals made by the doctors, by the kids. Promises were always the biggest, most real part of you.'

Greeley's gaze snapped to Frank. 'You hear that. You hear it and understand it. He doesn't break his word.'

Jones tried to sidestep him but Greeley hauled him back. 'You have to think very carefully about how hard you're going to push me into making decisions here, Jeven. The people I'll hurt will be blameless but I will hurt them for your sake.'

Jones fought to get clear, bracing spread fingers against Greeley's shoulders. Greeley pushing him back when he tried to slide by, holding him at arm's length until he stopped struggling. Only when he stood still again did Greeley back away. 'I'll be out in the hall when you're ready to do this,' he said firmly. 'The longer you delay, the more people you'll put at risk.' He picked up his cane and limped away, the door closing at his back with a dull, hard slam.

Jones took a deep breath, sniffed and wiped at his nose.

Frank snorted. 'You enjoying yourself?'

'You don't want to get trapped in this,' Jones hurled back at him. 'You have to talk to him. You have to reason with him.'

'You know he's not going to listen to me. Look how far he's gone to try to save you.' Frank turned for the door himself. 'You've lost this one, Jones. We all have. Make the damned deal.'

Jones' life on Beta had mirrored *The Bliss* perfectly: same long corridors, same communal rooms, same mess hall, the same deals made, the same promises for all those little things that made life worthwhile. On *The Bliss* his life had depended on every up and down swing of his performance, on Beta the only thing he'd feared had been Greeley; a certain shadowy look in Greeley's eyes, the same brooding displeasure he saw in them now as he headed towards the games table. He'd given in, valuing what he could set free over his own inconvenience. He'd decided to call it that. He glanced at Frank. The man sitting there with his face set into that null expression mask he favoured lately. The one person he shouldn't be near was being dragged in deeper and deeper.

He sank down. He examined his own upturned palms for a moment before he dared cast a furtive glance over the tabletop to Greeley's expectant expression. 'I'll make the deal but with one concession.'

'Which is?'

'I want a time limit. Two weeks' full cooperation then I'm free of all obligations.'

Greeley banged his cane down on the table. 'No.'

'I'll behave, for two weeks I'll do exactly what I'm told.' Jones watched Greeley's eyes rage. 'I'll deal for all the things you said, all of them, but I won't cooperate forever. I can't do that. I won't.'

Greeley rested back into his chair's cushions, pausing for a long-drawn-out moment. 'One month. One month is the deal, or you'll spend longer locked up in holding on Pak's ship. This deal isn't for my convenience, it's for yours; it's for the members of this crew. It's to make life bearable for all of you. And, may I remind you, the less time you deal for the more time you *will* spend locked up.'

'Locked up but free of obligations,' Jones threw into the face of that.

Greeley hissed out an aggravated breath. 'Don't delay this with childish arguments, Jeven. I want you all up and out of here as soon as Pak's ship is ready'

Jones snagged a breath; surrender an unbearable weight in his chest. Greeley knew a hundred and one tricks of his own and they all revolved around honour and respect. He'd shown the man precious little of either lately. 'I promise. I swear. Ship's crew for one month,' he said it as if he was back at the institution, dealing for candy, for treats, for nothing at all that was worth a damn.

Greeley nodded, looking relieved. 'Then I swear to let Durham and Hodge and the himmer free,' he returned. 'And I'll compensate—' The comp room's door slammed. Haine came hurtling across the mosaic, Max three steps behind him.

'Are you just going to just sit there and take this crap?' Haine bellowed at Frank. 'This isn't some milksop green kid just getting by, Greeley.' He jabbed a hand Jones' way. 'He's a killer, a liar.'

Frank got in the way in a hurry, blocking the man's way forward. 'We can't have that damned lab rat running loose on our boat, Frank.' Haine yanked his arm clear of Max's grabbing hands. 'He'll do damage. He'll do us damage.'

'Control your crew, Pak.' Greeley stood up, aiming the end of his cane at Haine's chest as if the thing were a weapon.

Frank pushed both fists into Haine's chest to force him clear. 'Out. Now. Or you're off my ship. You got that? We have to do this, we don't have any choice.' He hushed the rest up as best he could. 'Do you think Greeley's going to leave any loose ends behind here? Do you seriously want to be one of those?' With that Haine let himself be shoved back two paces. 'No choice,' Frank repeated.

Haine glared at Jones one last time then spun about. Max trailed out after him.

Frank sagged back down into his chair just as Greeley's coin beeped for attention. 'We'll be set in twenty to thirty minutes, sir,' a voice said over it.

Greeley looked over to Jones, sorrow in his eyes suddenly. Betrayed, lied to, made a fool of, and yet there he sat still hoping to see a glimpse of the boy he'd lost, the one he thought he'd known.

The one who'd never existed. 'I want you to go and rest a while, while I talk to Mr Pak.'

'Will he attack Mallin?' Max asked softly in Jones' room. He paced up and down as they waited, one hand wrapped around the ear-piece in his left ear, the other hand constantly scrubbing through his short-cropped hair. 'Kill him to leave things tidy here?'

Jones sat on the bed, distracting himself with a stray knot in the himmer's coat.

'Jones?' Max prompted when Jones didn't answer.

'I don't know.'

'Do you think Mallin's Confederation?'

'Does he have ties to it when he's importing to Alfa?' Jones let the question hang. Max was smart enough to work that one out. Greeley's security looked like black-suited Special Ops. He had no idea how many more the man had left waiting on his ship.

The himmer squeaked deep down in its throat. 'Quiet,' he whispered to it. It sat by his leg, tight in, nudging its head under his fingers. 'What are they saying out there?' he asked Max.

The man paced back across the room again. 'Not much. The Calders. Christian MacKay. He's left Delta. He's looking for you. Who isn't?' Every word out of Max's mouth was like a whip-crack. He stopped pacing to rub two fingers across his brow where that bird's-claw frown sat marking his obvious anxiety.

'Where's Haine?' Jones asked.

Max pointed at the ceiling as if Haine ought to be hanging from it. Up top, he meant, safely out of the way for now. Max paused, listening intently for a moment. 'Frank wants me. It sounds like we'll be moving out soon. Stay put.'

As the door closed Jones started work on another knot. Best to

stay busy when thinking led to all manner of dead-ends. The himmer trembled, moaning softly under his palm as if picking up on
his unrest. 'Stop it. Stop crying. You'll be safe. You're in with the
deal. Lucky you.' Tangle still moaned, brushing at eyes that couldn't
leak tears in a pantomime of human upset. 'What's the matter with
you?'

Far away a solid boom sounded that made Jones teeth click
together, a boom that reverberated through the walls. He'd heard
explosions before, on *The Bliss*'s last day they'd come often enough,
shaking the metal, making the lights flicker and fail.

The himmer squeaked.

'Shh,' Jones hissed at it. It had to be a ship coming into the mainland dock. Just a sonic boom, an innocent, everyday sound, he persuaded himself. Still his muscles locked solid, and he held his
breath. By his knee the himmer sobbed and shook.

A slaver might get attacked. The criminal hierarchy sometimes
attacked each other for the sake of money or power. Maybe some
of the missing people Mallin stole away had relatives looking for
them. Or maybe the cops had paid a few visits asking for some
kickbacks to keep things quiet. The cops would likely make their
visits a well-armed surprise. Mallin must be playing all sides against
the middle, or why let Frank roam around so freely?

Another boom: a solid, rolling roar that sounded worryingly
close.

Tangle bolted, dodging his stretching grab for fur. He dived after
it, tearing his fingers into pelt as they reached the door, feeling taut
sinew and muscle tense beneath it. Tangle shrieked, mouth wide,
glistening teeth snapping at Jones' wrists. It snaked its paws around
the door handle and pulled. One more almighty gnash of teeth at
Jones' wrists and it twisted itself free and fled.

In the hallway outside, men ran this way and that, men sliding com-links onto their heads, men holding guns skywards. The dull throb of motors echoed: up above the dome was closing, sheets of metal rising to shield the composite. The lights went down half a shade and rose again, something, somewhere draining power for a length of seconds.

Frank appeared, pushing by the running techs and rushing across the hallway. He prodded Jones back from the doorway. 'Sit down, shut up and listen.'

Jones sank back down onto the bed, mutely watching Frank throw things out of one of the chest of drawers in the room's far corner in a rapid chase to find something inside it. Jones waited and didn't say a word. 'There's something incoming from the mainland,' Frank explained finally. 'Something small, that's not talking. It's throwing off a weapons lock.'

'Whose firing on it?'

'Mallin's defences.' Jones stayed silent, Frank's harried expression suggesting there might be more and worse details coming. 'Greeley's ship up top has another target. A ship's just exited the gate. It isn't broadcasting an ID either.' Frank threw a packet down onto the bed: clothing in a plastic pack. Rain gear.

'Is this something to do with Mallin or something to do with Greeley?' Jones asked, pulling the packet into his lap.

'I don't know. Not yet.' Frank turned for the door. 'Hurry up and get dressed.'

Frank rushed back to the comp room. The blips on a comp screen never did it for him, getting those images as a holographic visual was better, he could see it all in 3D then, he could imagine the distances, the vectors.

Let them be more Durhams and Hodges, please God, he thought. Let this be a small-scale, desperate job, like Nash's. Nothing huge, nothing organized.

Another explosion, and he instinctively ducked down, the world shifting uneasily under his boots. Dislodged blue brick dust floated by, the overheads glittering off its aimless fall.

'A missile's just hit the south, south-west side of the island.' The tech in charge of the monitors leaned over the boards to hit keys. 'Our defences didn't track it. All our sensors are blind.'

'Military tech,' Frank muttered out. Not good news for his small-scale theory.

The 3D halo had died with the blast; half the monitors now black screens, the rest showing either normality or a pile of fallen native trees. A second blast was a flash of light on the furthest left screen. 'That was the dock,' the tech reported dourly. 'Still no ID and still no weapons lock on that inbound ship. Techs do have a visual. We're down to manual aim.'

Frank gripped at the board's edge as another explosion hit. The walls shifted, pictures swayed then fell from their hooks, a falling lamp shattered with a loud, echoing pop.

'You need to get out,' Greeley stood to Frank's left, glistening blue dust coating his hair and shoulders. He limped over to the door and yanked it open.

Outside, pictures lay tipped at twisted angles on the walls of the hallway, one tech cherry-picking art to pull clear and lay flat on the tiles.

Another blast, and the house shivered again.

Frank stared at the ceiling; tiny cracks streaking across the blue brickwork. 'The damned house is going to fall apart.' A drum beat interrupted, engine noise pulsing dully against the walls. 'Hell.' It had to be that ship from the main dock, too close to the house now to safely kill without endangering them all. Civilian-grade tech never trumped military; it never stood a chance.

More noise sounded from above.

'They're putting men down on the roof.' Greeley stared upwards too, wiping blue dust from his eyes as Mallin appeared from one of the off-leading doorways, out of breath and sweating.

'Foley reports the ship's taken a hit,' he announced over the noise. 'The enemy ship,' he clarified hurriedly. 'He says it's backing off. Greeley's boat's trailing it, warning it it'll get worse if it doesn't clear out.'

'Military-grade tech down here but not up top,' Frank muttered. 'Does this planet have a garrison?' he asked Mallin.

'Barely. A fifty-man outpost, if that.'

'I think it's visiting us on that smaller boat,' Frank said.

The sound of smaller explosions came from above their heads – sharp cracks interspersed with thuds against the metal-protected dome. Someone screamed, the sound shrill and full of panic. 'The main body of the roof is booby trapped,' Mallin said. 'I'm getting people up there now to secure it.'

Greeley rounded on him. 'I want my cargo out of here. If Pak's ship is secure I want him on board. Now.'

Mallin planted his feet and leaned into Greeley's personal space. 'And what do I get for that? Do I get to stay alive at the tail end of this?'

'I've no intention of killing anybody here.'

Mallin snagged a breath, laughed. 'Of course not. I can match you, Greeley, believe me.' He glanced to Frank. 'There are secure shelters all over the island. I can hide you and your cargo until this—'

'I *said* I want him on that ship,' Greeley said. 'Now. No delay.'

'We'll leave,' Frank cut in hurriedly before an argument started.

Mallin frowned at him. Nodded and stepped back. He pulled out his com-link and began relaying instructions, long seconds passing as more dust shook loose from the ceiling.

Frank checked round, searching for Max and Jones. They stood within a group of waiting techs by another doorway. Max raised his hand; by his side Jones looked as about as ashen and fretful as Frank had ever seen him.

'Go.' Mallin's sleeve billowed as he jabbed his hand towards a doorway. 'East passageway. My men are waiting below to brief you. They'll try to get you a clear run down to the coast.'

One of the off-leading doors was pushed open, Mallin's men filing down the flight of stairs beyond it, Greeley in a limping rush to join them. Mallin snatched at Frank's arm before he could follow. 'Listen to me,' he hissed, his eyes never leaving Greeley's back. 'This could have nothing to do with him. You can still change your mind and stay. I've had visits, Frank; from people telling me whose side of this war I ought to be on when things escalate. I told them they could deal with me as a free agent or not at all. This might be just another attempt to pressurize me.'

'I can't risk that,' Frank returned. He didn't wait to hear any more, he was still too wary to trust the man. He turned away, the hair at his nape bristling.

Max stood with Jones at the top of the stairwell. They'd stood waiting for him and they'd clearly heard every word said. Max stepped forward. 'Frank, if we don't know who—'

'Move,' Frank barked at him. He grabbed for Jones' arm, their footsteps clattering down the stone stairs as they followed after Greeley.

Long minutes of walking followed; footsteps and panted breaths echoing hollowly, Mallin's techs a clump of dark backs up ahead of them. Frank saw the metal of a blast door starting to slide open, hearing as the men filed inside a familiar grating voice bellow out. 'Greeley. Damned Greeley himself is here. Where's your brat, Greeley?'

Nash.

'Shut that man up,' Frank yelled to the techs in front of him. He tightened his hold around Jones' arm.

They passed through the doorway, the room they entered full to the ceiling with crated stores to the left; metal bars shone in the glare of the overheads to the right, row after row of close-knit primitive metal cells lining the room's length. Nash's face appeared, unshaven and bruised, his hollow cheeks pressing between one set of bars. 'Pak? Jones? Hell, have you two started a war all of your own? And Greeley himself is here. God almighty, did he come all this way to wipe your backside for you, brat?' Nash grinned. 'I'm still holding on to that info for you. You want me to tell you where *The Bliss* is these days?'

Nobody glanced aside to the man; nobody stopped moving. Frank towed Jones past Nash's cramped little cell as a tech rattled his gun butt across the bars to warn the man back. Nash dodged forwards instead, his shoulder rattling the metal, one lunging hand grabbing for Jones' jacket. His stretching fingers found no grip. 'You're the only one left.'

Frank swore as Jones spun about.

'They're all dead. All your little friends are dead. Didn't Greeley tell you? A little agreement they all got together on after you upped and left them. A suicide pact. Haven't you told your precious kid the truth, Greeley? They'd had enough, Jones. Hope was gone. You were their damned *hope*. You had a nice little job on the station, a real life, just like they wanted, and you screwed that up royally.'

Greeley elbowed through the swarm of men up ahead. 'Shut him up.' He grabbed hold of Jones' jacket himself. 'Move him to the outside door. Now.' Jones opened his mouth to object, throwing a hand back towards the bars before Mallin's techs enveloped him.

'He's lying.' Frank heard Greeley say as Jones started to yell, Mallin's men pressing in around him. 'You know he's lying.'

Nash stood wide-eyed, spittle on his lips, blood on the knuckles of the hands he wrapped around the bars. 'Is Greeley taking his lab rat home?' he rasped out in a low, dark voice just to Frank. 'If he isn't you'd better listen to me, Pak. Alexander wants that kid back. He's J series. The biggest bunch of mess-ups of all. But Alexander wants him, and he wants him fast before his damn head implodes.'

A muffled yell of frustration and the snarl-up of men heaved into the stacked boxes, the upper ones teetering dangerously under the onslaught. Jones wanted to come back and listen and Jones was fighting for it. 'He's lying.' Greeley's voice rose to the ceiling. 'Pak,' he bellowed, Mallin's men now moving further and further down the room in fits and starts. 'Get over here.'

Frank didn't move, his stare still locked into Nash's wide pupils. The man had been drugged, he'd been asked questions by Mallin, and Mallin had claimed he knew nothing worth knowing. Nash snorted. 'Friendly warning, friendly advice, get clear before all of this buries you and your precious crew.'

'Pak.'

This time Frank moved; he hurried forward, pushing through the crush of Mallin's men. At their centre Greeley stood leaning in close to Jones' ear to impart something he clearly didn't want over-heard. He had a lump of Jones' collar in a stranglehold, his other white-knuckled fist held under Jones chin.

'You hear me,' Greeley spat the words out. Jones squirmed side-ways and got shoved back into the wall. 'Do you hear me?'

Drained of colour, Jones nodded hard and fast twice over. 'Yes.'

They reached an open door, the shadows of other men shifting around in the night outside it, air rushing into the corridor that smelled of grass and trees and salt.

'It's clear.' One man stepped into the light, his waterproofs dripping fat droplets of water onto the tiles.

Frank nodded gravely. He pressed his way forward, his progress stayed when Greeley caught his arm. 'The boy's sick, he won't be able to run.'

Jones cast an anxious look out into the cold and the weather then back again in Nash's direction.

'I'll get him where he needs to be,' Frank said. 'I don't have much of a choice.' He pushed forwards, tightened his fingers into a wad of jacket at Jones' elbow and pushed him into Max's care. 'You move and you keep moving,' he said in a low voice. 'You don't ask questions. You don't make any noise at all you don't have to. You put one foot in front of the other, and that's all you do.' Frank leaned in closer, staring hard into Jones' eyes. 'Nash lied. He lied for the sake of getting to you, to me. What colour is he, Jones? What damned colour is he?'

Blood-warm drizzle slid through his hair and down his face, yet Jones still shivered. There was no sign of the house from their exit point, the tunnel's doorway a half-hidden oblong within a man-made hillock, the eerie shadows of windblown grass moving to and fro between thicker clumps of scrub around it. Greeley stood framed in the doorway flaring oranges and reds, Frank by his side flared indigo and black – but each man to his core was another solid colour: Greeley azure, Frank always calmest blue.

'Jones.' Max nudged at his shoulder, urging him into the cover of some of the lower-hanging branches of the trees surrounding them. Jones leaned his back into the rough bark of the nearest, Max yanking up the hood of his jacket for him as if he thought he wouldn't think to do it for himself. 'You all right?'

His face had turned blank and slack, Jones knew it, he knew his eyes were empty – and Max could see it all. The man wore night vision goggles strapped about his eyes, those optics protected from the rain by the cap of his hood. Max, like the techs, wouldn't take any chances in the darkness – but they hadn't given Jones any equipment. They'd hadn't given him anything at all.

Jones nodded a belated reply. Engine noise drowned out the rain's patter now, the breeze blowing the sound in, the enemy likely still trying to unload men onto the island. The pop of gun-fire started up, a louder explosion causing Mallin's techs to glance about themselves restlessly.

'You tracking?' came Max's gentle prompt. He stood checking his gun, the thing belted at hip level over the top of his rain gear. 'You hearing me, Jones?'

Jones gave another half-hearted nod.

'Good enough. Make sure you stay tuned in.'

Frank turned around and spoke to the tallest of Mallin's techs. A hand signal from him, and they started to move out. Jones glanced back to the figure in the doorway. Greeley waved farewell, Jones knitted his teeth together and didn't return the gesture. He stared out into the gloom between the trees instead, telling himself to do exactly what Frank had told him to: move and do nothing else. Don't think. Don't wonder.

They walked into the tree line, the darkness deepening as they went. The land, hidden beneath the low-growing grasses, dipping away unseen. Jones' line of sight so inhibited that safe footfalls were impossible. He slipped. Max caught him, using a low-growing branch to steady himself before he heaved them both back on track.

Shouts came from far away to their left. Shouts when com-links would have been more sensible. Not Mallin's men, the enemy, men stupidly giving away their position. More engine noise came – a deep throaty growl and a small black lozenge shape rose up into the sky, a cone of light dropping from its belly.

'Decoys are going out to every compass point,' Max hissed out. 'We have bug killers, ID killers, even with the tech they'll have up there they won't know the difference between us and them.' Max got hissed at himself by a man ahead of them.

'I can't see,' Jones said, his feet sliding again. 'I need some gear.'

'Sorry, Jones,' Max managed to sound apologetic. 'Not my orders.'

Vegetation cracked under Jones' weight, branches slapping at rain gear that whispered with every step. Leaves snagged at his arms and legs, some of the native species spiked all the way to their frond ends. His feet kept on skating across hidden patches of mud, his every breath a harsh, panted rush. The muscles in his legs grew tighter and tighter, cramp threatening as the earth beneath his leaden footfalls slewed into more and more of a precarious downward slope.

Noise came from behind them, laser sights hitting distant tree trunks in a frantic chaotic dance. Jones was bundled into cover, a circle of four men crouching about him with their guns raised. Their leader sank low, speaking into his com-link before waving two of the men close to Jones clear. They circled around and dropped back into the gloom. Moonlight seeped downward, as if on cue, giving Jones a clear glimpse of Frank to his left speaking to another tech. Jones choked a swallow down, feeling more and more hemmed in.

He heard the pop of gunfire: three rounds.

'Clear,' someone hissed, and Max hauled Jones forwards again, their shielding escort stepping away.

Too dark without night vision; cavernous black spaces opened up between the spills of moonlight, the trees dipping lower, the mud and grasses tangling around his boots and ankles. One cord-thin branch dipped low unseen; it tangled into his rain gear, thick leaf needles trying to gouge into his shoulder. He cursed, heaving sideways into Max's side and pushing the man off balance. Max staggered two steps and went down with a grunt and a splash of muddy water. 'Dammit, Jones.' Max used a tree trunk to aid the slippery climb back to his feet. He took a second's rest, puffing hard while settling his upset sidearm back into its holster. 'Stay clear of the brush, all right.'

'I can't see the brush.' Jones curled his fingers into the flapping tear in his jacket the branch had left behind, rubbing at the bruised flesh beneath. *Move and do nothing else* had begun to feel like an order for a blind, dumb fool. 'I need some gear. I need a gun,' he panted out. No response, no reaction. Moonlight intervened, Max's face taking on more detail: white cheeks, a set, downturned mouth. His eyes hidden by the dark curves of his rain-spotted optics. 'I'm crew – and I'm asking for a gun.'

'No'.

'Something might happen out here.'

A hissed instruction interrupted, the lead tech waving Jones back and down, Jones deaf to the com-links instructions, deaf and blind to it all. Max sank into a crouch, pulling Jones down with him while the rest of Mallin's men started to filter into the trees.

Frank came running back to them. He crouched low, his goggle-masked eyes turning Jones' way. 'We've got men between us and the coast. The techs need to clear the way. We need to haul up here and wait.' Frank resettled his com-link into his ear, shaking water from his fingers when the thing wanted to slip. Ten long seconds of listening and he let a little more information loose. 'Last report says it's a five or six-man hunting party. It sounds like they're spreading themselves thin trying to cover all the decoys. The good news is their ship's been holed. It's heading out. No info on if there've got anything else heading in. Mallin's weaponry still can't track those boats, all his techs can do is wait for a visual.'

'No night vision, no gun and no com-link,' Jones sent back. 'What the hell kind of crew am I?' The two men before him glanced at each other, no true reaction readable behind hoods and goggles. 'I need some gear.'

'You do exactly as you're told you won't need any gear,' Frank replied sharply.

'You don't *trust me* with any gear, isn't that closer to the truth?' An odd feeling of displacement followed that statement that had nothing to do with Frank's stubbornness. *The Bliss*'s secrets were apt to throw out warnings. The hairs rose on his arms, his thoughts tugged a certain way, into a certain place. He raised a hand and pointed into a patch of darkness, forgetting to duck as the first shot came inward. Max dragged him down with one hand, aiming and firing his gun into the trees with the other.

'That's dart fire. They know who they're damned well firing at.' Frank hauled at Jones' jacket as another shot hissed by. 'Find some cover.'

Jones moved where he was being shoved, back behind a tree's broad trunk. He shrugged down, hair not covered by his hood a wet snarl in front of his eyes.

A one-man assault, surely. One man who'd circled around their guard, one smart enough not to give away his position by using his weaponry's laser scope.

More fire started from behind them, great spats of it, going out and coming inward; it seemed Mallin's men had found some trouble. If their own assailant wanted to creep closer now he had enough noise to hide behind.

'Hell.' Jones heard Frank snap. 'Max, stay here. Stay down.' Frank squirmed out into the grass, climbed into a hunched run and disappeared.

The whine of a dart followed, a two-pronged dart striking a tree close by. A whistling hiss and it deployed an electrical charge into the bark with a curl of white smoke.

A waiting game, then, as more fire barked out in the distance ahead of them.

Max suddenly yanked off his hood, pulling the com unit from his ear, sounds coming over it: a man's screams of pain issued in tinny, hawking rasps. 'That's the group behind us. Someone's down, they've left their com channel locked open.' The noise died on the link, a voice taking over. Max tucked the unit back into his ear. 'Sounds like they're in real trouble back there.'

Silence then; Jones counting heartbeats, Max's gun all the time sweeping across the vista of darkness before them. Max, who suddenly swung in close, twisted up a fistful of Jones' collar and hung on tight. 'You have to stay here,' he said firmly. 'That's an order: you stay down low and you don't move. Frank's on the com and he needs my help.'

'A gun,' Jones said. 'At least leave me with a gun.'

'No deal. I have to follow orders just the same as you do.' Max moved out, tracing Frank's footsteps all the way until he disappeared from view.

CHAPTER 16

Jones' rain gear captured his body heat well enough, but still his shivering refused to stop. He crouched lower, pressing himself harder and harder into the spongy bark of the tree at his back.

Small targets were harder to hit, targets down in the tangle of grass might be harder still to hit even with night-vision-equipped weapons. It made sense for his attacker to try to circle around his hiding place to get a clear shot. It made sense too for Frank to have left him sitting there as bait.

Spooks in the undergrowth left and right, movements Jones' eyes could barely catch that might be the wind's breath, that might be something else. The gunfire in the distance went silent, *The Bliss* twisted gifts trilling across his skin: a cold, cold shiver stirring fear in overheated blood.

Bait?

Another spook· a flash of brown in bright moonlight heading towards him at speed, a thing that chittered and flashed white teeth.

'Tangle, get down.' Jones motioned frantically. 'Get down.'

Tangle flattened, creeping up on him in an eager rush. It took hold, starting to yank at his arm in quick, hard jerks. Himmer

293

instinct: take your own, run and hide. As trained as the creature was, it would count anyone in Mallin's blue room as its own.

'No.' Jones knitted his teeth around the word. 'No.' Still the himmer hung on tight and strained backward. Jones' *Bliss*-born instincts flared another warning. Bait or not, if someone was coming it might be wise to move out from under their path. He let himself be dragged, beginning to run into denser cover, the himmer getting under his elbow, his ailing body fighting to cope with their haste. Pain shot up from his ankles and knees with each thudding footfall. Minutes of running and he glanced back, sure a black splotch of undergrowth to their left was being pushed aside with more force than any Telemar breeze could muster. He kept low, kept moving, letting the himmer guide him deeper and deeper into the darkest patches of the night. Another glance back; the distant shapes of men were visible now. Men under helmets, in full gear, who found cover fast and hesitated, hearing the same thing Jones did: gunfire from where Frank had to be.

And if Frank and Max wandered back all unknowing into that space . . .

Jones pulled the himmer to a standstill behind the cover of a stand of thick brushwood. He motioned back and around, drawing a circle in the air, hoping the himmer would understand where they needed to go. The creature's huge eyes were white-rimmed. It hissed and snapped its jaw. Jones pushed it away, pushed it again harder, his hands engulfed by sopping-wet pelt. He caught his breath when the creature charged back at him. Threat posture: arms raised, teeth bared. Jones palmed its chest, the himmer so close its hot breath steamed up into his face. He kept eye contact, challenging its dominance as it challenged his. He knew this game, but this wasn't a black-skinned, yellow-eyed demon; he didn't know if he was being understood. He motioned again; back and around, back and around. The himmer backed off a step, teeth still bared to show its rage. Then it sniffed the air, jerked its head and lowered its gaze. Surrender finally.

Jones moved off. He didn't look back, trusting it to follow him.

Another splash of fire from where Frank must be, two quick volleys, too loud for a dart gun . . . and silence.

Jones checked back the other way, waiting to see those strangers heading in. Worried he might have been seen. He ran; heaving down air, counting seconds to try to judge distance, worried he might get turned around in the darkness and lose all sense of where he'd been and where he needed to go. A count of three hundred and sixty and he needed a rest. A feeling flared as he stood and panted, a downright uncomfortable flush of it that made his insides jolt. A shadow appeared, a helmeted man with a raised dart gun pushing forward out of the chest-high bushes right in front of him.

'Stand still. Put your hands above your head.' He barked the order just as the himmer darted around Jones' back. More threat posture, more arm waving. The man didn't hesitate: he drew his other gun and fired, the silenced barrel letting off a dull pop of sound.

The himmer slumped.

Jones dived at the man in mindless reaction. The man dodged aside, swinging his gun butt around, the collision of metal and bone a dull crack in Jones' ears. He fell into gloom, into drenched grass and mud, his stunned senses floundering. He rolled onto his back, rain in his eyes, a dizzying vista of white cloud broiling in the cobalt-blue heavens above the tree's sway. Light shone into his face, light so fierce and bright he recoiled and cried out.

'This is unit three-one-one,' the man said into his com-link. 'Come in, control' A spitting hiss of static returned. 'Come in, control. Can you hear me? I've caught a straggler – a kid. Likely he's the target.'

Jones curled himself up, tried to focus, nausea rising. He saw a dull image of the man's legs, the sheen of rain on waterproofs, the darkness of the man's goggle-covered eyes. No *Bliss* input came to him, but mindless outrage surged. He attacked, wet hands slipping for grip as he shoved into the body before him. He got a curse for his trouble, followed by another numbing blow across his head. Not a gun, a fist. He dropped back into the grass and watched the clouds broil, watched them rock and spin.

No one else grabbed for him, no one else came running to help, a man alone for certain. The damned fool had dropped his comlink. He searched across the undergrowth for it, his gun holstered, his gloved hands turning vegetation back in an impatient hunt for it. 'Son of a bitch,' he grumbled, bending lower still.

Jones feigned agony, clutching at his head as he waited for the man to bend lower still. One long, low dip to the grass and Jones rolled onto his knees and pushed off. Two paces to reach the man and he kicked out, sparing no force. The man collapsed, harsh wheezes and little else escaping from his crushed windpipe. Jones ducked in close and hitched the man's gun free. He turned it about, swinging it butt end first at the man's forehead. He winced when it met resistance, his assailant nothing then but a silent, dark lump half hidden in the grass.

'Tangle?' Jones whirled towards the himmer. He dropped down and rolled it over. A breath bubbled from the creature's lips, limbs flopping aimlessly, its head lolling over. 'Tangle?'

Tangle came alive with a shuddering cry. Not dead; not halfway dead when that shot would have killed a human being outright. Tangle gripped at Jones then at its own chest where a hole leaked blood. Too much blood. Jones tore off his rain jacket then his other jacket under that. Fast getting drenched, he peeled off his shirt, wadded it up and pressed it hard into the creature's chest.

Tangle shot backwards. 'Hold it,' Jones mimed the motion, and Tangle pressed fabric into blood with visible distaste. 'We have to move.' Jones said, shrugging back into both jackets with a chilled shiver.

He helped the himmer along as best he could. Something else coming to him, the sense of something familiar, something he'd lost that tugged at him. He searched for it as the bushes between the trees swayed, grasses making phantom shapes as the dawn gathered. Colour smothered the trees now, their bark alive with fungi that spread out in tattered umbrellas of glossy deep red and sallow yellow.

He lost his balance with a grunt of shock, lost his grip on the himmer too. It fell away from him as he dropped onto his knees, his stolen gun slapping into a pond of slimy leaf mould. He struggled upright, chest heaving, shaking debris from the gun, *Bliss* senses making him look left and wait. Just wait.

Movement: the sway of leaves in the distance, a solid shape pushing through a knot of bushes. No more gunfire echoed, the shift of branches being pushed roughly aside all he could hear bar the rain's splatter. The shape broke free, it stood wavering, gaining detail: no helmet, no bulky gear.

Finally a flare of colour: calmest blue.

'Frank?'

The figure surged towards him, hands reaching forward to wrap around his chin and lift his head. No black-eyed goggles now, Frank's dark eyes were sharp. 'Max told you not to move.' Frank reached the gun Jones held. 'Where did the hell did you get this?'

'Took it; stole it,' Jones blurted. He pulled back, letting the gun go, Frank searching his face as if he were insane or a liar. Max appeared, standing guard over them all, his blond head a bright target in the new light.

Jones pushed by to reach the himmer. It sat hunched over itself, blood on its coat from chest to thighs despite the wad of fabric it clutched on to so tightly. He fell to his knees at its side. 'We have to help it.'

'We don't have time,' came Frank's tense, sharp reply. 'It can skirt around and run back to the house. Mallin will take care of it.' His fist clamped around Jones' arm and hung on.

Max moved to his other side, wrenching his hands clear of the creature's coat. Max's voice low and tight. 'Mallin's tech's have cleared the way. We don't want to get cut off again.'

'No,' Jones protested, Max pulling him upright, Frank sliding between him and the ailing creature. He still tried to jerk free. *Bliss* echoes ran riot. Everyone dying. Memories and data streaming into his head, anything and everything, just a maelstrom of images and endless output he was too exhausted to fight against.

'Dammit. Stop it,' A slap of sound, a sting across his cheek, and he flinched, peering out into a world turning ruby-red and blue-grey now, a world with a sun at its centre. 'Stop it.' Frank leaned closer. 'Stay with me, all right. Stay here. *Here*, you understand? In the *right now*.'

Frank could see it. He could see it all. Jones bit his lip so hard he tasted blood, using the pain to force it back and back, forcing it away so hard he could barely get a straight breath into his chest.

'Stay with me,' Frank hissed. 'You're—'

Not alone. *Not any more.*

Frank needed to haul in a few breaths himself. *Bliss* images and data, a flickering, endless assault. He took another jolt then, seeing himself bathed in colour, the palest, sweetest blue. And something else, Lord only knew what that was; it felt like an itch under his skin, something crawling into him and catching hold like a para-site. 'Jones,' he snapped, hauling at rain jacket as if he could pull Jones out of the onslaught.

The himmer watched, whining in distress, blood beginning to drip from between its lips. 'Go home, Tangle,' Max told it harshly. The creature bared bloodstained teeth. It went, the slowest it was able, head low, forever turning back to look at them, its fingers pressed to its chest where the bullet had lodged.

Jones rocked on his feet and Frank shook at him. 'Stay with me,' he snapped. 'Or you'll kill us both.' He shot wary glances all around; worried they'd be caught off guard. The man who'd attacked them had been a scout definitely, one more interested in getting clear to report their position than getting involved in a fire fight. Up to their eyes in trouble and here Jones was half in one world, half in another. His flesh crawled, that weird sense returning that some-thing awful had caught hold of Jones and dragged him under, some big ugly leech of a thing that he just couldn't escape. 'Jones.'

Jones steadied, nodded, the input dying away finally. Frank hauled him into an unsteady walk.

They kept moving until the trees petered out, until they reached the edge of the island, only grass here resisting the breeze's jostle, rough shale under their feet instead of mud.

'We have to go down,' Frank said, making every syllable count as he stared down towards the rolling ocean. There was a sloping pathway down the side of Mallin's little island. The footing down its fall nothing but mud dressed over with the slime of rotting leaf mould. Mallin's work crew had only had time to remove the very worst of it from Frank's escape route. 'You stay clear-headed and you stay alert,' he said into Jones' stark white face.

The vegetation left behind on the cliff side helped their descent, Frank taking great chunks of it in hand as he led them down. His gun banged his hip, Jones, on his other side, forever sliding and bumping into him.

There was little grip underfoot but the odd rock jutting out of the earth; a hard enough descent for a healthy man, harder still for Jones. Thankfully the rain had stopped, they had enough light to see by now, Frank able to avoid the greasiest spots, the hand he had clamped permanently in a lump of Jones' jacket already cramping so badly he had to catch his breath.

A hard night, a hard damned few days, and still no definitive ID on the enemy from the house; just a warning only minutes earlier that the scrambled com-links might have been compromised, that they were now to be used for essential coded information only. Frank didn't know Mallin's codes. He planned to call the house soon whether the links were secure or not. He planned to call Foley too. They needed to know what the hell was going on up above them.

He winced, images flashing again, Jones skittering between past and present when the flaring data died down enough to let him. His face was stained with drying blood, a fresh stream of it leaking down from under his hairline. He'd taken a knock somewhere, sometime. Not sane, Frank thought, not altogether anywhere at all.

Jones stifled a cry and slid again, crashing down onto his shins, his fingers snatching at the wall of vegetation behind his back, dirt-caked chest heaving as Frank hauled at him. 'Get up. You damned well get up. You hear? Anything happens to us it's your damned fault.'

Cruel, downright pitiless, when you'd realized just how much a paradox Jones was. The cold-blooded assassin who couldn't bear to hurt anybody, or anything, if he could help it.

Jones' livid eyes locked into his own. Temper that would help. Jones fought to get up, yanking with soaked hands on slimy root tendrils.

'It's not much further,' Frank said. A damned lie, they stood halfway down, no lower. Jones spent, Jones on reserves of sheer bloody-mindedness. Frank gripped at his jacket as Jones' feet landed straight again.

A third of the descent left, and Frank turned about, setting his back to the cliff face. The slope was rocky now; they had more grip. Jones' head had dropped, his open mouth wheezing in air as if his lungs meant to burst. He stood facing the drop too now. Two paces out you hit fresh air, the rocks below promising to shred you down to the bone. Max had started to talk, a low-grade mumble for Jones' sake, to keep him shifting his weary feet.

'Near the bottom,' Frank said minutes later, watching the tide lap onto the tiny stretch of beach below. 'Nearly there.' He glanced up to the edge of the headland way above, seeing a figure up there he squinted at.

'Company,' he snapped out. By his side Jones tensed, looking up into the dizzying rush of the ruby-flecked sky above them. Frank forced to lean into his weight as Jones' legs dropped out from under him. He went down again. 'Dammit.' Jones blinked up at him, nothing in his eyes, all emotion spent, Frank floundering for another way to force him to move. 'You don't want to kill us. You don't. They get close to us we're dead. They won't be darting us. Crew don't get each other killed. Now get up.'

The two men holding on to him on both sides hurt him as Jones fought to rise, their fingers bruising. He grabbed the mess of vegetation behind him, his exposed skin clammy, the rest, trapped under the heat of his rain gear, burning hot. Runnels of sweat trickled down his back and chest, his heart a thundering crash against his ribs.

Shouts came from up above them: men's voices loud and insist-ent. The thuds of fire sounded. Darts rained down, metal spinning off the path's rocky edge and falling away. One hit straight into the dirt, discharging with a whine and a bright white flash. Frank unclipped his gun and sent volleys of fire upwards, Max pushing Jones hard into the overhang of the cliff face so he could do the same. And still they edged downwards. Jones grunted with every step, pain firing through every muscle.

Finally they reached the slope's end and the softness of the sand below, grey, ugly sand that cleaved to his boots. The ocean was a roar to his left, a miasma of sound that blanketed all else: his coughs, his sobs for air, the shouts and fire from above. Frank and Max still held on to him, but he moved of his own accord, pulling each foot from the sand's grip, fighting it, fighting himself. Both men still fired upwards, trying to dissuade a fast pursuit from the men above.

'There.' Frank pulled him hard over to the right, Jones' feet find-ing more purchase, the sand giving way to fawn-coloured pebbles. He shuddered, colder air hitting his skin as they moved under an overhang and deeper in, the darkness of a cave a sudden shroud. A different smell lingered within the fetor of vegetation and salt – metal, machine oil.

Around a wide bend the cavern walls were filled with a glossy white-grey shape. A ship. A tiny, thin-skinned pleasure orbiter, no more than that. Jones lurched into its side.

'Inside,' Frank ordered as the door in the shuttle's side hissed open.

More cold then, ship's cold that echoed, and vibrated with foot-falls. Max ran up to the seat at helm. 'Turning the lights on, and powering up,' he called back down the bay.

Bright white light sheared. Jones threw a hand across his water-ing eyes, collapsing to his knees on the plating. The ship's bay was tiny, nothing to it but seats and baggage webbing. Frank pushed at him. 'This boat has no grav. You need to buckle in. You have to move. Dammit.'

Engine whine, a loud throb of it thrown around the metal walls, and Jones moved one shaky hand and pushed off the plating. He crawled to the seating down the bay's middle and hoisted himself up. Frank pulled him up to a sit and buckled him in, the man forced to fight for balance as the ship's floor canted under his sand-crusted boots. A hard squeeze on Jones' shoulder, and Frank rushed away.

Up at helm Max's fingers flashed over the ship's controls, Frank sliding into the chair next to him. 'You know what you're doing?'

Max chewed his lip and nodded. He'd admitted to never owning a licence but he'd said he could pilot a shuttle confidently enough.

The ship moved, slowly edging out of its confines, buzzed warnings going off every few seconds. Max with the ship set on primary control, the comp making its own decisions about how far away the cavern's walls stood from the orbiter's delicate hide.

A tilt of the ship's body, one long scrape of metal on rock, a push of Frank's back into his seat, and they were free and climbing, climbing into sky streaked the colour of blood.

Frank reconfigured the com. 'Foley, tell me what the hell's happening.'

'We're clear,' Foley returned. 'Suspect ship stood down. Honestly don't know where the hell it is. Wherever it is Greeley's boat went with it. As soon as I can lock on to your position I'll vector in.'

The ship lurched, Max cursing and hitting keys. 'Got a ship aft. By the size of it I think it's their shuttle.'

Their holed shuttle, the shuttle the scans couldn't catch?

She was there all right, the shuttle now a blip on the ship's scan, info piling up on one side of ship's singular monitor. Frank grimaced at the stats. He couldn't read a single one.

'Do you think she'll fire?' Max asked.

'Last I heard she had a hole in her side. Looks like she lost her stealth capability with it.' There was lots of ocean below them right then. A splashdown landing might preserve the prize; it might well not. 'Ramp up the power and get us out of atmosphere,' Frank said. 'Likely the state she's in she won't be able to follow.'

More buzzes from the boards; a louder warning that they were vectoring out at the limit of the ship's capacity. 'Shuttle's still closing,' Max said. He ignored the comp's warning and hit the power.

A harder shove of Frank's backbone against his seat back then a hard bank to the right that leaned him over so fast his neck clicked and a shower of rainwater fell from his hair.

'Leaving atmosphere,' Max said. 'The monitor lost its picture to a snowstorm of static; the ship's singular camera retracting into the safety of the hull.

Frank glanced back into the bay. Jones sat slumped over, his body rocking aimlessly with the ship's motion, the baggage webbing lifting from the ship's sides as they lost gravity. Frank scraped water off his face, water that floated away now, spinning rainbow colours as it went. The monitor came back to life to the blackness of a star field. Frank hit the com. 'Foley, we're out. Watch our back trail. We're heading in.'

Jones raised his head, coming back to the tight grip of the seat's belt. Too tight, it hurt, it hurt his chest and middle, and those places hurt enough already. He eased himself back and heard another sound: the clang of metal. A sense of presence interrupted long before Frank touched his shoulder.

'We're about to make dock with *The Nova*,' Frank said.

Jones tried to answer, but his throat was full of sour half-tastes, his ears full of low whispered hisses. 'Listen to me,' Frank said in an undertone. 'When we get clear, you're going to tell me everything. Everything they did to you. Everything you ever saw. Everything you can do.'

Jones shook his head, Frank hanging on tight.

'I'm not a coward, remember. I'm not. I'm sick of being dragged along by this damned mess. So I want the truth. I want every bit of it.'

Jones sucked a breath down, his exhale freeing an exhausted sob he couldn't prevent.

'You hang on and you hold it together.' Another hard squeeze on his shoulder came with that. Frank didn't walk away, he floated, turning mid-push-off to reach a circular doorway set low down in the wall: the dock access way. The most basic dock, nothing but a push along down the ribs of a tube-way, bare inches between atmosphere and hard vacuum. Max floated by as Frank keyed up the controls and spoke into his com. 'How's it looking your end, Foley? Got a red light on the tubing here, oxygen and heat are running. I'll send Max over first.' A buzz sounded, and Frank unlocked the door, pulling it open with a slow spit of misplaced air.

Max moved hand-to-hand down the walls, its width riddled with indentations. He pulled himself down level with the opening, going down it head first, feet kicking off the door's surround, sand floating free from his boot soles.

Frank spun back to the seating. 'I'm going to move you now.' Frank undid the seating's safety straps, and Jones floated free. He allowed himself to be towed behind the man, Frank hauling them both across notches in the ceiling then down the wall to reach the doorway out.

Dim light in the tunnel, no indication of its length: it was just greyness, a void filled with the promise of ghosts. Jones curled his fingers over the access way's lip hard enough to hurt.

'Grav plates will be off on the other side,' Frank said. 'Push yourself out and let Max guide you.'

He pushed himself down into the maw; let it swallow him. He closed his eyes and felt for the ribs, pushed off, kicked off and cannoned off the side of the thing, lacking the skill to judge how much power he needed. He cried out, his crazed pulse pounding through his temples.

'Jones. Slow down. Just push off with your hands. That's all you need.' A hand on his ankle, Frank's touch an infusion of calm, tranquil blue he kicked hard against.

Frank swore at him, grabbed for his ankle and hauled him backwards. Slammed him back into the tubing and crawled right up over him, shoving him back all the way. Frank just hung there then, staring at him. Clearly not happy with it all either. Nothing to discuss, no words needed, just a hard-eyed look.

A shove then, and Jones hooked his fingers into the tubing sides and pushed off. He reached the tube's end. Max grabbed at him, pulling him free and attaching him to a handhold close to the floor. They were in the guts of *The Nova*, down by the freezer and the gun bay. Red warning lights on down there because the gun was out and armed, its motors a constant, humming whine.

Frank pushed free, ignoring them both as he headed for the wall com. 'Grav, Foley.'

It was a pull on every organ; a yank to the ground as the plates came on, the resettling of a mind suddenly understanding where down truly was.

Jones shrugged up, let his head sag to his knees. He'd reached zero finally, feeling nothing, seeing nothing, letting nothing in, time running forwards without him caring to touch a single second of it.

Frank pressed his back into the cold metal of the lift as it climbed towards A deck. He didn't want to look at Jones in a heap in the lift's corner, Max down by his side, talking again while Jones sat there looking like he didn't have a clear thought left in his head.

Frank forced a swallow down. Not your problem, Frank. Not your damned mess to unravel and look at you diving in. A carrier grunt, full of damned fool notions, seeing visions and deciding he'd like a full detailed explanation, please. A damned ship full to the brim with broken people, and here you are trying to add to it the most twisted, broken soul you're ever likely to meet.

Good old dependable Frank. No matter how heavy the load he'd haul it all up and carry it along. He nearly choked on his next swallow, anger rising. But he had had enough. He was sick of being blindsided and used.

The lift landed, the door open, Kady out in the corridor waiting to give him a hug he knew he didn't have the resources left to handle. He didn't let her get close, he held her an arm's length away. 'Take Jones to the med bay. Clean him up.'

She stared at him, frowning hard but not saying a word. She stepped into the lift with Max instead and started to help with Jones.

Frank turned towards helm just as Foley bellowed from the boards. 'Greeley's on the com. We've got contact from the island.'

He hurried in, glancing to Haine as sour-faced as ever sitting in the nook of the gun bay. Foley nodded a welcome before waving him in urgently.

'Pak here, Greeley.' Frank leaned over the boards as Foley opened up the link.

'Monitor the jump-gate,' came Greeley's sharp reply.

Frank glanced to Foley, who gave a swift nod. 'We're doing that,' Frank said. 'Have you any info on who's attacking us?'

'They seem half military, half civilian. We don't have any details – not yet. Put Jeven on. Let me talk to him.'

Frank looked back through helm's open doors towards the med bay. 'He's not up to talking right now.'

'Is he all right?' Greeley asked.

Frank slipped into the free chair, moving one dirt-caked hand to the board's edge to brace himself upright. 'He's . . . fine.' He said around a clenched jaw.' You want me to carry your cargo, Greeley, you need to tell me the truth. Is there anything you missed out? Anything you want to confess?'

'I don't know what you're talking about, Pak. Maybe you ought to start confessing a few things to me.'

Maybe he'd deal for that info one day, Frank thought bitterly. He'd tell Greeley all the parts of Jones he'd missed along the way. 'Did you lie to your cargo, Greeley? The rest of the kids from that boat, are they alive?'

'I didn't lie. Do you understand what I've risked to keep him safe – to keep all of you safe? Get out of this system. Get your IDs changed and disappear.' The com light went out. Frank glanced up to the monitors, to Mallin's orbiter on autopilot, its docking tube slowly retracting as it headed into a safe computer-piloted orbit ready for pick-up. 'The gate, Foley. We need to get out fast.'

'Got that.' Foley blinking at him, concern on his face. 'Are you all right, Frank?'

Frank couldn't find an answer. He turned for the med bay instead.

Inside, Jones lay on the bed, curled up nose to his knees, mud-caked and silent. Frank went in no further than the room's doorway, staying clear for now, stealing a little more time to settle himself.

Kady touched Jones' head, running her fingers gently over his scalp to find the source of the blood that stained Jones' face. 'Just cleaning you up a little.' She glanced to Frank. 'Are you hurt, Frank?'

Another question he baulked at. Hurt, he thought. No, I'm torn to pieces.

'Got a call in from Mallin,' Haine bellowed down from helm. 'He confirms it's a military attack with a few add-ons. That holed shuttle's came down, it took a lump of the mainland dock with it. No survivors. Mallin's just said something about the himmer. Damn thing's dead.'

Jones bucked on the bed, feet and bloodstained hands jolting.

'Shut it down, Haine.' Frank yelled.

'Just keeping you informed,' Haine returned.

Max leaned over the bedside. 'You couldn't have saved it, Jones,' he said softly.

Too much sympathy in Max's voice, too much Frank could connect to, and he railed against it. 'Max, get up to helm. Take care of the gun.' He sent a cold-eyed stare after Max as the man exited.

'What's going on with you, Frank?' a barely audible whisper came from Kady. He glanced up and got snarled up in her eyes. 'Please, don't do it again. Don't pull clear of us. We're all trapped in this thing with you. Talk to us; tell us what you're thinking this time around. We know there's stuff going on between you and this kid.'

Frank glowered at her, his standard glare, the one he always used on her when she was pushing him beyond his limits.

'Frank?'

'I need a clear head,' he barked out.

'Trouble,' Foley's yell from helm cracked on the word.

Frank sucked a breath, watching Jones' head rise from his pillow as if that word could pull him from the depths of hell.

Trouble: a small, dark angular vessel that sat right on the apex of the gate, blocking their escape. Frank stood at helm, breathing hard and staring at the monitors. The rest of his crew gathered there too, right behind him.

'She just exited the gate,' Foley said. 'No ID signature. She's running dark.'

Trouble was a military frigate. She had to be one of the ships Jones had warned him about. A Reaches admiral on a small fleet ship-killer. There wold be fewer than fifty on board her, a ship not so much bigger than *The Nova* herself.

Frank sat down at the gun controls and started flipping switches.

'Frank, what are doing?' Foley asked worriedly.

Frank glanced back to his crew, the plating vibrating beneath their boot soles as the gun dropped out of the hold. Frank checked monitors, ones he knew well, an odd comforting feeling in the middle of his chest. The ship had already started angling herself over to fire. Here was something he'd been trained how to do. No thought needed, nothing strange to unravel or wonder at.

'Frank, you can't attack her.' That came from behind him: Max.

Chatter came over the com. The island, she'd picked up that in-system blip and was trying to talk to it.

'Frank?' Jones' call: he stood right at his shoulder, ragged, mud-streaked hair in his eyes. Looking battered and beaten and worn now to nothing at all. Jones, who'd seen that frigate and raised his chin. That familiar keen-eyed sharpness returning to his gaze as if he spent his entire life waiting for moments like these. 'No target lock,' he said. 'Something's wrong with her. Standard operating procedure would be to lock her weapons onto everything in system as soon as she left the gate.'

A carrier grunt knew that much.

'No target lock,' Jones repeated, his voice hitching as he flinched. The frigate had fired. A silver-hulled missile went shooting across the black.

'Firing wide of us . . .' Foley snapped out. 'Firing wide . . . of everything.'

Everything save a fast burn-up entering the planet's atmosphere

'A warning?' Kady wondered aloud.

More chatter from the island, more and more from Greeley's ship in close orbit.

'Call her, Foley,' Frank ordered.

Foley hit the com. 'Unidentified ship, this is *The Nov*—this is *The Purcell*. Unidentified ship, this is *The Purcell*.' He repeated over and over.

The frigate fired wildly again at nothing at all.

'She has to be on auto,' Foley said.

'No,' Jones said, taking a grip on the side of Frank's chair. 'Somebody has to have fired.'

The com crackled to life. 'Ten seconds. Hurry up.' A young voice yelled out in raw panic. 'Calling all ships. This is *The Amity*. We are under attack. Repeat, we are under attack. There are fifteen of us holding helm. Command corralled everybody else down in the cargo bay. Command said it was a drill. Repeat, Command said it was a drill. They are trying to lock on missiles from the armoury bay to fire on all ships. Repeat, to fire on all ships. We are countermanding weapons lock from helm. Get clear. Repeat, get clear . . .' The voice broke off, a pounding noise sounding. 'We don't know what's happening. We're just trying to hold helm and find help.' Gunfire popped, men shouting in the distance. 'Calling all ships. Alert the nearest garrison. Alert . . . Alert . . . Alert . . . We are being attacked.' With that the silence came back.

Foley hissed a breath as a hole appeared in *The Amity*'s side, debris spilling out, turning and twisting. 'They've holed her.'

'You need to move,' Jones said urgently. 'They get into helm they'll fire on us. You have to get out.'

'Can you get by her,' Frank asked in a rush.

'Hell if I know,' Foley said.

'Try it, Foley.' Frank leaned across, hitting keys to get a link to the island. 'Mallin, Greeley?'

'We're getting out.' Greeley came on. 'Is Jeven there?'

Frank glanced round.

'I'm here,' Jones said faintly.

'Stay safe,' Greeley returned hurriedly. 'Keep your word and stay safe. I'll bring you home. I promise.' The com cut out.

Foley puffed out air, hitting keys, his head snapping down and then back to that ship, just hanging there. A direct move right by her, close, so close the cameras were already filling to the brim with her. Her missile turrets, her flat, sleek hide, the debris that spun away from her wounded side. 'Dammit, drift out a little more,' Foley snapped at her. 'Give us some damned room.'

Warnings sounded. The screaming pitch of a siren Foley swiftly silenced. Hull scrape. That close. A whine of sound that set Frank's teeth on edge. 'Foley?'

'Dammit. Dammit.' Foley hissed. 'Come on. Come on.' He hit other keys, getting a frenzied, harried look. 'Gate lock. Gate's cycling.'

'This is *The Amity*,' the voice came over the com strongly. 'All ships stand down. We are commandeering all ships. Repeat, all ships stand down. Do not resist. This is Admiral Pender of the Charris Confederation.'

'Going to jump,' Foley hissed. They had *The Amity* only on their rear camera now, those cameras retracting at the very last second, leaving them blind. 'In five . . . four . . . three . . .'

Frank heard a sucked breath behind him: Jones, who might just die one day during jump. He shot up from his seat, hauling Jones into it as the ship started to groan around them.

'Two . . .' Foley counted down. 'One . . . We're out. We're out.' The gate sucked them in. Grey-faced Foley glanced around to Frank, as everything in *The Nova* seemed to shift and spin before their eyes. 'They really are starting a damned war back there,' he said shakily. 'Do we even have the vaguest notion whose side we're on?'

Finally, a question Frank could answer. 'We're on our side,' he replied tightly. 'That's the only side we can trust.'

Today . . .

'Jones?' somebody said.

More mental sifting. Where was he this time? *The Bliss*? The Institution? *The Nova*? Was that still her name?

'Do you hear me?'

The cold rushed in; he had a blanket wrapped around him but he still felt cold, an icy, biting chill. His head throbbed, his arms ached, every shift of his ribs hurt something. He looked around and saw greyness. Grey little cell: his bed in holding.

Exactly where he'd started out.

He remember the frigate but he had no memory of moving down from helm. 'The feeds? War?'

313

'There's nothing on the feeds. Not yet.'

A tall form hung above him he fought to focus on. His *Bliss*-born senses flared a warning. Frank. It was Frank. Just Frank.

He jolted. The man's hand wrapped about his arm, his senses flaring another warning; sharper, more primal, fear plying into his bloodstream in a thick, blinding rush. He sat up and pushed himself back.

'We're still en route. Foley has a port picked out, a little backwater piece of nothing. We'll be safe. We have to sit back a while and work this out.'

Another reach for his arm. Calmness came back with the man's touch, a sense of floating on an ocean of it: wide and endlessly serene.

An ocean so deep you could drown.

Pull back, he told himself. Get away. Escape. He pressed himself against the wall, longing for flesh and blood to ooze into the metal.

'It's time, Jones.' Frank sank down onto the bed's edge, as if he expected to be there a while. 'This is just between us. You hear me? I want you to tell me everything, right from the beginning.'

Jones shook his head, trying to hold the dam back, trying and trying to hang on to it all. Tell Frank. Confess everything he'd hung on to, hidden for years, the secrets that burned through him. Start at the beginning: *The Bliss*, walking down a corridor wearing blue pyjamas, a woman holding his hand. Milo. Lieberman. Species K. The ship's last day, the memories of it had come back to him in a blinding rush and filled him to the brim with vengeance. Vengeance that tore him up inside and never let him rest.

Frank snaked a hand forward, he hung on to his arm. A good man. One he could trust. 'Tell me,' Frank said, and the urge grew and grew. 'Tell me so I can help you. So I can try.'

Not alone. Not any more.

Jones sucked a breath, hung on to it, forced a sob back. He could do it, he could let it all go. 'I was five,' he began shakily. 'My name was Jake.' A cold, hard breath and he forced out the one thing he really needed Frank to know. 'My name *is* Jake . . . and I think a doctor called Lieberman left something behind in my head.'